Praise for KATHLEEN EAGLE
and
THE LAST GOOD MAN

Also by Kathleen Eagle

WHAT THE HEART KNOWS
FIRE AND RAIN
THE LAST TRUE COWBOY
THE NIGHT REMEMBERS
REASON TO BELIEVE
SUNRISE SONG
THIS TIME FOREVER

Coming Soon in Hardcover

YOU NEVER CAN TELL

KATHLEEN EAGLE

The Last Good Man

AVON BOOKS
An Imprint of HarperCollinsPublishers

This is a work of fiction. Names, characters, places, and incidents are products of the author's imagination or are used fictitiously and are not to be construed as real. Any resemblance to actual events, locales, organizations, or persons, living or dead, is entirely coincidental.

AVON BOOKS
An Imprint of HarperCollins*Publishers*
10 East 53rd Street
New York, New York 10022-5299

First Avon Books paperback printing: May 2001
First William Morrow hardcover printing: August 2000

Avon Trademark Reg. U.S. Pat. Off. and in Other Countries, Marca Registrada, Hecho en U.S.A.
HarperCollins ® is a trademark of HarperCollins Publishers Inc.

Printed in the U.S.A.

10 9 8 7 6 5 4 3 2 1

*To Honor the Memory of
Mary Pierson*

*To Mama, with love
Kathy and Jill*

Chapter 1

The queen bees of Sunbonnet, Wyoming, were all abuzz.
Savannah Stephens was back, in the flesh this time.

How long had it been since the last time they'd pulled Savannah, dressed only in satin bra and lace panties, out of their mailboxes? She'd been quite the regular fixture on the cover of that mail-order catalog for quite a while. Of course, everyone knew all about how those pictures got touched up. But they had to admit, Savannah had the basic equipment. And it was all natural. She was born and raised right there in Sunbonnet. *She* was all-natural. That dewy-eyed smile had been just the right counterpoint for the flawless body of a woman who didn't have to think twice about walking around in broad daylight wearing nothing but pretty underwear.

Then suddenly she'd vanished. Air-brushed clean away, as though somebody had thrown a coat over her and dragged her back into the house. Had it been three years ago, maybe five?

The drones had noticed right away when it happened, but they hadn't said much. Once Savannah was gone, the men had gotten their catalog back. If anybody was to order anything, it was probably going to be a man. He'd send for something black and lacy for his own lady, something she would put on for him, just so he could take it off. The next morning she would tuck it away in a drawer, and he'd never see it again. Then it was back to the mailbox again. Sure, the men missed seeing Savannah, but there was still plenty of diversion on the cover of *Lady Elizabeth's Dreamwear Catalog*.

Still, the women pondered aloud on occasion. What ever became of Savannah Stephens?

Some had heard she'd found greener pastures, but there were all sorts of tales about the nature of green. A movie mogul with a pocketful of green had her stashed in a cottage beside the green sea. Or she'd starved herself like they all did to stay slim, taken to eating nothing but lettuce and drinking green tea, and she'd just wasted away. Some said she'd made so much green herself, she'd been able to retire and get fat. Heck, she always was pretty sassy.

The ebb and flow of such comments depended on the weather and what else was in the news, but they never sloshed through the door of the Sunbonnet Mercantile, owned and operated by Billie Larsen, the only relative Savannah had left in Sunbonnet. Or anywhere else, as far as anyone knew. The old general store was a gallery of pictures of Savannah dressed in pretty suits and glamorous evening clothes. The catalogs were stashed underneath the counter. Billie was proud of those, too, but she didn't tack them on the wall.

Whenever anyone asked, Billie said that her niece was taking some time off from her modeling career. The response hadn't changed in five years. Conventional wisdom calculated that it had probably been five years since Billie had heard from her once-famous niece, and the conventionally wise were not surprised to hear she'd finally come home with her tail tucked between her legs. It just proved that New York City was no place for a nice girl from Wyoming. It was bitch eat bitch in places like New York and L.A., or so the females of Sunbonnet had heard. And so they were fond of saying.

The males of Sunbonnet still weren't saying much. They couldn't imagine pastures any greener than the pages of *Lady Elizabeth's Dreamwear Catalog*. The thought of *that* tail and *those* legs coming home to Sunbonnet seemed too damn good to be true. They'd have to see to believe, and so far, the sightings had been few.

But she was surely back.

Even if every person Clay Keogh tipped his hat to hadn't mentioned it hard on the heels of saying how quickly the weather had changed this week, he would have known *she* was close by. Suddenly the clean, dry Wyoming air carried her scent again.

He'd parked his pickup in the shade of the loafing shed behind the Sunbonnet Mercantile, which was the oldest building in town. He was careful not to glance at the upstairs windows as he unloaded the tools of his trade. He had as good a buzz on as any bee, and he hadn't even had a drink in weeks. His face flamed in the shade of his cap as he took a quick inventory of the handles in his toolbox. He could have sworn he had Tabasco sauce coursing through his veins, a notion that made him chuckle. Dearly did he love anything spicy, but cayenne in his blood? Not likely. Wyoming dirt made him red-blooded, pure and plain.

Was she upstairs in her aunt Billie's spare room, fixing a face that never needed any fixing? Or was she downstairs, helping out behind the counter, the way she used to when they were kids? He hadn't noticed any cowboys lining up to buy a pack of gum they might never open or a postage stamp for a letter they'd surely never write. If he hurried, maybe he could be first. Just go on in and say hello before he worked up a sweat over Billie's old mare's shoes.

He'd seen Savannah only twice in more than a dozen

years, but he was counting on one of those hummingbird hugs she'd learned to greet people with since she'd gone away to New York, and he didn't want his shirt to be sticking to his back when she touched him. Right now, his hands were clean and his shirt was dry. He ought to go into the store and announce himself, see if there was any *kuchen* fresh-baked, ask about the new rasp he had on order. Any other time, he'd do just that.

Anybody but Savannah inside, he wouldn't be acting like he'd never ventured past the county line. He figured he'd see her sooner or later, and later would give him time to imagine the scene a few more ways. The tune he'd just heard on the radio swirled around in the secret part of his head, where he came upon Savannah alone in the store, wordlessly took her in his arms, and welcomed her home with a slow two-step.

He whistled the same tune as he wrapped his leather apron strings behind his back, switched and pulled the ends to the front, and tied them below his belt buckle. He reached for his hoof knife. In his head he was noticing how they still danced well together. He'd improved on the steps she'd taught him long ago. He'd practiced a bit. She hadn't. *It's been years since I've danced,* she told him. He asked her why, and she said she hadn't had a partner.

He was smiling when he rounded the corner of the storage side of the shed and came knee to face with the most beautiful little girl he'd ever laid eyes on. Standing in the open doorway, she looked up at him, chocolate eyes as big as soup bowls, likely startled by his size, the way most little people were when they hadn't seen him coming. She carried a mewling kitten in each hand. He got his smile going again.

She took a small step back, tucked one gray tiger against her neck, lifted her chin, and said, "Hello." She sounded all grown up and proper, like she was the lady of the house, rather than a little girl playing with kittens in a storage shed. She gave him an astute once-over. "Are you the horseshoe man?"

"Yes, ma'am, I'm the horseshoe man," he assured her. She was eyeing his hand and the curved hoof knife he'd all but forgotten about. He quickly slipped it into its pouch on the apron, which was more like a pair of knee-length leather chaps.

"Aunt Billie told me to watch for you. She said you were coming to put new shoes on Dolly and I could watch."

"She did, huh?" He took a frayed blue halter down from a hook just inside the doorway. "Is Dolly all ready for me?"

"I think so." She squatted behind the grain box and tucked the kittens into a wooden crate, under the narrow slits of the barn cat's watchful eyes. The mewling ceased. The little girl hurried to catch up with the new activity. "How does she have to get ready?"

"She usually gets Dollied up," Clay quipped as he unhooked the chain on the corral gate. The child laughed behind his back, and he stepped aside to let her slide under his arm and through the gate ahead of him. "The way all women do when they go shoe-shopping."

"Does she get to pick them out? Can I pick for her?"

She was grinning up at him now, bright-eyed, and he was thinking he knew her from somewhere. Feeling more than thinking, maybe, because the somewhere wasn't as far off as the some*time,* which didn't make a lot of sense. Sun-kissed round face, gleaming dark hair swept up in a ponytail, eyes full of puckish sparkle—unless he missed his guess, the child was at least part Indian, and that was the part he knew without knowing, the part he felt connected to. Clay wasn't Indian himself, but his brother was.

"My shoes only come in one color," he said. "As far as style, well, we're going to fix her up with a little wedge because she doesn't have much heel left on her."

"You're going to give her high-heeled shoes?"

"Gonna give her some of them hi-igh he-e-eled slippers," he crooned as he cross-tied the swaybacked sorrel in the loafing shed.

"She'll look silly like that." The little girl squatted next to his wooden toolbox, hands clasped between her knees, trying hard to look things over without touching. "Are her shoes in here? Can I watch you put them on?"

"How do you feel about that, old girl? Spectators generally aren't allowed, are they? Especially strangers."

"*I'm* not a *stranger*." She deserted the box in favor of delivering her point at close range. "I live here."

"Is that a fact?" Clay repositioned the toolbox. "I've lived in this town all my life, and I'm pretty sure I know everyone else who lives here. But I don't know you."

"You know my mother. Aunt Billie says you do."

"And who's your mother?" He knew what was coming, but he had to let it unfold. This was the child's way of introducing herself. By way of invitation, he slid her a glance.

"I'll give you a hint." She beamed, full to bursting with her secret. "My mother is the most beautiful woman in the world."

"The *most* beautiful?"

"In all the world." She shot up, stood straight as a soldier, and folded her arms imperiously. "You know her. She used to live here, a long time ago."

He raked his fingers through the mare's mane. "The most beautiful woman who ever lived here before, hands down, is Savannah Stephens."

The little girl was smiling now, like the teacher satisfied with her student's answer. He wanted to follow up with, *But you can't be her daughter*.

He shouldn't have been surprised that she looked like his brother. Savannah would have followed Kole to the ends of the earth when they were kids, and that was exactly where he was now, as far as Clay knew. But Kole had left Sunbonnet long before Clay and Savannah were even out of high school, so she'd have had to hook up with him somewhere, somehow . . .

He wasn't surprised, hell, no. It didn't bother him, either.

They were two wondrous adventurers, Kole and Savannah. Two of a kind, although it was hard for Clay to put them together as a pair. Clearly their paths had crossed at some secret place. For Kole's sake, it had to have been a secret place. He'd been dodging some powerful enemies longer than this little girl with the proud grin had been alive. So they'd gotten together, and this child . . .

This child was her own person, and she was the one conversing here, not her mother, and not Clay's brother.

He smiled. "But if you're living here now, I couldn't say who's the most beautiful anymore. You'd have to ask that ol' mirror, mirror on the wall."

" 'You are, my queen!' " she quoted with delight. Then she tilted her head and folded her arms even tighter, and right then he saw her mother in her, in that self-assured little pose. "Oh, but he lies sometimes, that mirror. That's what my mother says. If you're a queen, he might *have* to lie."

"That's not the way I remember it. Ho, Dolly." Clay knelt in the straw that covered the dirt floor, balancing the little mare's front hoof on his other knee. He was definitely too tall for this job. "The mirror has to tell it like it is. He'd say you and your mother are both very beautiful."

"And I'm not a stranger."

"I still don't know your name."

"Claudia Ann Stephens."

"Clay Keogh." He touched the bill of his cap. "Pleased to meet you, ma'am."

"You don't have to call me ma'am. I'm only six, you know. *Almost* six."

"I wouldn't have guessed. You seem very grown up. But even so, we generally don't allow specta—"

The sound of her feet shuffling in the straw brought his head up to check the child's proximity to the horse. His hands had already made quick work of trimming dead tissue from the sole of the first foot, and he'd begun to shape the hoof. He dropped a crescent hoof paring.

She dove for it. "Can I—"

Clay felt a shift of equine muscle. He dropped the hoof knife and snatched the girl out of the way of a warning kick from a back hoof. The move threw Clay off balance and toppled him on his side, but he managed to cushion the child's fall with his shoulder. He glanced up at the horse, who lowered her smug nose for a sniff at his boot, then dismissed the flattened humans with a snort.

"You okay?" Clay asked, ignoring the twinge in his lower back as he lifted the child away, checking for damage he was pretty sure hadn't occurred.

Two big brown eyes stared back at him, surprised and unsure, little head nodding anyway. "Are *you* okay?" she asked, her voice small but steady.

"Yeah." He retrieved the hoof knife and offered her the paring she'd been after. Still staring, she shook her head. "Dolly's kind of a cantankerous old gal sometimes," he explained.

"Maybe she doesn't want shoes."

"Want and need are two different things. You still want to watch?"

She nodded bravely.

"Then what I need is for you to help me out just a bit so Dolly thinks you're part of the act." He moved her to the far side of the toolbox, which stood within his reach. "Do you know anything about shoeing horses?"

"I didn't even know horses wore shoes until Aunt Billie told me to watch for you." She eased back into her conversational tone. "Aunt Billie said the reason we've been making a mud puddle by the water tank every day was because you said Dolly should stand in mud. Why did you want her to get her feet muddy like that?"

"Well, mud's good for frogs."

"Frogs? Dolly's a horse." She risked a small laugh.

The sound of it made him feel better. He knew he'd scared her, knocking her down like he had. He wasn't sure she realized how close that hoof had come. "Horses have frogs in their feet," he told her. He plucked a gray curl of dried cuticle and dropped it in the shallow tin tray on top of the toolbox.

"*Frogs* in their *feet?*"

The way she sniffed at the dead tissue reminded him of the way Dolly had sniffed at his boot, and he laughed when she reacted with a puckered-up face, as though he'd given her a lemon drop. He wondered if he had any in the pickup.

"The mud softened her frog so I could trim it easier."

"*That's* a *frog?*"

"That's part of it." He patted Dolly's flank, picked up the hoof again, and showed Claudia the T-shaped protrusion in its base. "This is a horse frog." He grinned. "It can't sing because it has a sore throat."

"Are you teasing me?"

"Would I do a thing like that?"

"You're not supposed to tease."

"Who says?"

"My mother. When boys tease, I just walk away."

"That's a sure way to leave them feeling stupid."

"Boys *are* stupid." Daintily she nabbed the bit of frog between thumb and forefinger. "Sometimes." She spared Clay a glance before she examined the tissue specimen more closely.

In his mind's eye he saw Savannah, golden hair gleaming in the summer sun as she traced the shape of a petroglyph etched on the rock wall of their favorite hideout, which was tucked up in the hills of his north pasture. Exploring fingers, ever-curious eyes, bright, lilting laugh. He was seeing more and more of her in this child.

Savannah, where have you been these last years? That

woman on those slick pages who looked like you, and now this child who doesn't . . .

"What did your mom have to say about you watching for the horseshoe man?"

"She's resting," Claudia reported quietly, as though her mother were bunking in with the kittens on the other side of the wall. "She's a lot better now, but she still has to rest. She used to be a famous model, you know."

He nodded, flipping the *better now* part over in his mind. *Better after what?*

"You've probably seen her picture in magazines," Claudia said as she squatted behind the foot-high box and peered over the top and into the open side. "A lot of people still remember. Aunt Billie has her pictures on the wall in the store. Have you seen them?"

"Sure have."

He'd also purchased more than a few fashion magazines over the years on the chance of finding similar pictures. Not for the clothes, but for Savannah. He thought of it as staying in touch with a friend.

Claudia tucked the frog peel in the pocket of her bib overalls. "What do you want me to do?"

"See that long, flat thing?" He nodded when she laid her small hand on the steel handle. "That's a rasp." He extended a hand after repositioning the trimmed hoof on his knee. "It's like a nail file, only big and heavy, so take hold with both hands."

"I hope my job is more than just handing you things. That's what people always want kids to do, but I can do a lot more than that." She demonstrated by doing exactly as he'd instructed. "I help my mother all the time."

"I'll bet you do." He tried to imagine Savannah doing something domestic with this little girl in tow. He filed, and he shaped, and he pictured short fingers and long fingers, clippers and polish.

Quietly she watched his every move. Patiently she waited her turn.

He put the first hoof down and leaned back. "I'll want you to be the keeper of the nails," he told her while his practiced eye appraised the angle, hoof to cannon bone. "Now, if you don't think you should be handling nails, just say so. This is a job I wouldn't trust to a kid, and you aren't quite six. You said so yourself."

"I'm used to handling all kinds of sharp things. I'm very careful." She took out the small box and shook it to hear the nails rattle. "Why does a horse wear shoes?"

"Dolly's an old horse. She's got some problems with her feet. I make her special shoes that help her walk with less pain in her feet. That helps her legs, her back, makes her feel better all over."

"Is she too old to ride? Would that hurt her? Aunt Billie said maybe I could try riding her after you put her shoes on."

"Have you ever ridden a horse?" He glanced at her as he reached for the nippers. She shook her head. "If it was up to me, this isn't the one I'd start you out on."

"This is the only one we have." She opened the nail box and took a peek inside. "But I won't ride her if she's sick. I'll take care of her, just like I took care of my mom when she was sick. She's a lot better now, though. A *lot* better."

"So . . ." *How sick was she? How long did it last? How much pain did she . . .* He clamped a back hoof between his knees. "How do you like Sunbonnet?"

"It's okay. My mother says we won't have to move anymore, so that's good. But the only playground here is the one at the school, and Aunt Billie says there's no swimming pool. I want to take swimming lessons."

"You might have to go to Dubois or Lander for swimming lessons, but we have other things."

"There's no hospital, either. When is it going to be time for the nails?"

"I have to finish trimming her hooves first," he explained, wielding the nippers on the mare's overgrown toe.

"Yikes! Don't cut her foot off!"

"I'm just trimming her toenails."

"She doesn't have toes. How can she have toenails?"

"Hooves are a little bit like toenails."

"Oh." She shook a single nail into the tin nail tray, and he thought it was clever of her to figure out what the tray was for. "Do you have any kids? I haven't found anybody to play with yet."

"I have, uh . . ." *Have?*

Hell, yes, have. They didn't live with him anymore, but he'd helped raise them, hadn't he?

"My kids, my *wife's* kids—" Damn. Exactly how did he want this reported? "My *former* wife's kids, well, they're a little older than you."

"That's okay. I can read, you know."

"Maybe you can teach them," he said with a chuckle. But the gibe didn't set well with him. Making fun of the kids was not his style. "Just kidding. They read pretty good. They just don't do it very often."

He glanced up from his rasping. She was arranging nails in the cupped tray, head to head and point to point. "You think you'll be staying in Sunbonnet for a while? Going to school?"

"Oh, yes. I took some tests. They put me in the second grade."

He whistled. "Pretty damn good for a six-year-old."

"That's not a nice word, Clay," she admonished with a frown, sounding like a very young mother.

"Beg your pardon, ma'am. You're right about that."

"I suppose you might be wondering why I don't have a father."

"I wasn't—" *Damn,* she was perceptive for a kid. He wouldn't insult her intelligence by denying the thought. "I wasn't gonna ask."

"I just don't, that's all." She shrugged, then set about reversing every other nail in the row she'd made. "Some kids don't. I have my mother, and now I have Aunt Billie, who's really my great-aunt."

"And that's a nice family right there. I don't know where this town would be without your aunt Billie. We'd have to drive fifty miles whenever we ran out of toilet paper."

She brightened, indulging him. "That's funny."

"You wouldn't think so if it was you who ran out."

Now they were laughing together.

She was a quick study, this little girl, and he set aside all her connections, real and imagined, and simply connected with her interest in horses and their shoes. He explained to her that old Dolly had worn her heels down, just the way kids did sometimes, but in Dolly's case it was the heels of her feet, not of her shoes. The important part of his job was to get her hooves shaped just right, so he took his time and checked the angles. He stood the rasp on end next to the first hoof to show Claudia what kind of an angle he was looking for. Then he asked for her opinion on the next one. Her perception amazed him. He showed her how he prepared the wedge pad to elevate the horse's heel and let her measure out the oakum he would use as caulking. He mentioned that as long as he talked and moved quietly, Dolly was willing to tolerate him.

"Don't put those in your mouth!"

He jerked the nail away from his teeth and clucked to himself. "Force of habit. I forgot I had an assistant today."

"That's very dangerous, Clay. I guess I know how to handle nails better than you do."

"I haven't eaten one yet." He lined the nail up with the first hole. "Okay, one at a ti—"

"Don't!"

He jerked his head up and came face-to-face with terror.

"You're going to put the nails right into her feet? That's what they did to Jesus."

He smiled, but he didn't laugh. It was no laughing matter. "Jesus didn't have hooves. It's okay to put nails in hooves if you do it the right way."

She scowled, unconvinced.

"I won't hurt her. I'm the horseshoe man, remember?"

The scowl was unchanged.

He nodded toward the tray. "You're in charge of the nails. If you think I'm hurting her, you can keep the nails away. Now, watch her face and tell me if you think she's getting mad."

"I'm the keeper of the nails," the little girl muttered, eyes firmly fixed on the old mare's head.

"That's right. Give me one at a time."

She watched closely as he tapped in the first one.

"Okay, one at a time."

Chapter 2

Tap tap tap.

Savannah threw one arm over her eyes, wrapped the other around her waist, above the surgical scar, then rolled from back to belly, twisting in the bed sheet like a corkscrew.

Tap tap tap.

Woodpecker? Some kind of pecker.

Tap tap tap.

Rude pecker. But then, weren't they all?

Savannah burrowed deeper, telling herself it was almost dark, almost night. She knew it wasn't, but she wanted to sleep. She'd hardly slept at all today. It was too hot in the small rooms over the store. Hot and still, even with the window open a crack below the roller shade. But if nothing else, it had been pretty quiet before the pecking started.

Tap tap tap.

What kind of a pecker was that, besides rude? Aunt Billie once had a clock that played a different birdcall every hour, but Savannah vaguely remembered breaking that herself when she was practicing the Baltimore oriole's song. She wouldn't have known a Baltimore oriole if one had landed on her nose, but according to Aunt Billie's clock, those birds had a pretty whistle. She'd seen high school kids imitating birdcalls on the *Tonight Show,* and she was planning to try out. Maybe Aunt Billie had replaced the clock, or maybe the broken one was still around, stuck at the pecking hour. She couldn't remember what hour that was.

Some damned daylight hour.

She thought about getting up. If she got up, she'd have to put her clothes on and brush her hair. She brought her face up from the pillow and looked at the big shirt and the shape-less jeans draped over the arm of the white wicker chair sit-ting under the window. She could get up now and put those on. That was all she had to do for now, just that much. *Don't worry about the brush. Start with the jeans. One move at a time. Do one small thing; one thing leads to another.*

She dropped her face back into the crook of her elbow, hoping the thought would go away. It was so blessedly quiet in this town that you could actually hear natural sounds. She'd never appreciated that about Sunbonnet. The absence of horns was nice. She almost smiled as she amended that thought with "car horns." Animal horns abounded, but they weren't noisy, and they weren't rude as long as you kept your distance. Neither was the meadowlark tweedling some-where out back. That was one bird she could actually recog-nize. It had a lovely voice that demanded nothing of her. No bread for lunch, no going to the playground, no look-see what that boy was doing out in the hall. They had Aunt Bil-lie now, and Aunt Billie would look-see.

Aunt Billie, look. See what Mama made for me to wear to the Christmas program? She says it's my color. Blue is my special color.

Mama used to say that Savannah's good looks and her singing would get them out of Sunbonnet. Savannah couldn't sing worth a nickel, but Mama had been right about her other assets. The world loved a beautiful woman. People dressed her up and took her picture, praised her and paid her well. It was a curious kind of love. First it made you warm, and then it turned you cool and slick. But it gave you a living, as long as your assets were intact.

Savannah's were not.

Tap tap.

Rude tapping. Crude tapping. Restless, impatient tapping. Just what she needed. From the inside out, her body wanted tapping. The urge came on her like an itch, small enough to be ignored at first, but real, growing, nagging. It would go away.

Tap me gently, tap me slowly.

Like an ostrich with her face in the bosom of her pillow, hidden even from her own reproach, she slipped her hand between her legs. *Slight, slow, steady, and soft.* It was her hand no longer. Not her own doing, but that of some faceless tapper, nameless banger, voiceless pecker who would tap her and touch her and take her away, take off with her, off the bed off the roof off the planet, and bring her . . .

. . . blessed release.

Savory, sweet, soothing, suspended in pleasure for a moment. But the pleasure evaporated, leaving her nothing but a sour aftertaste. She shoved herself up, quitting what she'd done, what she'd had to do. Relieved but not satisfied, she couldn't lie on the white sheets any longer with that sense of self on self. Without Claudia to urge her along, disgust was an effective way to drive herself out of bed and force herself to get dressed. She hated the prodding, hated herself for needing it, but there it was.

She'd made it this far. She could take one more step. She'd taught herself that the hatred would recede if she simply managed to move along. She remembered to duck this time. Getting up on the wrong side of the bed was hazardous with a sloped ceiling, but that was the side she favored. It was like burrowing into a pocket.

She raised the white vinyl window shade and surveyed the backyard. A colorful array of small pants and shirts waved at her—*Come and get us*—from the clothesline. *After nightfall,* she thought. *If you're still there.* Then maybe she would venture into the ramshackle shed.

All she could see was the storage side, which shared a wall with the loafing shed, a makeshift barn inside the split-rail corral. Maybe she'd say hello to Dolly, who was Aunt Billie's only livestock now, her only dependent. Savannah wondered where the old mare was and whose pickup was parked next to the shed. But it was only a vague and idle wondering, as inconsequential as her memories of riding Dolly or riding around in a pickup, riding deep into the foothills that looked as distant from her small window as those times felt.

She'd forgotten how many different shades of brown those hills wore, relieved only by broad slashes of blue-green pines. Somewhere out there was a configuration of round hills and tabletop butte that some pioneer had thought looked like his wife's sunbonnet. Savannah couldn't see the bonnet any better than she could find images in cloud formations.

She remembered lying up there on a summer afternoon with Clay Keogh and Kole Kills Crow. Such a long time ago. Kole was in high school, but she and Clay had barely hit their teens. Clay knew every inch of those hills. Their father's cattle grazed up there, and while Kole saw the Keogh ranch merely as temporary bed and board, Clay was the consummate ranch hand. He knew livestock, and he knew the land. He could always find a patch of grass, a good place to stop, a chance for the horses to "laze and graze."

Laze and graze. That was Clay's way of slowing his half brother's pace. Kole was their hero, so much older and wilder. He hung out with his juniors only when he had nothing better to do. When they went riding, as soon as they got away from the house Kole had to cut loose, "run for the sun," he called it, chasing what was to be his unsettling destiny. The order was always the same—Kole champing at the bit out in front, Savannah dragging on the bit and bringing up the rear, Clay bridging the two. He never let Kole leave them in the dust, but neither did he prod Savannah to go faster than she dared. He stretched himself like a piece of rubber, banding them loosely together.

Sooner or later Clay would convince Kole to stop for a cigarette. Clay smoked only when his brother was around. According to Patty Keogh, Kole liked to corrupt Clay every chance he got, but what Kole actually liked was aggravating his stepmother. The part of the corruption Clay liked was the chance to share a bit of Kole's space, any fragment his brother would allow. Savannah wasn't sure what her part might be, except to worship the ground Kole's shadow graced, to come to attention whenever he called her name. She didn't want a whole cigarette. Just a puff. She was eager to put her lips where Kole's had been. She knew Clay was watching her, reading her the way he always did. He was the more subtle competitor for Kole's attention. Subtlety had never been Savannah's strong suit.

She could see Kole leaning back on his elbows in the grass, blowing a long stream of smoke at the cotton-candy clouds in a blue china-bowl sky . . .

"Okay, you guys, what do you see up there today?"

"A kangaroo," Clay said immediately. "See the tail and the two humongous springer legs? And there's one little front leg, see?"

"Where's the other front leg?" Kole challenged. Savannah was still looking for the "springer" legs.

"Down in the pocket."

"Playing with his balls?"

The boys guffawed.

"Playing with her baby," Savannah said. She couldn't see it in the clouds, but she liked the way Clay's vision took shape in her head.

"Yeah," Clay said. "Only the females have pockets."

"The males have the balls and the females have the pockets," Kole said. "Why didn't we think of that? Makes for a much more interesting game of pocket pool."

"Jeez, Kole."

Savannah giggled. She didn't have to see Clay's face to know that he was blushing. "I think I see a snowman," she said.

"Yeah, right there." Clay pointed overhead. "Hat, nose . . . I only see one eye. No, he's winking."

"I meant there. Those two . . . clouds. They're just clouds, Clay. One on top of another."

"A girl after my own heart," Kole said. "She sees clouds mating."

All she heard was *A girl after his heart*. Nobody was completely sure Kole Kills Crow had a heart, although a fair number of girls had searched him high and low for one. Savannah would have gladly given him hers, but he'd warned her not to be falling for any guy until she was at least eighteen. She'd taken that as a hint that he might be ready for her then.

Meanwhile, she and Clay would have followed Kole anywhere. He'd jerk his chin toward his battered blue pickup, and they couldn't pile in fast enough, with Savannah happily sandwiched between her two best friends. She remembered how safe she'd felt. Barreling down Main Street, Kole would slap at her hand when she'd reach over and toot the horn at some kid from school. But he'd always miss, and Clay would always laugh and wave with her. Hanging out with Kole Kills Crow was a rare and risky privilege, even for them. He was gone by the time they were eighteen, and in the years since, he'd looked back only once, as far as Savannah knew. When he'd sent for her and given her his child.

She jumped at the sound of more tapping, this time on the bedroom door. She grabbed her shirt off the chair.

"Savannah, are you all right?"

"I'm getting dressed."

"Figured I'd check and make sure you're still alive." The door creaked on its hinges. A frizzy gray head eased in. "You are, aren't you? It's been pretty busy downstairs today. Hope it wasn't too noisy for you."

It was an exchange they'd had every Saturday morning when Savannah was a teenager. "Noisy enough to wake the dead, Aunt Billie." It always felt like a daring comeback, a challenge for any ghost that lingered in the old rafters. Especially her mother's.

"Guess you're alive, then." A hundred creases went into the making of Aunt Billie's soft smile. The old floor creaked as she stepped into the room on crepe soles. "Leanne Ames came by a little while ago, said to tell you to call her or stop in at her shop anytime. She runs a beauty shop in her house now, and she does them long fake nails. You ever try those?"

"I've never had acrylics, no."

"Natural beauty from the minute you were born, just like your mama always said."

Savannah zipped her jeans. "All babies are beautiful, Aunt Billie."

"If you like that pruny look. Babies look like tiny old people, all wrinkly and bald. But not you. Your mama would have put you into TV commercials right away if she'd been livin' anywhere but Wyoming."

The two sisters had lived in Wyoming all their lives, like their mother before them. They had inherited the store, but Caroline Larsen's dreams had not included storekeeping. She'd run off with Jack Stephens, the driver of a produce delivery truck, when he'd bought his own rig. Jack was going places, she'd said. Two years later she'd returned, battered suitcase in her hand, bruises on her body, baby in her belly.

Like mother, like daughter, Savannah thought, except that the men driving Savannah's getaway vehicle hadn't been truckers. Nobody had ever dared hit her. And, heck, she'd had nice luggage. She wished her mother could have been there to see the dream she'd invested in her come true.

There. I did it. Are you satisfied?

"Did you think about getting Claudia into it?" Aunt Billie asked cautiously.

Savannah dismissed the question with a cool look. She'd never do that to her daughter. For Savannah, *it* had started with her first beauty pageant. She'd barely been out of diapers. Aunt Billie had never thought much of her sister's obsession with little Savannah's "career." But her mother had been right about the money she'd earn someday. In a few short years she'd earned more money than her mother had seen in her entire life. Then came Claudia, and Savannah had quickly discovered what it meant to be a mother. She had plenty of money, so she took time for her baby. A year stretched into two, then three. About the time she decided to go back to work, she discovered the lump she'd dreaded, the one that might kill her the way it had killed her mother. Then came the two longest years of Savannah's life.

What was that old saying about money? Easy come, easy go? That was bullshit. Fast, maybe, but not easy. There'd been nothing easy about it.

"Well, she's a beauty, too, like her mama. Only she's got her own . . ." The old woman glanced at the rumpled bed. "Well, she's got her own pretty coloring."

"Yes, she does."

Aunt Billie was fishing again, but Savannah had never been one for explaining. She had a six-year-old daughter whom she hadn't told anyone about. With her body widely displayed in full, slick color, she had become fiercely private. She'd quickly learned to protect her tender places and cut all chafing ties. She'd seen no reason to send out new-baby announcements. No amount of explaining would change the fact that Claudia was hers and hers alone. Maybe she should have handled things differently, but she wasn't planning on having her body turn on her during prime time. Who would? So Aunt Billie could stop dropping these hints any time now, stop giving her that sad little why-didn't-you-tell-me look.

Because it did make her feel bad.

"I'm going to help out here, Aunt Billie," Savannah promised quietly. "Just as soon as I get my bearings, I'm going to quit being a mooch."

"For all the business we generally get, Claudia could run the store. Folks want to drive down to Lander or all the way to Casper for a loaf of bread these days."

"I'll start tomorrow. I promise."

"You don't have to promise nothin'." The old woman's voice was thin and tight. Savannah wasn't big on explaining, but she'd promised things before, like calls and visits. "You take it easy on yourself," Aunt Billie said.

Savannah turned to the window again. "Where's Claudia?"

"She's out there with the kittens."

"By herself? Where's that cranky old mare?"

"Where she always is."

"That's not your pickup out there, is it?"

"All I got to drive is that old van," Aunt Billie said, obviously enjoying the fact that she had a few mysteries of her own. "That pickup belongs to my farrier."

Tap tap tap.

"You have a farrier for old Dolly?" Savannah cast a furtive glance at the bed. The pecker wasn't a bird. It was a blacksmith. "But nobody rides her anymore."

"Somebody looks after her, though. Only the best for my Dolly, and Clayton Keogh is the best farrier in the state. Best in the whole region."

Clay? "I thought he'd joined the army."

"You know full well he did, but that was about fifteen years ago. We've all found ways to keep ourselves busy since you left."

Savannah spared her aunt a smile, but it was the pickup that held her attention. "Clay Keogh," she mused, imagining the boy, wondering about the man. Another tie she'd cut, simply by not answering his letters.

Forget I asked, he'd said. *I don't know what I was thinking. We'd be stuck in Sunbonnet forever. We've both got things to do, places to see. Only, please write to me. It's pretty lonely in boot camp, even though I've got guys with funny accents either yelling in my face or breathing down my neck all the time. How about you? (Ha ha.)*

"I hope he hasn't changed too much," Savannah said.

"Go on down and find out."

"I should get Claudia out of his way. She'll talk his ear off. I should . . ." She watched, wishing he would step into view. But he was working. Her old friend was busy doing a job, and her daughter was down there watching him, conversing with him. Savannah could do that. "Oh, but not today."

"I expect his ear'll be gone by tomorrow."

Savannah closed her eyes and smiled indulgently. "I'm not ready, Aunt Billie. The woman in those pictures downstairs doesn't exist anymore, and when she did, she was never . . ." She searched for understanding in Aunt Billie's eyes, glistening pale blue behind glasses rimmed with gold wire. She'd forgotten how utterly reliable those eyes seemed. "I don't know what to say to people. Things haven't changed here."

"What things?"

"People don't—"

"People *do*." Aunt Billie laid hands on her arms and gave her a quick shake. "People do, Savannah. Maybe I've been an old maid since the day I was born, and maybe this store ain't never gonna be no Wal-Mart, and those hills sure don't plan on moving, but just because we're still here don't mean we've been sittin' on our hands."

"I know."

"No, you don't. But you look around, you're gonna find out. Clayton Keogh isn't a soldier anymore. Leanne Ames isn't working as a waitress in Cody anymore. Lucille Bosch—remember my friend Lucille? She was in this morning, too. She isn't county superintendent of schools anymore, you know."

Savannah swallowed the *So?* "She finally retired?"

"They finally stopped appointing her when the teacher they stood for election refused to serve, but if you asked her, that's not the explanation she'd give you. 'Course, she ain't exactly world-famous," Aunt Billie allowed, lifting one bony shoulder as she let her hands slide away. "But her picture got published regularly in the weekly *Sun-Bee,* right next to her school attendance report. So she was pretty famous around here, even though a lot of people didn't exactly know about the deal she had going with the county auditor to keep her in that job when she wasn't technically qualified. It's a nice title, county superintendent of schools, and Lucille had an annoying need to go bandying it about. I know she still misses that title, but she's able to hold her head up pretty good in public now."

With her own head full of fuzzy old images, Savannah had no idea which one went with Lucille Bosch. All she knew was the eyes. Everyone had eyes, and the minute she went downstairs, the eyes would turn.

"You don't think people wonder about me?"

"Oh, they've been wondering what happened to the modeling, but they won't be asking you right off." The old woman folded her arms. The skin in the crook of her elbow crinkled like tissue paper. "They'll ask you where your husband is first."

Savannah groaned.

"But not Clayton," Aunt Billie said. "He'd be a good one for you to start with."

Savannah stared out the window. The tapping had stopped, but there was no man, child, or horse in sight. "He'll ask, unless he's already figured it out. Please go down and bring Claudia in for me, Aunt Billie. I can't do the catching-up thing right now. I just don't feel up to it."

Billie headed for her backyard corral. Her pace was purposeful, not because she'd been sent, but because she was running out of patience. For over a week Savannah had been holed up in the bedroom of her childhood. Homecoming was a fine thing, but Savannah's seemed like an attempt to return to the womb. Sooner or later she was going to find out that there was no womb here for her. There was shelter and food and an old woman who still cared what happened to her, even though Savannah had all but ignored her for years. But no womb. Billie Larsen's female plumbing had been ripped out before she was thirty. Not that it would have been any use to her without a man.

But she'd raised Savannah. Caroline was the mother the girl missed and mourned and romanticized, but Billie had done the practical part. She'd kept the store going, kept food on the table, kept the roof over all their heads. After Caroline died, she'd managed to convince the strong-willed girl to stay in school until she graduated. Billie hadn't favored the modeling idea—that was Caroline's dream—but she'd given in, because it was what Savannah said she wanted. She'd found a nice family for her to stay with in Minneapolis, and she'd paid for the six months of school and the makeup and the portfolio and the rip-off contest fees. She hadn't favored any of it, not one bit, yet had had to do something to keep the damn truckers away. She'd had a little savings and no children except Savannah, whom she loved.

So did every camera the girl had ever met.

The dry hinges on the gate announced that Billie was letting herself into the corral. She heard little Claudia suggest

it might be her mom, so she called out before she made her
appearance, just so everybody could relax while she hooked
the chain around the gatepost. That little one had spunk. It
was Billie who'd enrolled Claudia in school and taken her in
for her starting-school shots. She'd acted so grown up about
the whole thing, Billie could hardly believe the girl hadn't
even turned six.

"How's Dolly holding up?" she asked as she approached
the big man and the small child, who stood side by side, admiring the swaybacked mare's unremarkable feet.

"Not too bad for an old gal with worn-out heels," Clay
said, greeting Billie with one of those easy, sparkly eyed
smiles of his. He swept off the sweat-stained Sunbonnet
Mercantile cap he'd been wearing since Billie had given
them out five years ago to celebrate the store's centennial
anniversary. " 'Course, I had me some help," he allowed as
he wiped his face on his faded blue shirtsleeve. "Claudia
wouldn't let me put the nails in my mouth."

"It doesn't hurt at all when he pounds nails into the
horse's hooves." Claudia got busy with the nails left in the
tray on the top of the shoer's toolbox, putting them back in
their package as though the kit belonged to her now, too.
"Where's Mommy? Is she still resting?"

"Well, she's . . ."

"She's awake now? I'm hungry. I bet she is, too. I bet we
could have some lunch together now." She looked up at
Clay. "Would you like some lunch?"

"I already had mine, thanks. But I—"

"I did, too, but I'm gonna go now, okay? Thank you for
the horse frog." She patted the big pocket on her chest as she
backed out of the shed and into the afternoon sunshine. Her
hair suddenly gleamed like black satin. "I'm gonna show it
to my mother and tell her how I helped you put shoes on
Dolly."

"Tell her . . ."

Claudia tipped her head expectantly, eager to carry something to her mother.

The man wanted to tell her himself. Billie could see the wanting in those bright blue eyes of his. But, big as he was, Clay Keogh was never one to push, so he just said, "Tell her Clay Keogh says hello. She might remember me."

"I will," Claudia promised, squinting against the sun. "Bye, Mr. Horseshoe Man!"

He'd already taken the child to heart. Billie could see that in his eyes, too, the way he watched Claudia scamper across the corral, dodging little piles of horse apples. She climbed over the bottom rail and took off for the house.

"Of course she remembers you."

His smile dropped away when he looked at Billie, expecting truth now. Bottom-line truth. "Is she okay?"

"She had an operation, and she's taking her sweet time about getting over it."

"So she's home to recuperate?"

"She's home. That's all I can say for sure."

He put his cap back on, pulling it down to his eyebrows, then shoving it up about an inch. "Maybe I oughta pop in and say hello myself."

"Well, she's . . ."

He waited, and when she didn't say any more, he smiled. "You said that already."

"I did, didn't I? She's as stubborn as ever, is what she is, but the truth is she's here because she doesn't have anyplace else to go. She hasn't worked in quite a while."

"Because of her health?"

"If you ask me, which you just did, I'd say it's mostly because of her head. Everything else seems to be in working order."

"What kind of—"

"That's for her to say, Clayton. But I'll warn you, she sure don't say much. The last few years I barely get a 'Merry

Christmas' out of her, and when I call, half the time it's not her number anymore, so finally I just give up. Then she comes home with a child. Where did that child come from? She let me know pretty quick, just with that look she can give sometimes, you know? Ask her no questions, she'll tell you no lies. That's about what it amounts to." Billie wagged her head. "Sweet little thing, that Claudia. Savannah has to be doing something right, I guess, but I couldn't tell you for sure what she's done or what she'll do next."

"I only meant to ask about her health, Billie."

"I don't want to push too hard, you know? That's on the one hand. On the other, I'm gettin' too old to beat around the bush." She eyed her niece's childhood friend. He'd been as lanky and rawboned as a young hound back in the days when Savannah used to run around with him and his half-Indian brother. She'd sure be surprised when she saw him, if she ever got around to sticking her head outside that room. Billie figured Clayton had put on at least thirty pounds of muscle, mostly because of the kind of work he did. No longer awkward and gangly, Clayton Keogh had grown into his paws, all right.

Yessir, Savannah was sure to be pleasantly surprised.

"What Savannah needs is a husband," Billie said, flattening the beat-around bush with both feet. Clayton's eyes doubled in size. Billie shrugged. "Stands to reason, don't it? She's got a child. She's had more than her share of trouble lately, and she needs someone to lean on. She's got me, of course, but a man, the *right* kind of man, would be so much better for her. She needs a good husband, pure and simple."

Clayton stared at her for a moment. Then he laughed. When he quit laughing, he stared again, but the laughter lingered in his eyes. "You got somebody in mind, Billie?"

"Yes, I do. Indeed I do, and it can't be just anybody."

"But somebody, pure and simple."

"Somebody who loves her. Somebody who loved her long before he had a chance to see her in her underwear." She stood her ground, lifting her chin high so she could look him in the eye when she handed his own words back to him after nearly fifteen years. "Somebody who's always loved her."

"That was supposed to be our secret. You just ruined my faith in sweet little old ladies."

It was Billie's turn to laugh.

Clay nodded, smiling. "I was, what, about eighteen? Since then I've *been* a husband, and I'll tell you what, it ain't simple. Plus, I couldn't save myself forever. I'm no longer exactly pure."

"You've got the purest heart in the county, Clayton Keogh. Your ex-wife would be the first to say so." Billie jabbed a finger in the direction of his square chin. "And that's a sure sign right there. You're blushing."

"I don't think I've ever been sweet-talked quite like this before. I don't know what to think."

"There's no need to think when you know how you feel. Besides . . ." She laid a hand on the man's arm, adding a warm touch to that *feel* part. She knew just exactly what words Clay would take to heart. "Savannah needs you."

Chapter 3

There was a place in the hills west of Sunbonnet where dreams had been etched in pale stone for thousands of years. Nearly blinding in the sunlight, it was a place Savannah remembered for its brightness, even at night, when moonlight washed sheer rock and sand floor, took away hues and values, and made all faces young, clean, colorless, and utterly innocent.

The memory drew her inexorably, like magnetic north. She would find her way by moonlight, while Claudia and Aunt Billie slept. Rather than prowl the house another night like a restless cat, she would prowl the hills the way she had as a teenager, when summers had been long, Sunbonnet had been insufferably quiet, and Savannah had desperately needed to escape the confines of her tiny upstairs bedroom. Back then, she'd cherished the company of dreams, both day and night. But now that she was using sleep to shut out the daylight, no dream-bearing sleep would come at night.

She slipped her aunt's keys off the hook inside the cupboard to the right of the kitchen sink and grabbed a bulky cardigan off another hook in the pantry. She sneaked out the back door into the clear and peaceful Western night, where cricket voices ruled instead of cars and crowds in perpetual overdrive.

At first, of course, the glaring, blaring city had thrilled her, captured every scrap of her imagination. She'd absorbed the energy like a sponge and used it to re-create herself—a thrilling, shiny, seductive, and sassy self, the perfect picture. But the flash and the flattery had dimmed along the way, becoming one more threat to her fragile balance.

She was hanging on by a thread, but a thread was better than nothing. And at least it wasn't a loose thread. It was more like a sunbonnet string. Maybe she couldn't distinguish the shape from a distance, but she could see it in her mind. It had a sheltering brim and a long, loose ribbon tie, one end anchored to Wyoming rock, the rest fluttering in the wind. Hang on, she told herself as she turned the key in the ignition.

The roar of the old van startled her, so deep was she into her own head. She glanced up as she passed Aunt Billie's window, remembering a time when she'd swiped the same van, before she'd gotten her driver's license. Poor Aunt Billie. *Girl, you wreck that van, neither one of us will be goin' anywhere for a good, long while.*

Come to think of it, Savannah didn't have a license now. It had expired.

Oh, that thread was flapping like crazy. This was risk-taking at its finest. She smiled as she pulled into the quiet street.

The Sunbonnet Mercantile anchored the town at the south end of Main Street, which was four blocks long—or two long and two short. Fewer than a dozen streetlights illuminated the whole strip. If not a "white way," it was a least a *wide* way. Or seemed so, even with the covered plank walkway that flanked the two middle blocks on both sides. The false-front buildings were no more than two stories high, so the street seemed long and wide. And empty. Everything was closed except the Naughty Pines at the north end of the street, where the bartender was certainly announcing "last call" right about now to three or four half-shot cowboys. Sunbonnet was a town that slept at night.

Several of the buildings were vacant. A couple of plate-glass windows had been replaced with plywood. Savannah was glad to see that the bank and Grumpy's Café were still in business. She remembered the first time she'd gone to Grumpy's without an adult to pay the bill. She and Leanne had ordered the same supper—hamburgers and Cokes, with a large side of onion rings to share. Grumpy's was famous for onion rings.

God, how long had it been since she'd eaten an onion ring? Since she could stomach an onion ring?

The half-moon took over where the lights of Main Street left off at the North Fork Bridge. Savannah gunned the engine, enjoying the power of being behind the wheel again. She was tempted to spend the rest of the night just following the headlights. But there was the magnet, the memory of the way the hills felt at night, that persisted in pulling her off the blacktop. She drove as far as she could—first over gravel, then over tire tracks in the sod—before she had to park the old van in the brush and hike.

The night was cool and still, powerful and soft, if not silent. It surrounded her like water, and she soaked it in. Below, she could see Sunbonnet glittering in the distance. It was late, and the lights were few, but each one counted for something—someone or some family. Scattered like quartz crystals spilled from a child's jar, they made the town seem bigger than it was. But the night was bigger still—big, quiet, and gentle.

The hills were easy on her, giving her a gradual incline and a rocky handgrip or a toehold where she needed it. She'd taken to wearing loose shirts with long skirts that tented her. She had to pull the fabric between her legs and tuck it in her waistband to keep the hem from snagging.

The image of her destination burned blue-white in her brain, but she was less certain of the path. She sought the big sunbonnet. Maybe she couldn't make it out from her bedroom window, but she knew it was there. She'd been there. She'd crawled inside and cuddled in the deep pocket and played with the strings. She was prepared to pass the night searching for the narrow passage she sought, but the hills kept pulling her along, drawing her directly to the secret place.

Glittering shards of stars brightened the black velvet sky above jagged chalky, moonlit spires that enclosed what might have been a lunar garden. Savannah had dubbed the place Artemis's Castle, even though Kole had pointed out that the Old Ones who had painted the petroglyphs on the walls were hardly Greek. But Clay had thought Artemis's Castle was a fine name for a place that was, after all, *his* discovery. A secret place shouldn't have a name, Savannah had said, looking to Kole for approval. Still, she'd cherished the fantasy of a moon goddess living in the shallow cave that was tucked into the corner of the rock garden, hidden within natural walls.

She found their rock. It was one of many that had tumbled from the high ridge during some primal upheaval, planting themselves in the barren saucer, like specimen shrubs. At first Kole had refused to leave his mark, but when they'd discovered two nineteenth-century inscriptions on another rock, they'd agreed that there was a kind of brotherhood across the centuries going on in this place. They'd tested several surfaces before they'd found one they could scratch their initials into. No dates, Kole said. Petroglyphs were sacred things. He didn't think dates were sacred, but names might be. They had arranged theirs in a circle.

With the pad of her thumb she traced the boys' K's and C's, but she couldn't find her own S's. Panic fluttered in her chest. Had her name vanished from the rock the way her face had disappeared from fashion magazines? Here one month, gone the next. She'd found out how expendable she was, hadn't she? But this was stone. It was rugged and hard, and it held fast, a permanent marker.

Maybe she'd never been here. Maybe she'd never been anywhere but that little bedroom.

She heard the scratch of gravel, turned, and caught the shift of shadow, a moving shape separating itself from a stationary one. It was a horse.

"Where did you come from?" Savannah asked, approaching quietly, assuming it had wandered up there on its own, and she was all set to welcome the company. Then she got close enough to make out the saddle.

"The Lazy K."

The deep, dearly familiar voice seemed to issue from the mouth of the cave.

"Clay?" She jerked the hem of her skirt free from its mooring in her waistband and let it drop. Another shadow emerged, bootheels scraping with each step as though they were taken reluctantly. He looked bigger than she remembered. "Clay, is that you?"

"The real me." He touched the brim of the cowboy hat that was pulled low over his face. "Are you the real Savannah Stephens?"

She laughed a little. "I was hoping it wouldn't matter up here."

"It matters to me." He reached for her hand. "Welcome home."

He seemed to surround her entirely with a simple squeeze of the hand. She stepped into the shelter of him, her nose a scant inch below his square chin. She had yet to see his face clearly, to assess his life by counting lines, but it didn't matter. She knew Clay Keogh. Reflexively she lifted her free hand, her fingertips seeking something of him, finding a belt loop, a bit of smooth leather. All she wanted was a proper greeting, a quick embrace, but she heard the sharp intake of his breath, and she knew she had the upper hand. She'd turned the surprise on him. He was big-man sure of himself one minute, shaky inside the next, simply because she'd stepped a little closer than he'd expected.

A power surge shot through her.

She lifted her chin, remembering times gone by and aiming for a little humor with her old dare. "You can do better than that, Clay," she purred. Her own throaty tone surprised her. Having no humor in her, she couldn't help but miss the mark.

He touched his lips to hers, tentative only for an instant. His hunger was as unmistakable as hers. His arms closed around her slight shoulders, hers around his lean waist. He smelled of horsehide and leather, tasted of whiskey, felt as solid as the Rockies, and kissed like no man she'd ever known, including a younger Clay Keogh. She stood on tiptoe to kiss him back, trade him her breath for his, her tongue for his.

"Savannah . . ."

She couldn't understand why he was trying to pull away. There'd been a catch in his breath—she'd heard it distinctly—and it was that small sound that had set her insides aflutter. The surprise, the innocence, the wonder of it all. Good Lord in heaven, how long had it been since she'd been kissed?

"Shhh, Clay," she whispered against the corner of his mouth. "It's so good, finding you here."

"Glad to see—"

"But don't talk yet. Just hold me. It feels so good."

She knew Clay. She trusted him more than anyone she'd ever known, and she would not suppose any change. Not now, not here in this timeless place. They were the same as they'd always been, two trusted friends who would do anything for each other, and right now she needed her trusted friend. She needed him to serve one specific part of her, satisfy one fierce want, and she wanted him to serve the way he always had. Unselfishly.

"You're not married or anything, are you?"

"I'm something." His deep chuckle sounded a little uneasy, which wasn't what she wanted. She wanted him easy. "But not married."

"Let me see you," she said, reaching for his hat. He started to duck away, but she flashed him a smile, and he stopped, looked at her for a moment, then bowed his head within her reach. "Girlfriend?" she asked as she claimed his hat and slid her fingers into the hair that tumbled over his forehead.

"No."

"Me neither."

"How about boyfriends?"

She laughed. "Completely unattached," she assured him, learning the new contours of his cheek with her hand.

"Well, I've never been to New York, but I hear there's a lot of variety there."

"There's variety everywhere, Clay. Don't tell me you've turned redneck on me. I won't have that."

"You won't, huh?" His smile glistened with moonlight. "Not much has changed here."

"That's what I was counting on." She reached to the right to set his hat on top of their rock, felt the tug in her armpit, the sharp reminder of the way she'd been carved up and rearranged. But her secret was safe in the dark, as long as she took care of it, and she wasn't letting him go. She had her thumb tucked in his belt, and she had such racy thoughts. "Have you changed, Clay?"

"Hard for me to tell."

"It wouldn't be hard for me to tell." She leaned against him, hip to hip, lifting herself on tiptoe as though straining for his ear, but it was the contact she wanted, the deep stirring. "I think you're hard for me," she whispered.

He grabbed her by the shoulders, as though he had to steady himself, and she heard him swallow. He wanted more. She moved again, just a little, just enough to get a good rise out of him. She smiled in the dark when he uttered her name like a soft prayer. Then he muttered something about this being an idea and not a good one, words not strung together quite sensibly, but she got the drift. She let it drift away. His fingers trembled as he touched the back of her neck.

"Shhh. Just let it be what it is, okay?" On tiptoe again, she lifted her face to his. "I'm so glad to see you."

"Same here." He moved her hair, kissed her gently, then leaned back and looked into her eyes, where she knew her hunger mirrored his. He kissed her again.

He nudged her cardigan aside and kissed her neck, her collarbone, his warm breath stirring her, tightening her skin everywhere and sending shivers shimmying straight to her groin. He lifted his head and their eyes met, his questioning, hers questing. She pulled his head down, seeking his lips. He groaned, surrendering to her, hungrily embracing her and her madness. His hat tumbled to the ground as he sat back against the rock and pulled her to him, his solid thighs bracketing her, like a fork in an oak tree.

Safe place, that fork. She felt like climbing a tree. She felt wild, free to please herself beneath the velvet blanket of night. She felt like sitting herself right down on that fork and giving herself over to the height and the breadth and the sway.

But she couldn't let him touch her. When he tried, when he threatened the top button on her shirt, she nearly tipped them off the rock in her determination to distract him. He stiffened, caught his breath again, this time as though she'd dealt him some pain. *This won't hurt a bit,* she mentally promised him. Kissing him, straddling him, she fumbled with his belt buckle, then his zipper.

Kissing her, supporting her, he inched his butt down the side of the rock, which became his backrest as he became her chair. He made one more attempt to get at her breasts with his hands, managed to pull a bit of her shirt from her waistband before she stopped him again. She made him lift his hips so that she could work his jeans down far enough to frce his penis. She arched her back and rocked against him, showing him what she would do for him when she had him inside her. He tried to put his face between her breasts, but she took his head in her hands and kissed him, spearing her tongue into his mouth until, with a groan, he admitted to being as needy a man as ever lived. Possibly as needy as she was.

She took his hand and guided his thumb to her crotch, to the leg band of her panties. "Nothing fancy, just cotton," she whispered.

"Nobody's taking any pictures."

He slipped his hand beneath the scrap of cotton and caressed her. She shivered again, looked to him for understanding, and found it in his eyes. He bit his lower lip like a boy bearing the pain of a broken limb. If this was the game they'd invented years ago, he hadn't forgotten the rules. He would explore her and touch her any way she wanted him to, any way that pleased her. He would stroke and pet her until she let herself go in his big, sheltering hand, never asking anything in return. Except for that one time when he'd held her desperately tight and come in his jeans. She remembered it with a smile because he wouldn't look at her. Even as a boy, he'd taken great pride in his iron control.

And he had every intention of controlling himself this time. She could tell. That assurance was in his eyes, even though his penis stood rigid and ready in her hand. But she had another surprise for him. She leaned forward, forcing him to pull the cloth in his hand aside as she lifted her hips over his and boldly ran herself on his kindly sword. Now he was rooted in her, growing in her. Oh, but it was she who would bloom.

For a moment they neither moved nor breathed. He filled her so completely, she could feel his head bumping against her heart. If she moved at all, she would surely shatter. Slowly, slowly she took the risk. Slowly he responded to her signal. Slowly they found a good fit and made it better, flesh within flesh moving stronger and quicker, closer, coming closer, coming, coming . . .

She tipped her head back and cried out to the spinning stars, then collapsed as the earth opened up. He was part of the rock, joined to the earth's hip, and she was joined to him, grounded by him, taken by him, taken safely into him, into the haven of him, where she curled up, gave up, and wept.

Clay's heart slammed against its trembling confines. To, fro. Yes, no. *Slam-bam, slam-bam.* Thank you, ma'am? Hell, no. *Thank you, sir.* Jesus, Savannah. *Damn you, Savannah.*

Thank you, Jesus. It really *was* Savannah. Every inch, every hair, every blessed breath Savannah, still just as wild and beautiful as ever and maybe twice as crazy. If she'd come home to drive him mad, too, she wouldn't have much trouble. Right now he felt like the clapper banging madly in her bell.

Be damned if he'd let it show, though. He cradled her against his chest, rocked her, told her that he was sorry, promised her that he would make it right, all the while trying to slip his hand into his lap and save his cock from the teeth of his zipper. That done, he kissed her eyes and quietly rocked her some more.

He didn't know what else to do. It wasn't as though a woman like Savannah came along and skewered herself on him every day. She had to be hurting pretty bad. Damn, she'd gone berserk, and he'd taken advantage when he should have been trying to do something, like . . . like . . .

He wasn't sorry. He was saying he was, but he was lying

through his teeth. God help him, he wasn't a damn bit sorry. Savanna was back, and she'd come to him, and God didn't seem to want to help him at all, so he'd helped himself.

He was only sorry if he'd failed her, and he was pretty sure that was what he'd done. He'd failed her, and he'd thrown his back out to boot.

But once again she surprised him. She looked up with a face full of glittering tears and thanked him, like he'd just pulled her out of a ditch.

"My pleasure," he told her, but even that wasn't altogether true.

He couldn't remember a time when making love to Savannah—finally going the full distance, soup to nuts— hadn't been near the top of his list of dreams, but he'd never dreamed it this way. He figured he'd brought his ingredients to the party, put the soup and the nuts on the table. She was the one who'd left something out. Probably herself.

He skimmed her damp cheek with his thumb. "I don't know what this was all about, honey, but if some guy's broken your heart, it'll be my particular pleasure to break his neck. Even if he's related to me."

She took a swipe at her tears with the back of her hand. He could feel her shaking.

"I mean that," he insisted.

"I know you do, Clay, and I love you for it." She was laughing now, laughing and crying at the same time, which was something he figured only a woman could do. "But how did my shameless behavior lead you to that conclusion?"

"I met your daughter." Might as well just say it with a smile. "She's got her daddy's eyes."

"Yes, she does."

Her barely audible admission underscored the stillness around them. He suddenly felt awkward, a feeling she must have sensed or shared, for she chose that instant to slide off his lap. They sat hip to hip now, facing each other. Back pain shot down his right leg, there and gone in an instant. *Be damned if he'd let it show*. He hooked his arm over her legs.

She laid her hand on his knee.

"And how is my brother?" he asked.

"I haven't seen him since Claudia was a baby."

I'm almost six, the little girl had told him. Six years was a long time. Savannah hadn't been with Kole in six years? Hadn't been in his bed with him, slept with him, made love with him in six years? Not long enough.

Clay tipped his head back, resting it against the names on the rock, and looked up at the sky. Countless diamonds on black velvet. Forever. God, she hadn't seen Kole in six years. His reckless brother, chased to the ends of the earth by the law and the outlaw alike. His hapless brother. *His only brother.* She couldn't say that he looked okay, that he was healthy, maybe a little bit happy, maybe putting his troubles behind him.

Six years was too damn long.

He tried to come up with another smile. "I haven't seen or heard from him since he busted out of the pen, so you're the one who saw him last. It's good to know he's still alive. But if he's hurt you, I'll track him down and make him wish otherwise."

"He gave me the very best part of my life, so put your dukes down." She was smiling now, too, eyes glistening. "She's beautiful, isn't she? No one told you she was Kole's daughter? You could tell just by looking at her?"

"You and Kole," he said, reluctant to picture them together, unwilling to think of him as the best part of Savannah's life. Her crush on his older brother had been hard for Clay to ignore when they were kids, but he thought he'd done it on the outside pretty well. On the inside he'd felt all those sad things he didn't care to name.

But Kole had always treated her like a kid sister. Even now when she said, "It isn't what you think," he could almost hear Kole's voice rather than hers.

"Where is he?"

"I can only reach him through a friend," she said. "I really don't know."

"But he's okay?"

"As far as I know, he's fine."

"I miss him, too. Worry about him. Don't understand why he doesn't trust me enough to give me a damn phone call."

"We're a lot alike, Kole and me. We've both been wrapped up in ourselves for so long, we forget—" She laughed abruptly, gave her head a quick shake, and he realized for the first time how short her hair was. Short for Savannah. "That's not what I meant to say. We don't forget. We're simply thoughtless." She reached for Clay's fallen hat. "Do you come up here often?"

"No."

"What brought you here tonight?"

"The same thing that brought you here. I don't forget, either."

"But you've never been thoughtless."

"Sure I have. I can be as thoughtless as the next guy. Hell, I didn't even think to bring a condom."

"Caught you unprepared, did I?" She laughed again, soft and easy, as though his stupid remark had melted some of the years away. "Oh, Clay, I wasn't prepared for this, either. It was a wonderful surprise. I haven't . . ." She cradled his hat close to her chest and confided, "It's been so long since anything my body did felt that good."

"Interesting way of putting it."

"Did I remember to say thank you?"

"You did. And I told you—"

"Gallantly that it was your pleasure."

"Claudia said you'd been sick. Are you . . ." When she turned her face away, he could tell that this topic was just one more thing she wasn't ready for. He lifted one shoulder. "If we'd started with a proper hello, I would've asked you how you were, and you would've told me you were fine. Seems like we skipped right over that part."

"We chose to show rather than tell, and you showed me just how fine you are. You're better than ever."

"We used to tell more and show less, all right. I don't remember us ever quite reaching the grand finale."

"Well, we're not kids anymore. And the finale was fine."

"If you say so." He touched her upraised knee solicitously, the way he would have touched her breast if she hadn't pushed his hands away. "Are you okay now?"

"My cue? I'm fine." She ran her hand up the back of her neck and flicked at her hair in a quick, fidgety gesture, giving little laughs but no looks. "This is a magical place, isn't it? A place where all the rules are suspended. I was thinking about the three of us. The Three Caballeros, remember? And then I looked up and there you were, like a gift."

He took his hat from her, then took her hands in his and made them be still. They felt small and cool, a little shaky. He waited quietly until finally she looked him in the eye. *Get real, Savannah.* As long as he had her attention, he knew she could read his mind. It was only fair, since he could read hers. It was how they'd always been with each other.

"Yes, I'm okay now, thanks to you."

"Healthwise," he said.

"I'm fine, healthwise. I had some surgery, and it turned out fine, so now I'm fine." She was looking up at the stars, and he knew he'd lost her again. "It was a female thing, you know. Men have their war injuries; women have their female things. Let's talk about your back."

"My back?"

"Your back gave you trouble during that balancing act on the rock."

He chuckled. "I thought that was a pretty smooth move, getting us both to the ground without losing our pucker."

"It was. How's your back?"

"We'll see when I get ready to stand up."

"Shoeing horses must be especially hard on a tall man."

"It's hard on the back no matter what, but I enjoy the work."

"What about the ranch?"

"Still here. I'm still part of it, just like you and Kole always said I would be." He chuckled again. "I enjoy the work."

"You always did. What else do you enjoy these days? I thought you'd be married."

"I was for a while. Didn't work out."

"Work you didn't enjoy?"

"I wanted it to work, but Roxie didn't particularly enjoy marriage. I think the kids did, though."

"You have children?"

"She already had them when we got married, but I feel like I'm still their dad. They never see any of their other dads. So I'm not completely unattached, but I'm not hitched, either." He grinned. "How do you like that?"

"Do you still love her?"

"I care about her." He tried to shrug off the question and the queasy feeling it gave him, coming from Savannah. Made him feel as though he was cheating on somebody. Damned if he knew who. "Roxie didn't have much use for what I had to offer. Truth is, I don't want to talk about my marriage any more than you want to talk about your operation."

"Fair enough."

"Let's talk about my niece."

"No, let's talk about . . . what brought you here in the middle of the night."

"Memories, just like you said." He jerked his thumb at the names carved behind his head. "Same as what brought you here. Memories rest easy here."

"Up here they don't get knocked around by wishes and regrets," she said.

"And time doesn't screw around with them."

"But I do."

"Is that what you're up to? Screwing a memory?"

"I don't know what I'm doing, Clay, and I didn't come up here to figure it out." She sighed. "I'm just here. That's all I know. I'm here."

"Will you be here tomorrow night?"

"I don't know. Come by and see."

"Can I come by the house tomorrow?"

"Nights are better. I'm a better person at night these days." She stood suddenly, fluidly, like a cat picking up on some small sound, stretching, then bending to offer her small hand for the hauling up of his large body. "Come by the hills tomorrow night."

She got him all the way to his feet without a hitch. All it took was her levitating smile.

"What about Claudia? I'd like to see her, too. She's dying to ride that old mare of Billie's, but I'd rather put her up on a nice—"

Her smile slid away. "Claudia's not dying for anything. She's not deprived of anything. I've never fallen down on— I've never—"

"I didn't say you had. I just thought I could let her ride a good horse. Poor ol' Dolly's seen better days."

"So has poor ol' Savannah, but she still has her good nights." She stepped closer. "This has been one of them. A good-night kiss would top it off like a sweet red cherry."

He bent to the task, loving the taste of her and fervently wishing she'd take her hands off his chest and the wedge of her arms out of the middle of his embrace. There was no getting around the fact that she wanted him only so much. Still, the kiss was good.

"Sweet enough?"

"You are the sweetest, reddest kisser." She backed away, but he caught her hand. She squeezed as though she were bleeding a sponge dry, dropping it, backing away. "Do you still blush the way you used to whenever anybody teased you about me?"

"I got over it after you left. Good thing, too. I'd've been permanently red once those underwear catalogs started coming out."

"That wasn't my first job, you know."

"I know. I liked the blue jeans ads."

She laughed. "Which blue jeans ads?"

"The ones . . . hell, I don't know what kind they were. Blue jeans are blue jeans until you put a woman in them." He pointed to his horse. "Come on. I'll give you a lift."

"I've done enough straddling for tonight." She blew him a kiss. It was Savannah's kind of exit, a kiss before vanishing in the dark.

He wasn't going after her. He'd already gone far enough. "Good night," he said.

From the dark came the words, "You're still my best friend."

Which wasn't exactly what he wanted to hear, but he'd been called worse.

Chapter 4

Sunlight poked around the edges of the window shades and pressed against Savannah's eyelids.

Get back down. She had no sense of time or place, but she knew it was too soon for light. Where was her sleep mask? She'd unpacked everything, and she was without her personal blinds. One more small piece of herself dropped somewhere along the twisted trail to this comfortable old bed. Face to the wall, she dove deeper into the slanted niche.

Then she heard soft movement behind her back.

"Claudia?"

The movement stilled.

"I'm sorry," came the precious whisper. "I was being very, very quiet."

"It's okay, muffin. I should be awake now. What time . . ." Savannah rolled over, forgetting for a moment that she had no clock beside the bed. Claudia stepped in front of an open dresser drawer, hands behind her back in guilty-girl fashion.

"What are you doing?" Savannah asked, sitting up slowly.

"I'm not putting it on, Mommy. I'm just putting it out here on the dresser for you, in case you wanted to use it." Claudia moved to the side to display the makeup she'd care-

48

fully arranged on a flowered metal tray from Aunt Billie's kitchen. "See? Lipsticks here. Brushes here. These round things—what are these again?"

"Paint. Little pots of paint."

"But not like the kind for painting a picture."

"Sort of." Savannah plowed her hand through sleep-pressed hair. "It makes a picture of a woman."

"It makes a woman's face into a picture?" Claudia cast a wishful glance at the tray. "A girl's face, too?"

"Girls are already pretty. You don't need paint, and you know what?" Savannah extended her hand, an invitation to her daughter to come sit with her on the bed. "I don't think you ever will."

Claudia hopped onto the bed. "But you said I could use it when I get a little bigger."

"If you want to," Savannah promised, letting one of Claudia's thick ponytails, made by another woman, slide through her fingers. Everything about her daughter was bold and exotic, from her warm chocolate eyes and raven's-feather eyebrows to her bow of a mouth. Everything about Claudia was so different from Savannah, so vibrant, so perfect and natural. She kissed the top of the child's head. "I'm sorry I keep sleeping so long. What's Aunt Billie doing? Is the store open already?"

"It opened a long time ago. One red-haired woman came to get some chocolate chips and walnuts to make cookies, and Aunt Billie said that got her own mouth all set for some chocolate chip cookies, too, and maybe somebody around here ought to mix up some cookie dough today." Claudia looked up at her mother, puzzled. "And she asked me if we went anywhere last night after she went to bed. I told her we didn't." Her little-girl frown made puffs instead of wrinkles. "Was that right?"

"We didn't. That's right."

"Can we go someplace today?"

"There's really no place else to go, honey. What you see is pretty much what there is of your mom's hometown. Here . . ." She stood, her voluminous black T-shirt falling mid-thigh as she laid her hands on Claudia's shoulders and guided her to the window. A jerk on the shade sent it wheeling to the roller. "Look straight out there at those hills. Do you see anything resembling a sunbonnet?"

With due respect, Claudia searched the horizon. "I don't think so."

"Right there somewhere, the way those hills are shaped. It's supposed to look like a sunbonnet, with a brim and a—" Savannah described it with her hands. "Kind of like a baby's bonnet."

"Like I wore when I was a baby?"

Savannah nodded. *When I was a baby* was a favorite topic of Claudia's, one that Savannah approached with great care and tenderness. "Do you want to look at pictures?"

"Okay! Where did you put the box? I want to see the pictures of you, too. The ones from the magazines."

"I didn't bring those, honey." Savannah flipped the trailing chenille bedspread out of her way and reached under the bed for the box they'd decorated with Claudia's artwork and cutouts from greeting cards, then decoupaged and tied up with satin cord. "Those big ol' portfolios were too much to carry. I just brought the ones of you."

"Did you leave them in New York?"

"I left them with Heather."

Her friend had actually pulled the multivolume leather-bound history of her modeling career out of the garbage. Savannah had had visions of watching the garbage truck devour the damn things, but Heather had told her to cut the melodrama. She'd taken the portfolios. She hadn't asked, but she'd known she didn't have to. They were hers if she wanted them.

Savannah had been able to hide a lot of things by isolating herself from her friend, but face-to-face, Heather Reardon saw right through her, just as she had one rainy afternoon in their new-to-the-city days, fondly remembered as "the lean and green days." They'd recognized the common green right away. It was the way you hailed the cab, one said later; no umbrella, said the other. They had only to make eye contact to recognize the lean part, the common hunger for something bigger than life as they knew it. They'd shared a cab they'd barely been able to afford between them, and within moments had discovered that they were both missing home, friends, and job prospects. Heather was fresh out of college, a budding journalist. Savannah had been carting a skinny portfolio around.

"Are we ever going back to New York?" Claudia asked, as though she'd taken over for Heather, reading Savannah's mind.

"Do you miss the city already?" Savannah took Claudia's little shrug to mean *yes* so that she could indulge in some guilt. She'd indulged in so many other things during the first years of their lives together, mainly money and time, spending both lavishly with her small daughter. She smoothed a wisp of hair back from Claudia's face. "We don't have a house there anymore, muffin. But here we have Aunt Billie and the store."

"And we have Dolly and Ladybug and all her kittens."

"Kittens?"

Claudia splayed her fingers wide. "Five kittens. Do you wanna go out to the barn and see? Or else I could bring them up here."

"They need to be with their mama. I'll go soon, I promise. First I think—" More guilt. She slipped her arm around Claudia's shoulders. "Maybe we should make those cookies."

"Oh, yes! Cookies!" She wrapped her small arms around Savannah's middle and dove in for a hug, face between her mother's breasts, elbow in her gut. Savannah stiffened instinctively. Claudia jerked back. "I'm sorry. Does it still hurt?"

"No, sweetie, it doesn't. I'm all healed up now." Savannah wasn't sure which of her tender spots Claudia was talking about, breast or belly, but either way, she had no business flinching anymore when her child tried to hug her.

She put her thumb between Claudia's eyebrows and rubbed the frown away. "Stop worrying. You've got your worry face on again."

Claudia dropped her head back and closed her eyes, enjoying every stroke. "I'll make the cookies for you and Aunt Billie."

"I'll help." Savannah kissed the spot she'd massaged, Claudia's "mad spot," where thunderclouds sometimes gathered.

The child's face brightened. "Maybe we could give some to the horseshoe man for giving Dolly those nice new shoes. Did you know that a horseshoe brings good luck if you put it over your door?"

"I've heard that." Savannah held up two long fingers, forked wide. "With the open end up so the luck doesn't fall out." The two fingers took a playful snip at Claudia's nose. "You're my good luck, muffin."

"I know I am," Claudia said, wrinkling her nose like a bunny. "But I think you need a good-luck cookie today."

Clay caught a heavenly whiff of sweetness on the Mercantile's front porch. He could see Billie through the front window, working behind the counter. He didn't think she'd seen him yet, so he backed away from the front door, hopped off the end of the porch—cursing his stupidity when the landing registered sharply in his lower back—and headed for the outside stairs at the rear of the building. If he was going to hint for a handout, he wanted it directly from the baker.

The door stood open on the tiny landing, the scent wafting though the screen. He felt like an eagle trying to perch on a barn swallow's nest. Or maybe a giant. *Fee-fie-fo-fum.* "Do I smell cookies baking?"

Claudia looked up from her task at the doll-size kitchen table and waved her spatula at him. He took it as an invitation to step inside.

The old screen door chirped as he removed his straw cowboy hat. "You know, that's just like dropping a fishing line, letting that aroma drift out the window like that."

Claudia's laugh turned her ponytails into bobbers. "A fishing line? There's no water to go fishing in."

"No, but there's air, and the air around here is filled with bait for hungry boys."

"I don't see any boys." She glanced behind him, making sure he wasn't trying to sneak one into her wee-small blue-and-white domain. The eagle no more, he was clawless but bear-hungry, a big teddy bear who'd fallen into the dollhouse kitchen.

"Nothing turns a grown man back into a hungry boy faster than the smell of chocolate chip cookies." He eyed the neat rows she'd made on the cooling racks. "What do I have to do to get one of those?"

She smiled, delighted with her authority. "Say the magic words."

"Please, may I have one of your cookies, ma'am?" He took a seat at the table, thinking it wasn't right to tower over the one in charge. She wore a flour-dusted yellow apron tied high across her chest that covered her from armpits to ankle socks, but she had the bearing of a princess.

She pointed with her spatula. "You can have . . . how old are you?"

"I'm thirty-three." He grinned. "Almost but not quite thirty-four."

"I can't give you that many. I could give you three or four, but not thirty-four."

"All I need is one. But make it a big one." He smiled when she chose the biggest one she had, groaned with wicked pleasure when he filled his mouth. He caught a broken piece before it hit the table and quickly put that away, too. "Did you bake these yourself?"

"You shouldn't try to talk with your mouth full," she said imperiously. "If they were store cookies, you wouldn't be able to smell them. They'd just be cold, hard, and only about this big." She formed a small circle with her stubby fingers.

"Your mom didn't help you?"

"Yes, she did. She helps me measure, and we share stirring, and then I drop the spoonfuls on the pans. But she takes them out of the oven."

"Where is she?"

"She's resting." Claudia glanced toward the hallway, letting Clay know he'd just missed seeing Savannah's fleeing heels. "After we just made these cookies, she needed a little rest. They're good, aren't they?"

"Delicious. Chocolate chip is my all-time favorite."

"Me, too. Did you come to see Dolly again?"

"I came to see Billie, but it looks like she's pretty busy, so I had to follow my nose. And now I don't think I can quit at one."

Claudia waved her spatula over the racks. "I'll trade you all these for a horseshoe."

"A horseshoe is only worth . . ." Clay helped himself to another cookie, but he was still eyeing the racks. "Well, maybe . . ." He claimed a third cookie with his left hand, fed his face with the right. "What do you want with a horseshoe?"

"I want to put it up over my mother's bedroom door for good luck so she won't get sick again."

He paused in mid-chew. His throat felt funny. She was looking up at him, wide-eyed, and he was thinking no cookie ever made was as sweet as this little girl.

"Will you trade?"

Trade? He'd happily cover the house with horseshoes if it would make Claudia happy and keep her mother healthy.

He swallowed, then smiled. "Sounds like a good deal to me."

"Can I have it right now?"

"We can go out to the pickup, and you can choose. If you don't find one you like, you can have one custom-made. But that'll cost you another batch of cookies. I could even help you put it up. You might not be tall enough."

"*I'd* be tall enough," said a voice from the hall.

Clay and Claudia glanced at each other, then turned simultaneously as Savannah appeared in the doorway.

"But I don't think Aunt Billie wants us pounding nails in the wall," she told her daughter while sparing Clay a quick look.

"Mommy!" Hurling herself at her mother's legs, Claudia transformed instantly from miniature adult to normal-size child. She gazed straight up, her dark eyes gleaming with unqualified devotion. "I was just giving the horseshoe man some of our cookies. He says he likes them a lot."

Savannah laid slender hands on the child's cheeks, a slender smile on the visitor. "Hello, Clay."

"Look, Mommy, I put all the cookies on the racks, and they're cool enough to eat now. I'll get you one."

With the child scurrying between them, the adults exchanged frank looks, hers at once wary and defiant, his . . . well, he couldn't see his. He felt like a man who'd just taken a hit. Off what, he couldn't say.

"Claudia said you were resting," he said, noticing the shapeless tunic over the long skirt and thinking, *Savannah? Was that you last night?*

It might have been the same skirt she'd worn the night before, but daylight washed all the mystery out of it. Was this Savannah standing there with a limp, colorless rag tied around her?

Smile, Keogh. What the hell is wrong with you?

He obeyed himself promptly. He hoped to hell the smile looked real. He hoped it wasn't showing, the way his heart was acting up. That puppy was due for some heavy-duty obedience training, but his head was in no shape to do the job at the moment. He was fairly reeling over the sight of the dark hollows under her eyes, the gaunt cheeks, the wiry shoulders—hadn't she taken that shirt-thing off the hanger? Damn, she looked like a reed.

Damn, this was Savannah, and he was staring, and she could see every stupid thought in his thick head.

Then see this, he willed. *No matter what's going on with you, I'm sure glad you're here.*

But he said, "I didn't mean to disturb you."

She folded her arms around her breasts, as though she was protecting herself from him. But she did manage to smile, first for him, then for Claudia, who placed one carefully chosen cookie on a napkin, displacing not one crumb, and took it to her mother.

"Thank you, muffin." She smiled at her daughter, then looked at the cookie as if it were a curiosity rather than food, a pretty bit of rubble the child had found.

Eat it, Clay thought. That and any other nourishing thing we can find. God, she looked so fragile and frayed.

"They're really good, Mommy."

Savannah opened her mouth for a bite. Clay felt like he was watching a horse with serious foot problems take its first steps on shoes he'd custom-made. He glanced at Claudia. She was hanging with him on the hope that a taste of cookie would please the sad-eyed woman they both adored. *Still* adored, he thought. Any doubts he'd had last night were gone for sure now that he could see Savannah's blue eyes. They were pale-water eyes, stunningly calm and crystalline, like a secret lake. Irresistible. He waded in without a second thought.

"It's my daughter's trading our cookies off for horseshoes that disturbs me." She touched her finger to her lower lip to catch crumbs, then to the tip of her tongue, savoring, smiling. "Next thing I know, she'll be trading the cow for a handful of beans."

Claudia giggled. "We don't have a cow, Mommy, and anyway, looks like the giant came to us."

"With cookies like these—" A forgotten last bite had all but melted in his hand, but he nibbled to make a point. And to taste crumbs on his tongue. "With cookies like these, you don't have to grow a beanstalk."

"And you could put up a horseshoe without standing on a chair," Claudia said.

"Easy. And I wouldn't have to use nails." He flashed Savannah an inviting smile. *Come to the table.* "You'd be amazed at what I can do with a horseshoe."

"You were always amazing with horses." She glanced away, softly adding, "And other neurotic creatures."

"Horses aren't neurotic. They're a little unpredictable sometimes, but that just makes life more exciting." He put the toe of his boot to the leg of the other vinyl-padded chair and pushed it away from the table, eyeing Savannah. *Come sit by me.* "Some days I need a little extra rest myself, because sometimes they keep me up nights, pondering." *Take a step, closer to the cookies, closer to me.* "Especially if they have violet eyes."

"Violent eyes?" Claudia sidled up to his shoulder. "That's scary."

"*Violet,*" Savannah said, visibly relaxing, drawn to the table.

Clay gave the chair another nudge with his toe. He could tell he'd sparked the right memory, the one to put some sparkle in her eyes.

"Like purple," Savannah continued. "Have you ever seen a horse with purple eyes?"

"A *horse?*" Claudia shrieked giddily. "With *purple eyes!*"

"You remember the horse of a different color." Savannah chucked Claudia under the chin as she seated herself in the creeping chair. Clay recognized the line from Savannah's favorite movie, *The Wizard of Oz,* which, he'd lay odds, was Claudia's favorite, too. "Clay was my best friend when I was in school," Savannah said. "We used to study together sometimes."

"She used to make me study for those awful science tests. I wanted to be a veterinarian, and your mother said I had to be able to pass those damn science tests, even if they had nothing to do with animals. Mars, Venus, Earth, Mercury, Jupiter, Saturn, Uranus, Neptune, Pluto. 'Mary's violet eyes make John stay up nights pondering.' " His recitation and his smile were for Savannah. "See? I still remember."

"Mercury comes first," Claudia said gently. "But that's okay. You just got the two M's mixed up."

"Damn." He snapped his fingers. "That's why I never went to veterinary school. I choke under pressure."

"No, you don't, Clay," Savannah said. "You're the coolest head I know."

"Really," he said, trying to think of one truly cool move he'd made under pressure the night before.

"Really," she repeated, trying to finish her cookie.

"Maybe not the coolest guy in school, but dependable." Which she'd remembered last night, but how about this morning? He gave her the sly eye. "Like a jack-in-the-box. You just turn my crank, and I pop right up."

Savannah blushed. Staring hard at the remaining cookie fragment in her hand, she turned rose red. God, she was pretty. Heartbreakingly, guilt-makingly pretty. *Turn my crank.* What the hell was he thinking? His face was heating up, too, and it served him right.

"He popped right upstairs when he smelled our cookies."

Savannah was startled by her daughter's contribution, as

though she'd forgotten that Claudia was there. Her pale, guileless blush matched the child's innocent remark.

Damn, he could be such a country clod. The woman he was looking at now was far more fragile than the one who had come to him under the night sky. This one could no more climb those hills than a wounded bluebird. Hell, the Savannah who was perched on the chair, her knee a few scant inches from his, would no more perch herself on his dick than . . .

His face flamed as he stared at the racks of cookies and faked an easy smile. "Why try to resist anything so wonderful?"

"Take some more." Claudia slid one of the racks toward his side of the table.

"One more before I head down the road to Lander." He helped himself to an excuse to linger a little, but he told Claudia, "Babies need new shoes."

"Baby horses?"

"Not babies, really. Colts in training." His eyes met Savannah's. The blush had already deserted her face, which would have been a relief to him if it hadn't left her looking less like herself. Oddly, he found relief in talking. "I'm on the road a lot. I can always use some company, if anybody's interested in a ride to the big city."

"I am!" Claudia clapped her small hand on his big shoulder. "But you'd have to wait for us, because I don't think we can take the train back, right, Mommy? The train doesn't get this far."

"The train doesn't get to Lander, either. In Wyoming it's mostly cows that ride the train, not people. People ride in pickups here."

"And on horses," Claudia said. "That's why horses need shoes. Mommy, I'll bet you could find a new doctor in the big city."

"Lander isn't a very big city, muffin, and I'm not sick anymore. I want you to stop worrying about that."

"Just in case," Claudia insisted.

"How about Casper or Laramie?" Whatever this sickness was, Clay was on Claudia's side. Get Mommy to a doctor. "They'd have more doctors there, and I've got plenty of—"

"I don't need a doctor!"

Savannah grabbed the edge of the table, ready to take off.

The hand on Clay's shoulder tightened. He looked up at Claudia, and what he saw surprised him. Determination rather than fear. The little girl was all set to do the mothering.

Savannah glanced from one to the other as though they'd trapped her where she sat. Then she took hold of herself, mastering her face and her voice as if somebody in the room were holding a camera.

"Thanks for the offer, but I don't need a doctor. I don't need transportation. I'm not going anywhere today." The hand that had clenched the table now softened as she lifted it to entreat Claudia, a small quiver betraying the effort. "We'll go another day, muffin. I promise. Let's wrap these up for Clay to take on his trip, okay? Then we'll make some more. As many as you want."

"I know!" Claudia jumped to the task, pulling a paper sack from a rack inside a cupboard door. "We'll make big ones, like the kind they sell for two dollars, and we'll put them in Aunt Billie's store. All she has is those icky ones in the box. I bet we could make a lot of money, Mommy!"

"My little Mrs. Fields," Savannah said, her face so clear and pale it seemed to take on the child's enthusiasm like a mirror. "You know what? I think that's an excellent idea. Don't you think so, Clay? What this town needs is a place to go for a good cookie."

"How much money do you think we could make?" Claudia wondered, cheerfully sacking all her potential profit. "A lot, huh?"

"Forget the horseshoes. I'd pay top dollar," Clay said. "You'd better save these for—"

"We'll make more. We love to bake." Savannah laid a hand on his arm, even as she stood and backed away. "It'll make her happy. Please."

"Thanks. Like I said, I'm on the road a lot. Anytime you need to go—"

"I'll let you know. I can't . . ." She backed into the doorjamb, teetering on slippered feet, holding him off when he reached to steady her. "I'm just a little tired," she said softly. She seemed to be fading. Not just retreating from the kitchen, but fading, like a shadowy hologram princess, until only her voice remained. "Have a good trip, Clay."

Befuddled, he looked down at the hand she'd rejected. He could've sworn she was almost enjoying the conversation. Had he said something? Was she feeling sick? Had he gotten too close? What had happened between them last night had been so unreal, so miraculous. But even then she'd rejected his hands. She'd taken him deep inside her, but she'd denied his hands.

"My mother's just a little tired," Claudia explained in what was no longer the tone of a little girl. He turned to her, embarrassed by his thoughts, and found her happily holding the paper bag up to him. "Are you really going to put shoes on baby horses today?"

"I could use an assistant. Maybe your mom would let you come along."

"Oh!" For a moment he thought she would leap into his arms with the cookies, but then she shook her head. "Oh, I don't think so. I know you're not a stranger now, but . . ." She glanced toward the hallway. "She needs me, too."

Clay tucked the cookies in the cooler on the backseat, along with his bottled water, beef jerky, and strawberry licorice whips. The requisite sunflower seeds were in the glove box. He was getting a late start, but with a good breakfast and a handful of soul-nourishing cookies al-

ready under his belt, he wouldn't be looking for another
real meal until he'd put in a day's work. He shifted into re-
verse, preparing to back away from the Mercantile hitch-
ing rail, when Claudia stuck her head out the door and
waved good-bye to him with the horseshoe she'd picked
from the box.

Damn, he could have given her those licorice whips.

Next time, he thought as he waved back. He had to get to
work, but next time he'd stop at Billie's counter and load up
on lemon drops and licorice and hair ribbons before he went
upstairs. He remembered blue ribbons tied long ago in her
mama's golden hair. He'd choose yellow for Claudia.
Maybe red.

It was hard to believe the child was only six, two years
younger than Dallas, his youngest. *Roxie's* youngest, but he
felt like they were his. Dallas was a boy, of course, which
made a difference in maturity, but Claudia seemed to slide
back and forth between little girl and young woman almost
the way Dallas's sister did. Cheyenne was twice Claudia's
age.

Clay loved those kids. The divorce had broken his heart,
but it was more from the loss of his kids than his wife. He
still saw them often, but he missed having them around the
house. They hadn't been easy keepers, to be sure, but they'd
livened things up around the Lazy K. He thought he'd been
a pretty good father to them, even though Reno, the fifteen-
year-old, was suddenly doing his damnedest to get himself
arrested just about every weekend. Reminded Clay of his
brother.

No, *Claudia* reminded him of his brother. It wasn't something he wanted to think about too much, Kole being her father, but it was pretty hard to miss that little reminder of
Kole's sloe-eyed smile.

Looks were one thing, deeds something else entirely. It
was because of Reno that Clay had to stop at Roxie's on his

way out of town. He'd taken her car and gone to Dubois, where he'd parallel-parked his rear bumper into some tourist's grille. Then he'd tried to take off. Roxie had called Clay this morning, first thing. He woke up with Savannah on his mind, feeling five kinds of frisky until he picked up the phone and got his ear fried by his ex-wife.

"I should have reported my car stolen," Roxie grumbled by way of greeting as Clay mounted the wooden steps to the little porch of her shotgun house. She herded Reno through the screen door ahead of her, then whapped it shut to add punch to her pout. "They couldn't be holding me responsible if I told them he stole it, could they?"

It was a question best ignored. Clay turned to the gangly, shame-faced boy and spoke solemnly. "What's the damage?"

Reno hung his head. "Can't hardly see no damage on that dude's ol' Caddy."

"You picked a Cadillac?"

"Hell, it's an eighties model. Big fat barge, sittin' way the hell out there, three feet from the—" Voluminous shirt-sleeves flapped around his bony elbows as he flung his scrawny arms just about three feet apart.

"Reno, what were you thinking, taking your mom's car into Dubois?"

"I dunno."

"What was *I* thinking," Roxie complained, "letting you talk me into letting him get that permit?"

Hell, what was she thinking, dying her hair the color of fresh blood? It was hard to look at her without cringing, so Clay shoved his hands in his back pockets and looked down at his boots. "He's old enough for the permit. He needs some practice."

"You said you'd let me drive your pickup," Reno muttered.

His mother jammed a hand to her hip as she chimed in with, "Yeah, let him wreck *your* vehicle."

"Not without me," he told the boy. "Doesn't sound like anything's been wrecked this time."

"The guy wants three hundred dollars," Reno said, barely audible.

"For what?"

"He'd rather have the money than file an insurance claim," Roxie said. "He was claiming that Reno left the scene, but he's willing to drop that."

"I was only trying to get out of the way," Reno said. "There was no place to park, and I didn't want to leave the car in the middle—"

Roxie was in the boy's face with her version before he could finish telling his. "You didn't think anyone saw you. You thought—"

"Were you trying to run, son?"

"No," he told Clay, and then, to his mother: "I ain't that stupid."

"No, you're not," Clay said. "And neither am I. I'm gonna loan you three hundred dollars, Reno, because I know you're good for it. But it's between you and me. I won't accept payment from your mother." Not that she'd offer, but this way they could all pretend.

"I . . ." Reno nodded, swallowed, his Adam's apple bobbing like a Ping-Pong ball in a storm drain. "Maybe I should just sit in jail if that's what they want. I don't know if I can come up with three hundred dollars."

"What are you doing right now?"

Reno gave him a blank look, then realized what the deal was. He screwed up his face so his zits all ran together. "Aw, maaan, I don't wanna haul bales today. It's gonna get too hot."

"That's for tomorrow." Clay clapped a hand on the boy's skinny shoulder. "I've got fifteen horses waiting for shoes and the day's half gone. If I help you out, you can start working it off today."

"I need him to watch—"

Clay silenced Roxie with a look. "That's my offer, Reno. Take it or leave it."

"I'll take it. I'll go change my clothes."

Clay was thankful for that. He didn't care how worn and faded they were, but a few sizes smaller would be an improvement in the jeans.

The screen door slapped behind Reno, leaving Clay and Roxie standing in silence until she finally said, "Thank you, Clay."

He nodded. He was glad to do it. Her kids were a handful, but never as much of a handful as Roxie herself. She knew it, too, yet there was no chance she would ever change. He figured she'd given it her best shot with him, but she just wasn't the marrying kind.

"You should have been their father," she told him.

"I tried."

"And you don't give up." She laughed. "God, you love to punish yourself, don't you? What I meant was, I wish I'd . . ." The hard-life lines around her eyes and mouth softened with the kindhearted look she gave him. ". . . started with you."

"Ah, Roxie." He shook his head, slipped his arm around her, and drew her against his side. "You were too much woman for me."

"Why don't you just say it, Clay? Say what you're thinking. Too old, too fast, too wicked, maybe, but I was hardly too much woman for Clay Keogh." She looked up at him, pouting again. "You never really loved me. You felt—"

"Come on, Roxie, don't start that."

"Have you seen her yet?"

"Who?"

"Savannah Stephens." She gave a tight smile. "The Dreamwear Girl herself. Rumor has it that she's back in town, but I don't think anybody's actually seen her up close."

He glanced away. Up close with Savannah was his privilege, then, his secret.

"You have, haven't you?"

"I was over at the Mercantile earlier." He lifted one shoulder. "I saw her."

"So how was it?" She teased him with a smack on the hip. "Was it good for you, Clay?"

"She's an old friend. It's always good to see an old friend."

"How does she look? What was she wearing? Does she dress like—"

"She looks like Savannah. A little older, a little more uptown." A little white lie, followed by his own unshakable truth. "She's still Savannah."

"And you still get pie-eyed just thinking about her."

"Like every other guy in the universe."

"And don't you forget it. You think *I've* been around, boy, you can just about imagine how many—"

"Don't." He warned her with a look. "Don't go there, Roxie."

She smiled, as though his quiet warning afforded her some kind of victory.

He shrugged. "It's no different from you getting all giddy over George Strait, except that you saved his picture. I never did that as long as you and me were—"

"You didn't have to, Clay. You had her memorized."

He was grateful for Reno's timely emergence from the house. "Come on, sport, we're burnin' daylight." He handed the boy his keys.

"You're letting me drive?"

"Got your permit on you?"

"Yeah." Reno studied the keys, then bounced them in his hand and bolted exuberantly for the driver's seat. "Yeah!"

"He just needs practice, Roxie," Clay said. "There's always a price. Three hundred dollars isn't much."

"Right." She backed away. "It is when you don't have it. It's one more headache."

"You do now, and I'm taking your headache with me." He nodded toward the front door. "Spend some time with Cheyenne and Dallas, huh?"

Chapter 5

It was Savannah's habit to ignore mirrors, but after she'd left Clay in the kitchen that morning, she'd caught a glimpse of herself in the one above the dresser. Oddly, it was her hair that drew her back for a second look. She had blessed the night for cloaking the details, and now she'd exposed them in daylight because she'd heard Clay's and Claudia's voices. They'd been talking about her, yes, but she hadn't realized that right away. It was the sound of their voices, the two of them talking together, laughing together, cheerful tones that had drawn her out of her hole. Unless the mirror was lying, she had gone out looking exactly like someone who'd been living in a hole.

At least put some lipstick on, said the maternal voice in her head.

She looked pallid, maybe even a little scary. Clay hadn't seemed too shocked, but that was just Clay, looking sympathetic on the outside, but probably thinking, *I fucked that? Damn.* He was likely on the phone with his shrink right now. *I think I've got a little necrophilia trouble, Doc.*

The thought made her smile. She noticed the immediate difference in her reflection. She still had her smile. *They can't take that awaaay,* crooned another voice in her head. More of a kid voice. *Clay's in love with sti-iiffs, Clay's in love with sti-iiffs!* It was the kid voice, her brat voice, making her laugh now. God, where had that come from?

The same place the notion of Clay having a shrink had come from, obviously. He was a rock. An earthquake could rearrange everything on the Lazy K except Clay. If a tornado came through, Clay would be the one wall on the place left standing. Clay Keogh would never end up in Oz.

She hadn't done much with her hair lately. She'd almost forgotten how. Head tipped to the side, she assessed with a little finger-combing. Her hair had become thin and scraggly during her chemotherapy, but she hadn't gone totally bald. She'd had it cut professionally before her surgery, said good-bye to her once-famous palomino mane, ended up with a chic, chin-length style. She'd been pretty upbeat about the whole thing then. A few months later she'd scared her daughter to tears when she'd taken the shears to what hadn't fallen out and whacked it off like a gardener going after a hedge. She'd been left with hacked-up yellow fuzz.

It had grown in thicker than ever, more body, more wave. More forgiving, maybe, but she didn't know what to do with it. It had been too long since she'd cared beyond keeping it clean, and even that took supreme effort sometimes. The hedge had grown, crept down her nape, odd pieces poking out here and there. If she put a little gel in it and slicked it back, it might look like planned disarray. Photographers loved that.

Of course, she'd have to find some gel, or make do with something else. What could she use? She caught her reflection smiling again.

"Well, don't you look nice," Aunt Billie said, peeking around the door. "Got a date?"

Savannah glanced down at her plaid, jumper-style dress. It wasn't fancy, but it was clean. She'd changed clothes after two rounds of cookie-baking. "I just thought I'd try . . . Do you have any hair gel, Aunt Billie?"

"Hair gel?" Billie screwed up her face for some serious pondering. "I know we've got some stuff for men, but you wouldn't like the smell. How about hair spray? I'm pretty sure we've got that. 'Course, it might not be your brand."

"Old men's stuff or young men's stuff?"

"I wouldn't know the difference," Aunt Billie said with a laugh. "Around here they all wear the same thing on their heads."

"A hat, which is what I need." Savannah drew a deep breath. One step at a time was easily said, but she felt a step coming on. "I thought I'd help out in the store."

"We just closed, honey."

She'd waited long enough, then. "I thought I'd close out the register and straighten up."

"Closing is a start. Maybe you could open tomorrow. There's a group of women comes in on Thursdays to discuss books."

"Books?" Savannah smiled. Aunt Billie was the queen of clubs. "What kind of books?"

"The kind we read. The kind we sell right here in the Mercantile. Fact is, we read all kinds of books in Sunbonnet." Billie slipped her arm around Savannah's waist and steered her toward the stairway to the store, chattering as she herded her into the stairwell like a calf in a chute. She snapped the light on. "We have a reading group that meets here, a whist club, and the King Me Boys are still going strong. What would a general store be without old men playing checkers? They've all been asking about you. You might not remember every one of them, but they—"

"Of course I do, Aunt Billie. That's why I'm here. I remember what 'normal' was like, and all I really want is to get back to it again. That's all I want."

The accumulation of old boxes and tins on the side opposite the railing left only a narrow passage, which Savannah descended carefully, inhaling deeply of what she thought of as the "granny" smell that pooled in the stairwell. She re-membered her mother's complaints about the junk on the stairs, but Billie always said that it wasn't junk. It was a col-lection of "discontinued sundries," a century's worth of Mercantile samples stored on the stairs, squirreled away by their mother and her mother before her. Savannah had vague memories of her grandmother, only a photograph of her great-grandmother, but she'd always liked the musty, an-tique smell and the close embrace of the stairwell.

"I talked to the doctor yesterday."

Savannah paused. Her aunt's quiet voice rolled over her from above. She felt like a bug trapped in a vial. She skit-tered down the remaining steps and broke free behind the store counter.

"Dr. Schmidt?" *Shrug him off. What could he know?* "He must be getting up there." She found the ledger where it al-ways was, on the shelf below the old cash register.

"Paul Schmidt retired. We got a woman doctor now. Comes to the clinic once a week. You'd like her, honey, she's about your age, and she . . . well, she can't do what you need done here at our clinic—which, the way things are nowa-days, we're lucky to have open even once a week—but she can check you over and refer you for—"

"I know, Aunt Billie. I'll get to that. Right now, if I could just count the money in the till and sweep the floor, that would be"—she pleaded with her eyes, her voice losing steam—"something."

The ledger columns looked daunting. Brain work. She used to do this all the time. She closed the book, stroked the nubbly green cover as though she might iron out the bumps, then turned to the broom closet. "Good exercise, for one thing. Reaching and stretching is just what I need. That's why I've been . . . sometimes when I can't sleep, I'll come down and—"

"They've come a long way since your mother, you know,"

Aunt Billie said quietly. "The treatment, the rate of survival, it's all so much better now. I try to keep up with the latest news about—"

"I know all that, Aunt Billie." She pulled the broom out of the closet, gripped it in both hands, and told herself to be patient. The old woman meant well, but she didn't know the half of it. "I'm not afraid of dying."

Billie looked her niece in the eye. "How about living?"

"I'm not afraid. I'm just . . . unsure. I start to take a step, and then I stop and think, No, I can't go there right now. Maybe if I . . ." She laughed, realizing she had a death grip on the broom handle. "I just want to sweep the floor. Can't I do that? Let's see if I can do that. If I manage that in broad daylight, then . . ." A thought. A care. An appendage was missing. "Where's Claudia?"

"Feeding the cats. I promised to take her to Bingo with me tonight. She even painted my nails, so now I can daub in style," Aunt Billie said with a sad smile as she extended one pink-tipped hand. This had to be a first. Savannah had never known her to wear makeup. "Poor kid. She's all excited about going to Bingo."

"I used to get excited about going to Bingo with you, too. We won a Barbie doll once, remember? You said you liked baby dolls better than 'babe' dolls, but it was my choice. Don't say, 'Poor kid,' Aunt Billie."

"Come with us."

Savannah retreated to the corner, where colorful bolts of cotton fabric stood on the shelves behind the long display-and-checkout counter. She'd come out either sweeping or fighting.

"Come on, girl, we know you can clean. You're the midnight cleaning fairy. You've got this place cleaner than it's been in a hundred years and disgustingly organized. You've got your days and nights all turned around."

"Maybe we should try staying open a few nights a week."

"This is a one-woman operation, and *this* one woman's got a social life. Are you gonna take that shift?"

"I think I could. I think . . . I'm going to start earning our keep, and I know I have to get over this . . ." Lacking a word, she offered a gesture. *This thing, this stupid thing.*

"You're my family. You don't—"

The bell on the front door jangled as the door opened and closed. A simple, everyday occurrence, but it sent Savannah's heart into a tailspin.

"Billie? It's just me."

"Hey, Leanne."

"We're closed," Savannah whispered, more a plea than a reminder.

"She called ahead. We stay open for people who call ahead." Billie blocked Savannah's escape as she slid a small paper sack across the counter and called out, "I've got your order ready for you, Leanne. Watkins liniment, Tylenol, and you did say white shoelaces?"

"Yeah, thanks, Billie. I couldn't get away from the shop today. Back-to-school haircuts and two . . ."

The voice had not changed. Like a talking doll, Savannah had said once, and she'd gotten Leanne to say, "Hi, Mama," when she'd pretended to pull a string from her back. It had seemed funny at the time, but times had changed, along with appearances. Leanne had put on some weight, exchanged her glasses for contacts, added some curl to her flaxen hair. She was wearing a red windbreaker with her first name and a bowling pin machine-embroidered over her left breast.

"Hi, Savannah." She still gave that tentative smile to start with, as though she wasn't sure people would want to see her teeth. "I heard you were here, but every time I've stopped in—"

"Leanne, it's so good to see you," Savannah cut in quickly, reaching both hands across the counter, which served as her defense.

Flustered, Leanne extended the paper bag, then her free hand. They both twittered. "You look as beautiful as always," Leanne said. "Your hair's real pretty like that. Nice and thick."

"Thicker than ever, actually. One of the better side effects, in my case."

"Of what?"

Savannah shrugged, testing the extreme. "Shaving my head."

"No kidding. Completely? I saw pictures of you with dark shoulder-length hair, and the next time it was real long and more blond, and I wondered. So they make you wear wigs?"

"No. Well, sometimes. I haven't worked in over two, three—" *She knows. They all know. Just say it and get it over with.* "I'm not a model anymore. I'm trying to get Aunt Billie to hire me as her"—Savannah stole a glance at her aunt—"stock supervisor. That's what I want to be when I grow up, Aunt Billie. Stock supervisor for the Sunbonnet Mercantile."

Billie laughed. "I don't know that I've got a tag like that in the drawer, honey, but I can make one up for you."

"Aunt Billie says you have your own beauty shop, Leanne. That's wonderful. I'll have to make an appointment soon." Savannah ruffled her hair. "I haven't done anything with this in a long time."

"You don't have to. I'm sure you could give me some tips on the latest styles. I try to get down to Casper every now and then—that's where I went to school to be a stylist, you know—but it's hard to keep up." Leanne folded her arms and lifted her chin a notch, studying with a pro's eye. "Did you get a tattoo when you shaved it off? I did a foil for this one woman—you know, she wasn't from around here, but she stopped in for a foil—anyway, she had a tarantula tattooed on her head. Wouldn't that just make you feel crawly every time you thought about having a tarantula in your hair?"

Savannah was smiling now. Leanne was still a talker. Shy at first, but once she got going, the silences were brief.

"It's like nose rings," Leanne continued. "You don't see them much around here, but whenever I do, I can just feel it, you know? It's like I see that ring and I can feel somebody poking a hole in my nose. People do the weirdest things to their bodies sometimes."

"Sometimes," Savannah agreed, thinking about how difficult a "tram flap" was to explain. *This thing that looks like a breast is really my stomach muscle.* "The weirdest things."

"I thought about piercing ears, but I'm afraid someone would come in wanting a nose job, and I just couldn't handle that. I just can't imagine . . ."

"Putting your fingers in people's noses," Savannah said with a chuckle.

"Yuck, blood and snot both."

The barriers tumbled as the years slid away. They were both laughing now, friends again, no topic too revolting, no body parts or fluids barred.

"No way, Nellie," Savannah said, one of the many expressions they'd coined that she hadn't used in years. She moved without thinking, out from behind the counter. "You don't need that. You must be busy enough, being the only hair stylist in town."

"Some people think you have to go to a city to get your hair done right. I can do nails, too, but there isn't much demand except around prom time. Roxie Keogh—used to be Keogh, except I think she's back to Fischer now—she gets her nails done in Casper, but she lets me do the fills." Leanne reached for Savannah's hand, gave a warm smile. "Yours are natural. I was gonna offer to give you a free set of nails, but I wouldn't cover these. I'll do your hair for free anytime, though."

"Thank you."

"You'd have to thank me by telling people you got your hair done right here in Sunbonnet."

"I could do that." Savannah shrugged diffidently. "I haven't seen many people yet. I'm sort of sneaking home through the back door."

As if on cue, the back door flew open, then slammed shut. Claudia came bounding in, reciting the latest names she had chosen for the kittens and explaining why she was changing them again and how she didn't think the one she called Sandy was really a girl. Her face lit up when she realized that Aunt Billie wasn't the only person listening. Here was her mother—downstairs, all dressed up, and talking to a customer!

Savannah nodded, smiled, felt a little sheepish about getting such a big hug for such a small accomplishment. "Leanne, this is my daughter, Claudia."

Leanne was staring. Claudia looked up at her mother, puzzled.

"Leanne was my best friend back when we were in school," Savannah told her.

"My best friend in New York is Rachel Woods, but after we moved from Manhattan to Brooklyn, I never got to see her," Claudia said. "Now she's really far away, but maybe I'll see her next summer."

"Are you going back to New York next summer?"

"Maybe. If my mother gets well and finds her head and gets it back on. Not her outside head, but her inside head. Right, Mommy?"

Savannah nodded dumbly. Her own words, more or less.

"Bingo," Billie quipped. "Claudia and I are headed for Bingo. Anybody who cares to come along is welcome. We're going to see if we can win ourselves a babe doll."

"You mean a pig? I don't think so. I'm going to win something like . . ." Claudia tugged on Aunt Billie's sweater as they headed out the door on the words "for my mother."

Quickly turning her back on Leanne's inquiring eyes, Savannah scanned the display on the closest shelf. "I was just about to check the hair products to see if we have any gel."

"She's a little doll," Leanne said. "She looks like somebody I know, and it's not you. Not that you're not a—"

"You don't know." Savannah selected a long box off the shelf. "Don't suppose anything, okay?"

Leanne allowed two beats of silence to pass before she tried again. "Nobody's actually seen him in years."

"Listen," Savannah warned as she whirled around, box in hand. Leanne's eyes widened expectantly. She was all ears, ready for any detail. They had traded many fantasies years ago, imagining all kinds of sexual summits and what it would be like to scale them with a *real* man. Savannah's fantasies had always included Kole.

She sighed. "This is exactly why I've stayed away. This place is like a box. A box full of boxes, and if you don't fit, if you don't *want* to fit in a box, you can't live here. How do you breathe inside a box, Leanne?"

"I'm sorry. I didn't mean to pry." Leanne touched her arm, and it was all Savannah could do to keep from shrinking away. "She's beautiful, Savannah."

"Yes, she is. But she's not Kole's, Leanne, she's mine. Okay?"

"Okay."

"And I wouldn't have brought her here, except that . . ." She glanced at the front door, with its window, its bell, and its lock. "Well, Aunt Billie's the only family I have. They say you can't go home again, and if that's true—"

"Okay, so I *told* you that Roxie Fischer has acrylic nails. That's like the kids say. Duh. Plus, she only lets me do the fills, and she was never my best friend. I always thought, like you told your little girl, that we were the kind of friends that don't forget, you know? Even if they don't stay in touch. And, yeah, I've bragged about my friend being a big-time model. But I don't tell tales. I always knew you had a crush on Kole, but I never said a word, and I'm not about to now."

"I know." Savannah offered a tight smile. "I'm nothing to brag about these days. I haven't done anything in years, except—"

"So what's this about getting well?"

"I had breast cancer."

There. Amazingly, she'd said it. Most women probably said it easily, but Savannah wasn't most women. She didn't look like most women, didn't act like them, dream like them, live like them. She wasn't built the same.

How many times had she said that, oh, so easily? *I'm not most women*. What a joke! Again she came up with a tight smile.

But Leanne wasn't laughing or smiling or looking horrified. She wasn't even asking questions. She simply took Savannah's hand in hers, held on, and kept quiet.

Pity.

Savannah gave a quick, dismissive squeeze and pulled away. "I had surgery. I'm fine. I don't want to talk about it, and I don't want you talking about it. I don't want people thinking about cancer whenever they look at me."

"People look at you, and they think about—"

"I really don't want people looking at me anymore. I want to be invisible."

"I don't think that's gonna happen, Savannah. Not you. How long ago?"

"The surgery? Almost two years."

"You're gonna be fine. I mean, two years? That's the magic number, isn't it? Or is it five? Anyway, you're gonna be just fine."

"I need to get my head on straight." Savannah laughed as she slid a tube out of the box she'd taken off the shelf. Was it two? Was it five? Was there any magic number to take the worry away? "I guess I must've said that a few times in front of my daughter."

"I don't have any children," Leanne reported sadly. "I wish I did. I was married for a while, but I got out of that little situation without too much skin off my nose. I always wanted, *wished* I could be more like you. Independent."

"It isn't all it's cracked up to be." Or maybe Savannah wasn't and never had been. She turned the tube of men's hair dressing over to look at the instructions. "How about this stuff? It says *gel formula.*"

"Do you want to smell like ol' Stout Trout?"

Savannah grimaced. "Is he still around?"

"Moved up from vice principal to the big kingfish. And that stuff right there is pure fish oil."

"Genuine Trout stink?"

They looked at each other, each mirroring the other's mock horror, then echoing the other's laughter.

"Come with me to the shop," Leanne said, taking the tube and the box away as she urged Savannah toward the door. "I've got stuff that smells like lily of the valley and stuff that smells like blueberries on the hill. I've even got stuff that smells like a sea breeze, although you couldn't prove it by me, seein' as how Salt Lake is as close as I've ever been to any sea."

"I don't—"

"Come on, now. I want to make sure you can find the place when you get ready for your next haircut."

In the old days Savannah had been the one to decide what to do, where to go, and Leanne would follow. Now it was Savannah's turn. *Don't think, just go,* she told herself. They were two old friends, simply going out for a little hair gel.

The woman who had never seen the ocean gently urged her once-worldly friend across the street of their hometown on the promise of help for her hair. In the dimming daylight

Savannah felt her insides tremble wildly as she watched Leanne unlock the front door of the Tip Top Shop. She'd made it. She'd crossed a street, *two* streets, turned one corner, dying to turn back with each step, but she'd kept going. She felt as if she'd run from one end of the state to the other, even though she'd only walked the country equivalent of two blocks. She'd made it!

She relaxed the minute they stepped into the lavender-and-white parlor and shut the door. It was a small, cozy shop with a feminine feel. Leanne gave her a choice of products, and they experimented with a slick-back do and a drawer full of makeup samples. It was just like the old pajama-party days, Leanne said. When they left the shop together, it was dark outside. There was no need for Leanne to walk her home, but Savannah didn't object to having an escort. Nobody was crowding her. *That's what friends are for,* Heather had said to her once too often after one too many favors, and Savannah had thought then that it was a wonder she had any friends left.

"Would you like to take a walk down to the Naughty Pines and see what kind of night life we can scare up?" Leanne suggested.

"What kind can we expect?"

"Music, merriment, and men. They still outnumber the women in this state. We can expect a lot of the same ones who used to party out at the old Sherwood shack after ball games. Remember? I'll go if you will."

"And no taking your tattletale sister along," Savannah recited from memory.

"And no taking off and leaving me with some creepy octopus."

Savannah laughed. She had turned an honest-to-God corner before the sun had left the sky and the night had come to protect her. "I'll take the walk, but no music, and no men."

"No Naughty Pines?"

"Definitely no Naughty Pines. A makeover and a stroll are plenty of excitement for me."

Clay brought Reno home after a good, long day of working together. The light was on in the kitchen, the TV flickered in the living room window, and Roxie's car was in the driveway, which meant there was a good chance that she was home with her kids. Clay was glad. He half wished it were him coming home, that they'd be walking in the house together, like father and son. The ol' man would get the bathroom first. His back could sure use a tub full of hot water.

The boy had worked off some of his restlessness. He'd been sullen to begin with, but by the time they'd trimmed half a dozen sets of hooves, he was telling Clay about a girl he'd met at a softball game.

He hadn't exactly *met* her. She'd hit him in the back with the ball. Reno proudly displayed the green-and-yellow bruise and explained how sorry the girl had been and what great tits she had. He described every detail of the little top she'd been wearing and how he could tell she wasn't wearing a bra, but he "didn't say nothin' stupid or stare or nothin'." Clay had given him credit for his good manners.

The drive home had felt altogether different from the drive out. On the way home they were two guys who'd put in a good day's work together. Respected equals.

"You were a real help to me today, son," Clay told the boy as he slipped him a ten-dollar bill. "You won't have any trouble working off your debt."

"I will if I take this."

"That's extra. When a guy does a good job, sometimes he gets a little something extra."

Reno muttered his thanks, shoved his hands in his pockets, turned on his heel, then swiveled back again. "It would be easier if I could stay with you until I've paid you back."

"I don't think so."

"She'd let me if you—"

Clay shook his head. "School's starting soon. You going out for basketball?"

"I dunno. Maybe."

"I sure like to watch you play. You remind me of my brother."

"Kole? He was good, wasn't he? Mom says they took his picture out of the trophy case, but I heard he was real good."

"He was all-state. Hell of a guard, just like you. Nobody told me they took his picture down. Guess I'll be having a little talk with the principal."

Reno's eyes lit up. "You mean, the fish?"

"Mr. Trout. A guy makes all-state on a championship team, you don't ever take his picture away. Not in this town."

"Mom says it's because he got put in the pen for whatever it was he did before he killed that other convict."

"He didn't kill anybody. If he did, it was self-defense. Look, it's no good being in prison, Reno. I went to see him there, and I'll tell you what . . ."

No, he wouldn't. He hoped the boy would never have cause to find out what that place was like. He laid a hand on Reno's shoulder. "I'll tell you what. You make the basketball team, I'll be there at every game."

"I know I can make the team. I'm just not sure I want to play. If we move . . ."

"Is she talking about moving?" Clay felt a little sick when the boy nodded, but he shrugged it off. People came and went; that was life. "I haven't heard of too many high schools that don't have basketball teams. That's something you can take with you wherever you go."

"I guess." Reno jerked his chin in the direction of the borrowed stock trailer hitched to the pickup. "Why'd you buy that horse, Clay? That's the sorriest-looking one yet, you know."

"I do believe you're right," Clay agreed, peering between the slats of the trailer. "But I'll tell you what, this horse was a beauty queen in her day. Ten years ago she was winning blue ribbons for some Four-H kid. She's a little head-shy now, but she's a grand and gentle lady. She's got the makings of a baby-sitter, that horse. She's suffering from saddle sores and stone bruises right now because of the way they were using her, but you just wait. She'll clean up and feed up real nice." He tapped his knuckles on the trailer's wheel housing, shoved his hands into his pockets, and turned to the boy again, smiling. "She deserves that much."

"Damn," Reno said. "You ain't got two words to say the whole way back from Lander, but say something bad about your brother or that ol' nag you wasted your money on—"

"I wasn't talkin' much because I was listening. And I didn't pay much for her."

"That's what you always say. Your back's bothering you, ain't it?"

"A little. But that comes with the territory."

Clay didn't hang around after Reno bounded up the porch steps. He was a hopeless sucker for a damn porch light, and this one wasn't burning for him. He had his own porch light, and it was attached to a place he loved. If he wanted to go home to a porch light, he could turn the thing on easy enough. A whole lot easier than a woman, he reminded himself as he slowed for a stop sign. He could turn them on, but he couldn't seem to keep them . . .

Two women strolled around the corner, and another light came on for Clay. He didn't really recognize her—she looked different from the woman he'd seen that morning—but he knew her. No matter how she looked, he would always know her by the way that light came on.

Before he realized it, he was hanging out the window like a teenager dragging Main.

"Evenin', ladies. Will you be needing escort services tonight?"

"We might," Leanne said sweetly, even as Savannah elbowed her in the ribs. Leanne giggled, returning the jab as she crooned, "Are you available?"

"Yes, ma'am."

The pickup engine idled so loud he couldn't hear Savannah's demurral, but he could read it on her fully juiced-up lips. *Just out for a walk.* God, she looked beautiful, her hair glistening under the streetlight, all slicked back like she'd just surfaced at the edge of a mountain lake. She didn't say, *Take a walk, Clay,* so he kicked the parking brake and cut the noise.

"It's a fine night for walking," he said. He'd almost said "for swimming," which it wasn't. It was coming-fall nippy. "Your hair looks cute, Savannah. Leanne does good work."

"I'd like to take the credit, but all I did was supply a little gel," Leanne said. "How's your mother, Clay?"

"She's doing all right. Try to get her to slow down, but she says she doesn't have time to be sick."

"Clay's mother had surgery, too," Leanne told Savannah. "Hers was for . . ."

"Heart bypass," he supplied. "I swear. They opened her up and there it was, a real heart."

"I owe her an apology," Savannah said, her voice as soft as the night breeze. "The last time I saw her, I believe I said she was a heartless woman. I think I may have said 'shriveled up.' She was mad at me because you enlisted."

"She was mad at everybody back then. She's over it now."

"That's good. For the sake of her health, don't tell her I'm back."

He laughed. "She knows everything that goes on in this town. Her best friend runs the general store."

"Her best friend? Aunt Billie? That's right, they're friends, aren't they?" She stepped back, took refuge behind Leanne.

Odd thing to say, he thought, wondering how much of her was really back. But he smiled and took the conventional approach. "If her best friend wouldn't mind me leaving a horse in her backyard for a little while, I could buy you two ladies a meal or a drink or whatever you've got time for."

"We were just out for a walk," Savannah said, shrinking into the shadows. "Aunt Billie took Claudia to—to the church, I guess. For Bingo. They'll probably be home soon."

"I already suggested the Naughty Pines," Leanne said.

"I should be getting back. Claudia isn't going to last long, I'm sure."

"Why don't I take you over to the church and we can see if she's ready to quit? I picked up this mare, and I'm thinking maybe she'd—"

"The church or the bar. This is way too much variety." Savannah gave a nervous laugh. "I have to be getting back now."

"Savannah . . ."

"It's such a beautiful night, isn't it?" She touched Leanne's arm. "Thank you. This has been so good. I haven't been getting out much. Thank you," she repeated, draining away in the dark like clear, cool water. "I'll see you both later. Or maybe even sooner."

By the time Clay was out of the pickup, she was gone. He stood with Leanne and listened to her retreating footsteps. "What's going on with her?" he asked, more of himself than of his companion.

"You'll have to ask her," Leanne said. "It's just not my place. I'm sure she's going to be fine."

"Judging by the way she's acting, I'm not so sure." He climbed in behind the wheel and slammed the door, resolving to buy *himself* that drink. "But I'm damn sure gonna find out."

She was alone in the house when he came knocking at the door. At first she thought it was Aunt Billie, whom she was fully prepared to scold for keeping Claudia out so late. Maybe she'd forgotten her key. By the time Savannah got to the kitchen door, the knocking had moved downstairs to the front door. She went to the front bedroom window and spotted Clay's pickup.

"Savannah?" He was rapping on the store window. "Savannah, I know you're in there. Let me come in for a little while. We'll talk."

Her first impulse was to close the window, close the bedroom door, close herself off. He had no business pushing her, no right to come unbidden.

"Savannah? I'm not leaving until we've had a talk, so you might as well open up."

Is that so?

She raised the window shade and stood in the dark room, dark window, watching the dark street. There would be no opening up. Not unless Savannah felt like opening up.

"I'm still here, Savannah. I'll bust this door down, I swear to God I will."

She shoved the window all the way up. "What is the matter with you, Clay?"

"What's the matter with *me?*" He jumped off the porch, spun around, and took a few steps back until he had a clear view of the upstairs window. "Hell, there's no matter with me," he claimed for all the world to hear, thumping his chest like an indignant gorilla. "It's you. You're the one who's acting—"

"Have you been drinking?"

"Not much."

"Well, you're disturbing the peace pretty much."

"I wouldn't be if you'd answer the door like a normal person. You could do something like a normal person, just to surprise me. So far, you haven't surprised me at all, Savannah."

"I'm not trying to."

"But you've damn sure disturbed my peace, so I guess it's only fair for me to disturb yours."

"Is that so? I might have to call a peace officer."

"Go right ahead." He stood there, head tipped back, watching her, waiting for her to make a move. "You're not gonna call anybody."

"You're not gonna bust any door down."

He glared at the door.

She waited for him to make a move.

"I should," he grumbled. "I should do it just because you're so sure I won't."

She almost laughed. When she remembered this tomorrow, she probably would. "The store is closed, Clay. Do you see any lights on here?"

"The back porch—"

"I left that on for Claudia and Aunt Billie, who should be back any time."

"Good. Two women who know how to be polite."

"But you'll be gone by the time they get here because you *also* know how to be polite."

"I wanna know what's going on with you."

"I took a walk, straightened up the store a little bit, and now I'm going to read." She paused, then added in a near whisper, "Maybe I'll see you later."

"What's wrong with right now?" he demanded, oblivious to a set of approaching headlights.

"I don't feel like talking," she said. "But obviously you do, so here comes your chance."

He looked over his shoulder as the sheriff's car slowed for a U-turn in front of the Mercantile. It surprised Savannah when the car stopped.

It infuriated Clay. "Did you really call—"

"I don't feel like talking to them, either, so would you just explain that it's all your fault and you won't let it happen again?"

"What's all my fault?"

"The prowler," she said, smiling. "I'll see you later, Clay."

She closed the window and watched the sheriff's deputy approach him. She couldn't hear the conversation. Clay could take care of himself, and he was in for nothing worse than an awkward moment. She imagined herself a puppeteer, watching from above, wondering what he'd say before he realized she hadn't really called anyone. Knowing Clay, she figured he'd probably confess to prowling.

That she was capable of setting up such a scene made her feel at once omnipotent and cruel, self-important and disgusted with herself. She stood there, watching and wallowing in the brew she'd made.

They were laughing now. It didn't take much for men to explain away a woman's power. Crazy chick. Too suspicious, susceptible, sensitive. More laughter rumbled below. Too sexy. Too damn sexy for her skirt.

But not her shirt.

What did men know about the flesh beneath a woman's shirt except for how it served them? Seduced them, they might say; stimulated, sometimes succored them. What did they know of the fear, the dreaded word that turned a woman's supposed assets into an awful liability?

He did *not* want to know what was going on with her. He said he did, only because he didn't know and couldn't know, not really. He was a man, pure and simple. Clay Keogh was about as pure and uncomplicated as a man could get. He always had been.

Chapter 6

He waited in the secret heart of the hills, sheathed in shadows. He was the shadow of a shadow, the part of himself he hardly knew, the part that was all hope and expectancy. The fragile part. Like any sane man, he protected this part of himself from harsh daylight and from all scrutiny, including his own. But he took it to the hills and let it rise in him there, let it mingle with the timeless dreams that lived there. If she came, he wanted to be there. If she didn't, then he'd misunderstood her, but no harm had been done. No one would know. He would tuck this fragile, foolish self back inside where it belonged and get back to being down-to-earth and dreamless by sunrise.

Loose rocks rattled beneath a climber's feet. Kole, the hunter, would have known whether the climber was four-footed or two-. Follow your nose, Kole would say, but Clay, who took everything Kole said as the literal gospel, could smell nothing but river and pine. Take the first shot, Kole would say, and Clay would lift the rifle to his shoulder, try not to notice the soft, dark eyes as he took aim at the heart. He always allowed for wind and recoil and momentary astigmatism.

Take the damn shot, Kole would say, and Clay would

squeeze the trigger, envisioning the missed shot. A miss imagined was a miss achieved.

Nice try, Kole would say.

Clay was no hunter, but tonight he was a seeker. Tonight he followed his heart. Listening within and without, he peered through the shadows and past the rocks for a climber with only two legs. They were hidden beneath a long, loose skirt, a change from the schoolgirl dress she'd been wearing earlier in the evening. He remembered the slim jeans and the short skirts she'd worn when she'd actually been a schoolgirl. He remembered the clothes she'd worn later in pictures, some crisp and polished, others satiny or diaphanous. This voluminous, layered, monkish garb was a new style for her. *Must be what they wear for hill climbing in New York,* he told himself as he stepped from the shadows.

He didn't give a damn what she wore. Those long, fine legs were under there somewhere, striding across the rock-strewn basin, bringing her to him.

"You came."

She laughed as she touched his cheek. "You knew I would."

"I don't know anything about you except that you're determined to drive me crazy."

Her cool fingers made his face tingle. "I will if you'll let me," she promised with a soft, colorless smile.

"You know I will." He reached for her, eager to hold her in his arms. "But this time you'll let me—"

She grabbed his hands, held them tight, and drew him toward the rock den they'd used as a hideout when they were kids, a place to meet, to trade secrets and dreams. "I have rules," she warned.

"I'll figure them out as the game progresses."

"You can't play with me the way you used to, because I'm not . . ." She released him. He nearly got hold of her shoulder, but she slid away, circling him, teasing him with a smile. "And anyway, why would you want to? All those mysteries, you've solved them all by now. It's my turn to play with you. Are you game for that?"

"Why not?" He chuckled. "Long as I came all this way."

"You came before, too."

But not the way he would have chosen to.

Savannah lay her head on his back, put her arms around him, pushed his denim jacket aside, and caressed his chest while she pressed herself against him from behind. If he'd had a care for his sanity, he would have taken himself out of her hands then and there. But she was hugging him so hard, rubbing her face between his shoulder blades, hanging onto him for dear life. *Her* dear life. To him there was none dearer.

She jerked his T-shirt up and slipped her hands beneath his belt, teasing his belly button with her thumb. Her fingers undulated like caterpillars headed for some sheltered underside. He sucked his belly in, just to be polite, but his rude cock grew faster than Jack's beanstalk. Delighted either with the stalk itself or with her own green thumb, she made a soft, sweet, female sound. Every cell in his body thought it belonged in his groin. Exquisite torture.

"Shall I unbuckle your belt?"

"Allow me." His hands were dying for something to do. This wasn't it, but he'd play along.

She played with him delicately at first, then got firm with him. He'd get his turn soon. Play along, play long, get long, *go long*. But he wasn't prepared for her pass, did not anticipate her shifting, sinking, putting her mouth into play. He didn't want it to stop, couldn't stand for it to go on, couldn't move between the rock at his back and the soft place before him.

He laid his hands on her head, blessing her, thinking to hold her there longer, and still longer, the way he was growing. He could go on growing, grow forever if forever would please her. He touched her hair. It felt crisp, which surprised him. Crisp, like a delicate cookie. He felt her tongue stroking, remembered her tongue licking crumbs from her lips, sugary crumbs on the sweetest lips, sweet, sweet . . .

"Savannah," he groaned as he sank to the ground, extricating himself, like taking the bottle from the baby's mouth. And like the baby who was used to having all she wanted, she looked surprised.

He put his hand on the back of her neck and drew her to him, forehead to chest. "God, Savannah, this isn't right."

"Not right?" She laughed a little. She still had him in her hand. "Have you gone and gotten religious on me, Clay?"

"I've always had religion. I might misplace it once in a while, but that's got nothing to do with—" She was stroking him insistently now, as though she had a point to prove. "Savannah, it doesn't work like this."

"You coulda fooled me. Am I doing it wrong?"

"Doing what wrong? What are you trying to do? Get milk?" She rooted under his jacket, playfully bit his flat nipple.

"Ouch!"

"It does work, Clay. If it's up and ready, it works for me." She pushed his hands away and positioned herself over him. "For me, now. Please?"

Even in the dark he could see the strange look in her soft, sad eyes. *Please take the shot.* Please put me out of my misery. Please give me what I don't have. Please take me by letting me take you.

He couldn't keep anything from her. Anything that would please her was hers for the asking. It always had been. He would go down with her, on her, under her, whatever she needed. No more protests, no more questions. He had always had only one answer for her, and that was *yes.* Have it your way, have it all, have it now.

She took him deep inside her body, but she would not permit him to touch her or kiss her like he wanted to, so he gave that over to her as well. He poured all his desire into one strong, sure rhythm, one search, one seizure, one trigger, one release. He would have her soar and shudder and gush and keen with pleasure. If nothing else, he would have her helpless, coming and coming and coming all over him before he joined her.

She lay back against him afterward, his shoulder pillowing her head, her hands holding his, fingers interlaced, at their sides. He thought it strange that she refused the parts of him she'd once enjoyed and admitted the part she'd always turned away. His hands were bigger and stronger than they'd ever been, but he longed to show her how deft such hands could be.

She shifted gingerly in his lap.

"Did I hurt you?"

"Not at all." Softly she kissed the side of his neck. "You're incredible."

"How so?"

Her laughter bubbled deep in her throat. "So like a man."

"What do you mean?"

"How are you incredible? Let me count the ways. Incredible strength and size and self-control. Incredible—"

"Don't do that, Savannah." He sighed. "I'm not *like* a man. I *am* a man. I was afraid I'd hurt you, the way you . . ."

He swallowed the rest. Only he and the stars had heard the cry she'd made, and the pleasure it gave him knowing that she felt him, felt him good and hard, that pleasure also hurt him. How long he'd been waiting, and how strange and terrible and wonderful the moment was.

"I know you've had some kind of trouble. I don't know what it was. I just know it left you tender in places you don't want me to touch." He pressed his lips to her hair. "I don't want to do anything to make it worse."

"So unlike other men," she whispered, and before he could ask what that meant, she added, "It's been a long time for me, Clay. I've kept myself . . . apart. There haven't been other men. I want you to know that, even though I might seem . . ." She looked up at him. "Do I seem crazy?"

He smiled. "Just slightly off plumb."

"Things haven't been going well lately."

"Tell me."

"Well . . ." She laughed. "For one thing, I'm not strutting around in my underwear for a living anymore."

"Leaving a lotta guys around here downright heartsick," he acknowledged. "But where does it leave you?"

"Without a job."

"There are other jobs," he said, and she nodded. He had to ask. "What happened? Did you turn shy?"

"Sort of. I became a mother, for one thing. And then I had some . . . complications. Physical, medical complications."

"That's the part you need to tell me about."

"No, I don't. Not here, Clay. I don't want to bring that stuff up here."

"You haven't been willing to talk to me anywhere else."

And she still wasn't. Her silence made that clear. She'd had some kind of surgery, something she wasn't going to let him get close to. He remembered how standoffish she'd been when her mother died, and if he'd had to guess, he'd suppose this surgery had been a ripple off that long-ago plunge.

He wouldn't presume to guess, but he figured he had the right to ask at least one question. "Are they all over with now, these complications?"

She turned, smiled, released his hand so she could touch his cheek and trace his mouth with her fingertip, all the while looking at him like he was some sweet, simpleminded boy. He almost pushed her hand away. But he didn't. He closed his eyes and sucked her forefinger into his mouth.

"I'm not dead yet," she said. He opened his eyes, and she laughed. "That's when all the complications end, don't you think? That's why it's so peaceful up here in these hills. The mysteries of this place overwhelm philosophers and scientists, so there's no point in our struggling with them. Up here we can be at peace without being dead."

It wasn't like Savannah to wax philosophic. She was neither fanciful nor fatalistic, so her words scared him some. "I don't know how close you came," he said, "but you're alive now, and you look fine to me. Better than fine."

"You haven't seen me in my underwear." She laughed again, turning in his lap to face him. "You've fucked me, but you haven't seen me—"

"Jesus, don't say that, Savannah. I wouldn't call it that."

"No, you wouldn't, would you?" She straddled him, wrapping her long legs around him, her arms around herself, tucked beneath her breasts. "What would you call it? If somebody asked you, under oath, whether you'd fucked Savannah Stephens—"

"I'd punch him in the mouth," he said flatly, wishing she'd stop saying that word. "Case closed."

"Contempt of court."

"So arrest me." He put his arms around her. "Whatever it was, it left you with a scar."

"Yes, it did."

"Seems like they'd need models to show off more than just underwear. Just a little while ago when you sashayed across this rocky plot, I thought, Damn, that woman makes a gunnysack look like a party dress."

He'd made her smile. She let him touch her under the chin, where he used to tickle her with purple locoweed and tell her the next person she looked in the eye would go crazy. She'd look directly at him and laugh when he made some silly face. He leaned over now, touched his lips to the corner of her smile. "Where's the scar?" he asked.

She lifted one shoulder. "There's more than one," she said in a small, soft voice, the kind that could never utter a word like "fuck."

"Show me. If it's looks you're worried about, let me—"

"I think the worst one is in my mind. You can't see that one, and you can't flatter it away."

"Okay." He leaned back against the rock wall. "Then tell me about Kole. Not about you and Kole, just . . . tell me how he's doing."

She shook her head. "I haven't seen him."

"You must hear from him." He had his answer when she turned her face away from him, and he knew he shouldn't be asking. Not now. "He knows about Claudia, doesn't he?"

"Yes, but . . ." Her sigh rang hollow in his ears. "I hear very little from him. Even after all these years, he has to be careful. All I can tell you is that he's alive and well."

"And probably hiding out on some Indian reservation."

Clay had studiously ignored his brother's political activities, even as Kole had made a name for himself in the news. They'd called him "The Renegade," and for a while he'd been a hero. But he never quit his protesting, and finally he'd gotten himself into a mess he couldn't muscle his way out of. Clay didn't know much about Indian land and treaty rights and all the concerns that used to get Kole so riled. What he knew was that Kole was his brother. He'd stuck his fool neck out once too often, and Clay never heard from him, and now this with Savannah—Kole just never quit doling out the heartache. But Kole *was* his brother.

"I think he still moves around quite a bit," Savannah mused. "He has a lot of loyal friends."

"And determined enemies." The prison sentence was supposed to last only a couple of years, and Kole had nearly served his time when another inmate had turned up dead and Kole had escaped. "I'd help him any way I could, if he'd only let me."

"He knows that. He doesn't want anyone else to get hurt."

"The FBI used to keep tabs on us, thinking he might show

up here. They haven't bothered us in a long time." He paused. "They didn't know about you?"

"No, and they don't know about Claudia. That's one complication that never occurred to me—that anyone might connect her with Kole if I brought her back here. I don't even connect her with Kole anymore. She's my daughter. Period. End of discussion."

"Were you with him very long? Was he—"

"Alive and well," she repeated firmly as she slipped off his lap. "End of discussion."

"You're not still—"

"*End* of discussion."

They sat side by side in silence for a few moments.

"You're not fucking your brother's girl," she said finally, quietly belying her decree.

"You like that word? Okay, *she's* fucking *me*."

"That's not who I am. I'm not—"

"Who are you, then?" He turned to her, tried to get a good look at her there in the dark. He had to keep his hands off her or he might end up shaking her, which would do his cause no good. "Who are you, Savannah?"

"I was hoping you knew." She dropped her gaze along with her voice into the chasm between them. "All I know is who I'm not. I'm nobody's girl, that's for sure."

"You're somebody's mother."

"Yes, that much is also for sure. I'm somebody's mother." She looked at him again. "But it isn't *somebody's mother* who's here now, doing this . . . with you. This is . . . it's *nobody's girl*."

"Where's *Savannah?*"

"I don't know." She leaned slightly toward him. "Sleeping in her bed, maybe?"

"Is this my dream or hers?" He put his arm around her and drew her close. "It must be mine. Except in my dream, Savannah wouldn't be using the word—"

"We won't say it again, Clay." She put her head on his shoulder. He could feel her hesitancy, the way she barely let her head touch, then gave in. He wanted to laugh, until she said, "This is the closest I've come to feeling like a woman in a very long time. Thank you."

"For what? Rising to the occasion?" He tipped his head until it touched hers. "Always glad to oblige."

"There's no one in the world I trust more than you."

He gave a slight head-to-head nod.

He knew it was true, but somehow it didn't make him feel all that great to hear her say it. In secret places she trusted him with her secret places, needs, desires, but in public they were "just friends." Everybody trusted Clay. Good old solid Clay. He was everyone's friend. He had so much more than that to give Savannah, but he'd always understood that, solid as he was, he was part of Sunbonnet, part of the hills of Wyoming, part of Savannah's springboard.

And she could always read his mind.

"I never thought I'd say this, but it's good to be home. I feel safe, like bad things can't get to me here." She sighed. "At least not here, right here in our hills. There's magic here."

"What bad things?" he coaxed, but she offered no answer. "Let me help you, Savannah. What bad—"

"Speaking of . . . How's your mother?"

"Not bad." He looked at her now, and they laughed. "No, she really isn't. The surgery kinda knocked the wind out of her for a while, but she's probably about eighty percent now."

"Eighty percent human?" she teased, and he laughed again. "I'm sorry. She took me for a hundred percent Jezebel."

"She caught us skinny-dipping in the stock dam."

"You were just as naked as I was."

"Yeah, but a Jezebel is one hundred percent female, which lets me off the hook."

"And you're her darling son."

He shrugged, mock innocence. "Can't help that."

"How did she get along with your wife?"

"*Ex*-wife. They mostly tolerated each other." Another diffident shrug. What could he say? "I don't have the best luck with women. I understand horses a whole lot better."

"You understand both, I think, but I won't argue about your luck."

"What about yours?" He wasn't going to give up. "I promised to help your daughter hang a horseshoe over your bedroom door."

"Ah, Claudia, my little angel." She nodded, glanced away. "She worries. Six-year-olds shouldn't have to worry. We should make that a rule in this world. Worrying should be for adults only."

"Sounds fair."

"Put something like that up and the next thing she'd be worried about is having it fall on my head. But we're going to be fine now."

"You're back home."

She nodded again. "Tomorrow I'll go to work in the store. I really think I can do it tomorrow."

"You mean, today?"

"Today or tomorrow. I'd better go back." She used his shoulder for leverage as she stood up. "Thank you."

He wished she'd stop thanking him. Next she'd be slipping him a tip. But he had to bite his tongue to keep from asking whether she'd be wandering the hills again tomorrow night.

He'd be there. Damn his foolish heart, he would be there waiting.

"Aunt Billie, Mommy won't wake up!"

Claudia tripped on her shoelace, caught herself, and knocked two bottles of green dish soap off a shelf. Aunt Billie dropped a blue can on the floor, and Claudia hopped over it as it rolled toward the soap. "I don't know if she's pretending, but she said to wake her up this morning, and I can't."

Aunt Billie didn't move very fast. Claudia wanted to push her a little bit as she followed her upstairs, but she waited until they reached the top, and then she grabbed her hand. She was glad to have Aunt Billie there. At first it had seemed funny to have another person living with them and doing things like fixing her hair, especially when she didn't do it the way Mommy did, but it was getting easier to ask Aunt Billie for things. Mainly for help when she needed it, which was only sometimes.

"Savannah?"

Claudia stayed close to the door. She was glad to see her mother sitting on the edge of the bed, but she didn't like the way she looked, holding her head in her hands, sicklike. It scared her. She didn't want her to start throwing up all the time again. Then she'd start telling Claudia not to come in the room, and then Claudia would have to wait and wait because she didn't want to do anything else until she saw her mother looking all right again.

But she liked the way Aunt Billie made her mom straighten up a little bit, just with her stern voice.

"What foolishness is going on here now? Are you all right? Savannah?"

"Hmmm?"

"What's wrong with you? You're scaring me, scaring your little girl. You're . . ." Aunt Billie snatched Mommy's brown skirt off the chair and threw it on the bed, right next to her. "Get dressed now, girl. You're seeing a doctor today, and there's no argument."

"I'm okay. Just a little groggy." Savannah glanced at Claudia. Not mad, but a little bit sorry. She looked tired. "I'm okay, honey."

"You told me to wake you up."

"I know. I'm glad you did. I wasn't sleeping, and I was a little sore, so I took some . . ." She showed Aunt Billie the plastic pill bottle on the nightstand. "You can buy them over the counter. It's aspirin with a little something to help you sleep. It's not like *drugs*."

"It's not *like* drugs. It *is* drugs. I don't care where you buy them." Aunt Billie tossed a wrinkly shirt on top of the skirt. "And the reason you can't sleep at night is because you sleep most of the day. I don't know what they do in New York, but around here we go to bed at night so we can be awake during the day. It's only scoundrels and sixteen-year-olds that go sneaking around in the middle of the night."

"My mother's thirty-three." Claudia opened the second dresser drawer, looking for a better shirt for her mother to wear.

"Well, that's what I thought, too," Aunt Billie said. "It's been a good, long while since you had that operation. You're gonna get yourself a checkup, Savannah. Claudia says it's been a long time since you've seen a doctor."

"Claudia doesn't know everything, Aunt Billie. She's a *child*."

Claudia chose a white shirt with some lace. She knew her mother would want to wear a sweater with it, so she went to the third drawer. She knew for sure that her mother hadn't seen a doctor, but she also knew when to keep quiet.

"That makes two of you," Aunt Billie said, "but she's the only one with any sense right now. You're going to see a doctor if I have to throw you down and hog-tie you."

"You can't, and you won't."

"You don't think so? You think I'm too old, too feeble? You've got another thing comin', young lady."

Claudia put the clothes on top of the dresser. It sounded like they were going to have a fight, but all of a sudden her mother laughed and said, "You sound just like Mama."

"And so do you." Aunt Billie wasn't joking around. "I'm

not gonna let you do what your mama did. I should have taken a hand with her, but she kept telling me to mind my own business, and that's what I did. And that's why she died."

"Oh, for heaven's sake, it is not. She died because she was afraid to face the fact that she had a lump. I faced the damn lump, and I did what I—"

Claudia backed out of the bedroom, escaped through the kitchen, and rumbled down the outside steps, feet pounding hard. She ran toward the barn, pumping her legs as fast as she could. She didn't want to hear their talk anymore. She wanted to be with the kittens.

They were mewing for their mother, who was gone from the box. Ladybug had to get away sometimes, too. Five kittens was a lot, and their voices were loud when they got to mewing all at once. Claudia plucked the orange-and-white stripey one from the box and tucked it into the crook of her arm. Its tiny claws pricked her as it clung to her shirt.

The roar of an engine drew her attention to the gravel driveway. It was the horseshoe man pulling a trailer behind his white pickup truck. He parked, got out of the truck, touched the brim of his cowboy hat, said hello, and called her by name. Her mother had told her to be careful around big men who acted too polite, especially around a kid, but she liked his eyes. They were really looking at her, sparkling kind of friendly-like, and they didn't look tired or sad.

"Hey, guess what I brought," he said.

Claudia hung her head, rubbing her nose in the kitten's fur. She didn't feel like playing guessing games right now.

His eyes went soft as he hunkered down to her level. "You okay?" he wanted to know. He waited for an answer, so that meant he really wanted one. He wanted her to be okay, or at least he actually wanted to know if she was. She nodded. She wasn't hurt or anything.

He smiled like he was trying to get her to smile, too. "I brought you a surprise."

"What is it?" She didn't care much for surprises.

"Well, it took a horse trailer to carry it, so you can probably guess. I called your aunt Billie this morning, and she . . ." He smiled some more, like he was trying to get her in a good mood. "How's that kitten doing? Looks like they're growing pretty fast."

"They nurse on Ladybug all the time."

"That's what kittens do. Does this one have a name?"

"Charlie."

"Can I see him?"

She could tell he was asking about the kitten mostly to be nice to her, but she edged closer anyway, offered the orange tabby.

He took it in one big hand and held it up, hind legs dangling. He gave her that smile again. "Charlie's a girl. Did you know that?"

"Of course. Charlie can be . . ." Her lips trembled. Prickles started creeping up the back of her throat, making it hard for her to breathe right. She squeezed her eyes shut tight, but she couldn't stop the tears from coming. "Noooo," she wailed.

He put one arm around her, but she kept shaking her head, so he didn't pull her tight, just rubbed her back a little bit when she admitted she didn't know which ones were girls. She was trying to stop crying, her words coming out in bubbles and blips.

His came out smooth and soft. "It's okay, honey. Uncle Clay has big shoulders for cryin' on if you feel like using them."

"You're not . . . m-my uncle."

"You could adopt me for one if you wanted to."

She nodded. Hard, because she was crying hard now, and everything seemed hard, including the big man's chest, but his arms didn't squeeze hard when they came around her, and his voice wasn't hard. It was deep and quiet, telling her it was okay to cry. So she did.

A little bit, but not too much. "I don't want my mommy to see me," she confided, trying to wipe her face with her hands.

"Go ahead and use my shirt," he said, and it seemed okay because it was a big, soft T-shirt, and the sleeve was handy, so she went ahead and used it. He was asking, "Why don't you want her to see you?"

"It would make her feel bad."

"Yeah, but you're feelin' bad. Maybe she oughta know about that."

Claudia shrugged. "She won't go to the doctor."

"Does she need to?"

"Aunt Billie says she does. Aunt Billie says she sounds just like *her* mama, and she didn't take a hand to her, and that's why she died." Saying that scary word made more tears come. "I don't want my mommy to die."

"I know you don't." He held her a little bit tighter this time, but not too tight. "I don't, either." He sounded like he meant it.

"I can't hug her too tight because of her breast," she whispered. "It still hurts sometimes."

"From her operation?"

She nodded, mopping her face with his shirt again. "Because that's where she had that tumor thing that the doctor took out. She says she's all healed, but sometimes I think it still hurts. She's supposed to take medicine."

"Does she?"

"I don't think so. I think she ran out of it. It costs a lot of money." She sniffled. "We used to have a lot of money, but we don't anymore." Another sniffle. She knew she shouldn't be sniffling. And she knew she shouldn't say things about money. "I mean . . . well, we're not poor. I didn't say we were poor."

"No, you didn't. I wasn't thinking that at all."

"I don't want her to be sick anymore."

"And she doesn't want you to worry anymore. She loves you with all her heart."

"I love her, too, but sometimes she makes me . . ." The child pushed her lips together tight because she didn't want to say what she was thinking. But when she saw in his eyes that he kinda knew anyway, she just blurted it out. "A little bit mad."

"I know what you mean." He smoothed her hair back. "Tell you what, Claudia. I'm gonna take your mother to see a doctor. I don't care what she says, she's going."

"How can you make her if she doesn't want to? You won't—"

"I won't twist her arm very hard. I promise." He smiled, but she scowled. "Okay, no arm-twisting. I'll be firm but gentle. I'll get her there, and that's a promise, too. I always keep my promises. You believe me?"

She really wanted to, so she nodded.

"You'll put that worry out of your head now?"

She wanted to do that, too, but that would be a lot harder. She didn't want to lie anymore, so she shrugged.

"You wanna see what I brought?"

This time she nodded good and hard.

They put the kitten back in the box. Ladybug was back on duty, and Miss Charlie couldn't reach her fast enough. Claudia had to run a little bit at first to get beside the horseshoe man on the way to the trailer, but then he slowed right down. His big hand seemed a little bit empty, and it was just right there, so she slipped hers into the hook of his fingers. He smiled at her, and she had to smile back. It was like he had magic wands in his eyes, the way they twinkled.

He told her to stand beside the trailer wheel and not to move, just to watch. By this time she'd figured out that the surprise was going to be a horse, but she didn't know it would be a *golden* one with white mane and tail. She'd never seen such a beautiful horse.

"I asked Billie if I could keep her here for a few days. She said I could, if Dolly approves of her, which I know she will."

He took the golden horse into the corral, and then he came back to get Claudia, who hadn't moved the whole time. It startled her when he lifted her high in the air and set her on the corral rail. She wasn't sure she liked being up there, but he stood close and held onto her, and it seemed okay.

"Aw, see there," he said as they watched the two horses touch noses. "Dolly's been wishing for a girlfriend. Haven't you, old girl? That's why you always seem a little crabby."

"What's her name?" Claudia asked.

"You know what? On paper she's got kind of a stupid name. I think she needs a new one. What would you call her?"

"Angel," Claudia said without a moment's hesitation. "To me she looks like a golden angel, so that's what I'd call her."

"Angel it is."

"Where did you get her?"

"It wasn't exactly heaven, but any place in Wyoming is God's country, so it's the same neighborhood. I want you to get to know her a little bit before you try her out."

"You mean . . . ride her?"

"She belonged to a girl who used to ride her in horse shows. Then she grew up and went away to college and couldn't keep Angel anymore. The guy who bought her was using her pretty hard. She's got some saddle sores. But we're gonna take care of those, aren't we? Find her a saddle that fits her right, a small one." He gave Claudia a little squeeze on the shoulder. "One your size."

Her size? She turned to him, checking to see if he was saying what she was hearing. "For me?"

"I sure can't take her home," he said with a shrug. "My mom would have a fit. She says I've got too many horses already."

"Really?"

"He's telling the truth," Aunt Billie said.

Claudia hadn't heard her coming up behind them. They both turned when she spoke, but Claudia wasn't going to take her eyes off the golden horse for very long. She whipped her head back around to make sure the horse was still there. The horseshoe man laughed when she whapped him in the face with her ponytail.

"Patty Keogh has been my best friend for over fifty years," Aunt Billie was saying. "When it comes to throwing a fit, Patty's a corker. But you sure didn't need another horse."

"Nobody *needs* another horse," Clay said, and he patted Claudia's shoulder. "But Angel needed us."

"Did she, now." Aunt Billie laid her arms over the top corral rail and stepped up on the bottom one so she could rest her chin on her arm. "Tell you what, she ain't the only one."

"With a horse, all you have to do is hand over the money and sign the papers," Clay said.

"A lot of things work that way, you get right down to it."

He was quiet for a minute. Then Claudia could barely hear what he said.

"She won't have me. You know damn well she won't."

Was he talking about Angel? He wanted Angel, but she didn't like him? He seemed sad about it, maybe a little embarrassed, so she pretended not to hear. For sure Angel would like *her*, but Aunt Billie might say Angel couldn't stay. Claudia stared at the beautiful horse. If she kept quiet and made wishes, maybe they would come true. Maybe magic would happen and Angel would really stay.

"I don't know any such thing," Aunt Billie said. "What I do know is that she's scared and mixed up and desperate, like a cornered wild thing, and I can't help her."

"What makes you think I can?"

"I was there when you were born and I watched you grow

up, Clay Keogh. I know what you're made of." Aunt Billie's voice lowered now, like they were telling secrets. "And I know how you feel about her."

"Yeah, well, as long as you're making so damn many assumptions, what do you know about her feelings for me? Maybe you know something I don't. Maybe she's sworn you to secrecy, huh? About her love for me?"

"She doesn't know what she wants or who she—"

"She knows who she *doesn't* want," he said.

Aunt Billie stared at him with that same disbelief Claudia's mother got in her eyes sometimes. *How do you know that?*

"I've already asked her, Billie, a long time ago. I actually put it in writing. She never even answered me."

"I know she's not the easiest person to love, Clay. I know that from my own experience." Aunt Billie bumped Clay's arm with her elbow. "But you really don't have any choice, do you?"

"No," he said, "But it's up to me what I do about it."

Chapter 7

"Where is she?" Clay asked Billie quietly as he outfitted the little palomino with a bareback pad, taking care to keep the cinch away from the sores on her belly.

"Where she's been mostly since she got here." Billie glanced up at the bedroom window. "But she's out of bed, so we've made some progress."

"You think you could give Claudia a little ride?"

"While you . . ." She hiked one wild gray eyebrow above the gold rim of her glasses.

"While I get the princess out of the tower."

He raked his fingers through the white mane he'd painstakingly groomed that morning after he'd tended to the mare's superficial injuries. Angel was going to make another fine kid horse. He'd been reminded that the Lazy K pastured a few idle kid horses already. *We don't have any kids,* his mother had reminded him.

He hadn't responded. He wasn't ready. But he liked the idea of having a horse especially designated for Claudia on the ranch. *I've got the right. She's my niece, and I want to do something for her*. He'd imagined the look on her face, how excited she'd be, how pleased her mother would be. He knew the last part of his vision was pure fairy tale—

Savannah's pleasure was hard to figure—but it was his damn fantasy and he'd have it his way.

"Like Rapunzel?" the little girl asked him.

"Who's Rapunzel?"

" 'Rapunzel, Rapunzel, let down your hair!' And she threw her long braided hair out the window, and the handsome prince climbed up it so he could save her from the tower." She demonstrated the toss and the climb with outstretched arms and walking fingers. "See, braids are like ladders. How big are your feet?"

"I think I'd better use the stairs." Clay chuckled as he lifted Claudia onto the pad, which was made for learning to ride bareback. He showed her how to use the handle. "How does that feel?"

"Fine. Who's the princess?"

"Your mother, of course."

She was all wide-eyed. "You're getting *my mother* down from the tower?"

"Either that or I'll have to kidnap a doctor and bring her over here. But I made you a promise. How do you like her so far?" He could tell he had Claudia thoroughly confused. "How do you like Angel?"

She assessed the distance to the ground. "You might have to get me down from *this* tower."

"Say the word, and you're down. Your wish is my command."

"My mother's the princess, remember?"

"I can answer a lot of commands. I was a soldier before I got to be the horseshoe man. You want down?"

She shook her head. "But I want to go slow."

"That's your aunt Billie's only speed," he teased as he handed Billie the lead rope. "I'm not coming down without her, which means you've probably got all day."

He could see through the window that the kitchen was clear, so he walked on in and called her name. He'd never heard such loud quiet, but he knew she was there. He could feel her, just as surely as he'd felt her presence in the hills last night before he'd heard her footsteps. He'd conjured her up so many times, he figured he'd finally developed a sixth sense just for her.

He dragged a chair away from the table and took a seat to let her know he wasn't going away any time soon. He stared at the window, but his mental focus was on the bedroom he knew she occupied. "I've got a proposition for you, Savannah."

"Let me guess."

The sound of her voice surprised him. He turned to find her standing in the doorway. Damn, she moved quietly on those pretty little bare feet. She was wearing jeans under a big white shirt that hung halfway down her thighs. Her hair was slicked back again, and her lips were shiny and sweet-looking, like she'd been eating pancakes with plain Karo syrup, which, for no good reason, reminded him of last night, which made him feel hot in the face and hard between the legs.

She smiled. "You've been talking to Aunt Billie, and you think you're going to talk me into seeing a doctor."

He cleared his throat. "I think I'm going to talk you into something even more daring than that."

"Not today. I'm not in a daring mood." She gave him that look he'd seen in some of her photographs, the one that said, *I dare you to turn this page*. "But maybe tonight."

"Tonight might not work." He braced his hands on his knees and stared at the blue linoleum in the space between his boots. He imagined a diver looking into a pool of water and wondering how deep it was, how cold, how long the drop. "We'll need a license."

"To catch fish? Shoot antelope?"

"To get married." He lifted his head, looked her straight in the eye. "I'm proposing marriage, Savannah."

She didn't laugh, though it took her a moment to respond. "You and me?"

"No, I want to marry your aunt." As soon as he pushed to his feet he wished he'd stayed in the chair. He was trying to keep it light, but now the ceiling seemed to be pressing down on him. "I want you to make an honest man of me."

"You've never been anything else, so don't try to change that now." Her eyes warmed with a real smile, the natural Savannah. Yet she protected herself with folded arms. "I don't know what this is about, Clay, but I'm going to give you the benefit of the doubt and assume you spent the morning at the Naughty Pines."

"What, you've got something against marrying a guy who takes a drink once in a while? Or is it more personal?" He glanced away. "Is it just—"

"It's very personal," she insisted, stepping closer. "I don't want to ruin our relationship."

"If it doesn't work out, you can always ditch me. I make a damn fine ex-husband. Just ask Roxie."

Now she laughed. "Knowing you, you're probably paying child support for *step*children."

"Hell, I'm not that good."

"You are. You're good, and you're soft, and you're . . . you're my good friend, my oldest and dearest, so you're too important to risk."

"Have you already tried this? You sound like somebody who's been burned."

"I know better than to put my hand on the stove, but you—" She started to check her swing, yet couldn't quite resist following through. "Wasn't once enough?"

He shrugged. Hell, he was no baseball player, no high diver. He was a plain and simple cowboy. "You get bucked off, I'm a firm believer in getting back in the saddle."

"On the same horse. Isn't that the way it's supposed to be done?"

"Don't try to take these clichés too far, Savannah. I know what I'm asking. I learned a few lessons about marriage. Like, you don't expect more than a person is able to give. I was pretty naïve the first time around. I figured you could just go by the vows the way they were written, the way they've been repeated for hundreds of years. Now that I've got a little experience under my belt, I'd want to start with a bargain. Lay it all out right on the table." He submitted his two big, empty hands, palms up, for her inspection. "Here's what I have to offer; here's what I expect in return. If we're honest about everything right up front—"

She looked surprised, probably because he usually didn't prattle on this way. And now he knew why. Prattling made a guy look and feel like a jackass.

She laid her hands in his. "Why would you do this, Clay?"

"It's like you said . . ." He swallowed hard as he closed his hands, slow and easy, nearly forgetting the quote he'd had in mind. "We've been friends for—"

"That's not enough and you know it."

"All I know is that you haven't said no, which means you see some merit in my offer." He hung onto her hands while he sat down, drawing her to his lap, which she resisted only briefly. More support for his supposition. "I was talking with Claudia a few minutes ago." He was avoiding her eyes, but he could feel her wary glance. "Don't worry, she didn't say anything she wasn't supposed to. You can always tell when a kid's been told not to tell anybody about the things that worry her, and the person who told her is the person she loves more than anything, the person who—"

Her hands flew up. "Uncle!"

"That's right, isn't it? I'm her uncle, and I have—"

"*I mean* you're laying it on so thick, I can't breathe. I surrender."

"You'll marry me?"

"I'll tell you my big, bad secret." It was her turn to look

him in the eye. Her arms formed an X across her chest, her hands clasping her shoulders. "I have—*had*—breast cancer."

"That's what I figured." He glanced past her for a moment. "Well, I had it narrowed down. You're due for a checkup or something, aren't you?"

"Yes."

He covered her hands with his, tried to move them off her shoulders, but she stiffened up all over. He might have been holding a mummy in his lap.

"It'll be okay, Savannah. Lean on me a little. Let me take you to see a doctor." He massaged her hands until they slid from her shoulders like suspenders gone slack. He rubbed her shoulders and offered a smile. "Afterward, we can apply for a marriage license."

"I'm a disaster, Clay. Anybody with any sense . . ." She looked at him sideways. He waggled his eyebrows and got a smile out of her. "You're crazy. You know that, don't you?"

He shook his head. "I love my brother, too. I don't know where he is, haven't seen him or heard from him since . . ." His gaze drifted to the back window. He couldn't see the yard, of course, except in his mind, where a dark-eyed little girl sat astride a golden horse. "I see him every time I look at her."

"You'd want to replace Kole?"

"No. He can have his place, whatever and wherever the hell *that* is. I'd want my own. I'd take care of you. I'd take care of *both* of you, Savannah. That's something my big, bad brother doesn't seem to be doing."

"He isn't supposed to. It's what I'm supposed to be doing, what I claimed I could do quite well all by myself." She sighed. "I've been thinking about Claudia's . . . security. I'm all she has right now, and I'm a little iffy. That's why I came home. But Aunt Billie . . ."

"Ain't no spring chicken."

"Whatever that is. And Kole is simply not an option. I was hoping you'd let me name you her guardian in case—"

"No deal. I want the whole package," he told her. "I want both of you."

"I don't need a guardian."

"You could use a husband. I'm offering you my home, my health insurance, my financial support, companionship . . ."

"Mother-in-law." She smiled a little.

"I was gonna hold that one in reserve."

"Sex." There was no more smile.

"Marriage bed," he said, thinking it sounded romantic. He hadn't given much thought to the actual living arrangements. A guy could climb only one mountain at a time.

"I'd want my own bed."

She was dead serious. He didn't know whether to rejoice—this sounded like she was maybe thinking about it—or to mourn. "I figured that would be the least of our problems," he said, half to himself.

"Then you haven't figured everything quite narrowly enough. I'm not in the market for a marriage bed."

"But we've . . ."

She wouldn't look at him. She was going to let him supply the word, and the word was . . . the *truth* was . . .

"F-fine," he said.

"Fine?"

"Fine. As long as you don't end up in anyone else's bed, fine; you can have mine all to yourself."

Jesus, what kind of a thing was that to tack onto a proposal? Right away he felt like an asshole. And she rightly looked horrified.

He shrugged, but he wasn't taking it back. "Not that I'm thinking you would, but that's the promise I'd be asking you to make to me."

She nodded slowly, eyeing him with dismay and pity, as though he were losing his marbles right before her eyes.

"A reasonable request tacked onto an absurd suggestion," she said as she moved to the window, leaving her warmth, a tracing of herself, in his lap. "Women don't do things like that anymore, Clay."

"Like what?" He followed her. "Marry guys they've known all their lives?"

"Marry for security. You expect to marry for . . ."

He grabbed her shoulder. His stubborn eyes held her gaze as he braced himself for the word, for her to name the feeling she was missing before she brushed him and his proposal off. She'd have to look him in the eye while she was doing it; he'd take his hit straight up.

What he saw in her eyes was not a lack, but a frenzy of feeling. It was end-of-the-rope fear and frustration, confusion and defeat, all brimming in tears too scant to fall. She couldn't even come up with the word. Apparently she had no expectations.

"Security doesn't look half bad right now, does it?" he said, shamelessly pressing the advantage he was sure he'd detected. He wanted to smile, but the backlash of hitting the nail on the head had him smarting.

"No," she said, her voice raspy.

He wasn't going anywhere unless she pushed him away. "No, what?"

"No . . . kidding." She drew a deep, unsteady breath, then slowly released it. "Security looks pretty damn good right now."

He nodded once. "You wanna try it on, see how it fits? Pretty easy to do that nowadays—just try it on."

"You think so?"

He didn't, but he would take a *yes* any way he could get it.

"I have a child, Clay. I'm not about to be trying on husbands. I'm not . . ."

"That desperate?"

"That *bad*." She looked away. Her voice dropped. "I'm not as good a person as you are, but I don't think I'm quite *that* selfish."

"I am," he admitted. "I want both of you. You think about it while you do whatever you need to do to get ready. I promised your little girl I'd get you to a doctor, and you've got no choice in that particular matter. A promise like that isn't negotiable."

It wasn't that she'd decided *not* to get a checkup. She didn't want to think about it that much. She was going to get it done, but not today. Today was never a good day. It was going to cost money she didn't have and bring news she didn't want. Either the disease had spread, or it hadn't. The waiting was all. She hated herself for being so pessimistic, so indecisive. She even hated herself for hating herself. But choosing seemed impossible. Lately she could not make a choice to save her life.

It felt good to let go, to let the choice be taken and made by someone else, someone she trusted as much as she trusted anyone. It felt good to know that Clay was that some-one, that he was willing. When they were kids, he had al-ways been willing. Whenever she'd had a plan, he was game. Whenever she'd needed a friend, he was there. His willingness was so commendable, she'd decided to emulate it when Kole had asked her to help him out.

Raise my child. She'll be safe with you. You're the only one I trust.

Kole should have asked Clay. She'd always wondered why he hadn't, even though he'd given her more explana-tions than he was accustomed to offer for his actions. Ex-cuses aside, Clay was the logical choice. When it came to being trustworthy, Clay was the model. After the original, only the imitator. At this point she felt like the mere shell of an imitation.

Clay said little on the drive to Lander except that he thought she'd like the doctor she would be seeing. She started to tell him she'd never met a doctor she didn't *dis-*

like, but he had that Mr. Fix-it look in his eyes, and she
didn't want to burst his bubble. She would tolerate the exam
and the doctor for his sake and for Claudia's. It was easier to
tolerate these things than to choose them. Take the menu
away and bring on the soup, she thought. No need to mention what's in it.

"Nice, huh?" he whispered when he ushered her into the
waiting room, which was decorated in cheery seaside colors.
"If I spent more time in the house, I'd have a fish tank like
that."

To Savannah, it was a doctor's office like any other, but
since Clay was pleased with it, she agreed to be pleased, too.
She took a seat next to the fish so that he could watch them
while she filled out the new-patient forms. She hardly had to
think about the answers anymore. She felt as though she had
become her medical history.

The nurse who came for her greeted Clay by name and
asked about his mother. "Doing fine," he reported. "But I
brought you a different patient this time."

"Let's get this over with," Savannah muttered as she
bolted out of her seat and handed back the clipboard.

Dr. Charlotte Mears was a plump, attractive woman
whom Savannah judged to be older, more clever, and ultimately more sophisticated than Savannah, which was why
she could afford to be so damn patient and friendly. She also
seemed to know what she was doing. She didn't seem to
mind when Savannah asked for a cloth exam gown instead
of the skimpy paper thing. Cheerfully the doctor promised to
get Savannah in for a mammogram *that day,* which amazed
her since she had checked the part marked "No Insurance"
on the form. Maybe Dr. Mears had missed that part.

The doctor had never examined a patient who'd had
"tram flap" surgery, and she was far too interested in the results. Savannah scowled when the woman referred to her
body as "fascinating." She said that the *procedure* was fas-

cinating, but she was looking at Savannah's body. She was examining the part of her that had once made plain white cotton look like fine lingerie and which now was a medical miracle. The nipple that had been an enticing shadow beneath a sexy bra was gone, replaced by a bit of scar tissue with a tattooed areola.

Dr. Mears wanted to know where she'd had the surgery done.

"The Mayo Clinic," Savannah said to the wall. She always turned her face to the wall and stared at it hard, mentally taking herself out of the picture while her body was being examined. Usually she refused to talk until the physical part of the exam was finished, but Dr. Mears's easy manner was disarming. "Back in the days when I could afford to be choosy," she added, which put the brakes on the inquiry.

Savannah's smug satisfaction dissolved quickly. The woman was trying to help her. She was lucky she could find someone to do this at all, to look at her this way. She was lucky Dr. Mears was interested in the procedure she'd chosen over the lumpectomy that had been suggested. Because the lump had grown beyond the smallest phase, a mastectomy was offered as another option. *Take it all off,* she'd demanded.

But she didn't want any implants. No silicone, no saline. The tram flap had appealed to her because her own body would supply the replacement part for her treacherous breast. The surgeon had moved muscle and skin tissue from her abdomen to her chest. The procedure had been explained to her by using a doll with two zippers—one on its tummy, one on the depleted side of its chest. All the doctor had to do was rearrange a little stuffing.

Savannah's zippers weren't as neat as the doll's. They had changed color, size, shape, and now, bunching and sagging, they seemed set to spit the stuffing out. The scars looked awful. Not that it mattered. Awful was what scars were all about, and nobody was ever going to see them. But Savannah had become paranoid about physical changes. She tried not to be, but any new bump or sag shamed her. Worse, she didn't understand her body anymore, didn't trust it, and that scared the stuffing out of her.

She swung her legs over the side of the exam table as she sat up. "So you wouldn't actually *know* whether this bulge in my abdomen is normal," she said, gingerly touching the part of the scar that had become a sad sack, a lazy slouch.

"Since the muscle was used to build you a new breast, I'd say—"

"You'd *guess?*"

"No, I'd *say* it's normal. And I would suggest more exercise, but I wouldn't promise that exercising would eliminate the problem entirely. Does it hurt? Does it—"

"Not anymore. It just looks bad."

"In a bikini, maybe. I guess the exposed belly button is in with jeans now, too, for some women, but most of us will be happy to let that fad slide right by." Dr. Mears gave a little laugh. "I know I will."

Savannah was busy covering herself up, but she spared the woman a glance. Like most redheads, Charlotte Mears was a blusher. Was it the mention of the belly button or the idea of exposure? Surely no one would expect a doctor to wear sexy jeans. Especially not a chubby doctor. She had nothing to blush about. She had everything else going for her—brains, confidence, job security. Why should she worry about a little flab?

"Did your surgeon recommend a mastectomy?" the doctor asked.

"He suggested a more conservative approach. I told him I wanted the whole thing removed. I thought about having the other one taken off, too, just for good measure."

"Because of your family history?"

"Because of my mother. Because she was all I had, and I'm all my daughter has. Because—"

"You were scared. So am I. I'm a doctor, but I'm also a woman, and the idea of breast cancer terrifies me. My older sister just had a lumpectomy."

Savannah sighed. "That's probably what I should have done."

"But you didn't. You chose what you were comfortable with."

"Comfortable?" Susannah snorted. "I don't remember what that means!"

"What do you do, Savannah? You look so familiar."

"I grew up in Sunbonnet."

"I grew up in Ohio," the doctor said. "I thought maybe I'd run into you where you work, or—"

"Or maybe you've seen my picture somewhere."

Savannah couldn't believe she'd said it. She used to love the where-have-I-seen-you-before game, but not anymore. Still, she'd tossed out the hint, and now she was offering the enigmatic smile. There were real smiles and there were camera smiles. Her body was a disaster, but Savannah could make her face do exactly what she wanted it to. She had never taken a bad head shot.

Some people had their health. Savannah still had her smile. For some reason, she felt like lauding it over the chubby doctor. *Recognize me. Eat your heart out.* "Maybe I'm wanted, dead or alive," she teased. "Maybe I'm a Before and After. Or maybe—"

"You're a model."

"Were." She laughed, surprisingly easily. "I *were* a model. I gave it up to stay home with my baby. This"—she waved a hand over her breast—"had nothing to do with it. Now I'm unemployed and uninsured. The bad news is that I have no idea how I'm going to pay for this visit. The good news is that I intend to find a way." She raised her brow. "Good incentive for you to keep me alive. I could use something to help me sleep. Do you have any samples?"

"I was going to suggest that medication is one way to deal

with depression, but maybe we should try another approach first, like—"

"I didn't say I was depressed. I said I can't—" She lapped the soft cotton gown tightly around her. "Never mind. Where do I go for the mammogram?"

"Just across the street to Radiology." Dr. Mears handed her the order for the X-ray. "We should have the results within a few days, and we'll either send a card or call."

"You'll only call if you see something suspicious, in which case don't bother. I'm not going through it again."

"Everything looks good so far, but the radiologist will be able to tell us . . ."

Savannah nodded stiffly.

"What have you been taking for sleep?"

"Long walks, right around midnight."

"And during the day?"

Savannah's silence answered the question.

"You do need to turn that around. You can get dressed now."

The doctor left the exam room, but she was back before Savannah had her shoes on. She handed her a small bag. "Samples. If they help, we'll do a prescription for—"

"I don't need a prescription. I need one good night. Lately that's about how far ahead I can think."

"Okay, here's a prescription for tamoxifen," the woman said, pen and pad in hand. "You've taken it before?"

"Yes, but I—"

"You're on the honor system with this. Get on 'er and stay on 'er." She smiled broadly as she handed over the prescription for the drug that, according to the studies, would improve Savannah's chances in what she had come to regard as the lottery of her life. "It's the best defense we have right now. The research is very encouraging, but it's a lifetime commitment."

Savannah accepted the paper wordlessly. The stuff in the bag was a sure bet, a ready knockout. The stuff on paper was a long shot. She valued the bag right now, and she especially liked the price.

"You're here with Clay Keogh?" the doctor asked, shyly lowering her gaze when Savannah said that she was. "He's a wonderful person, isn't he?"

There was no mistaking the kind of "wonderful" she meant, so it didn't surprise Savannah when the woman walked her to the waiting room and greeted Clay with one of her pink-faced smiles. Savannah ignored the pleasantries they exchanged, but she kept track of their duration.

Her patience lasted at least half a minute. "About the bill . . ."

"There won't be one this time," the doctor told Savannah. Her tone changed slightly as she turned to Clay. "We're trading services?"

"You're about due, aren't you?"

"Overdue. Apgar threw a shoe this morning, and I'm not letting anyone else reshoe her."

"I'll take care of her."

"Honey Bear just needs a trimming. She's in foal. And the rest—"

Clay smiled. "You gave her the full six-horse treatment?"

"Soup to nuts."

"We missed you during that last course, Clay." Savannah realized that she was the only one laughing, mainly because it wasn't much of a joke. But she kept her chin up and pretended it was. "I couldn't resist. I'll pay my own bill, thank you, but you'll have to—"

"*Billing* is another department, and there won't be one this time. Have you been to a survivors' group, Savannah? I know it's a long drive, but we have some meetings here."

"I've done the psychiatric thing. It doesn't stop cancer. So." She cast Clay a pointed look. "Now I've had my checkup. I don't want to talk about it anymore or think about it or read about it. I just want to get past it."

"I'll do the work," Clay promised the doctor. "But not today. We're—"

"Getting married," Savannah put in brightly. She hadn't felt the words coming, but there they were, along with the photogenic smile. Not that she hadn't thought about them, thought, *I don't know what else to do,* but she hadn't said them out loud. She welcomed the hint of disappointment in the other woman's eyes. "If I pass all my tests. I'm not going to saddle this cowboy with an unsound nag."

Dr. Mears turned to Clay. "Congratulations. This is very . . ."

"Good news," Clay said, reassuring Savannah with a look that lacked proper astonishment. "We've known each other since we were kids. Savannah went away, but . . ." He smiled. "Now she's back."

"Back in your arms again, hmm? Well, I wish you both the very best. As I said, if you get the mammogram today, I should have the radiologist's report within a couple of days." Suddenly all business, the redheaded woman offered a pamphlet. "If you change your mind about talking with people, either in a group or one-on-one, here's some information."

"I know the drill," Savannah said, waving the information off. "Believe me, I've had the best."

"So I gather, but it doesn't hurt to have options." She slipped the booklet into Clay's hand. "I'll call with the results. I enjoy springing good news as much as the next person."

"I thought you said you weren't involved with anyone," Savannah snapped as soon as the pickup doors were closed.

"I'm involved with you." He looked puzzled. "Charlotte? Charlotte's a friend. I've done a lot of work for her. We share an interest in horses. She raises—"

"I don't care what she raises, she's interested in you."

"Given a chance, I can be pretty interesting. I do have

friends, Savannah. I have . . ." He was studying her now, watching her as though he wasn't sure what she was up to, what she might do next. "Good friends. You didn't have to say that. She would have trusted you."

She stared at the building across the street. "I might as well go put myself in the vise."

"Now, wait a minute. I'm not—"

"I meant the mammogram. They put your boob in a vise and snap a picture. It's great fun." She turned to him. "I didn't have to say what? Have you changed your mind?"

He stared. She could always tell what Clay was thinking, but not this time. He just sat there and stared. When she couldn't stand it anymore, she lowered her gaze to her hands. Bare hands. Empty, useless, wretched hands. Thin and thorny. Ragged cuticles. Soft skin. No skills to credit them with.

"I'm sorry," she whispered finally. "I was awful, wasn't I?"

"It's a hell of a way to accept a proposal, if that's what you were doing." He reached out to her, covering her hands with his. "But I'll take it any way I can get it."

She gave him a stiff smile. "Are you sure it's what you want?"

"Absolutely."

"Let's do it today, after we're finished here," she said, surprising herself again as she grabbed for his hand. "Let's be impulsive. Is there a blood test? A waiting period? You don't have to get counseling, do you? Do you have to—"

"We don't fool around in this state." He was laughing. "No waiting. Sign your name, pay in cash, carry her out the door."

"You've done it before," she recalled, and he nodded. "But you're absolutely, positively, completely divorced and free to do it again."

"Absolutely, positively."

"Then let's do it all now. If we tell people, they'll try to talk us out of it. If Charlotte had had two more minutes with you, she would have told you what a bad risk I am."

"That wouldn't be right. You're her patient."

"Oh, but she likes you much better."

"If she does or she doesn't, that's got nothing to do with her being a good doctor, which is why I brought you to her. As for the other—"

"You didn't expect me to take you seriously."

He smiled. "I never know what to expect with you, but I sure hoped you would. I'm ready when you are."

The look in his eyes said he'd been ready for her all his life.

Chapter 8

He took her to a jewelry shop called Gold from the Hills.
A quick stop, he promised. He wasn't about to give her time
to change her mind, but he decided to squeeze an amenity or
two into the plan. A ring was a solid token, made by a crafts-
man like himself. Built to last. He wanted more than a piece
of paper to commemorate the dream he'd never quite given
up on. He wanted pure gold.

"Choose anything you like," he said quietly, working
hard to maintain his cool when he felt like a pup who'd
cornered his first rabbit. The thought made him shake his
head, chuckling. She gave him a funny look, and he nearly
confessed that if he had a tail he'd be looking for a place
to sit.

"Don't worry, I'm not a big jewelry person. Anything but
Black Hills gold," she said, referring to the popular pink-
and-gold jewelry that filled the display case she was passing.

It was a reminder of Kole and his aversion to the style of
gold jewelry crafted from the mines in South Dakota. Pi-
rates' booty, he'd called it. But this was one time Clay didn't
want to think about Kole or his causes, for he was about to
marry Savannah Stephens. He figured there might be hell to
pay down the road, since his bride was the mother of his

127

brother's child, but he wasn't going to worry about that now. That bill would not come due today.

"What did you have before?" she asked as she gave each section of the case a cursory inspection. "What kind of ring?"

He didn't want to think about Roxie, either. Couldn't it just be the two of them for the moment? They were surrounded by gem-sparkle, and he would have dearly loved to see her get a little starry-eyed. "I've never worn a ring," he said. "It's a hazard in my line of work."

"I meant for your wife. I don't want mine to be the same as hers."

"It won't be."

He didn't feel like telling her that Roxie had picked some honking thing that looked like it belonged on a Christmas tree. But she was looking at him for some kind of an answer.

He shrugged. "I don't remember right offhand. You pick whatever pleases you, Savannah." He could tell she was trying to be subtle about checking for prices, and he didn't want that, either. "Just go by what you like."

"I'm not fussy. They're all pretty." She pointed to a plain gold band. "This one." The clerk tried to hand her the ring box, but she deferred to Clay with a soft look. "It's simple and elegant."

He nodded. He wanted her to be fussy, damn it. At the very least, he wanted her to get the ring she really wanted. They hadn't talked about money. He'd never cared much about it, and he didn't have a lot. He was a rancher; he had assets and debts. But he shoed horses for spending cash, and he'd find a hundred new customers tomorrow to foot the bill for the best ring in the store.

All he said was, "Whatever you like."

"This is a very nice choice." The elderly man took the ring from the box himself, since nobody else seemed eager to touch it. "There's a matching band here for the groom," he said as he unlocked another sliding door on his side of the display case. "Where did that bugger get to? Oh . . ." He set a blue box on the counter. "The same ring, on a much larger scale. This is a good style for you. Substantial, like yourself."

"That's a lot of ring," Savannah said.

Clay snatched the big ring out of its velvet nest, pumped some bravado into his voice, and tried the thing on for size. "Like the man says, this is a lot of finger. We don't want to break up the set." It would be his gift to himself—a ring to match the one Savannah would wear.

The first time around, he'd bought a set of rings for his bride, then picked up one for himself a few months later, thinking a married man ought to wear a ring. But Roxie hadn't given him one, and he'd been afraid she'd laugh at him for buying it for himself, so he'd never worn it. He'd had a ready excuse.

"But if it's a hazard . . ."

"I won't wear it when I work."

"I want you to wear it," she whispered. "It's just that . . . would you mind paying for both until I can pay you back?"

"You don't have to—"

"I want to give my husband a ring."

Clay drew a deep breath. The warmth in her blue eyes gave them more luster than any jewel in the store. His chest was suddenly a tight fit for his heart.

On the way to the city building they stopped at a shop called Roses Are Red, where they were all out of roses but were able to tie some ribbon around a pretty bouquet of white spider mums. He almost offered to buy her a dress, but he didn't want her to know he didn't like the tenty little combo she was wearing. She knew more about style than he did. The top of the outfit was white, and it had some lacy stuff around the neck, and Savannah was in it, so that was enough.

Her lack of identification with her picture on it almost stopped them cold, but she produced enough cards to convince the clerk that she was who she said she was. The marriage license was issued, and the justice of the peace was open for business. The ceremony took all of ten minutes, and that included posing for the clerk and her Polaroid camera. The tiny woman insisted on "big smiles," first for the camera, then for each other. By this time Clay's head was spinning. Savannah Stephens had just taken his name. For better or for worse, richer or poorer, in sickness and in health, she was now legally Savannah Keogh.

He opened the pickup door and offered her a hand up. She looked a little surprised, but she indulged him. It should have been a limousine, he thought, or a carriage. Had Rapunzel had a carriage? He'd have to ask Claudia. Was she his daughter now? When a guy married his niece's mother, did that make him Uncle Daddy? That sounded as strange as his own left hand resting on his own steering wheel suddenly looked with that gold ring flashing in the sunlight.

He slid a furtive glance to his right. Sure enough, Savannah was staring at the ring on the third finger of her own left hand.

"Would you like to go out to dinner?" he asked.

She shook her head. "I'm really tired. I'd like to go home now."

Claudia was the only one they managed to surprise with their news, and she was truly flabbergasted.

"You married the horseshoe man?" She climbed into the chair next to the one Savannah wearily claimed at the kitchen table. "I thought you were just going to see the doctor."

"I did. I got checked out, and everything's looking pretty good. So, um . . ." Savannah brushed at the wisps of hair around her daughter's sweaty-cherub face. Her tongue was purple, and she smelled like grape Popsicles and dusty horsehide. Savannah smiled from the pure pleasure of having her this close. "So it seemed like a good time to get married."

The look in Claudia's eyes warned that nobody would be putting anything past *this* kid. "You don't look like you got married."

"I have a wedding ring." Savannah shoved her hand under the child's small nose. "How do you like that? Isn't it pretty?"

"You wore *that?* You're supposed to wear a pretty white dress with a long train and a veil, and you're supposed to have flowers and music and—"

"I do have flowers. Clay gave me flowers, and I brought them back for you. And we . . ."

She sought some kind of confirmation from Clay, who was standing in the doorway behind Aunt Billie, a two-person gallery. This was her explanation to give. All he supplied was the wilted flowers.

"We've waited a long time, honey. Clay asked me to marry him a long time ago. I wasn't ready then, but today, when the doctor told me everything was going to be fine, I just couldn't wait." She smiled, gestured with her ring hand. "I know it seems sudden, but it really isn't. I've known him all my life."

Claudia flashed Clay a quick frown and spoke of him as if he were standing behind a glass wall. "But he said he *had* a wife."

"He was married before, but he got divorced. You remember your friends Jennifer and Paula? Their parents were divorced and their dad was planning to get married again. He could do that because he wasn't married to their mother anymore."

"Paula was going to be the flower girl," Claudia recalled

pointedly, examining the flowers Clay had laid on the table, turning her little nose up at the bit of ribbon. "Remember those pictures of you in that bride magazine? You have to wear a bride's dress when you get married."

"You don't *have* to. A lot of people don't. Sometimes people elope. That's—that's another way to get married."

"Elope?"

Savannah arranged the Polaroid pictures on the table as evidence, pictures she'd pocketed quickly without really looking at them. They seemed a little tacky compared with the magazine spread Claudia had loved so much, with her mother posed as a storybook bride. Savannah knew how to smile, no matter who was behind the camera, but as a real bride, she looked sadly shopworn. In the magazine, her groom had gazed at her adoringly, even though he probably hadn't caught her name. In the Polaroids, her groom appeared a little shell-shocked.

But he'd said the words, said them with a tremor in his voice that moved her, electrified her like a soft bass buzz. He'd made the promises she'd read about in storybooks, the ones she'd read to her daughter.

Claudia studied the pictures. She looked up, confused.

"*Elope* means you just go get married, without all the frills. No frills, no bills. You don't have to put on a big show. Marriage is . . ." She glanced at her new husband, but still he offered no help. Damn him, he lifted an eyebrow. She smiled for her daughter. "Mainly when you get married you promise to stay together as a family and take care of each other, which is what we're going to do."

Claudia seemed unimpressed.

"We'll have all the frills when it's your turn." Savannah cupped her hands around her child's face. "Everything's going to be all right now, sweetheart. You don't have to worry anymore."

Claudia recognized the invitation to scoot down from the

chair and into her mother's lap. "You're not going to be sick?"

"They took some X-rays, and it takes a couple of days to check those out, but the doctor thinks I'll be fine. I got some more medicine. I'll be taking it every day. I'm going to . . ." *Don't hesitate. Be positive.* "I'm going to get better."

"So he's going to be my father now?"

"I'd like to be, if it's okay with you," Clay finally offered from the sidelines. "But you don't have to decide whether I'm right for the job right away."

Claudia peered up at him from the safety of the nest of her mother's lap. "What would I have to call you? I know your name is Clay, but . . ."

"But you still kinda think of me as the horseshoe man." He grabbed the chair she'd vacated, spun it away from the table, and straddled the seat. "I guess I've been called worse."

"That's not a name. It's a job," Claudia admitted, turning toward him. "Though I suppose I could call you Horse for short."

"You're gonna call your horse Angel and your new dad Horse?" He laughed. "I think I'll call you Funny Girl."

"No, you won't. My name is Claudia." She squared her shoulders and assumed a stiff, regal pose until he nodded; then she relaxed, finally giving a big shrug. "I guess you could call me Kitten, though."

Savannah remembered Claudia's friend Katie, who was never ready to quit playing when her mom came for her, but whenever her dad was at the door saying, "Time to go home, Kitten," she would run to him for a swing up, up, over his head.

"Kitten?" Clay grinned. "Oh, yeah. I see your tail, those pointy ears, that little button nose."

"Big, long head," she returned, her hands mirroring his gestures. "Big, heavy hoofs."

"You say the nicest things. Will you come live in my barn? Catch mice for me?"

"Barn?" She scowled. "*Mice?*"

"You wouldn't mind living on a ranch, would you? Cats, dogs, horses, cows, a few mice. The perfect home for a kitten."

She turned to her mother. "We're going to move again?"

"That's something else you do when you get married, but it's not very far from town, and it's a beautiful house with lots of room to play."

Claudia had to think about this for a moment. She had gone into the bathroom and cried over the last move. No arguments. No tantrums. She'd asked how far they would be going, and she'd said nothing more. But behind the bathroom door she had had herself a cry. Not a baby's cry, but a young woman's. She had moved before, and she had good reason to cry. Moving meant more retreat, more defeat.

Not this time, Savannah longed to say. *This is different. We're doing this for you.*

Suddenly Claudia slid off her lap and walked over to Aunt Billie. "I'll come to the store a lot," she said solemnly. "Every day. And you can come and see me. Do you know where he lives?"

"I do." Aunt Billie exchanged what-a-kid glances with Savannah. "I go there a lot. Clayton's mother is my friend."

"Your mother lives in your house?" Claudia asked Clay. "Did she say you could get married?"

Clay laughed. "She's got some say over the horses because that's part of the family business, but me and your mom getting married, that's our business."

"So you haven't told her," Billie deduced. "Why don't I go pay my friend Patty a visit while you get yourselves packed up? I'll go prepare the way." She touched Clay's shoulder. "It's going to be just fine. You belong together.

Anybody says any different is just plain wrong, and I'll tell her that myself."

"I was going to call her," Clay said. "Tell her we were coming. We don't have to move your stuff until tomorrow, Savannah. That might be better."

"There isn't much to move," Savannah said. "It's dark now. Night is the best time to relocate, I think. You wake up, and there you are. It's done. Everything's new."

"It's still the same ol' Lazy K."

"How will she take it, do you think?"

"The way she takes any kind of change. She'll bitch about it. You'll have to tune her out for a day or so, and then . . ." He shrugged. "I made a fool of myself over you when we were kids. She blamed you instead of me. When I went in the army she blamed that on you. She couldn't see that I needed to get away so I could grow up a little bit. I was bound to come back."

"As it turns out, so was I."

"I don't think so. You had a bad time lately, but you're gonna pull through it and come out stronger on the other side."

"Are you going to show me how?"

He shook his head. "I don't know how."

"*Now* you tell me. I was hoping you could save me."

"Jesus, don't get me started. That's one job I can screw up for sure."

She sighed, laughed a little. "Now you tell me."

With two drawers and a suitcase standing open and not much packed, Savannah sank to the bed, exhausted beyond reason, for she'd barely begun. She'd done little, so little. But her hand was heavy from the weight of Clay's ring.

She had done a stupid thing. She was a woman. She wasn't some lovesick kid who could be forgiven for eloping with the boy she adored.

She had done a smart thing. She was a mother. That was

the one good role she had left to her name. She had done the
right thing for Claudia. A responsible parent could not be
without a backup plan. If anything happened to her, Claudia
belonged with Clay.

Oh, God, she had done a stupid thing. This run-and-hide
kick she was on had gone too far. Marriage was too damn
far. She was a mother, but she wasn't *her* mother. She carried her mother's genes and she'd lived her dreams, but
she'd taken charge of them. She had gotten behind the wheel
of her life. She hadn't hitched a ride with a passing trucker.

No, she hadn't; she'd done a smart thing. She'd married
her best friend. Clay Keogh was not a passing anything. He
was a rock.

And Savannah was paper. Slick, glossy paper. Which
meant Clay was the one who had done a stupid thing.

She could hear Claudia chatting him up while he helped
her pack, and she knew that neither smart nor stupid had
much to do with anything lately. She couldn't tell the difference anymore. She scooped up an armload of clothing and
dropped it into the suitcase. Two more loads, and she was
finished. She didn't have much to pack, but she sure had
plenty of baggage.

Poor Clay. She gave him a sad smile when he appeared
in her doorway to see whether she had anything ready for
him to carry out to his pickup. She tried to hide the sad part,
but he saw it. Even if she could come up with a more practiced smile, he would see through it. He leaned a shoulder
against the doorframe and gave her smile right back to her,
complete with the sadness. Or pity. Maybe that was it. He
didn't say.

She didn't ask. She simply handed him her suitcase.

In the dark, the Lazy K would have blended into the hills
except for the three lights burning inside the big log-and-
stone house and the one outside on a pole, lighting the approach. The place had once seemed like the top of the world

to Savannah. She had embarrassed Clay when, in the presence of school friends, she'd called his home "Tara West." *How can you say you can't afford college? You live in a mansion, for God's sake.*

He'd said nothing, and she'd regretted her words, although not immediately. In those days it had taken time for some compunction to surface, long past too late to take anything back. She wasn't sure why she should remember that now. She was looking at the house for the first time as the place where she and her daughter would live, realizing that it wasn't as big or as grand as she'd remembered.

She'd lived in some very big, very grand places since she'd last laid eyes on the Lazy K. She'd lived in some shabby places, too. Either way, she'd always been a boarder, and this would be no different. This was still Patty Keogh's house. She hoped it was big enough for both of them.

It would have to be, she told herself as Clay turned on the light in the dark-paneled foyer. She sat Claudia on one of the heavy benches flanking the door, whispered to her to wait there quietly, and reminded herself that she was Clay's wife now. She hadn't come over looking for something to do. All she had to do was stay out of the old woman's way, and they'd get along fine.

Patty waited for them by the living room fireplace. Savannah could feel her presence, but at first all she could see were the leathery hands. The one holding the cigarette beckoned them. Since the only light in the room came from a lamp near the window, she had to venture closer. Oddly, some sort of inspection seemed required, but she was not going to be intimidated. She wasn't a teenager who had run off with the favorite son. There were no apologies to be made.

Still, she wasn't prepared for the difference between the woman she remembered and the one tucked back in the leather chair they'd once called her throne, which now dwarfed her. Her hair, once charcoal gray, was now pure white. Her face, once merely unpretty, now sagged heavily and bore no hint of gender. There was only age. The woman who had once filled a room with her presence now spoke from the shadows.

But she still had plenty of starch in her voice.

"I hear you got yourself married again," she said to her son. And then, turning surprisingly cordial, added, "Hello, Savannah."

Savannah stepped closer, leaving Clay near the door. *Guard my baby while I face the dragon.*

"Hello, Patty. You're looking—"

"Don't say *well*. I'm looking old and tired. You're looking pale and thin. Neither one of us is looking her very best, but I've never put a whole lotta store in a person's looks. Looks mean nothing." She moved, a shifting shadow in the big chair. "Billie and Clayton are the two finest people either one of us knows, but you won't find their faces on the cover of any magazine, now, will you?"

"I hope not."

Patty raised her voice. "I understand you have a child." Her inquisitions never included any real questions. She already knew everything. "Well, bring her in."

Savannah glanced back at Clay—*Is it safe? Is she okay around kids?*—who reassured her with a smile.

"Don't worry," Patty said. "I've been forewarned about who she favors and told to keep my mouth shut about it. Well, at least now we know the boy's still alive somewhere. He never bothers to . . ."

Claudia approached the throne with Clay, but she quickly moved to Savannah's side. The leathery hand summoned her closer. Claudia looked up at her mother, making sure she wasn't going anywhere, then took several bold steps toward the chair.

She favors *herself*, Savannah thought proudly.

"Well, well, well," Patty crooned, a real smile threatening the droopy corners of her mouth. "Aren't you the little princess."

"No, you're thinking of my mother. She's the one that, um . . . that Clay brought down from the tower and took off and married. I'm Claudia."

"Claudia," the old woman repeated carefully. "I'm Patty. This is my house, and Clay is my son."

"I thought this was *your* house," Claudia said to Clay, who stood beside her mother. "Are we going to get a different house?"

"I wasn't planning on it, but if anybody's not comfortable here, we sure can." He claimed Savannah's hand. "What do you say, Mom? Is it going to be too crowded?"

"Of course not," Patty said impatiently. She was having her conversation with Claudia. "You see how big this house is? It's just me and him and his uncle Mick. The last time he got married, he brought *three* kids. You're the only one this time, right?"

"My mother and me. We can sleep in the same room. We didn't at Aunt Billie's, but usually we do. And we're very quiet."

"You must be a lot older than you look."

"I'm almost six, but I'm big for my age."

"Smart, too."

"They told her she could skip a grade in school," Clay put in. "That's how smart she is. And wait till you taste her cookies."

"*They cook*," Patty crowed. "Hoo-wee, things are lookin' up now."

"My mom ain't exactly your storybook grandmother, but we can—"

"*Grand*mother! When have I been given a chance to— When have I ever had any grandchildren? Answer me that!" She stabbed her cigarette into the ashtray next to the arm of her chair, cleared her throat, and toned down again for Claudia. "Are you going to be my granddaughter?"

"I don't think so," Claudia said quickly, and Clay chuckled. Claudia glanced over her shoulder, then back to the old woman. "I've never been anybody's granddaughter. What would I have to do?"

"You'd have to treat me with respect, for one thing. No boom boxes, no stealing, and no cussing. Can you do that?"

"Jesus, Mom."

"*He* cusses, but he's my son. Grandchildren don't cuss."

"I don't use cuss words, and I don't steal, and I don't know what that other thing is." Claudia turned to her mother. "Let's go back to Aunt Billie's."

"Your aunt Billie is my best friend," Patty said. "She'll vouch for me. I'm just a little grouchy because my son didn't invite me to his wedding."

"I didn't get to go, either. I thought my mom was just going to see the doctor."

"So you understand how it feels."

Claudia nodded.

Patty nodded, too. Something in common. Suddenly Clay and Savannah were outside the circle of sympathy.

Patty jabbed a finger toward the ceiling. "Clay has the whole upstairs all to himself. Mick and me, we don't like stairs. So you'll have your own bedroom, even your own bathroom, and there's a nice den up there with a TV. We won't be getting in each other's way except at mealtimes. The last time we had a meal was Christmas, wasn't it, Clayton? We have a sit-down meal together every Christmas."

"You can see she hasn't changed much," he muttered to Savannah.

"I'll have my talk with the princess bride another time. She can judge for herself, and vice versa." Clay's mother levered herself out of the chair. "Billie helped me make some beef stew, if anybody's hungry."

Coming from her, those words sounded to Clay like a warm welcome. She said that she and Mick had eaten their supper when Billie was there and that Mick had gone to bed, but she had waited up. She had kept the pot warm.

Clay could count on one hand the number of times she'd kept food hot for anybody. "Come and get it or I'll throw it out," had been her call to supper, back when she'd regularly cooked supper. It was her way of acknowledging the fact that she wasn't much of a cook, her way of saying, *So what*.

They'd had a cook at one time, back when the old man was alive, an Italian woman named Rosa who had fattened everyone up nicely with her pasta, kept the house in order, and taught him and Kole how to give the finger in Italian. But when she'd started exchanging secret glances with the old man, she'd gotten herself fired. Then they'd gone back to his mother's overcooked stew.

Tonight's batch was pretty good, thanks to Billie, but Clay didn't mention Billie's contribution. He told his mother that the food was fine and promised to take his turn at cooking this week and make that pork chop casserole she liked so much. Savannah offered to do her share, and Patty asked if she knew how to can.

It was all Clay could do to keep from busting a gut. *Can?* The last time they'd had canning jars around was when Rosa was there. Even though Patty and Savannah were polar opposites, neither of them had much in common with Rosa. Now, *there* was a canner. But here they were, talking about putting up the tomatoes in Patty's garden before the frost got them, which it did every year.

"I can put up with tomatoes," Claudia said, "but only the little baby ones."

"I'm with you, Kitten," Clay said. "But if you two decide to do any canning, be sure and let me know. That's one show I won't wanna miss."

After the obligatory bowl of stew, they took their bags upstairs. Clay set Savannah's down at the door near the top of the stairs and took Claudia's down the hall. He flipped a light switch. "What do you think?" he asked the little girl. "How would you like to try this room on for size?"

Hands on hips, she stepped over the threshold and sized it up. "It's big."

"It used to be my brother's room." He glanced at Savannah, dismissed her wide-eyed warning with a shrug. He didn't much like keeping secrets. "But that was a long time ago. It's at least a little bit girlish now, huh? It was Cheyenne's room. My daughter. Wife's . . . ex-wife's, other . . . step . . ." He didn't like tiptoeing around that issue, either. "*Cheyenne*. You'll meet her sometime. She's gonna be thirteen pretty soon. She had some posters on the walls, movie stars and singers and whatever; she took those with her. She wanted to get rid of these colors."

"I like yellow," Claudia said as she tested out the frilly canopy bed. "Will she be mad about me taking her room?"

"Nah, she's got a different room now. But they come over sometimes." He shoved his hands in his pockets and shrugged again. "Not a lot. Just sometimes."

"The bed's big enough for two," Claudia said, and he wasn't sure whom she was thinking of offering the extra space to.

Cheyenne probably *would* make a stink over sleeping with a six-year-old, and the kids did stay over once in a while when Roxie went on one of her junkets. But he didn't have to deal with that now. Right now Claudia seemed to be pleased with her new room, and it pleased Clay to have her there, under his roof where he could watch over her. And her mother.

"I let Cheyenne take some of the stuff," he said. "There was a little TV. You don't want a TV in here, do you? I don't think television's that good for kids."

"I watch it sometimes when my mommy's sleeping."

"I won't be doing that now . . . so much," Savannah said as she sat beside Claudia on the bed. "The doctor gave me some medication. I'll be getting more sleep at night. So it sounds like I'll be doing some cooking. And other things, like taking you to school. Maybe helping out at the store. Maybe . . ." She looked up at Clay and smiled, and he saw a flash of the old Savannah—*young* Savannah—the girl with the dreams. "Maybe I'll become a rancher now. It's a lot of work, and I don't know how you do it all, Clay."

"I don't. Some things fall through the cracks, and these days we've got some pretty big cracks. C'mon, I'll show you our room."

Claudia hopped off the bed and started to follow, but she was distracted when Suki, the calico house cat, dropped in to see what was going on. Clay suggested closing the bedroom door so the cat wouldn't get away. "We'll be down at the end of the hall," he said.

The big corner bedroom had once belonged to his parents, but Patty had given it to Clay when he came home after his father had died. With a hardship discharge, he'd gotten out of the army a little sooner than he'd planned, but he'd always planned to return to the Lazy K sooner or later. Later would have been his preference, with his parents retired and spending winters in Arizona. He'd always hoped that he and Kole would take over as partners, but by that time Kole had become a notorious crusader. Patty, Mick, and the Lazy K were barely hanging on.

But with Clay in the driver's seat as well as the master's suite, they'd survived a three-year drought, a downturn in the cattle market, a U-turn in Patty's health, and Clay's crazy marriage. He had his weaknesses—he'd admit to horses being one of them—but he loved the Lazy K. He loved the big bedroom with its corner fireplace, heavy pine furniture, wide plank floors, thick rugs, and view of the Absaroka foothills to the north, the Continental Divide off to the west.

How much more he loved the room now that Savannah was there.

"This is lovely, Clay, but our agreement was—"

"You wanted your own bed. You can have this one." He turned away quickly. He hadn't forgotten the damned agreement. He took a firm hold on the doorknob. "The bathroom's here, and through that door on the other side there's a den with a big sofa. This way we'll be separate but still connected, which is what everybody's looking for nowadays, isn't it? Being well connected?"

"Isn't there another bedroom?"

"You've got your privacy; I've got my pride. And the beauty of it is, if you need me, you won't have to go looking for me up in the hills."

"I won't be . . ." She retreated from him, her voice shrinking, as though she'd been sucked into a hole. ". . . discussing that."

"Why not?" he bellowed. "I don't have to guess anymore, and you don't have to keep me guessing. We can—" Damn, he was scaring her. He lowered his voice, idly twisting the doorknob as he spoke. "You don't wanna sleep in the same bed with me, fine. But you *do* want—"

"I don't *want,* Clay, not the way you mean. What happened up there . . ." She'd dropped to a whisper. "If I have to explain it, if I have to justify it, if I have to put it into some kind of—"

"Okay!" He shook his head and backed off with a conciliatory gesture. "Okay, Savannah, we'll leave it alone. This is our room, but that's your bed. You're safe there. I won't bother you. I'll move some of my clothes into the den. Most days I'm an early riser anyway, so it's better . . ." He tried to reassure her with a steady look, an easy smile, but he wasn't feeling too easy, and he wasn't sure why. He'd had his eyes wide open throughout the whole day. "I'll go give Claudia a hand."

"I'll do that. That's—that's my job."

"She's probably a little bewildered right about now."

"Really." Savannah laughed. "You don't know Claudia. She's wise beyond her years."

He nodded. He thought better of saying he'd noticed. The last word was hers. He'd put his ring on her hand, brought her to his house, given her his bed. She needed to have the last word, the one meant to put him in his place.

She went to her daughter. He went downstairs to have himself a drink. He was deep into counseling himself to be a man about this bargain he'd made—*Be cool, be collected, be considerate*—when his mother startled him from behind with her brand of counseling.

"You could have at least had the balls to come and tell me yourself."

"The only thing I was short on was time." He took a bare-handed swipe at the Jim Beam he'd dribbled on the kitchen counter. "We just decided today, and we didn't see any reason to wait. It's not like we don't know each other."

"I guess not. You know she's using you, and you don't care. You care even less about it this time than you did the last time."

He drained the glass, set it next to the bottle, and turned to face his mother, who was also his business partner, sometimes his friend. He couldn't address her as any of those, though, not now. He didn't want to hurt her, but he knew her well.

"I'm gonna say this only one time. Savannah is my wife. Our marriage is our business. You either wish us well or you don't. You tell me now."

"What I wish and what's likely to be are—"

"I'm not interested in predictions," he told her calmly. "I'm interested in attitude. I'm asking you to tell me now, and I'm counting on you to be truthful."

She looked him in the eye. She was old and tired, but she

stood up straight, and her gaze didn't waver. "I want you to be happy."

"I know you do. But are you willing to let me be happy my own way?" He knew damn well it wasn't that simple, but he had to start with some kind of a bottom line. "We can't live under the same roof if you're not."

"Your father left this place in your name right along with mine."

"It's your home. I can make my home somewhere else."

"Is that a threat?"

"No, Mom, I don't do that. I don't make threats, certainly not to you. I try to do what feels right to me."

She nodded. She knew that about him. And more.

"I won't let you come between Savannah and me. Our marriage is for us to make or break. Nobody else gets a say in that." He drew a deep breath. "Tell me now."

"I wish you well," she said quietly, "with your new family."

Savannah slept with her daughter the first night in their new home. She pretended that it was Claudia who was scared. Claudia played along. They whispered in the dark like two girlfriends of an age somewhere between their own. They both noticed that the Lazy K was even quieter than Sunbonnet and that the house made them both feel small. They agreed that Clay's mother was a little crotchety, but that he was nice. They both liked him a lot. Claudia thought she'd call him Clay for a while, and Savannah thought that was a good plan, at least until everybody got used to each other.

"You should've let me carry your flowers, though," Claudia said, drifting off.

"You're right, sweetie, I should have," Savannah whispered. She pictured little Claudia in a pretty yellow dress, as frilly as the ruffled comforter they had folded at the bottom of the bed.

In her mind, little Claudia turned into grown-up Claudia, strong and confident and breathtakingly beautiful in a white gown, a diaphanous veil covering her seal-sleek hair.

"Please don't hold it against me when it's your turn to get married," she whispered anxiously. "I want you to have a big wedding with all the trimmings, and I want to be the best mom."

In the dark, a small, sleepy voice assured her, "You are."

Chapter 9

The little voice felt like a moth trapped in Savannah's ear.

"Mommy. Mommy, I went out there in the hall and guess what I smelled? Bacon. *Cooking*."

Good morning, guilt. Since when had she allowed cooked bacon to become such a rarity?

Savannah turned and tucked her knees to her chest. "I'm sure you can have some, sweetie. Go on down and see who's—"

"No. I'm not going down there by myself." A little hand clasped her shoulder and gave a little shake. "Come on, Mommy. You said you wouldn't sleep so long."

She had said that, hadn't she? How many times? Once was a good intention. Twice didn't really constitute a promise. It was more like you were trying, but it was still too hard.

"Momm-myyy." Shake, shake, shake. *Shake your booties.* Otherwise they start shaking you. "I don't even know how to get to the kitchen here."

Here. Savannah opened her eyes. A big, fluffy, yellow thing loomed above her head. Somebody had peed on a cloud?

Here. The Lazy K.

She turned her head, nose to nose with her hungry daughter. No Sunbonnet Mercantile, no Aunt Billie waiting to fix Claudia's droopy ponytail. Instead, there was Clay. Even better. *Go find Clay,* she could say. And then she could go back to sleep for just a few short minutes. Here at the Lazy K, under a pee-laden cloud, with Patty Keogh sitting downstairs on her throne waiting to say, *I told you so.*

"What's wrong with me? Of course you don't." Savannah dug deep, wound up, pitched back the covers. "Getting up now. Upright, right now. Clothes, where are my clothes?"

"You can wash your face in there if you want," Claudia said, pointing to the door on the far side of the room. Then she plucked her mother's skirt off the arm of a chair upholstered in cheery yellow gingham. "It only has a toilet and a sink, so I don't know if it's really a bathroom, but I like it, even if I had to stand on the little trash can to turn the water on. You can use my hairbrush. You might have to change into some jeans, though, because we might go see what's in Clay's barn."

Savannah dropped the skirt over her head, over her nightshirt. "Who said?"

"He said. Last night, when he was showing me the drawers and stuff in here. He said Angel was out by the barn and I could see her this morning and I might like to see what else he had in the barn. I didn't put everything away yet. He says he'll make me a toy box. Can we see the barn before we see where the kitchen is?"

Savannah listened with a smile. Claudia was happy. Her daughter's spirit, always a wonder to her, was in top form this morning.

"Knowing Clay, he's got horses in his barn. Horses in his pasture. Horses in his horses."

"*Horses* in his *horses?*" Claudia giggled.

"In the spring he'll have baby horses. You might find a

few cows here, too. This is actually a cattle ranch, but Clay's always been such a horse lover."

"Me, too. I'm a horse lover. But I think he's got kittens in his barn, too."

"Did he say so?"

"Kind of. He hinted. Maybe he has kittens in his kittens. That spotted cat gets to come in the house, but she doesn't have kittens." Claudia handed her mother a hairbrush. "Is he going to adopt me the way you did? I mean, *could* he? Could two people adopt me?"

"Let me do you first," Savannah said, making a stirring motion with the brush while she weighed her answer. Eagerly Claudia spun around and backed into the harbor between Savannah's knees. "They can, but it's a big step, and we're taking one step at a time with Clay. So let's hold off on that question until we get our bearings here, okay?"

"Bear rings? Do I get one, too? Is it like a wedding ring?

"Oh, muffin, you are such a joy," Savannah said with a laugh as she worked the hair band off the ponytail. "You lift my heart, you know that? I don't deserve you. You're too wonderful."

"But you're still gonna keep me."

"Yes, I am. And, you know, you're absolutely right. Everyone got a ring but you, and you should have one. A great big bear ring." She dropped her arms around her daughter, making a ponytail of her, bound in a loving armband. "Like a bear hug. See how my arms make a ring around you?"

"Yes!" Ah, the child was laughing, and for once Savannah was the cause. "But I still want a little one for my finger."

"And you shall have one. A bear ring." Savannah spun Claudia around like a top. "You've given me a quest."

Claudia crawled up beside her on hands and knees. "What kind of a quest?"

"I shall search high and low. I shall seek here and there. A-hunting I shall go, and I shall find . . . what?"

"What?" Claudia was wide-eyed, enchanted by the rhythm of her mother's impromptu verse, hanging on the rim of the rhyme.

Savannah repeated the ditty, stressing "there," angling for . . .

"A *bear!*"

"How about some breakfast first?" Clay said from the doorway, startling them both.

With a rousing cheer, Claudia shot off the bed like a rocket.

Savannah instinctively jerked the sheet to her chest, even though it was already covered. But without a bra under her nightshirt she felt naked. "We were just getting ready to follow our noses to the bacon."

"The bacon has come to you," he said, entering the room with a large tray. "I brought it home, fried it up in the pan, which sure must make me some kinda man." He winked at Claudia. "Not bad for a horseshoe man, huh? Figured a new bride ought to have breakfast in bed."

"Thank you." Savannah grabbed her blouse off the chair and slipped it on over her nightshirt. "I hope you brought enough for three."

"Probably got enough here for twice that, but I have to hit the road pretty soon."

"Oh, please share this with us." She moved a lamp off a small, round table and tugged at one side of it. "Claudia, let's move this. We won't be *in* bed, but we can be *on* the bed." She set the table beside the bed, then dragged the chair up close. "I was actually planning to get dressed, go downstairs, and face the music."

There was a hint of hurt in Clay's eyes as they met hers. "Now you don't have to."

"I didn't mean that the way it sounded. We really took your mother by surprise. I don't blame her for being a little testy."

"She *will* test you. That's just her way. You two are gonna have to get to know each other all over again."

"I don't think we ever got to know each other before."

"You might be in for a surprise. I've got coffee and juice out here, too. Be right back." He returned carrying a thermal carafe and a glass bottle with plastic cups upended over the top, barely missing a beat in the conversation. "You and Patty might find out you like each other. I know I like you both pretty well."

"You like everyone," she muttered as she settled Claudia beside her, using the bed for their bench.

"That's not true. I don't like mean people. Won't tolerate a bully." He looked at Claudia as he took the chair. "How about you?"

The little girl shook her head solemnly.

"I can't be wasting my time on a person who causes pain and doesn't give a damn about it. A person like that can't be trusted. But I like most people." Again Clay said to Claudia, "How about you?"

She nodded, also solemnly. "I do, but if she wants me to be her granddaughter, she'll have to be nice to my mom. Why do you have to hit the road?"

"I have work to do, horses to shoe." He grinned. "Damn, this poetry thing is catchy."

Sullen, Claudia nibbled a piece of crisp bacon. "But I haven't seen what's in your barn yet."

"Didn't I hear something about a quest?" Clay said. "You might want to start with the barn."

"You don't have any bears in there, do you?"

"I sure hope not."

"Mommy says you have so many horses, you have horses *in* your horses."

"*We*," he said emphatically as he poured her a glass of juice, "have quite a few horses. They're yours now, too. But you have to be careful around them. You take your mom with you when you go exploring the place."

"Or you?"

"Or me. But your mom knows her way around the Lazy K. Coffee?" Savannah nodded, and he proceeded to pour. "Like I said, not much has changed."

"Why do you call it the Lazy K?" Claudia asked.

"K is for Keogh. That's my name." He glanced at Savannah. It was her name now, too. Much to his surprise, she had become Savannah Stephens Keogh. She'd take that new name, she'd said, if he didn't mind. It was a chance to gain some privacy. She hadn't really been Savannah Stephens for some time, not Savannah Stephens the model. But the name was still recognized in some circles. She was glad to set that aside.

Claudia's name, however, was another matter.

"You don't seem lazy," Claudia told him.

Clay laughed. "Well, just look at me now. Here I am eating when I should be working."

"You already cooked breakfast," Claudia pointed out. And she'd already eaten all of her bacon. "I know how to wash the dishes, but I have to stand on a chair."

"You and I will take care of the dishes together," Savannah said. "And we have to see what's out there in the barn. Maybe you can think of some chores we could do, Clay. We want to help out."

"Patty's in charge of the house, and Uncle Mick has charge of the barn. Once you get settled in, we'll make adjustments. If there's one thing I've learned about women, it's that they're just as territorial as men are, but they'll work it out differently." He transferred his bacon to Claudia's plate. "With any luck."

"How's yours been running?" Savannah wondered.

"My luck? Stick with me, baby, I've got a truckload of horseshoes, and I just hit the jackpot." He flashed her a smile. "I should be home late this afternoon. What would you say to taking a couple of horses up in the hills? Claudia could get to know her new grandma a little bit while we—"

"I wouldn't ask her to do that, Clay."

"All right." He seemed to deflate a little. He finished off his scrambled eggs, took a couple of sips of coffee, finally looked up, and asked quietly, "Is there anything we need? From a store?"

It's a married man's question, she thought. He hadn't been married a full day yet, but he knew the drill. And that was just fine, because his current wife was a novice.

"I don't know," she said, just as quietly. "I don't need anything."

He nodded. "Me neither."

The last thing Savannah wanted to do was to ruin Clay's luck. Or his life, a prospect that truly troubled her. But fitting into his mother's routine, whatever that was, was bound to be a trial, and she had no defense at the moment. Better to retreat to the barn and find herself an ally.

She remembered Uncle Mick as the guy in the background, always working around the barn or the machine shed or out in the field. If you were taking any horses out, you checked with Uncle Mick. If you were getting into any mischief, you checked to see whether he was looking. Whenever anything mechanical needed adjusting, Uncle Mick was the man to see. He had pulled out a dent in the door of Aunt Billie's van after Savannah had banged it into a streetlamp. "She'll never know the difference," he'd promised, a rare pronouncement for Mick. He wasn't given to predicting anything but the weather or talking about much of anything except what was going on in the pasture. He couldn't tell you what yearlings were selling for, but if a motor was making a funny sound, he knew exactly what was causing it.

He was always working on Kole's pickup. "You oughta let the engine cool off once in a while, boy," he'd say when he had it running again. Kole would laugh, thank ol' Mick, and take off down the road. Clay would pick up Mick's tools, his tips on how to use them, and any slack left on the chores his father—Mick's brother—had assigned to the three of them.

Like everyone else, Mick had aged. His shuffling gait had gone stiff, and he stood stooped over, like a shepherd's crook. He'd always loved Savannah, but there was no hugging when she found him in the tack room after she and Claudia had tracked down the litter of kittens in the barn. He set whatever gadget he was repairing aside, took his hat off like the proper old cowboy he was, and bobbed his head.

"Savannah Banana," he called her. It was she who took his hand and gave him a peck on his leathery cheek. He blushed, bobbing his head some more as he looked her over. "Hoo-wee, what a sight for sore eyes you are, girl! Where have you been?"

"I went to New York, Uncle Mick. Don't you remember how I always wanted to be a model?"

"Well, sure, but you've been gone a long time." He settled his hat back on his head, carefully adjusting it. "I thought you'd come back to see us once in a while."

"I got kind of busy. I should have come back more often, but I started getting a lot of jobs, and . . . well, you know how time gets away from you sometimes."

"Well, now, some things do get away from me, but I don't lose time. I've always got plenty of time, especially for a pretty girl. I got something to show you." He opened an old metal cabinet door and proudly displayed a full-color page from a magazine, protected by a plastic cover and taped to the inside of the door.

Savannah remembered doing the shoot for Pure Co skin lotion. She remembered that the low-cut je bikini top were her idea. The old boots and batter hat were her own. The face was hers, the hair, t it was hard to remember feeling as confiden

in the picture appeared to be. It was hard to remember baring her soul like this. If the body was the temple of the soul,
she had surely bared her essence on a regular basis. And she
had been well paid.

"I cut it out of a magazine," Mick said. "This is part of a
bathing suit, isn't it? It's supposed to be showing."

"It's not underwear, if that's what you mean, Uncle
Mick."

"I never looked at them pictures that kinda got passed
around, the ones they took of you in your skivvies. Not that
I wouldn't look at pictures like that, but it's different when
you know who the girl is. It don't feel right. Feels like
window-peepin'. Not that I'd know what *that* feels like, you
understand, but I didn't . . ." He brushed a bit of dust off the
picture's plastic sleeve with the back of his hand. "I sure like
this one, though. Not a bad-lookin' little horse you got there."

The piebald head dipped over the fence behind her in the
picture. "It wasn't mine."

"Don't matter. Now you can have all the horses you want,
you and Clay. He told me the news this morning. Even when
he was married to that other girl, I thought, She can't stay.
Savannah's gonna come back." He closed the cabinet. "And
now here you are."

"I guess you were right."

"Sure I was. I don't like to say much, but I get a strong
feeling about these things sometimes, and when I do, that's
the way it turns out. Always. I mean, you can count on it,
ninety-nine percent."

"Not a hundred?"

"Well, no, only God can be a hundred percent on anything, and I don't know fifty percent of what most people
now. But I do know you and Clay make a good match, Sa-
nnah Banana. Always did." He turned at the sound of a
wling kitten and greeted Claudia with a smile. "Hey, I
d about you, little missy. I'm Uncle Mick."

"My name is Claudia, not Missy, and you can't make a rhyme out of it. There's nothing you can rhyme with Claudia. It's just Claudia. Claudia."

He laughed.

"We came out here looking for kittens," Savannah said. "And I'm also looking for work."

"You need a job?"

"I'll do anything. Muck stalls, haul water, stack bales. Anything."

"I'm supposed to catch mice," Claudia said.

"Speaking of which, since when did you want to be called Kitten?" Savannah asked.

"I said *he* could call me Kitten." She gave her mother a pointed look, then turned to Mick again. "My real name is Claudia Ann, but don't try to rhyme it."

"Got it." Mick tapped his temple with a stiffly curved finger. "Got it right up here. And we got plenty of mice you can chase, whenever you're not in school. You go to school?"

"That's another thing, Uncle Mick," Savannah said. "I need you to help me get her to school, at least for the first day. I don't have a driver's license, and Clay's so busy."

"I'd be glad to help out."

A shadow fell across the threshold.

They hadn't heard Patty come into the barn, and her sudden presence was a conversation stopper for everyone but Claudia. "Are you in a good mood now?" she asked.

"As good as it gets," Patty said. "I thought I'd have a little visit with your mother."

"I was just getting ready to feed the cats. You want to help me?" Mick handed Claudia a plastic dish. "First day of school, huh? Big day. When is it?"

"It's in two days," Claudia reported as they left the tack room together.

Savannah and Patty looked at each other for a moment,

alone now, sizing each other up. They were both pretty
small, an even score on the eye level. Patty had the home-
turf advantage. Savannah figured she had novelty going for
her. She was a hell of a novelty. But Patty Keogh was no
slouch, either, tough old mama cat that she was. Old cat,
young cat, both sickly and half starved, with one Clay pigeon between them.

"Clay told her about the kittens, so we had to come and
see," Savannah said with a pleasant smile.

"Stinks in here. Dusty hay and horseshit." Patty nodded
toward the door. "Let's go out in the sun. I'm supposed to
walk every day."

"I'd enjoy that," Savannah said, then followed her new
mother-in-law—God, that sounded weird—through the barn,
past empty stalls and stacks of bales and speckles of dust
dancing in shafts of light. "We'll be right outside," she called
out over her shoulder, then went on with, "I know this whole
thing is unexpected, Patty, but I promise not to get in the way
or—or disrupt your life too much. I won't try to—"

Once outside, Patty turned on her, couldn't wait, which
was just like Patty. She had a way of taking people by
storm. Innocent kids venturing into her parlor. Unsus-
pecting, naked, but still mostly innocent kids in her
hayloft . . .

"There's one thing I want to know." Patty thrust her hand
up abruptly.

Savannah jerked her head back, purely a reflex.

"Relax, girl. I'm mean, but not *that* mean." Patty cackled
as she shaded her eyes from the noon sun. "Considering the
way this all came about, I'm just gonna ask you straight out.
Do you love him?"

Again Savannah was caught off guard. She stared, con-
founded.

"Clay," Patty reminded her. "My son. Do you love him
at all?"

"Of course. He's the best friend I've ever had."

"And you love all your friends."

"I don't have many. But, yes, I do. I love my friends."

"So this is a friendship kind of love you got married on. Your part of it, I mean. I know damn well how he feels about you."

"The same way I feel about him."

"Not hardly." Patty surprised Savannah by grabbing her arm for support as she sat down gingerly on a cement feed bunk. So much for the walk. They'd gone only a few feet, and she was already tired. "Billie told me all about how you had breast cancer and got out of the modeling business and came back here because you ran out of money and options."

"That's about the size of it, yes."

"And she told me to prepare myself for some déjà vu when I saw the little girl." Patty patted the space beside her, and Savannah took a seat. She hadn't been invited to sit in the living room last night, so she took this as an unexpected bit of welcome. Two women sunning themselves on a cement bench. "How's Kole?" Patty asked, her tone curiously tender.

Savannah stiffened. "He's fine, as far as I know."

"Yeah, we don't hear from him, either," Patty said with a sigh. Then she saw Savannah's stiffness and upped the ante with cynicism. "He's the one you wanted, but in a pinch, you'd settle for his brother."

"I didn't want either one. I wasn't planning on getting married. Since we're talking straight, that's as straight as it gets." Savannah crossed her legs, adjusting her shapeless skirt over her knee. Two frumpy, grumpy women sunning themselves on a rock in the barnyard. "Marriage was Clay's idea. I didn't suggest it, and I didn't twist his arm."

"Did he twist yours?"

"I guess the hardest part for him was getting me to leave the house for the day. I'm sure Aunt Billie told you that I haven't been getting out much. I'm all wrung out most of the time. I'm . . ."

" 'Wrung out' is a good way to put it," Patty said, nodding thoughtfully, her gaze lost in the distance where brown foothills bumped up against blue sky. "I've been thinking more like *ragged*, like all my seams are coming apart, edges all frayed. Used to be rugged; now I'm ragged."

Savannah nodded in agreement, although she couldn't see that it was quite the same. Patty had to be seventy years old, or close to it. People expected you to be a little ragged at that age, and they forgave you for it. And surely you expected to *get* ragged by then, and you forgave yourself.

"You see those horses out there?" Patty pointed to the small pasture west of the corrals where a dozen horses grazed peacefully, tails swishing late-summer flies away. "They're worthless. Either too old or too crippled up to be useful to anybody. They don't do nothin' but use up the feed. Any good rancher would sell them to a canner. You sure wouldn't go out and buy a horse like that. But every time I turn around, my son's bringing another one home."

"He bought that palomino for Claudia."

"Good. Then there's one of them that has some purpose."

"They all do, don't they?"

"Oh, sometimes it's not hopeless; it's something Clayton can do something about. Sometimes it's a foot problem. So then he gives them some kind of special shoes, and he babies them along until they're sound again. Those are the ones he'll let go to the right buyer when we get overstocked, which we always are. You're overstocked on horses when you've got more than you can afford to feed. And who can afford to feed horses like that?"

"I can't see Clay selling horses to a canner."

"Of course you can't. And he can't see you any which way but perfect. So now he's got his princess, and you've got your softhearted fool." She clucked and wagged her snowy head. "Should be interesting."

"Clay's not a fool, and I don't intend to be useless, Patty. In fact, I was just about to go looking for you to ask what kind of job you might have for me to do." Savannah offered a perfunctory smile. "Besides staying out of your way."

"You won't be in my way. Nobody gets in my way." Patty offered an old-imp smile. "Besides, you can't help but be an improvement over the last one. You've only got one kid, so right there we've made progress."

"I'm not . . . I don't know Clay's first wife, and I don't want to—"

"Doesn't matter whether you want to. You will. She comes around pretty regular. She doesn't mind asking him for favors."

"I was going to say I don't want to talk about her."

"You will," Patty assured her in that infuriating all-knowing tone of hers. "Just so you know, she's the jealous type. It's funny, because she was the one stepping out on him, but every time another woman got near him, she was ready to kill somebody. Just so you know."

"You think I should pack a pistol?"

"Wouldn't hurt." Clay's mother shrugged. "He's got a lot of women in his life, to tell you the truth of it. I can see where it might wear on a wife some."

"Is that so?"

"Well, he shoes horses. Naturally, most of his customers are women. It's women who own most of the horses nowadays, you know. Women raise them and show them and pamper them, get them shod every six or eight weeks, just like clockwork. You should hear the messages on the machine. 'Clay, I'm desperate. Long John Silver threw a shoe, and I need you now, today, this minute.' " Patty's aping was a cross between Edith Bunker and Betty Boop. "Usually they're the rich ones from over in Jackson

162   KATHLEEN EAGLE

Hole. Everywhere he goes, the women know him. Roxie used to—"

"I don't want to talk about Clay's first wife, Patty. Seriously." Nor was Savannah willing to laugh, if Patty was trying to be funny. "And I'm certainly not going to worry about Clay having female customers. He isn't like that."

"He isn't like what? Like a man?"

"You know him as well as . . ."

"Anybody," Patty supplied. "And you're right. He's as good a man as you'll find anywhere." She pushed to her feet. "Do you cook?"

"A little," Savannah replied, following Patty's lead.

"Me, too. I hate to cook, and it shows."

"I can help out with that. My little and your little might add up to—"

"So is this just temporary?" Patty asked abruptly, then quickly put up a hand to ward off objections. "Okay, none of my business. You're not kids anymore."

"That's right. I'm not going to be a burden to you, and my daughter is as good a child as you'll find anywhere."

"Your daughter," Patty echoed, her eyes suddenly devoid of humor. "Is she going to call your husband Daddy or Uncle?"

Savannah glared. "I think they've decided on 'Clay' for now."

Patty nodded, muttering something that might have been an apology.

"She doesn't know Kole," Savannah said quietly, dipping into her reserve for more patience. "She knows nothing about him. I plan to tell her about him when she's older. I hope you'll—"

"You don't have to worry about me," Patty claimed, that hand up again. "I'm not one for interfering."

"That'll help all of us. My not being a burden and your not interfering."

They moved to the corral rail in stalemated silence. Two pens away, Claudia was watching Mick put a halter on her palomino. She turned, all smiles, and waved at her mother. Out of the corner of her eye Savannah saw Patty lift her hand in a tentative response.

"Clay said you had bypass surgery recently," Savannah said. Patty glanced at her askance, and Savannah added, "Actually, someone else asked after your health, and that's when he explained. You're looking very well, considering."

"You, too," Patty allowed, but she was looking at Claudia. "That cancer, that's a rough one."

"It can be."

"Well . . ." Patty slapped the pine rail with both palms and turned with a squinty smile. "Looks like we're both on the road to Wellville."

"We're both looking well, so we must be." Savannah nodded. "It helps not to think about it too much."

"It doesn't do any good to think about it."

"None, really."

"But you start thinking like you're exactly the way you were before, and your body soon reminds you that you're not. And you're never going to be that way again." Patty touched Savannah's shoulder, a surprising and tender gesture. "You're young, though. You probably—"

"No. I won't be the same," Savannah said quickly. "That's why I don't have a job."

"Mastectomy?" Patty asked. Savannah nodded. "Billie didn't offer any details."

"I don't talk about it." The headline was enough. Details were never to follow. "I try not to think about it, so I certainly don't want to talk about it."

"Maybe you should."

"I've had very expensive counseling. I've moved on from that. I just want to forget the whole thing and raise my daughter." She watched Mick put Claudia on Angel's back. "Differently from the way I was raised. She's smart. I want her to go to college and learn to use that wonderful mind she has."

"She's beautiful, too."

"Window dressing, that's all it is. Frosting." Savannah moved her hands close together on the corral rail and leaned in, unconsciously guarding her breasts the way she always did when they were under discussion. "But it was so important to my mother."

"As I remember, it was pretty damned important to you, too, so don't be hanging it all on that poor woman. She's been dead a long time."

"I'm not hanging anything on her."

"Billie would have sold the store to send you to college. As it was, she . . ." Patty glanced at Savannah, taking some kind of measure. "Well, you got the kind of training you said you wanted."

"I know that. I did very well. I don't—" She lowered her voice, unsure of how much truth she was telling or wanted to tell. "I don't regret it."

"That's good. Can you fry steaks?"

"Fry? They're much better broiled."

"Are they, now?" Patty laughed. "*That* must be what I've been doing wrong. A lotta times I just put the food out and let them fix it themselves. I'd rather haul hay than cook a meal."

"I'm not saying my cooking is anything to brag about."

"One thing I will say for the former Mrs. Clayton Keogh—she could sure make good chili. And she had this chicken-and-spaghetti thing that was . . ." She held her hand up again, waved away Savannah's impending objection. "Okay, no comparisons. I'll tell you what, I got the impression they were only happy together when they were in bed, which was her favorite place to be until just about noon every day. I don't think they disappointed each other there, but otherwise it was a mismatch from the start."

Savannah had never even laid eyes on the woman, but an unwanted image jumped into her mind, one she'd never truly entertained. Clay with another woman. It wasn't right, didn't work. It made her feel a little queasy.

"I don't—"

"Okay, sorry. You didn't want to know that. It's better if you don't think about it." Patty chuckled. "But you're the one that got him started, out there in the barn."

Savannah folded her arms, leaned her shoulder against the corral. "You know, Patty, this arrangement is going to be pretty difficult if you're going to insist on baiting me like this."

"Bait's about all I've got left. That and my bark. The bite's just a memory, which is why the steaks I've got for supper aren't the kind you broil. They're basically pre-chewed. Breaded and fried, they're not too bad, but . . ." Patty looked at Savannah closely, as though what she'd said had just registered. "Arrangement? Billie said you were married."

"We are. I meant—"

"He's done it again!" Patty slammed her palm against the corral rail and turned to walk away, muttering, "Damn it all, he can't even learn the hard way."

Savannah had half a mind to pack up and leave, but the other half wouldn't cooperate. The other half was telling her to dig in and hold steady. Clay was no fool, and she was no . . . well, she was no fool's wife, damn it. She was no teenager, either, and Patty wasn't going to run her off. She remembered looking at a picture of Calamity Jane once and thinking, If that mouth could talk, it would have a voice like Mrs. Keogh's, which had once actually scared the pants back on her.

Now *she* was Mrs. Keogh, and Patty was a little old woman with a weak heart. Savannah could take her on with one arm tied behind her back.

Better yet, with one breast more or less missing.

"Come here, Savannah Banana," Uncle Mick said, calling her away from the corral rail, where she'd been left stinging. "I've got something to show you."

She followed him into the barn. He'd cross-tied the palomino and set up a long wooden box for Claudia to stand on while she groomed her horse.

"Hi, Mommy." Claudia flashed her a gleaming smile. "Look how tall I am. Uncle Mick showed me how to use this currycomb on Angel. Isn't this a funny-looking comb?"

"I've got a brush here for your mom." Mick handed Savannah the big wooden brush, brown bristles filled with horse hair. "Patty's a bossy one, ain't she?" he remarked gently as she slid her hand beneath the strap. "Feels like she's my sister now instead of my brother's widow. Big, bossy sister. Sometimes I just gotta get away from her for a while, so I come out here and tend these old horses until I can't hear her voice in my head anymore." He nodded toward the horse. "Try it."

"She's not so . . ." Savannah shrugged. "I don't hear her anymore."

"In one ear and out the other? That's what she always says to me, like there's nothing in here blocking the way. Sometimes I wish there wasn't." Again the nod toward the horse. "Just try it."

Savannah stepped around the tethered horse and took up the chore with her daughter. As they chatted with each other across the horse's dished back, Savannah found the act of grooming, the scent and the sense of the animal, to be surprisingly soothing. She loved being with her daughter this way. She'd always loved horses. It felt good to know these things, to move her hands over the animal's body, feel the soft hair, do the service, and see the joy in Claudia's eyes.

She moved easily from grooming to showering to preparing chicken-fried steak for five people. She moved readily, of her own accord. No thinking involved. Just doing. It felt remarkably good.

She and Claudia set the table in the kitchen for five, but only three of the place settings were used. Clay had not come home yet. Patty took her food to her room so she could watch *Court TV*. She had her routine, Mick said.

"Guess we all do," he added, and Savannah agreed. Lately hers had been even more pathetic than *Court TV*, but she'd changed it now, for two days running. She'd seen a doctor, gotten married, and moved to a new place, all in two days. Not only that, but she'd eaten breakfast and cooked supper. She was on a roll. Her goal for tomorrow was to get out of bed on her own. She wasn't going to have Patty Keogh making comments about her staying in bed all day.

But it was good to be able to retire to a place of their own, to have the whole upstairs to themselves. It was big and comfortable and private, a place for Savannah and Claudia. They crawled into the big yellow canopy bed and took turns reading to each other from their favorite books until Claudia's eyelids began to droop.

"Sleepy?" Savannah stroked the little girl's forehead, brushing back downy wisps of dark hair.

"Uh-huh."

"Did you have a good day?"

"Uh-huh."

"Do you think you'll like it here?"

"Uh-huh. Where's Clay?"

"He's still working." *And he hasn't come home yet.*

"Putting shoes on horses?"

"Yes, that's what he does." *And he hasn't come home yet.*

Claudia looked up and smiled. "You don't have to sleep with me, Mommy. I'm not scared. You can go sleep in your own new bed now."

So independent, her little one was. So strong and so sensible beyond her years. So utterly right.

"Good night, muffin." Savannah kissed her and slipped away.

She crept down the hall, taking a peek through the open door to the den, connected by a bathroom to the room that was now supposed to be hers. The den was empty. Her room was empty.

The house was dark and quiet, and she realized that she was actively, keenly missing someone.

Chapter 10

Savannah heard Clay come up the stairs.

They creaked under his weight, which he eased onto each step in his careful, considerate ascent. She lay awake in the dark in bed, *his* bed. She listened, knew that he paused outside the bedroom door, heard him move on. He moved slowly, his bootheels heavy. He was tired. He entered the bathroom through the den. She had forgotten to close the door on her side, but he did that before he turned any lights on. She anticipated the shower, but no, he chose the tub.

She drifted on the soothing sound of running water, drifted until it stopped running, then listened again. Two soft plunks, a slosh, a soft groan. The water felt good to him. She imagined him sliding his big shoulders down the back of the tub, which then could not accommodate his long legs. He'd have to prop his feet on the tiled wall as he sought ease for his back in the hot water. She could feel the steam billowing in the space between his nose and his knees.

Water trickled with the movement of his arms. He sloshed it over his upper body, over a chest that was so much broader now than in the days when she'd teased and called him manly and tweaked his nascent hair until he'd yelped. He

169

had a wonderful body, which had always been at her disposal, even in their green season when she'd dreamed of his brother, the "older man." Clay, the unselfish. Kole, the enigma. Savannah, the dreamer.

What a genius she had for picking the wrong dreams.

She could easily get up now, glide into the bathroom—she was a great glider—give him one of her seductive looks, and slide right over him. She could overpower his big body with her small, once-perfect self. She could do that, and he would be thoroughly charmed and confused and controlled, and she would soon have her satisfaction. She wouldn't even have to take off her nightshirt. Wet, it would mold itself to her, give her the illusion of beauty, make her a piece of classic sculpture. She might let him touch the good breast, the left one, make her real nipple pucker and tingle. She could trust him. He had always played by her rules.

Big slosh. He was washing his hair. Water sluiced over his craggy face, a mountain stream over a rocky bed. He had a Western face, rough-cut and hard, an exterior so unlike the man inside. It was not a beautiful face, but it was a striking one, memorable, singular, features as strong as the man himself. He could lift her above all the mire. He wouldn't put her on a pedestal; he would *be* the pedestal. His hands would be full, but his tongue would be free, and she wouldn't have to do anything in her wet drapery but smile.

Oh, this was a good dream. A typical, selfish Savannah dream.

But what about this life he had now, with all the women his mother had mentioned? Healthy, normal, double-breasted women. He was doing her a favor, making her his wife. What kind of favors did he do for them, this generous old friend/new husband of hers? Did he listen to them talk about their problems while he trimmed their horses' hooves? Did he offer advice? Sympathy? Solace?

She needed solace. She needed sympathy and more. Why

hadn't he looked in on her when he'd stopped and stood briefly in front of her door? Maybe he would do that when he got out of the tub. Maybe he had been too grimy, wanted to get cleaned up first. If he toweled off and came into the room, he would be warm and damp and nude when he crawled into bed with her, and he would pull her into his arms, and she would turn to him, like a proper wife, a *real* wife.

Now, *there* was a new dream. She hadn't planned on marriage, any more than she'd planned on motherhood. When she was eighteen her life's goal was to fly over the rainbow. Her dream had been for Savannah alone. No dependents, no partners. Simply Savannah. She would do as she pleased and people would see how beautiful she was and they would give her all the love she needed.

Sure, they would.

He'd pulled the plug. The drain sucked noisily on the bathwater, gulping down her chance to be kinky and seductive. If he came to her now, his body would bear the citrus scent of soap and other gifts, and she would welcome him. She truly would, if that door were to open now, right now. She touched herself between her thighs where she was hot and damp from thinking about him being hot and damp, and she willed the door to open, because if he came to her now, she would be a good wife, could not turn him away, would not, *would not* . . .

He opened the wrong door and went out the wrong way.

Savannah snuggled under the covers and listened, but soon there was no sound rising within the house above the *lub-dub* of her own heart. A simply Savannah sound, far less appealing than the soft rustling of the big firs and the rattling of the cottonwoods outside the window. Sleep would not come, and neither would she. Simply Savannah was not enough tonight. Waiting was not her style. She needed contact with some warm-bodied, kindhearted creature right now, and her most recent sensual pleasure had involved petting a horse.

Well, why not?

She threw a robe on over her nightshirt, put on a pair of canvas sneakers, and headed across the backyard beneath a star-studded, wee-hour sky.

Pale mane and tail flashed in the moonlight as the old palomino trotted toward the fence. Either she recognized Savannah or she smelled the cracked corn in her hand. Savannah slipped a halter over the mare's soft nose and led her into the barn, left the door open so she could find the crossties. Then she took the currycomb from the grooming box and gave herself over to Angel.

She nuzzled the horse's neck as she palmed the egg-shaped rubber comb and moved it over the dished back in slow circles. She could feel the muscles recoil and rebound in response to the massage. Such pleasure. She'd been away from this too long. She'd always loved the hot, racy smell of a horse, the gentle nibble of its lips, the velvet nose, the downy hair at the base of its ears, the feel of its back between her legs. Ah, the intimacy.

Oh, letdown. Why had he gone the other way? He could have come to her. He would have discovered how desperately she wanted to be touched in the dark. Not everywhere. Only where it counted. Didn't he know that?

How was he supposed to know? She'd asked for her own bed. As always, he had given what she'd asked for, done what she'd asked him to do. And if he had done otherwise? If he had tried, tested her will, she would have welcomed him.

Whom was she kidding? She would have driven him from her.

If he got near her private parts, her *really* private parts, she would have to protect them, unattractive as they were. Like everyone else, he treasured her old image. She'd found one of the old Lady Elizabeth catalogs in the bedroom when she'd been putting her clothes away. She was pretty sure it hadn't belonged to his former wife. She wondered whether he'd ever gotten off on pictures of her in her underwear the way she'd nearly done listening to him take a bath. If he had, it was a good thing he'd hung onto the catalog. The reconstructed Savannah in her underwear would surely do nothing for him, would do nothing for anyone but Savannah herself, by her own hand.

"I love the way you smell, Angel," she whispered against the horse's neck.

"Wish I'da known."

She hadn't heard him or felt him closing in behind her until he was all around her, his hands sliding from her shoulders down her arms to her hands, his warm breath on the back of her neck. "I smelled just like your Angel before I took a bath," he said into her hair.

She closed her eyes, tipped her head back, thinking, *Yes, yes, you're here*, but saying, "I thought you went to bed."

"I thought you were asleep."

"I was . . ."

"Sorry. I tried not to be too—"

"No, you were fine. It was . . . I was restless."

His hands were on her shoulders, gently kneading. "The stuff you got from Charlotte isn't helping?"

"It's too soon to tell. So much has happened so fast. My head's spinning."

"Mine, too." He kissed her neck as he shifted the massage to the small of her back. "I saw you from the window."

"I had to . . . I had forgotten how good it is to . . . be around the horses and . . ." The massage migrated to her buttocks. He knew her so well. She pressed the currycomb against the horse's back with one hand, gripped a hank of mane in the other. "Clay?"

"Tell me what you need."

Ah, but he knew. He parted the front of her robe and slipped his hand between her legs.

"Is this it?" he whispered, and she made some silly, half-choked sound. "Tell me yes and say my name."

"Yes, Clay, but . . ."

"That's one word too many. This?" His fingers parted more folds and touched high and feather-friendly. "Ah, that's sweet."

"Clay . . ." The currycomb slid off the horse's far side and dropped to the dirt floor.

"Keep your hands where they are," he growled, a bandit's warning. "Hold on and leave the rest to me."

"Clay . . ."

He whispered to her, asking her to keep saying his name as he touched her deeply, inviting her to come to him, to let herself go and he would catch her. Part of her resisted while the rest pulled against all that would not yield, lean-ing his way, as though he were sunshine on her face. She felt deliciously stretched, slight, sketchy, a thousand tin-gling bits barely hanging on. She turned her face to his neck, pressed parted lips there, nibbled there, suckled there, wished aloud to suckle elsewhere, made him laugh and groan at the same time, even as he made her come in the cup of his hand.

He lifted her in his arms and carried her to a stack of square bales, piled like a child's blocks in steps that reached the rafters. He sat her on a folded canvas tarp that had been left on one of the hay steps, then turned away, looking for the blanket he'd grabbed before he left the house. He tucked it under his arm as he unhooked the cross-ties on the mare and turned her out the side door.

"I should have stopped you," she said when he returned to her.

"Why?"

"You must think I've gone crazy."

"You make it sound like something new." He chuckled as

he draped the blanket around her. "It's pretty nippy out here."

She gathered the blanket tightly about her. "I don't know why you'd want to put up with me."

"I don't, either." He took a seat beside her.

"You feel sorry for me."

"You're feeling plenty sorry for yourself, so I'm saving up my sympathy."

"For who?"

"Don't know yet. Just keeping it in reserve." Maybe for himself, since there was no tarp to keep the hay needles from poking him through his jeans. He drew her legs into his lap, taking one canvas shoe in his hand. "If that mare stepped on these, you'd have a broken toe."

"Then you'd feel sorry for me?"

"I don't waste pity on people who know better."

"Is that why you don't feel sorry for yourself?"

"You got it."

They sat together quietly, she huddled in the blanket and leaning against a backrest of bales, he with his big hand spanning her knees, his thumb stirring over her fuzzy leg. Moonlight spilled through the clerestory that ran the length of the barn. This was always quiet, this afterward part. He couldn't think of it as *afterglow*. It was often one-sided, or maybe separate-sided. He'd never shared blended satisfaction with her, the kind that was like sharing the same skin, slipping into the same sleep, having the same dream. He'd never quite reached that state with anybody. But he believed in it. He knew he'd get there someday.

"You were . . ."

He looked over at her quickly, hanging on the words that broke the silence.

"You were so late coming home," she said, her voice small.

"Had three calls over near Jackson, drove all over hell

looking for one place. New client. Plus . . ." He figured this was as good a time as any. "They've got a nice library over there, so I stopped in and read up on breast cancer and the treatment you can get for it."

No response. Maybe she hadn't heard. Maybe his voice was smaller than hers.

He cleared his throat. "I read that sometimes it's in the genes. If a bunch of women in the family have had it—got it young, like you and your mother—well, what I read was that some women in that situation decide to have their breasts removed, both of them, even if they don't have cancer."

"Sounds pretty radical," she said in that same small, tight voice.

"It's hard for a guy to imagine what it might be like. I mean . . ."

"I *had* cancer," she said carefully, as though speaking slowly might help a simple male out. "I had a stage-two tumor. I did what I had to do. Nothing more, nothing less."

"So you had them take out the—"

"I had forgotten how good it feels, being around horses. They make you feel quiet inside. There's something reassuring about a creature that big being so gentle." He could see her smile, soft and pale in the moonlight. "A lot like you."

"Do I make you feel quiet inside?"

"Not always."

"But I don't scare you."

"No." She shook her head. "Never."

"How about Kole? He's pretty dangerous. Did he ever—"

"Never," she said firmly.

He nodded, thinking he'd gotten the message to back off that subject. But he was wrong. He could tell by the way she touched his arm. He was forgiven, it was okay, he was allowed . . .

"I've never slept with your brother, Clay."

He was confused.

She gave his arm a little squeeze, like she was reassuring a kid. *Yes, Clayton, there is a Santa Claus.*

"You mean, like you've never slept with me."

She actually laughed. "I mean, like, I had a crush on him for the longest time, but he never . . . Well, once. He kissed me once. Then he said it was wrong, that he was too old for me, that his brother would kill him, which made me laugh because . . ." She sighed, while he was thinking, *Well, that's two laughs, one then, one now.* "He said it wasn't funny, and that if I didn't watch out, I was going to lose the best—"

"Then where the hell did Claudia come from?" The question busted out of him with more volume than he'd intended.

"From Kole," she said, a soft counterpoint. "But she's legally my daughter. I adopted her."

"Wha . . . *why?*"

"I took her because he asked me to. He called me and said that he had a baby, that her mother was dead, that he couldn't take care of her, and would I do that for him. I didn't know anything about babies, but this was *Kole.* Have you ever known Kole to ask anybody for anything?"

"He never . . ." Never came by, never called, never wrote, never said a word. "No, he never asked."

She heard the hurt he felt.

"He couldn't ask you, Clay. He wanted her far away from him and anyone related to him. I was somebody he trusted, and he didn't think anyone would associate me with him. He was concerned about Claudia's safety, because I think—well, I don't know exactly what happened, but I'm sure her mother was murdered."

Under any other circumstances, the news might have been a surprise, but not when it was Kole they were talking about. Clay's brother had had the worst kind of trouble most of his life.

"Who was she?"

"I think she was involved with his Indian causes or something. He wouldn't talk about it. He said the less I knew, the better. I could tell he was scared, and you know Kole doesn't scare easily. So I couldn't refuse him. I was doing very well then. I flew to Minneapolis and picked her up. Of course, I thought it would be temporary. I hired a nanny, kept working, kept thinking he would want her back any day.

"But then there were nanny problems, and I started taking more time to be with the baby myself, started learning what it meant to be a parent, to be needed by someone who—" Savannah leaned closer to Clay, as though she were confiding a cherished secret. "She didn't care who I was, what I looked like, what I did. She wanted *me*. I soon fell head over heels in love for the first time in my life. With my baby girl."

Clay couldn't speak right away. It was a lot to take in. "So you adopted her?" he asked finally.

"We worked it out through some of Kole's connections with an agency run by a church. He wanted no references to his paternity. Even now we keep our contact to a minimum, although he makes sure I always have a way of getting in touch with him, usually through a friend."

"Does he know . . ."

"He doesn't know anything about the problems I've had lately. There was nothing he could do, and I didn't—" She shook her head hard. "I didn't want to lose her. I really have been a good mother, Clay. I swear to you, I've given her everything I had to give except breast cancer."

"Oh, honey . . ."

He reached for her, but she drew back, clutching the blanket. "She doesn't have to worry about that," she said quickly. "Isn't that wonderful? It stops with me."

"We'll get you all the help you need." He closed his empty hand and reeled it in. "You're gonna be fine."

"I know. I know I am." She had that eager nod going, like she had a spring for a neck. "Do you think I could help you take care of the horses?"

"Sure, that would be great. You probably noticed we've got a few too many. I mean to get serious about breeding good horses, but I keep . . ."

"Bringing home the broken-down creatures you feel sorry for. Oh, Clay." She sighed. "You're a rescuer."

No compliment there. It was hardly an occupation, certainly not one that made for a good breadwinner. She didn't sound mad or disgusted with him. Maybe a little sad. By now she'd probably heard she hadn't married into much of a bank account.

"Some of them make good breeding stock," he protested. "Some make good kid horses." *Hell of a feeble protest.* He shrugged. "Some just need a place to hang out, which is not too much to ask, is it? They've worked hard. They've earned a rest." He offered a smile on behalf of his broken-down creatures. "They'd be grateful for any TLC you've got to spare."

"I made supper tonight. I wanted to wait for you, but Patty said not to."

"I found the plate in the refrigerator. I wasn't sure whether I should take it. It looked real good, though."

"Who else would it be for?" She swung her legs down. "You haven't eaten, then. Come on, I'll heat it up for you."

"I can do that later. Had a late lunch out to one of my customers. Did Claudia kick you out of her bed?"

"She reminded me that I've been given my own. And put you out of yours."

"One thing we've got in this old house is plenty of places to sleep." He slipped his arm around her shoulders. "Maybe we'd do better out here, you and me."

"You agreed."

"I agreed. No marriage bed." He drew a deep breath, blew

it out, trying to drain the heaviness from his chest. "So you and Patty came to terms on the kitchen. That sounds promising."

"She doesn't like to cook, so I think I may have gained some ground. But whether you gained any, you won't know until you try the chicken-fried steak in the fridge."

"You already passed muster with me. All it takes is a great chocolate chip cookie."

"I can do other kinds of jobs for you." Her hand stirred on his thigh. "Now, if you like."

"Tit for tat?"

"*Tat* for tat. Tit isn't up for grabs anymore."

He gave a dry chuckle. "I don't grab anymore."

"You never did. You were never the grabby sort. A little *grubby* sometimes, but you're a working man." She slid her hand slowly into the well between his thighs. His groin prickled. "You were never, ever grabby," she said.

"I clean up pretty good, too."

"You clean up very, *very* good."

"I never go to bed with dirty feet."

"I'm sure you don't."

"And they're never cold, like some people's." He pinned her hand still with his. "Hands, too. I could keep you warm, Savannah."

"You agreed."

"I agreed. No marriage bed."

"But . . ." She squeezed him inside his thigh.

"I'm okay," he told her, holding on tight. "Like the poet says, if you don't want my peaches, honey, don't mess with my tree."

"What poet?"

"I think it might have been Ringo Starr." He shrugged off her laughter as he folded her hand securely in his. "Well, he ain't no Shakespeare, but every so often he hits the ol' nail right on its big, square head."

"I can do that."

"So can I," he said suggestively, his mouth close to her ear. "I want to hit yours with mine. I want to drive it in so solid, you couldn't extract it with a crowbar."

"Now, *that's* poetry."

"What I'm saying is . . ." He straightened, turned serious. "I'll give you anything you want, anything you need. But I don't want you playing with me anymore, Savannah. I can't handle it the way you do."

"Then . . ." She tried to pull her hand away. "I don't want you playing with me."

"I'm not." He gave her hand a quick squeeze before he let her go. "I never have."

He burst into the kitchen the following morning, spoiling her surprise.

"What's this about Uncle Mick driving you guys to school for the first day?"

Savannah crimped the corners of a piece of aluminum foil around the rim of a platter of French toast. "It shouldn't tie him up too long."

"Tie *him* up?" Clay tossed his cowboy hat onto a chair, planted a fist on his hip and himself between Savannah and the table. "How about tying *me* up?"

"I don't think I remember that one. Could you hum a few bars?" She flashed him a smile as she handed Claudia the platter to set on the table. "You won't be—"

"I'll be taking you myself," he bit out, ignoring the joke as well as the smile. "I'll be meeting her teacher and helping her pick out a desk and making sure all the little boys know that if they start in teasing her, they'll be answering to me."

"But your work is—I know you're booked way in advance, and I don't want to interrupt your schedule. We made French toast."

"We make good French toast," Claudia reported, back for the next table transfer.

Clay wasn't interested.

"I'm not a surgeon, Savannah. My schedule can be changed. 'Course, it'd be nice if you'd tell me a day or two ahead, but I can handle short notice." He added quietly, "Unless you'd rather go with Mick."

"I'd rather go with you so you can scare those boys off," Claudia put in quickly.

"So would I." Savannah gave him a conciliatory look. "So you could scare everyone off. I'd like a private audience with the teacher."

He glowered at her. "Mick said you asked him to take you."

"I did."

"Sounded like I wasn't . . ."

"There's no school today. We don't have to worry about it yet." She tried another smile, a pointed glance toward the table. "We made breakfast."

He took the hint and turned to the table, where Claudia stood beside a chair, wide-eyed with apprehension. "Where are my manners?" he said, seating himself. "It smells great."

"Maybe you could take me, and Uncle Mick could pick me up."

"Sure, we can all go," Clay said as he helped himself to the French toast. "It's gonna be a big day for you, Kitten. Nobody wants to miss it."

It was true. Savannah would not have chosen to miss seeing her daughter through the front doors of her old school on that all-important first day for anything. When the day came, she woke up in a panic. She could barely force herself out of bed. But she helped Claudia get dressed, fixed her hair, walked her to the door, and put her hand in Clay's.

The child showed no surprise, but Clay was totally confused.

"I can't explain it." Savannah's eyes filled with tears. "I just can't go with you today. P-please . . ."

"It's okay, Mommy." Claudia hugged her mother's hips. "I'll tell you all about it when I get back. You don't have to go."

Chapter 11

"They grow up fast."

It was the last voice Savannah wanted to hear right now, from the last person with whom she had any desire to exchange maternal regrets. Her back stiffened as she drew a slow, deep breath.

"I'm not what you'd call the sentimental type," Patty said quietly, "but when I took Clayton in for his first day of school, I felt like I was cutting off a limb."

Savannah put her head down and turned away from the front door. She would simply shut the woman out as she set her course for the stairs.

But Patty surprised her with a cup of coffee, stuck it under her nose, and went right on spinning her recollections while Savannah dumbly took the mug in both hands. The steam tickled her nose with a pacifying aroma. She gave raspy thanks.

"His dad wouldn't go with us," Patty continued. "Said he paid taxes for bus service and I shouldn't spoil the boy. Little Clayton said he wanted to ride the bus, but I said no, not on the first day. He let me go into the classroom with him, but that was it. The teacher showed us where to put his lunch box and his brand-new bag with his pencil box and all that stuff we'd bought. 'You can go now, Mom,' he said. 'These chairs are all too small for you.'"

She laughed. "He was afraid I was gonna try to sit with him all day. He saw this one boy sitting all by himself at a table, crying these big silent tears, and he went right over and sat next to him. Everybody else was keeping a distance from the kid, like he might be contagious. Which they can be, you know, crying kids. But not with Clayton. He didn't say a word to the boy. He just sat right next to him, like he was taking up his post."

"That's Clay," Savannah whispered into her cup. Her throat felt like salted meat, and she needed to wet it down. She also wanted to get past Patty without looking up.

"Well, you were there," Patty said. "Billie was with you, I remember, and your mother was there, both of you all dolled up. You were already a beauty-pageant queen, so the first day of school didn't scare you a bit."

"It doesn't scare Claudia, either. Excuse me, Patty, I need to . . ."

Patty stepped aside, rested her knobby elbow on the newel post, and forced a close passing as Savannah mounted the first step. Abreast of her, Patty played the schoolyard bully. "Are you gonna cry now?"

"No."

"It's contagious with women, too, so try to keep it to yourself."

"I am." Savannah went up another step. "I'm not. I just don't feel very well. Otherwise I'd be . . ."

"You don't look sick," Patty said to Savannah's back. "You got something else that's contagious? Besides depression, which might not technically be contagious, but it sure does have an effect on the people around you."

Braced on the banister, Savannah twisted her body so she could look down at the woman. "Stay away from me, then."

"Hey, you *do* have some spunk left. Good enough. I won't follow you upstairs, but I'll still be here when you come back down. Want a little piece of free advice?"

"No." Savannah was on her way up again.

"I'll charge you for it, then. Stay away from that bed. Find something to do and make yourself do it. Anything but—"

"I said I'd do the cooking," Savannah snapped.

"Good."

"And I'm not going back to bed."

"Good." Patty laughed. "You wanna pay cash, or should I send you a bill?"

Smart-alecky old biddy.

Savannah felt bad enough about her shortcomings as a mother without Patty piling on the accusation that she was heading back to bed. Maybe she would have ended up there, but that wasn't what she wanted to do. She wanted to be the one to take Claudia to school. Part of her did, anyway, the better part of her. But today that part was too small to drag the rest of her around. She barely managed to haul the dead weight up the stairs.

She could feel it thumping along behind her, and she thought about an old parakeet Aunt Billie had had years ago who could say, "Welcome to the Mercantile," as clear as a bell. Beneath his tail, Petey had developed a tumor the size of a robin's egg. God, what an ugly thing. Savannah's mother had suggested getting rid of the bird, but Aunt Billie wouldn't hear of it. Petey was her greeter. "Hey, how's the Petey bird?" was the customary response from a local customer. Only the tourists asked about the tumor he dragged along behind him.

Savannah's weight was more like a cyst. It seemed to expand and contract. *God, what an ugly thing.* But today she would not stuff it under the covers. She would let it thump along behind her while she made herself useful, first in Claudia's room, where she paid for her inadequacy by cleaning, rearranging furniture, displaying Claudia's treasures, using scraps of wallpaper to turn an old wooden box into a pretty bathroom stepstool. Claudia would see these things and know where her mother's heart was. It wasn't until she was satisfied that the room reflected her daughter that Savannah went to the room she now occupied—really Clay's room—and got dressed. By now she had staved off the urge to retreat to the bed.

She went out to the barn to pay her debt to Clay. He'd taken her daughter to school; she would tend to his mostly geriatric horses. A pair of blue heelers greeted her when she let herself in through the side door. She called out for Uncle Mick, but the only response was the flapping of swallows' wings. If the dogs were there without him, Uncle Mick had to be operating the tractor that droned in the distance. She took out the grooming tools, set the bucket near the cross-ties, and headed out to the pasture to see which horse wanted to be first.

She talked to the animals while she worked the burrs from their manes and the tangles from their tails. She made plans with them, listed aloud what she would need to turn the barn into a horse spa. A whirlpool was probably out, but she'd heard that cows gave more milk when they listened to music. She needed better lighting, but nothing harsh. And the flypaper dangling from the rafters was coated with corpses. She vowed to change it regularly. By the time she'd ministered to half a dozen horses, she felt as though she'd had a successful therapy session. She was ready to take over in the kitchen.

Patty gave her a wide berth when she came inside, and Savannah returned the favor. She was washing up in the kitchen when Patty wandered in to tell her that Clay had called while she was outside. "Said to tell you he'd picked the little girl up from school," she reported, "but he has a stop to make before they come home. Guess he had to rearrange his appointments a little bit."

"I didn't want him to do that."

"What was he supposed to do?" Patty opened a drawer and rummaged around noisily. "I've never been to New York, so I don't know what kind of men they grow up there, but I hope you realize . . ." She located a ball of string, then slid the drawer closed with her scrawny hip. "He might not be the sharpest tack in the box, but Clayton works hard. He'll turn himself inside out for you if that's what you want."

"I won't ask him to—"

"You won't have to ask. He's not like us, Savannah. He's still giving even when his gauge reads empty."

"I agree with Clay's father." Savannah figured a dead ally was better than none. "There's nothing wrong with riding the school bus."

"After the first day."

Squatting, Savannah snatched a blackened roasting pan from the oven drawer. "There's chicken in the refrigerator. Do you like it baked?"

"I like it any way somebody else fixes it. I'll be out in the garden." Patty looked down her nose as Savannah gave the drawer a good pan-rattling shove. Locked in a stalemated stare, Savannah slowly rose to her full height. Patty finally raised her brow. "Could you use some tomatoes?"

Savannah was taking baked chicken out of the oven when Claudia burst through the back door. Clay followed, ruffling his hat-creased hair. The way he was grinning, Savannah knew Claudia's chatter had been nonstop for fifteen miles.

"I'm the littlest one in the class," she burbled as she climbed onto a stool across the counter from Savannah. Her ponytail sagged, and she was missing one of her pink barrettes, but she'd forfeited none of her pep. She covered the counter with crayon art and pages of penciled printing. "See all my work? One boy called me shrimp. I told him if he didn't call me Claudia, I wouldn't answer him."

"What was his name?" Savannah asked, taking care to wipe her fingers before touching the precious first-day papers.

"Lester Howard. I told him it sounded like he had two first names."

"Jim Howard's kid. Remember Jim?" Clay tucked the remaining counter stool between his legs and turned to Claudia. "Your mom and I went to school with his dad. Jim married a girl from Sheridan."

"Lester Howard took my crayons, but I made him give them back. But then I saw that he didn't have any, so I gave him three of mine to use. He broke one. I told him he presses too hard. He goes like this." She used an upended fork to demonstrate laborious pressing on one of her papers. "He called me shrimp again, so I took my crayons back, and he didn't finish his picture."

Clay glanced at Savannah, his eyes warm. "I guess that'll teach him to show Miss Claudia Ann the proper respect."

Savannah reached for a cup and offered him coffee with a wordless gesture. He nodded once, bright-eyed with appreciation.

Claudia sighed as she set the fork aside. "I guess I should have let him keep those crayons so he could finish his work. One was broken anyway. I heard some boys teasing him about his funny haircut. I told them it wasn't nice to tease." She looked up at Clay. "Why do boys act so stupid sometimes?"

"I don't think we have a reason for it," he admitted, "or much of a choice. We just muddle along, teasing and pressing too hard until some girl takes pity on us and shows us a better way."

"I tried to show him, but he wouldn't listen."

"Oh, I suspect the boy was listening. He'll probably try it your way when nobody's looking."

"*If* he gets some crayons. Maybe Aunt Billie would give me an extra box."

"We'll put that on our grocery list." He nodded as Savannah delivered coffee into his hand. "Right, Mom?"

"Right." *Mom*, Savannah mused as she gathered the papers for closer study. How easily he slipped into the role and used the terms. How practiced he sounded, and how smoothly he carried the parental end of the first-day-of-school conversation. "Yes, I've started a list. I see you gave Angel sort of a halo in this one."

"It's a horse halo, see? It's shaped like a horseshoe."

"Perfect. And the colors are so bright." Savannah smiled, slipping the horse picture to the bottom of the pile. "How do you like your teacher? Mrs. Carpenter."

"Mrs. *Lar*penter," Claudia corrected. "She's nice. She knows who you are, Mommy. She said—"

"Claudia, you have to stop telling people that I'm some sort of famous person. I'm not famous at all anymore, and I don't want people thinking of me that way." She shook her head. "I don't know any Carpenter-Larpenters. I probably should, but I don't."

"Try Wheeler-Dealers," Clay muttered over the rim of his coffee cup. "Remember Mary Wheeler?"

"She said she used to baby-sit you, and she gave you makeup," Claudia reported.

"Mary Wheeler, the Avon lady's daughter? She's your teacher?"

"Mary and her mother still sell makeup," Clay said. "That's what put Mary through college. She's Mrs. Larpenter now. She said to tell you hello. I saw Leanne today, too. Told her we got married. She'd like to come out for a visit." Savannah flashed him a warning look. He scowled. "We're not keeping it a secret, are we?"

"Of course not. Not in Sunbonnet."

"Somewhere else?"

"Of course not," she repeated, and then she laughed. "The best way to get the word out is through the beauty shop."

Clay grinned. "I'd like to put it on a billboard, send out fancy announcements. How about if I put it in the newspaper?"

"Why bother? I'm sure the story's been written by now."

She didn't realize how disgusted she sounded until she saw the light fade from his eyes, the boyish grin replaced by a hot blush. She desperately tried to think of a redeeming comment, something droll about women and beauty shops, something that would override her accusatory tone. *It's no secret anymore.*

She didn't want it to be a secret. She simply wanted it to be old news.

"Did you get any phone calls today?" he asked quietly.

She shook her head.

"Well, I have some to make. I've got some 'splainin' to do, Lucy," he aped, recovering his humor. " 'Bout some appointments I missed."

"I'm sorry about that, Clay. I didn't mean to mess up your schedule."

"There isn't as much call for shoeing in the winter, so business will soon be winding down. You're not messing anything up. I can take care of it."

Claudia held court during supper, regaling everyone, including Patty, with her descriptions of her classmates and her opinions about school. She thought she would like it, but she hoped they would get on to more challenging math and start reading out loud pretty soon. After supper she wanted to ride her horse before it got dark, and after that she wanted to play school. Finally Savannah told her that tomorrow was another school day and that nightly baths were required for schoolgirls.

Clay could hear them through the bathroom door. Claudia

was playing with some kind of toy in the bathtub while Savannah was trying to wash her hair. "Oh, sweetie, you're getting me all wet," she was saying, and he smiled, remembering a time when she'd shrieked nearly the same words at him.

But instead of "sweetie," she'd said, *Clayton Jonas Keogh!* She'd been complaining about the heat, and he'd just happened to have a squirt gun handy. He'd aimed for the cocker spaniels on her T-shirt. *That oughta cool those puppies off.* He'd soaked her good, too. Pinned those floppy ears back, couldn't resist pinging that one perfectly placed nose and making it poke out as though it smelled milk. *You stop that!* But, ah, the look she'd given him was pure, proud Savannah.

Where had that girl gone?

The plug had been pulled. The drain was sucking up bathwater. Claudia's laughter was like a rubber ball, bouncing away from him, rolling into the bedroom. Then the hair dryer howled.

On an impulse Clay reached for the phone on the desk and punched in Dr. Charlotte Mears's home number. She sounded glad to hear from him until he told her what was on his mind. "Savannah hasn't heard from you about those X-rays yet. What's the holdup?"

"When I have the results, I'll be calling my patient, Clay. You're not my patient."

"She's my wife."

"Already? When you make up your mind, you don't waste any time, do you?"

"When I've made up my mind, why waste anything as precious as time?"

"No reason, I guess."

There was no real reason for him to feel bad about the echo of disappointment, but he realized he did. They'd never been more than friends, though he'd known all along what

Savannah meant by "the look" Charlotte gave him sometimes. It made him uncomfortable when he thought about it,
so he didn't think about it. He pretended it was nothing more
than a smile from a friend who appreciated the work he did,
which he returned in kind, even over the phone.

Except when the work she did didn't seem to be getting
done.

"Which brings me back to the holdup question. Does it
usually take this long? Does that mean there's something
wrong? Can't they just tell us, or do they have to get a second opinion first? Isn't it—"

"Slow down, Clay, this isn't good for your blood pressure.
We may be a small operation here, but we're thorough. We
get more than one specialist to read the film. I don't know
anything yet, and when I do, I'll call . . . your wife. Can I
reach her at the Lazy K?"

"If it's bad news, I want you to tell me first."

"Repeating, in case you somehow missed it the first time:
you're not the patient. I don't know what it says on the marriage certificate, but the one-flesh deal doesn't apply med-
ically."

"Yeah, but mentally . . ."

"You've got one brain between you?"

"Very funny, Doctor." Being of one mind with Savannah
on matters of the flesh was a subject too touchy to joke
about at the moment. "We're talking about an emotionally
fragile woman, Charlotte. She hasn't been going to the doctor like she's supposed to, so she's gotta be worried."

"As anyone in her situation would be."

"Savannah isn't just anyone," he reminded her patiently.
"She's my wife, and I want to be here when she gets whatever news we've got coming."

"Either way, I think she needs to talk to someone who's
been there."

"Been where?"

"To the Ladies' Room. *Come on*, Clay."

He had to admit, Charlotte's smart-assedness could be pretty cute, coming from a doctor. "How many horseshoes would a house call cost me?"

"She needs more than just me. She needs to talk with other survivors and start seeing herself as one of them. A survivor. You can see what she's been through, but you can't really know unless you've experienced it yourself."

"I haven't . . ." Could he say this? Maybe just to Charlotte, who might be willing to educate him some. He tucked his chin and leaned forward in his chair. "She won't even let me see."

Long, loaded silence. Long, indrawn breath. Deep sigh. Finally: "What has she told you?"

"Not much." By now he was squirming. Damn, he was talking to another woman about his wife's tits. Breasts. *Breast*—just the hurt one. "Maybe you could explain it to me a little bit. Layman's terms."

"I'm not a layman."

"Doctor's, then. I'll take anything I can get."

"You'll have to get what you can from your wife."

"Come on, Charlotte, help me out."

"I'll be happy to talk with both of you when I get the report back, which could be tomorrow, could be Monday. But that's up to her. She's my patient."

"So am I."

"Two separate patients. How's your back?"

"Great. You never answered me about the house call."

She laughed. "That goes with your territory, not mine. Let's see what the X-rays show."

"Right." His friend was letting him know she was a doctor first. He had to respect that. "Once we get that out of the way and she knows everything's okay, she'll be her old self again."

*   *   *

Savannah stood outside the door, listening.

She was on her way to Claudia's room for pajamas. She heard him on the phone, didn't mean to listen, but the words charged through the crack in the door. *I'll take anything I can get.* What was that about? She heard the name Charlotte. He was talking to her doctor. He was trying to get something out of *her* doctor.

Her doctor, his friend.

Help me out. House call? What kind of a house call? Probably some private little joke between friends.

Clay was Savannah's friend, too, and what she'd heard was merely proof of his concern. Their marriage wasn't a regular marriage. He was helping her out, doing her a favor. He'd done her a favor by making her see a doctor, and he was following up on the favor. That was Clay for you.

That was Clay for *her*. He was a good man. Better than she deserved, useless as she'd been lately. She stood there feeling small, distant, nearly invisible.

Come on, Charlotte, help me out.

Easy, familiar, somebody he could turn to and count on. Charlotte was his friend. His helpful, smart doctor friend.

Charlotte wasn't pretty, though. She really wasn't very pretty.

So what? What a stupid thought. Her husband—technically, her husband—was chatting up a clever doctor, and his wife was standing outside the door *listening* and having stupid thoughts about who was prettier.

More than technically, she corrected herself. He was her husband. They'd consummated the marriage, hadn't they? They'd had sex. Did it count if it happened before the wedding? Did it count if he didn't get to see his whole bride? Did it count?

Who besides Savannah was counting? Savannah, the stupid thinker. But pretty, technically speaking. If he didn't get too close.

Savannah moved on. What was she doing eavesdropping? She'd call the woman herself tomorrow. Right now her business was to get her daughter's pajamas.

Clay stood outside the door, listening. His girls were reading together in Claudia's bed.

His girls. Savannah would probably laugh if he said that out loud, so he'd be careful not to say it. If she laughed, the bubble might burst. His thoughts were his own, and it was better to keep some of them that way. He'd keep *his girls*.

He could just picture them both in that big yellow canopy bed, dark little head pillowed against mother's pretty breast. If they were really his girls, he could tap on the door, and they'd tell him to come on in, and they would read to him about a girl and her mother nurturing a nest of orphaned pigeon eggs. Claudia was so smart, she could read much of the story herself.

Smart like her dad.

They weren't Clay's girls yet. They were still more Kole's than Clay's. It would take some doing to make them his, even if Kole stayed out of their lives and kept all his love and his secrets wherever he was hiding them.

Clay didn't much like secrets. He'd felt bad about calling Charlotte the minute he'd hung up the phone, felt like he'd done something behind Savannah's back and needed to confess. But the door was closed. They were doing their bedtime routine, which didn't involve him. Maybe in time it would, but they were just getting used to each other. They needed their privacy at night. Tomorrow they'd let him in. There would be things he could do for them in the morning.

Maybe pounding on her doctor's door was one of them. Maybe he was rubbing up against her privacy there, too, but she needed assurance, and he wanted to get it for her. It was his quest. He wanted an answer, and it had to be the right one. He wouldn't settle for less. If the disease was back, he'd fight that off, too.

After she'd first told him about it, he hadn't let himself think about it a lot. She'd chosen not to tell him too much, and since it was kind of a woman thing, he'd taken the hint to stand back from it. But then he'd sat in the waiting room while she was getting her breast examined, and he'd allowed himself to wonder how it felt. After two years, maybe she was used to it. She'd had good care. She'd gone to the best doctors. Maybe this was all routine now. He'd sat there with an old issue of *Sports Illustrated* on his lap, thumbing through pictures of football games that had long since been forgotten by everybody except maybe the guy who was getting wheeled off the field on a gurney, and he'd thought, *Like hell it's routine.*

He'd closed his eyes and imagined Savannah on that gurney, and he'd known in that instant exactly how she felt. Cold, crippled, and cornered. He'd felt it, too.

He'd bolted right out of the chair, gone outside, and grabbed some fresh, warm Wyoming air. *Damn.*

Within a few hours she had become his wife, and he'd realized how little he knew about this thing she'd been battling, how little he'd bothered to know, and how much it threatened should it ever come stalking her again, stealing into her, sneaking back *into* Savannah. He needed to know more about this enemy of hers, of *theirs*, so he'd gone and looked it up. He wasn't a frequent library patron, but he'd furtively fumbled around until he had found what he was looking for. A woman's disease, he'd thought, but he had learned that it was possible for a man to get breast cancer. Rare, but possible.

Savannah had described her tumor as stage two, and he'd found out what she meant. Not the smallest, but not the biggest, either. Definitely beatable. What she needed now was that all-clear sign. Okay, so it was a numbers game, and "all-clear" was a relative term. After two years it meant a little more than it did after six months. She needed that sign. And he felt a compelling need to get it for her.

God, he needed to be close to her now, to both of them. He needed to be welcome inside this room, to be sitting near the bed like a big watchdog, listening to them read. He needed this marriage to be real.

He needed it to last.

The next morning Savannah drove Claudia to the end of the road and put her on the bus. She didn't recognize the bus driver, but she could tell he was trying to get a look at her without being too obvious. She smiled and asked him to drive carefully; he nodded, touched the bill of his cap, and muttered something about precious cargo.

She spent much of the morning with the horses, first learning the feeding schedule from Uncle Mick as she followed his instructions in preparing Clay's customized blend for each horse, then bringing them into the stalls to feed and pamper them. They were like huge old dogs, some docile, others a little crotchety, but they all needed attention. As much as she'd loved riding when she was a kid, she couldn't remember when she'd done it last. She didn't know which of these might be rideable. Maybe the stocking-footed sorrel mare. Maybe the big black whose soft lips tickled her palm when she offered him apple-flavored horse cookies.

The horses gave her a peaceful feeling. It didn't matter whether she could still ride or whether they could still carry her. They served their life's purpose by being horses. Human purposes for them warred with their own instincts. But here she was, quite human, and here they were, giving her peace. She wanted only to return the favor.

When the phone rang that afternoon, Savannah ignored it until about the fourth ring. She'd made a couple of calls, but she hadn't received any. She didn't want to. But the insistent ringing finally got to her. Charlotte Mears, the woman said. It took a moment for Savannah to make sense of the name, and then she went still, felt nothing, said nothing except Yes, and Good, and Yes, and Thank you. She placed the receiver on the hook as though it were an egg.

And there it was. All that worry for nothing.

When Clay called to say that he'd be late again, she didn't mention the call from the doctor. She kept it from him like a sweet she had squirreled away. She said nothing to Claudia until after she'd heard all about School Day Two. After Claudia had talked herself out, Savannah took her turn. "The doctor said Mommy is okay."

Claudia didn't say much. She repeated the news, just to make sure she had it right, and then she put her head in Savannah's lap, arms around her waist, and stayed that way, so quiet, so still, while Savannah stroked her hair, rubbed her back, patted her bottom until she fell asleep.

Savannah looked at the illuminated red numbers on the clock when she heard Clay's footfalls on the steps. It didn't matter what time it was. She wasn't really waiting up. She simply hadn't gotten to sleep. He seemed to be keeping long hours for a horseshoer, but *that* was his business.

She waited until he'd bathed before she went down the hall—could have gone through the bathroom, but that didn't seem like the proper approach—and rapped softly on his door. There was no answer at first. Disappointed, she stepped back.

The door opened, reversing both the move and the mood. Backlit by the desk lamp, he suddenly filled the doorway. Her heart swelled instantly, and she welcomed the sight of him.

"Come on in." He buttoned his jeans as he stepped aside to admit her. His feet were bare, his broad chest damp and dewy, his hair a spiky wet mop, and his blue eyes bright with boyish surprise. "That was such a tiny knock, I thought it might be Claudia, and I was just . . ." He swept his shirt off the sofa. "Have a seat."

All she wanted to do was look at him. "You had a long day."

"Sometimes I have to do a lot of driving between jobs. This time of year there's a flurry of events to end the season, so the money's good. Did I wake you up?"

She laughed as she sat down where his shirt had been. "Are you kidding?"

"I could shower downstairs."

"No, please. I was listening for you." She pushed two bed pillows over to make room for him. "I thought you said this opened up. I'll bet it isn't very comfortable. They never are."

"It's fine. All I have to do is stretch out, and I'm out like a light." He sat beside her, his body skewed her way. "I was thinking about you all day. I gotta confess, I called Charlotte. Twice. Last night and again today."

"What did she tell you?"

"She told me to mind my own business, but I don't see why it should take them so long. Thought I'd lean on her, just a little." He plowed his hair back from his face with splayed fingers, gave her a lopsided, self-effacing smile. "It's kinda my business, isn't it?"

"You're paying the bill."

"Yeah." He glanced away.

"She called this afternoon."

"Charlotte?" He said the name eagerly, but when Savannah nodded, his gaze nervously ricocheted. "Goddamn, I told her I wanted to be here."

"It's okay." She covered the hand he'd braced on his knee with her own. "For now, everything's okay."

"*You're* okay?"

"The mammogram looks good." She pulled her hand back and substituted airiness. "Thank you for making me get that done. It's a relief, now that the results are in. I've turned into an awful coward lately."

"That's not the way I see it. You told Claudia?"

She nodded. "I waited a while, though. I wanted to tell you both at the same time. Kind of a moment, you know? Like Christmas morning. Finally I had something to offer. Finally I had done something right."

He gave her a curious look. "But it's not your doing."

"No. You're right. I don't know why I thought that. Finally my *body* did something right. Finally I'm not causing any trouble. Finally something's going on in here." She laid her right hand high over her chest, then slowly slid it down, pulled it cautiously to the right. "Good, maybe. I can't promise it'll last any longer than Christmas does, but right now I'm in pretty good shape." Holding onto herself, looking at him, promising him.

"How did Claudia . . ." He leaned closer, eyes locked with hers, fingertips meeting her knee, where her robe had fallen away. "Bet she turned cartwheels, huh?"

"What do you want to do?"

He smiled a little. "Put my arms around you."

"That's what she did," she whispered as she leaned into his embrace. She ducked under his chin, pressed her face against his smooth, warm chest, breathed the citrusy scent of the soap they shared. It smelled so much better on him. "And she held me for the longest time."

His arms enveloped her. "Bet I can go longer."

"I doubt it. She held me until she fell asleep, and I'm sure she wasn't as tired as you must be."

"I can hold you till you fall asleep. I can carry you to bed, put you down, and keep holding you." He rubbed his cheek against her hair, then put his mouth near her ear. His voice was low and intimate. "I could even carry you out to the barn. Into the hills, anywhere you want. I could hold you forever."

"As long as we both shall live?"

"*Forever*," he insisted, threading his fingers in her hair. She could hear his heart pounding beneath her ear, feel its redoubled efforts in the intensity of his body. "Let me love you properly, Savannah."

Properly would be good. Improperly would be fine, too.

But she demurred. "Claudia held me without saying anything. She took the news for what it was worth and held on."

"So I'm supposed to love you the way a child does?"

"Nobody can love that way except a child." She looked at him. "The thing is, I'm never going to be my old self again."

"What do you mean?"

"I can't be, you see. Even if the disease is gone for good, I'm never going to be the way I was. If it's Savannah Stephens you're looking for, you'll have to go looking in those old issues of *Lady Elizabeth's*."

He smiled and traced the line of her face with his finger. "What about Savannah Keogh? Where can I find her?"

"I don't know."

"Out in the barn? Up in the hills, maybe?" He indicated the bedroom with a shift of his glance. "Who's been sleeping in my bed?"

"Maybe nobody."

"Bullshit. I don't give up my bed for *nobody*." His innocent smile turned canny. "Savannah Keogh."

Her hand slipped to his lap, stirred, feeling over the denim for the length of his erection as she mirrored his smile. "Let *me* make love to *you* properly."

"Savannah . . ." The look in his eyes said that she could undo him if she wanted. He wouldn't stop her. There was hunger in his eyes, but pity, too. "I don't think you know what 'properly' means. It's not one-sided. If you could trust me, just a little, we might try—"

"I've always trusted you, Clay. More than anyone, including myself."

"Aw, come on, darlin', who are you trying to kid?" He dropped his head back against the sofa. "Probably both of us, but I'm too tired to appreciate the humor."

"I'm not . . ." Pity. *Pity*, for God's sake, as though she was too destitute to give him anything. Even pleasure. "I do know how to give a proper back rub," she said quietly, shifting. "Let me do that for you."

He didn't protest very much while she arranged his pillow and blanket on the floor. She winced at the catch in his breath, the soft sound of his pain when he got down on his knees. She felt a phantom pinch deep in her chest as she told him how good this would feel. He told her not to trip over him on her way out. Straddling him, hovering over him, she reassured him with words and hands, first thumping, then kneading his broad shoulders, long back, firm butt. When her touch made him groan, she attended to that spot until he stopped resisting. She could feel the tension melt and drain away from him. She devoted her entire focus, all of her care and energy, to his overworked muscles, forgetting her own.

His sleeping face reminded her of Claudia's, and she wasn't sure why. Innocence in sleep, surely. The shape of Claudia's ear was Clay's in miniature. Lips, too, maybe, but the resemblance was subtle. The echo of her own feeling was not. It was a pleasure to watch him sleep and wonder whether she had a role to play in his dream.

She considered lying beside him, but she went to his bed instead, satisfied that she had given his body some measure of comfort. Perhaps, too, her news had given his mind some ease.

Chapter 12

Savannah congratulated the woman in the bedroom mir-
ror for being up and dressed so early in the morning. She
was making plans for another first—cooking everybody in
the house a full breakfast—when Clay appeared at the door.
Not only was he clean-shaven, sweet-smelling, and smiling,
but he was wearing a white shirt and a sport jacket. He
hadn't been this dolled up since prom night.

"Don't you look fine," she enthused, giving him the ap-
preciative once-over from polished black boots to silver-
belly Stetson.

His eyes gleamed appreciatively as well. "That was nice,
what you did for me last night. Peeled myself right up off the
floor this morning, didn't hardly feel stiff at all."

"I guess I'm good for something, huh?" She laid a hand
on his lapel. "What's the occasion?"

"It's Sunday."

"Do we dress for breakfast on Sunday?"

"I . . ." Head lowered, he pulled at the brim of his hat.
"Sometimes I go to church on Sundays."

"Oh." Why did that make her feel funny, as though he was
noting that he bathed and she didn't? "Well, that's . . . that's
nice. You look great."

"Claudia wants to go with me. Is that okay?"

"Sure. I don't have anything against—" She stepped back. "We've actually been to church on occasion. It's been a while. She used to get pretty fidgety, but I'm sure she'll be fine."

She didn't know her daughter wanted to go to church. He must have been thinking, *What kind of a mother is this woman who won't even take her kid to church?* She gave a small excuse for a smile. "I didn't know you were a church-goer."

He lifted one shoulder. "They say they need me in the choir. Small town, small choir, they need all the bodies they can get."

"You sing?"

"Yeah. As a matter of fact, I do," he informed her with a touch of amusement in his eyes. "We used to sing together sometimes, remember? Kinda playin' around?"

"We did, didn't we?" She smiled now, tilted her head, and chirped, "Don't you break my heart."

"I couldn't if I tried."

His eyes challenged her to deny it, but she couldn't. If she had a heart, she was pretty sure it was unbreakable. Still, she wanted to respond to his challenge and the warmth in his eyes with another line from the song, if for no other reason than to keep him singing, make him stay another moment, "play around" a little more. But she couldn't think of any more words.

The door on the other side of the room opened, and Clay was the first to turn and look. "Hey, Kitten. Man, that's some dress."

"I want my hair down, Mommy." Claudia marched toward Savannah hairbrush in hand, arms deliberately swishing layers of pale blue organdy. "Can you fix it a little bit special?"

"Those pretty seashell barrettes would be perfect. I have

them in the treasure box." Savannah flew to the small wooden box on the dresser, flipped open the lid, and rummaged through buttons, brooches, and beads. "Here they are. We got these at Cape Cod, remember? You were about three. You probably don't."

"I remember the ocean." Claudia stood between Savannah's knees, old blue jeans bracketing fluffy blue skirt, holding one mother-of-pearl barrette in each hand and lifting her chin as her mother drew the brush through the luxuriant fall of black hair. She gazed at Clay. "Have you ever seen the ocean?"

"Yes, ma'am, I have. I joined the army to see the world. Got to see a couple of oceans in my travels from post to post."

"And that's where you learned to shoe horses, isn't it?"

"That's right."

"I didn't know that," Savannah muttered, wondering why Claudia knew this about him when she didn't. "The army still has horses?"

"A few. Mostly for show. I didn't get to be a veterinarian, but I got to be a veteran, and I did learn a good trade."

"I asked Clay where he learned so much about horseshoes, and he told me the army taught him. I might join the army, too."

"No way, muffin mine," Savannah said. "You're going straight to college, do not pass go, do not waste your precious—"

"But I might join the army *and* go to college," Claudia insisted.

"And she might become an astronaut," Clay said, exchanging conspiratorial smiles with Claudia. "She can do lots of things. You wanna go to church with us, Mom? We've got plenty of time."

"No," Savannah said quietly as she fixed the second barrette. She resented the chipper invitation, phrased as though it would be as easy to go as it would be to stay. "Not this time."

"We've got plenty of time," Clay repeated. "And lots of choices."

Through the bedroom window Savannah watched Clay ceremoniously open the pickup door and assist Claudia into her seat and her seat belt. Her feet barely dangled past the edge of the seat, but she looked so grownup. Of course she remembered the ocean. Claudia remembered everything. She remembered things Savannah didn't want her to remember, but the ocean and the Cape and the times with Heather, those were good times. Savannah had made some poor choices along the way, but she'd made some good ones, too, and Claudia was the best. Anything she'd had or been or done in her life paled in comparison with Claudia.

Impulsively she picked up the phone on Clay's desk and dialed Heather's number. They hadn't spoken since she'd left New York, but there were no apologies exchanged, no explanations. There was no need. They were speaking now.

"I've got some news," Savannah said. "I finally got that checkup that was overdue."

"And?"

"And I'm living proof that boobs don't regenerate."

"So who needs 'em? You may not have the one God gave you, but yours was handmade by a surgeon who could, if not walk on water, at least pass for Adonis."

"You never met him."

"I read his book," Heather reminded her buoyantly. "Which he should have called me to write for him, even though I'm not into medical stuff. For him, I might have made an exception. The most interesting part of the book is the physician-passing-for-author photo." Pause. "What else, Savannah?"

"So far, so good."

"No cancer?"

"Not today, thanks."

"Say it, Savannah. Cancer. *I've got no cancer*. Say it."

"Cancer, cancer, cancer." She laughed, surprised by a sense of unburdening. "Satisfied?"

"I'm delighted. I am ecstatic! Good mammogram, no new boobs popping out, and you sound better than you have in ages. No kidding. You sound wonderful. By the way, Dixon's still 'touching base' with me about every other week. God, I hate that term. Like I'd want to touch anything with anybody who throws that ridiculous term around."

Savannah shook her head. Trevor Dixon, from her agency. From her past. He'd given her hell for refusing work after she'd gotten Claudia, tried to make her feel guilty with words like "professionalism," "commitment," "timing." *You're a country girl, Savannah, so let's put it this way: we've got to make hay while you're in your prime.* Well, her prime had passed.

"What does he want now?"

"He wants to know how you are, and he says he's always on the lookout for jobs for you. You're still his greatest success."

"And his biggest disappointment."

"You never told anybody much about what was going on with you."

"I told *you*."

"And swore me to secrecy, which I've honored. But I'd love to write about you, Savannah. You know I'd handle it lovingly, and it would save lives. You know it would. We can't say it enough nowadays. We're so close to getting a handle on this thing through early detection. Women need to know, they need to realize that *anybody* can get cancer, and that it isn't something we have to—"

"Heather, don't." She thought better of questioning Heather's use of the word "we." "I know you'd do a great job, but I'm the wrong person to be the subject for any of your crusading journalism. I'm a big ninny, is what I am."

"Ninny nothing."

"Ninny nobody," Savannah averred.

"What*ever*. You know I'm not going to sit here and listen to you run yourself down. How's my goddaughter?"

"She's terrific, Heather." Savannah warmed to the new topic. "She likes it here. She has her own horse. She started school, skipped the first grade. She went to church this morning."

"You went to church?"

"Claudia went to church. *This* little piggy stayed home."

Heather laughed. "Have you been to market? Are you eating your roast beef?"

"I'm gettin' there, girl. Doing better. Getting some exercise, plenty of fresh air, a little sex, doing some cooking, some cleaning, a little horse grooming—got myself a groom, as a matter of fact."

"Wait, wait, wait, hold it right there. I thought you said getting a little sex. As in, *getting laid*?"

"I even got married."

"Wait, wait, wait." Silence. "I thought you said 'married.' "

"I did. I married my best friend."

"I thought *I* was your best friend."

"All this strenuous thinking is bound to give you a headache, my friend, so take it easy. I guess I have two best friends. But Clay Keogh came first. So I have a new address and phone number. Got something to write with?"

"You married Kole Kills Crow's *brother*?"

"He's not just Kole's brother, he's—"

"Claudia's uncle."

"You're the only person in the world who knows any of this, Heather, and you promised me you'd forget it. Obviously you haven't kept your promise."

"I promised not to tell anyone, and I have kept that promise. You got married without me, Savannah? How could you do that?"

"We just decided to do it, and we did it. Spur-of-the-moment civil ceremony."

"With strangers for witnesses?"

"Well, yes. Otherwise . . ."

"Otherwise you might have had time to think about it. For God's sake, Savannah, *married*? You can't just *do* that. It has to be—"

"Claudia adores him."

"She adores me, too."

"I know. But if anything happened . . ."

"That's no reason to get married."

"It isn't? What is, then? Seriously, Heather, marriage is a reasonable choice, a legal partnership, a good . . . *arrangement*. Sometimes it makes perfect sense."

"Are you in love with this partner you sensibly chose on the spur of the moment?"

"I told you, he's my best friend, I've always loved him, and you know I don't share your fairy-tale illusions about marriage."

"But you always said you couldn't see yourself as some guy's wife."

"I didn't see myself as some child's mother, either, but I'm Claudia's mother. And I'm . . ." His desk chair squealed at her as she angled away from the adjoining door. His bed pillow lay at the end of the sofa, mocking her. "I *am* married."

"He's a good man?"

"He's the very best, Heather. He's so much better than I am."

"When do I get to meet him? Better yet, when can I meet his brother? *That's* the book I want to write."

"I don't know if any of us will ever see Kole again, but

you're welcome here anytime. *Almost* anytime." She sighed. "I still need a little time, Heather. I'm not ready for prime-time company yet, but I'm doing better. I'm not half as ugly as I was a few months ago."

"Mommy!" Claudia's patent-leather Mary Janes clap-clap-clapped up the stairs. She burst into the bedroom. "We're back from church. I saw Aunt Billie. She said she's coming to see us sometime this week if we don't go see her. And I saw a little baby scream its lungs out because it didn't wanna get baptized. And I saw a woman—*two* women who said they used to know you. One of them said I looked like *cold*, but I wasn't cold. I had my sweater, but I didn't want it on. She said it to Clay kinda funny, like he wasn't making me keep my sweater on or something, but it's not even cold." She jumped up on the bed, bouncing onto the floor one of the cookbooks Savannah had been perusing. " 'Why, she looks just like *cooold.*' " Claudia imitated the woman at church.

Clay appeared in the doorway, hat in hand. His eyes met Savannah's immediately with a meaningful look.

Slowly the meaning sank in. "She looked like she was . . . Kole?"

He shrugged. "It's bound to come up."

"But I *wasn't*," Claudia assured her. "Not at all. And they had an organ donation in church, too."

"Really?" Savannah gave her daughter a bright smile. "In the middle of the service?"

"Pretty much in the middle. After the baby screamed, but before Clay sang by himself. Boy, you should have heard him."

"The baby?"

"No, Clay. He was even louder than the baby. The baby's voice was like way, way up, and Clay's was like—" Claudia tucked her chin in as she shifted from her natural high to her best imitation of his mellow low. " 'And He walks with me, and He talks with me.' It was like he was all around you," she said, arms outstretched, "and he didn't even have a microphone."

"Was he good?"

"Oh, yes, very good. He sang just with a guitar because the church needs a new organ because they can't fix the other one anymore because it's too old." Pausing for a breath, Claudia glanced at Clay. "And, um, we brought some kids home with us. They're downstairs getting into the refrigerator."

Savannah questioned Clay with a look.

"Roxie's kids," he explained. "Reno's going to help me with a job, and Cheyenne needed to get away from her mom for a while, and Dallas and Claudia already met at school, so I figured they could play a little bit, like kids are supposed to. After all, it's . . ." He shrugged, risking a sheepish smile. "Sunday."

"Oh. Sunday."

He nodded once.

She nodded, too.

"So you and Reno have work to do, which leaves me with Dallas and—what's the other city?"

"Cheyenne."

"I guess I'm out of touch with Sunday rituals. Do you often bring people home from church without any warning?"

"It's not like a tornado or anything. They're pretty much family."

"They weren't at church." Claudia filled in the details. "On our way back we saw them all sitting outside their house with nothing to do, so we stopped."

"Sometimes Roxie—" Clay folded his arms, making his stand in the doorway. "I like to take 'em off her hands once in a while."

"Your mother warned me that your ex-wife still—"

"I said that wrong," he put in quickly. "I like to see them

when I can. They're still, like I said, family. But it's not as if we have to baby-sit."

"Yeah, they're not babies."

"And you don't even have to meet them if you don't want to."

"Yeah, I'll tell them they can't come up here."

She looked at one, then the other, finally burst out laughing. "How long have you two been rehearsing this act?"

"We haven't rehearsed at all. Have we, partner?" Clay glanced at Claudia for ratification. She shook her head, dead serious. "Strictly off the cuff, I swear."

"Yeah," Claudia chimed in as she examined her sweater sleeve. "And Mommy can be a partner, too, right?"

"We'll change your clothes," Savannah said, extending a hand to her daughter. "And I'll try to remember how to be sociable. They're children. I'm fine with children." She eyed Clay. "Believe it or not, she's had children to play with. I haven't been keeping her—" She forestalled his protest with a gesture. "I even have dinner covered. Plenty for everyone."

"Hey, that's really—"

"Except you," she told him, teasing him now with a testy eye. "You might have to sing for yours."

The children came in three sizes, three shapes, and three shades of sullen. Dallas, the younger boy, sat in the corner and picked at a scab on his elbow until it bled, at which point he followed Claudia in search of a Band-Aid. She was telling him they could go out to see the kittens or play on the swing in the backyard, but he seemed intent on seeing how much blood he could squeeze from his elbow. "Quit messing with that," his sister barked after him as he disappeared down the hall.

Clearly Cheyenne wasn't sure why she'd come along. She took care to distance herself from the interloper, her stepfather's new wife, while her brothers went their separate ways.

Reno had a job to do, and Dallas didn't mind playing caboose to any engine ready to pull him along. Cheyenne, woman-child with the limbs of a spider and the eyes of a lemur, was the middle-maid. She bossed Dallas, was undoubtedly bossed by Reno, had little patience with either, but, like a wad of gum, was stuck between them.

From the looks of things, she was going to be left with Savannah, but it was clear from the way her huge eyes followed Clay's every move that she'd prefer to be with him. When he said he had to load some things into the pickup, Cheyenne hopped up and scooted out the door behind him. She was back moments later, looking rejected. "Clay says I don't have to watch kids today," she announced. "If they wanna go out to the barn, they'll be Uncle Mick's problem, not mine. I'm gonna probably watch TV or something, but at least I don't have to watch kids."

"What would you like to do?" Savannah asked, keeping her own reluctance to watch teenagers to herself.

"Nothing. I didn't wanna go with them anyways. I'd just be sittin' in the pickup all day."

"Would you like some lemonade?"

Cheyenne shook her head. "I need to use the john. Which one should I use?"

"Take your pick." Savannah stowed the lemonade she'd just made and nobody wanted in the refrigerator. "I'm sure you know your way around here better than I do."

"The yellow bedroom used to be mine." Cheyenne edged toward the door to the hallway. "I guess you've changed it all. Fixed it over for a little girl."

"It's still very yellow."

They looked at each other. Savannah gave a sympathetic smile, but Cheyenne couldn't bring herself to answer in kind. "Can I look? Don't worry. I won't bother any of your stuff."

"We don't have much stuff, and I'm not worried about it.

I'll take Claudia and Dallas out to the barn, and if Uncle Mick's out there, I'll be right back."

"You don't have to baby-sit me."

"I don't plan to. If you get tired of TV, I'll be in the kitchen."

Clay was going to leave her with this sulky child. There were times when Savannah wanted to wring his neck.

He'd seen the children sitting on the porch looking needy, and he couldn't drive past. There were times when she wanted to hug his neck.

She'd decide which time this was when she got hold of him. She headed for the pickup, which was parked near the big Quonset they called the machine shed. The pickup tailgate and topper stood open, as did the side door to the machine shed. She knew he was just inside, for she could hear him singing to himself, soft but not shy. He had a deep, rich, beautiful voice. She'd been around his singing; why hadn't she really heard it before?

She stepped out of the sunlight, into the dark shed, which smelled of metal and motor oil. But the sound was like heaven's vestibule, until he looked up from sharpening a pair of long-handled nippers.

"Don't stop," she said.

He looked at the tools in his hands. "Don't stop what?"

"Have you been hiding it, or is it just that I've never listened?" He was still puzzled. "Your singing," she said. "How have I missed that?"

"Maybe because I didn't go breakin' your heart, huh? I like to sing in the bathroom sometimes, but since you moved in, I have to be careful, because you're usually in bed when I . . ." He shrugged. "We haven't been together that long."

"We were together a lot, and we used to do all kinds of silly things." She smiled, remembering. "We'd go up to Artemis's

Castle and sing, get that acoustical thing going with the rock walls. I always thought we were kidding around."

"We were."

"But you really *were* good, and I never . . . Did I ever tell you before?"

"We were having fun. I wasn't any more serious than you were."

"I never did, did I? This is the first time I've really heard you sing."

"You still haven't heard me. I was only . . . that was more like talking to myself." He dropped the nippers into the toolbox on the floor. "Anyway, a lot of people can carry a tune."

"But I like the way you do it."

He looked pleased. It was too dark to tell, but she would bet he was blushing. "I think it's all part of the plan myself," he said. "One person gets a voice for singing, the next one gets a face for singing. Seems like we all get to sing pretty one way or another."

"A face for singing." She laughed. "What good does looking at a face do anybody?"

"All I know is, looking at you is good for me." He lifted his hand to touch her cheek, but drew it back when his gaze shifted from her eyes to his hand. He wiped it on his faded shirt and smiled sheepishly. "All I know is, the sight of your face takes me apart and puts me right back together, all in the space of one breath."

She could only stare. She had no words, no thought except the image he'd conjured, no will to draw breath and spoil the magic.

"A song can do that, too," he said quietly, stepping close. "Or a story. Or the touch of someone's hand." He shook his head, laughing at himself. "I can't believe I said anything that lame."

"I can't, either," she whispered. It seemed he'd captured her voice as well. She cleared her throat, squared her shoulders. "But it's sweet, so you can't have it back. I'm going to hold onto it. Write it down and keep it for my old age, when the sight of my face will surely be another matter."

"What other matter? It'll always be your face." He lifted his hand again, and this time when he hesitated she caught it and guided it to her cheek. His fingers were warm and gentle. She turned her lips to his palm and tasted his sweat, his salt, his skill. He whispered her name as he cupped her face in his hands and drew her into his deep, wet kiss.

"Mmmm-mmm." Grinning, Reno had caught them in the act. "Are you sure you wanna go to work today?"

"No." The smile in Clay's eyes was for her eyes only. "I don't know what I was thinking," he confessed.

"So let's cancel," the boy suggested.

"Can't do that." Clay sighed, drawing away. "But with your help, it'll get done today, and I'll be caught up."

"My sister wants us to take her back home. She says there's nothing for her to do here. I guess she'd rather go back and fight with Mom."

With a look, Clay dared to ask Savannah for help, and she remembered why she'd gone looking for him. It was that neck-squeezing thing.

"You guys go ahead," she said, picturing her arms around his neck, wishing him a parting kiss as she smiled for him. "I think I can come up with some way to entertain Cheyenne."

"You sure?"

"I suggest you take the offer and run. Don't invite second thoughts."

Clay picked up his tool box. "She doesn't really want to go home. She doesn't know how to act around you, Savannah. She's at that age where it's all an act, so what you need to do is give her a cue. One small piece of advice, though." He smiled and whispered, "Don't sing."

*   *   *

If karaoke wasn't an option, what did you do with a twelve-year-old girl? Savannah plucked a package of chocolate chips from the kitchen cupboard and plopped them on the counter. "I thought we might bake some cookies."

Cheyenne gave her a look of consummate indifference. Savannah knew exactly how much practice it took to achieve that look. It had been about twenty years since she'd mastered it herself.

"And do what with them? Feed them to the rug rats?"

"You're right," Savannah said, shoving the chips aside to make room for her elbows. "I need to expand my repertoire."

Cheyenne took a seat on the counter stool opposite Savannah. "I heard you were a model."

"That was actually a few years ago."

"Yeah, well, I've actually seen some of your pictures. When was the last time you ate a cookie?"

"A few days ago. Claudia and I made some. But you're right again." She looked into the face of surprise—a teenager twice credited with having a clue—and smiled. "I got out of the habit of enjoying food because I thought I had to stay a certain weight. And then I got sick, and I lost more weight, even though I didn't have much to spare." She patted the package of baking chips affectionately. "I love chocolate."

"It makes your face break out."

"My mother used to say that, so I always felt guilty about it, which makes it even harder to resist." Savannah could see she'd hit a Bingo. Cheyenne obviously had one of those mothers, too. "Okay, no cookies. I've got this ragout going for dinner, and I thought maybe cookies with ice cream for dessert, but that really shows no imagination on my part. I'm not a bad cook, even if I've forgotten how to eat."

"What's ragout?" Cheyenne asked dutifully, her tone betraying her lack of interest.

"It's just a stew. I used fresh vegetables from Patty's garden."

"I heard she had a heart attack or something. Funny she didn't have it when we were living here. We just about drove her crazy. Of course, we were only little kids then, and there were three of us. She probably doesn't mind having only one."

"I used to come over when I was your age. I just about drove her crazy, too. And now I'm back."

"What did you do?" Now Cheyenne was interested. "How did you drive her crazy?"

"By being a kid. With some people, that's all it takes."

"How come Clay isn't like that? You'd think she would've rubbed off on him. He likes kids, though. He hardly ever gets mad. When he does . . ."

"When he does, what?"

"Well, you can't push him." The girl shrugged. "He walks away. He has his limit, and when he reaches it, that's it. He calls it quits." Idly she pulled the bag of chips to her side of the counter, flipped them over, patted them flat. "That's what happened with us."

"Us?"

"We were brats. Reno set fire to a haystack once. I fell off a horse he told me not to ride and broke my collarbone. Dallas was always whining. Finally they got a divorce."

"I don't think it was because of you kids."

"Maybe it wasn't *just* us, but if we'd behaved better, they might have stayed together." Her small hand closed around the bag as she looked up, huge eyes connecting with Savannah's. "I don't know why I'm telling you this. Now he's married to you."

Savannah gave a tight smile. In the face of this displacement, she had to remind herself that she wasn't a homewrecker. "We've known each other a long time."

"Yeah, I know. My mother accused him of you once when they were arguing about something else."

"Accused him of me?"

"Wondered if he'd gone off and looked you up, said he'd

never get over you, stuff like that. He never said she was lying, so I guessed she wasn't. I can see why he wouldn't." Cheyenne glanced at her, then went back to petting the bag of chocolate. "Get over you, I mean."

"I haven't seen Clay in years, so I can tell you—and this is all I'll say—that it wasn't a fair accusation."

Cheyenne's thumb was the only thing that moved, caressing those chips. "That was my room, the one he gave your daughter."

"I know. I don't know anything about their marriage, Cheyenne, but I know he misses you kids. Obviously he— well, he brought you here today."

"Because he felt sorry for us."

"Maybe because he felt sorry for me."

Cheyenne looked up, puzzled. Interested. Maybe even caring, ready to listen.

"I don't get out much," Savannah explained, much to her own surprise. "I haven't been able to see many people since I moved back home. I can't seem to . . . it's like I'm afraid to face the people who knew me and know that I'm not . . ."

Not what? Not who?

"Did you get too old?"

Savannah laughed. It was an innocent question, coming from someone to whom thirty seemed old. She shook her head.

"Okay, then, why did you give it up?"

"I thought I could go back. Then I got sick, and there was no going back." Savannah lifted one shoulder, then smiled.

Cheyenne waited, hesitating out of respect or fear or sympathy. But she was listening. Waiting for more.

"I had breast cancer. The surgery . . ." Savannah's hand fluttered over her chest, accidentally catching her little finger in the placket of her blouse, which she quickly readjusted. "It was quite extensive."

"Do you have a fake breast?"

"Sort of."

"Gee." Cheyenne tried to read Savannah's chest from left to right, then back again. "They look the same. Are they both fake?"

"No." She couldn't feel the touch of her own fingers on the right side. "It's just this one."

Cheyenne's face was full of new, womanly tenderness, eager to reassure. "You'd never know."

"No one does. I don't ever talk about it. I don't want—"

"I won't tell anybody."

Savannah nodded. Her smile came more easily now. "I really need to get over this. It happens to a lot of women. It isn't such a big deal. You asked me, and I told you. Simple, straightforward. It's not like I'm *all* fake."

"Not nearly as fake as I thought you'd be. I mean, you're not at all, really."

Savannah laughed. "Except for that one part."

"Whatever. Not the part that counts. I've seen your pictures, and I couldn't believe somebody like you came from Sunbonnet. I thought you'd be totally fake. You know, totally stuck-up, like you wouldn't even talk to people." Cheyenne had suddenly become a chatterbox, embracing the role of confidante with new passion and profuse gestures. "I mean, because you think you're too good, not because—"

"Because I'm not as good as I used to think I was."

"Sure you are. You're still really beautiful, just like in your pictures. Even more beautiful because you're good but not *too* good." For the first time since she'd walked into the house, Cheyenne smiled. Her dark eyes lit up with privilege and promise. "I won't tell anybody. And if anybody asks—you know, like I did—you can tell them it's none of their damn business. That's what I'd say. Because you're still really beautiful."

"Thank you." Savannah imagined touching the girl, taking her hand or touching her face. She wanted to. Speaking of repertoire, she wished that kind of gesture were part of hers. She had only the smile, but at least it came naturally. It felt real. "Thank you for listening."

"Hey, no problem." Cheyenne bounced the bag of chips as though weighing them in her hand. "Tell you the truth, I don't know too much about baking cookies. I like Oreos. You don't have to bake those."

"Somebody has to bake them. I like them with the milk on the side."

"Definitely. Not all soggy. And no crumbs floating around in the milk, like my stupid brothers do. They do make your face break out, though."

"Your brothers?"

"No lie. Those two creeps for sure, plus just about everything I eat that tastes any good. Or else it's . . ."

"Before you get your period?"

The girl flushed, shrugged, finally nodded.

"That happens to all of us. Tell you what, you help me make cookies, and then we'll share some more secrets. I know every makeup trick in the book."

"Makeup?" Cheyenne slid off the stool, bright-eyed and willing. "Cool."

Before long they had makeup on one end of the kitchen table and cookies cooling on the other. Dallas and Claudia had come back from the barn, and Patty had gotten up from her nap, made a comment about the mess they were making, then dropped off a curling iron with a passing, "Might as well do the hair while you're at it." She'd gone outside, and Savannah and Cheyenne had exchanged looks and laughs. But Cheyenne had plugged in the curling iron, and they'd talked about school while Savannah worked over the girl's straw-colored hair, enthusing over its thickness and suggesting they pay a visit to Leanne Ames's Tip Top Shop together sometime.

The conversation meandered to the topic of first names.

"Stupid, right?" Cheyenne said. "My mother named us after the cities we were born in."

"It's not either stupid. I was born in Dallas and my dad was from Dallas," the little boy said.

"Savannah's the name of a city, too."

"Was your dad from there?" Dallas wanted to know.

"I doubt it. And I'm sure my mother had never been to Georgia. She said she was going to name me Tara but decided that was too common."

"I don't know any Taras. Or Savannahs, except you."

"And you're the only Cheyenne I know, so I guess our mothers succeeded. Uncommon names must make us uncommon women. You think?"

"There are Cheyenne Indians," Dallas said. "Like Claudia."

"I'm not a Cheyenne Indian, am I, Mommy? Is there a city named Claudia?"

"I don't know of one, but I'll bet there is somewhere."

"You guys all have cities."

Dallas was determined to be helpful to Claudia. "You're probably named after your grandma or something, huh? She might be a Cheyenne Indian."

"I told you, I'm not a Cheyenne Indian. I'm Sioux, which is also called Lakota. Right, Mommy?"

"That's right, muffin. Your father is Lakota." Savannah smiled at Claudia, then glanced at the other two. They shared an understanding of the elusive nature of fathers.

"Then why did you name me Claudia Ann?"

"Your name is the most beautiful name I know, and it fits you perfectly."

"I know, but . . ." Claudia studied her mother. To pursue or not to pursue, dig for facts or accept the fiction? As she glanced away, it was the child's voice that won out. "I want a city."

"Someday you'll build one yourself."

The children were enjoying themselves now, and Savannah was in charge. Her spirits took another upward step when she heard the back door open. Clay would be so pleased.

But it wasn't Clay. It was a shapely redhead with a hard face.

So this was the first wife.

"So you're the famous model."

"Not so famous," Savannah averred with an outstretched hand. "You must be Roxie. I'm Savannah." And she was still in charge. "Help yourself to the cookies the kids made. We were just experimenting with—"

"God, you need more color than that," Roxie told her daughter. She'd already assessed the experiment. "If Pillsbury needed a dough*girl*, this one would have the job sewed up. I hope you haven't fed her a bunch of chocolate. Ever since she started getting her period, I can barely keep up with the Clearasil. That stuff ain't cheap."

"We call her pizza face," Dallas said.

"How 'bout I call you—"

"Shut up with that now. It's annoying as hell." Roxie examined the makeup brushes and little pots of color as she chomped on a cookie. "These are pretty good. Where's Clay?"

"Him and Reno went out on a job. He said he was gonna take us back after dinner," Cheyenne reported. "Why . . . why are you here?"

"Well, I got done with what I had to do, so I thought I might as well pick you guys up and save him the trouble." Roxie turned to Savannah. "Hope they haven't been in the way of anything."

"Not at all."

"He's real good about helping me out with them. I was real busy this weekend. You know how crazy things get sometimes, and when you're the only parent . . ." She lopped the tip off a lipstick as she clumsily capped the tube. "Did I hear right? About you two getting married?"

"We're married, yes."

"That's what I thought I heard. Pretty damn sudden."

"We've known each other for a long time." Savannah spoke softly, standing her ground with a pointed look. *I knew him first.*

"Yeah, but you haven't been back very long, have you? I mean, everybody's talking, but hardly anybody's seen you."

"Famous people can't just go walking around in public," Cheyenne informed her mother. "They have to protect their privacy."

"I'm really not all that famous."

"I don't think you've got much to worry about." Roxie dropped the lipstick on the table and sent it rolling. "I've seen your picture, but I wouldn't have recognized you."

"I recognized her right away." Cheyenne caught the lipstick and carefully set it on end next to two other tubes.

"So did I." Patty appeared in the doorway with a colander full of ripe tomatoes. She glanced from one woman to the other before heading for the sink. "Leave it to Clayton to take off and leave me with a house full of stepkids and daughters-in-law."

"Oh, keep your shirt on, Patty. He'll be back." Roxie turned back to Savannah. "He's gone a lot, and you're stuck here, but one thing you can always count on is him coming back. If that's what you're looking for, he's real good about that." She winked. "Among other things."

"Bringing home strays is what he's good about." Patty peeked around the refrigerator door. "Damn, Roxie, is your head bleeding?"

"Bleeding?" She plunged deadly looking nails into blood-red locks, provoking a peal of laughter from Patty. Roxie scowled. "Hell, I ain't got time to exchange insults with you today, Patty. Maybe Clay's new bride can teach you something about style."

"I'm what they call classic," Patty said, flashing Savannah an arched eyebrow.

Roxie couldn't resist. "Why, because you've got a face that looks like it fell offa Mount Rushmore?" She laughed, grabbing a treat in each hand. "Lighten up, Patty. Have a cookie."

Chapter 13

"What the hell is she *doing here?"*

The sight of Roxie's car parked in her favorite spot—blocking thc view of the garden from Patty's bedroom window—caused Clay to forget for a moment that Roxie's son was sitting next to him. With a quick sideways glance he adjusted his cap by the bill. "Not that she ain't welcome, but . . ."

Reno grinned. "But you don't particularly want her raisin' hell with your new wife."

"I planned on making the introductions myself." Clay's grin started in his eyes as he arced the steering wheel. "If I could set it up with one of them on the ground, the other on a moving train. Savannah, Roxie; Roxie, Savannah."

"Sorry you two don't have time to chat." Reno aped Clay with a laugh.

"That's the idea." Clay shut the pickup door, tossed his cap through the window onto the seat, and hitched up his jeans. "Well, I'm going in. Cover mc, Reno."

But to his surprise, there was no flak flying in the kitchen, no holes in the wall, no smell of blood. At his back, Reno remarked about the fine aroma of "ugly-woman cooking."

Clay imagined Roxie waist-deep in a stock pot. He turned his head, arched a questioning eyebrow at Reno.

"I gotta figure you hired somebody," the boy whispered as the back door snapped shut behind him. "Women can't look good and cook good *both*. Mom says you only get one or the other."

So Clay entered the kitchen laughing. There he found, if not easy laughter, at least courtesy and passable humor. Roxie kept insisting that she couldn't stay for supper, but she agreed to try Savannah's stew while the kids were fed at the kitchen table. Pretty soon the adults were all standing around the kitchen with bowls in their hands, unable to commit to sitting down together, but sampling, eyeing each other, perching like birds around the counter, trying out a comment, eyeing each other some more. Clay felt pretty strange, but everybody seemed to be getting along and Savannah was doing fine, even though she was pretty quiet. She was so gracious he couldn't tell whether she was mad at him. When she disappeared suddenly, he figured she might be. Either that or she'd smiled all she could smile. Or she was tired of his ex-wife and her brood. Or just plain tired.

Or mad at him.

The hubbub had finally gotten to her. After a retreat to the bathroom, Savannah couldn't face the crowd in the kitchen again. She'd slipped out the front door and escaped to the barn. Claudia would make the excuses for her. She knew what to say; she'd said it countless times. *My mother's very tired.*

But Savannah just needed to get quiet inside. Uncle Mick's two blue heelers didn't help much. They were too excited to see her. She sought refuge in the paddock, where several old horses had gathered in the twilight to wait for their evening grain. Their quiet patience worked on her like a tranquilizer. "If I knew what to feed you, I would," she told

the mare snuffling around the feed trough. "But I could give
you a nice rubdown. How would that be?"

The sound of crickets cheered from the bushes beyond the
corral. The mare took a chuck under the chin as a hint and
followed Savannah into the barn, clomp, clomp, *What do
you have for me?* She dusted her off with a soft brush, then
tried a soft rubber tool, then hands only, assuming that
kneading fingers had to feel as good to equine muscles as to
human muscles. If nothing else, the contact was soothing to
Savannah.

Clay came into the barn without a word, rubbed the
horse's face in passing, and took up a post on the opposite
flank, where Savannah could see him across the horse's
back. A single bare bulb cast dim light and long shadows
over the alley between the rows of empty stalls. His first
glance was warm, the next a little wary. She liked that. She
played the game as long as she could, keeping a straight face
while she vigorously plied the currycomb—she wasn't
going to let him see her massaging a horse. But she would
keep him guessing whether she was angry or not. She
wanted to be, but she had truly enjoyed herself too much
today. Finally she let a smile crack the deadpan mask.

"What?" He managed to look wounded. "You think it's
funny watching me squirm through Sunday dinner?"

"It wasn't exactly a sit-down Sunday dinner like I'd
planned."

"Close enough. Close as I've come since I don't know
when."

"I believe you said Christmas." She reached into the tack
box and handed him a soft bristle brush. "I should have
taken charge, set the table, made everyone sit down."

"The way families are supposed to do?" He lifted one
shoulder before he started brushing. "One step at a time. It
might feel a little awkward, looking across the table at my
ex-wife while I'm sitting beside my new bride."

"You think so? 'Awkward' pretty much describes how I felt when she first walked in the door. Then you came along."

"And made it awkward times two," he said. "I still can't believe she came to the Lazy K. She hasn't been here since she moved out. I brought the kids over because they weren't doing anything, hadn't done anything all weekend, what with their mother busy doin' her usual weekend thing. I sure didn't expect her to show up here."

"Goes to church on Sunday, sings like an angel, suffers the little children . . . my heavens, have I married a saint?"

"Not hardly," he muttered sheepishly, then grimaced. "Damn, not *that* bad."

She laughed. "You're a bloody wicked saint, you are."

"Look, I'm sorry. I won't make a habit of springin' them—"

She took the brush from his hand and traded it for the currycomb. He wasn't doing much brushing, anyway. He was mostly watching her. "I think I did pretty well, don't you?"

"You did great."

"Meeting the kids first made it easier. Roxie's quite an interesting woman. How old is she?"

"She's lived long enough to become an interesting woman. She can be touchy about the details."

She had to be close to forty, which was a touchy detail for some women. Savannah couldn't imagine worrying about a thing like that anymore. If she lived to see forty, she would shout it from the hilltops. But Clay kept Roxie's intimate details to himself, which was just like Clay.

Oddly, Savannah had half a mind to see if she could wheedle them out of him, purge him of any vestige of Roxie. Especially anything intimate or wink-worthy. *Among other things?* The things Clay was good about were no longer Roxie's concern. Her things were no longer among his things, and his things wouldn't be mingling among—

The other half of Savannah's mind kicked in just in time.

She met his innocent gaze with her own. "Does this horse have a name? I was thinking I'd like to have a horse to ride, and this one seems to like me. She came right up to me."

"Yeah, I call her Sugarfoot because she's such a sweetie. And because she has such bad navicular disease in her front feet that she won't make you a saddle horse."

"That's a shame. She's so beautiful."

"That she is, but she's gimpy. You didn't notice?" He bent to pick up one hoof, rubbed some dirt off the frog, then let the foot down again. Savannah had no idea what he'd shown her, but she noticed that the horse wore shoes, and she wondered how much of his time he donated to shoeing horses nobody rode.

"She was a lot worse when I brought her home," he assured Savannah as he brushed his hands together. "She's got a gorgeous head, only six years old, came with a nice pedigree, and she won't even give me a colt. I've tried to breed her, but she won't settle. She's what you call a hay-burner."

"Navicular disease is incurable, isn't it? She had it when you bought her?" Clay nodded. "And you knew that."

He shrugged. "One little defect in the foot makes this beautiful creature useless. And around here, nobody can afford to keep a useless horse, even if it's a problem they caused themselves. This pretty lady's owner was way too anxious to turn her into a barrel-racer. You start a horse too young, especially if you're asking her to turn or stop hard, you're likely to do this to her." Tenderly he ran his hand down the horse's front leg. "Like I said, I thought she'd make a good broodmare."

"I probably should have mentioned this before." She turned to the tack box, carefully replacing the brush. "I won't make a good broodmare, either."

He stood waiting for her to turn to him again, waiting to question her with a look, rather than with words.

"As long as I take tamoxifen, which Dr. Mears put me on again, I won't cycle. So I won't be 'settling' or turning out a brood of little Keoghs. One small defect." She gave him a flicker of a smile as she patted the mare's plump rump.

"Guess it's a good thing you're not a horse."

Her smile broadened. "Good thing you can only keep one useless wife at a time."

"Useless? Hell, Roxie makes great chili."

"So I've heard."

"But I've always been a chocolate-chip-cookie kind of guy."

"Then how did you get hooked up with a chili pepper?"

"We're talkin' about two very different kinds of victuals," he said as he stepped around to her side of the horse. "They don't compare. Guess there's room for both, but not at the same time, and that's about as far as I can take this without getting into some serious trouble."

"You'll get no trouble from me. You were good enough to take us in. We're not about to question your judgment." She unhooked a cross-tie. "Are we, Sugarfoot?"

"I didn't *take you in*," he said quietly. "I don't look at it that way at all. We're . . ." He reached under the horse's neck, unhooked the far tie, and let the chain drop. It clattered against the wall. "I was thinking you might like to go somewhere next weekend and do a little shopping. Some new clothes, maybe."

"School clothes?"

"You goin' back to school?" he teased, and she regarded him with incredulity, pointing at herself. "Yeah, something for *you*, Mrs. Keogh. Not that you don't look good in what you've got, but it seems like nothing lifts a woman's spirits like a new outfit."

"Nothing wrong with my spirits. Nothing wrong with my clothes, either." She spread her jeans at the thighs. "Baggy is *in*."

"I know that, but . . ." He chuckled. "I *don't* know that. I don't know anything about what's in style. I thought maybe you'd lost a lot of weight since the last time you got clothes." He grabbed the same wad of denim she'd unfurled and jiggled it. "Like a hundred pounds."

"Damn, not that bad," she said, echoing his protest with the added touch of a playful swat to his chest. "I'm comfortable. Dressing for comfort is the definition of freedom in my book. Do you think a person feels comfortable sucking it in and tucking it under while she's parading around in her underwear?"

"Tucking what under?"

"One's ass."

"If you can find one back there, I was thinking you might enjoy tucking it under a new dress." He attempted a little rubbernecking. "Not so?"

"Not necessary, but very thoughtful. Thanks."

"So how 'bout a moonlight ride? I can saddle us up a couple of horses, *usin'* horses—sorry, Sugar, that lets you out." He proved it by turning the mare out, returning with an empty halter. "We could take a ride up to the castle in the hills."

It was because she wanted to go with him that she moved away, gathered up the grooming tools, and made no reply as she put them back in the tack box. She wanted to, but not the way she had lately. Not to escape or to seek some sensual relief. She imagined going willingly with Clay, being with him, touching him and being touched by him, doing what came naturally as they used to do, back in the days when her definition of freedom had had nothing to do with how she dressed. She remembered and imagined and, oh, there were so many hazards, even in fantasy. He would take control. He would touch her as he pleased, the way he used to please her, and soon there would be no more illusions.

And then where would she be? Who would she be?

Control over her body, such as it was, was vital to her now. It was her only chance for survival, really. For the sake of their cherished illusions, she had to stick to her terms, make the man mind.

"It's late, and it's been such a long day. I think I'll just say . . ."

He drew a deep breath, closed his eyes, and nodded, but not before she had glimpsed the precipitant sadness. It was gone when he opened them, replaced by something infinitely more touching, mesmerizing. He lifted her chin on the side of his finger. "Good night," he whispered, stealing the word, and more, from her mouth. "I'll see you in the morning."

How would he survive her indifference?

He poured himself a shot of Jim Beam. His back was bothering him again, so he'd popped a pill. Just one, since the pain was only three on a scale of ten. Ordinarily he'd tough it out at this level, but he was feeling sorry for himself. Turning into a double shot, Jim felt sorry for him, too. Who wouldn't pity a guy on his way to a makeshift bed in the room right next door to the room where his wife slept? Heaven was just a few feet away, but there he stood in purgatory, feeling the pinch of his promise.

He didn't want to turn the TV on and interfere with the ice queen's sleep, so he reached for a stack of magazines. It hurt him to reach. Feeling sorrier and stiffer, he sat down with his drink and his magazines—most of them about horses, but there were a few strays. He had other interests. Women's underwear, for example. He tossed the periodicals into the corner, hit the wall with the damn things.

Whoops, didn't mean to wake anyone up.

He sat sipping his whiskey, listening to see if he had disturbed her, hoping he hadn't, wishing he had. Damn, he was a sorry, mixed-up sonuvabitch. He stared at the floor, then at the wall, then at the corner between the two. He glared at the ice-blue eyes staring back at him from the cover of *Lady*

Elizabeth's Dreamwear Catalog, wondering who in hell Lady Elizabeth was and why in hell the pouty-lipped woman was giving him that come-check-out-my-bra look when there was no way in hell she'd let him put his grubby hands anywhere near that clasp. Some dream.

Still, he noted that it was a front-hook model. He pictured himself stepping into the picture. He carefully wiped his grubby hand on his grubby jeans before he laid the backs of his fingers in the valley between her breasts and deftly flicked open the clasp. She gave him the slowest, sweetest blue-eyed smile.

And the meanest hard-on imaginable.

He drained his glass. What he needed was sleep. He heaved himself out of the chair. What he needed was another drink or another massage or another kiss. He imagined the soft touch of those pouty lips on the small of his back, and he decided that would do it. Just that one small gesture. Her kiss would cure him.

Come down to earth and take your damn boots off, Keogh.

It hurt him to bend over. He reached for support from something solid. The closest thing was the TV on its swivel stand. Where the hell was his bootjack? Where the hell was his *boot*?

And why in hell were the walls shifting around him?

He heard the crash before he felt it. At first it was like watching some crazy film made by a falling camera. Delayed sound. Deferred pain. Suspended stupidity.

"Clay?"

Light from the bathroom flooded the den, exposing him for the numskull he was. Numb everywhere else, too.

Savannah fluttered over him like a bird, landing at his side. "What happened, Clay?"

A groan was the only answer he had for her. As soon as he could get his legs under his body, he'd haul himself up.

Or maybe not. Her hands felt cool and sweet on his face,

and she sounded so concerned, crooning to him, "Oh, my God, are you hurt? Clay?"

He couldn't tell. He decided to let her figure it out. Her fingers were tangled in his hair, feeling for blood, for tenderness, for signs of intelligence.

"Are you okay? Did you . . ."

He levered himself up on his elbow, but that hurt, so he flopped back down again. "Tried to get my . . . damn, clumsy . . ."

"Oh, sweetie, don't move. Can you move? Well, obviously you moved, but— Did you hurt your back?"

"Yeah, but it's nuthin' . . . except when I try to move."

She hovered over him, her nose twitching like a rabbit's. "Are you drunk?"

"Shouldn't be. Hardly had . . . just tryin' to get my damn boots off."

"What's going on up there?" The indignant demand came from downstairs. "Is somebody throwing things up there?"

Clay's merciful bird took off and flew away, but he could hear her chattering outside the door. "I'm sorry, Patty. I was trying to find my way in the dark. I should have turned the light on."

"I ain't puttin' up with any more tantrums."

"I don't do tantrums."

"Yeah, well, the first one did. Nobody's hurt, then?"

"I don't—"

"We're fine, Mom," he called out, working his thick tongue as carefully as he could. "Go on back to bed."

"If he's takin' them painkillers, he shouldn't be drinkin'," Patty grumbled. "Just so you know."

Biddie went away. Birdie was back, perched on his arm.

"Are you taking pain pills?"

"I only took one. Just one." He wasn't sure how much sense his tongue was making, so he produced a finger. He hoped it was the right one. Humiliating as his situation was, he didn't want to do anything to drive her away. She was stroking his arm, making his skin tingle, and he was enjoying it all over.

"How much have you had to drink? How—" She gasped. "Oh, Clay, you're bleeding."

"Damn TV musta fell on me," he grumbled. She was sliding away from him, slipping through his slick fingers. He closed his eyes and tried to fully appreciate the nature of spinning. "I'm okay. A little buzzed, is all."

"Did you hit your head?" she asked when she returned with a wet cloth.

She mopped his arm and taped it up with something and told him she didn't want him to go to sleep just yet. She kept asking about his head. He wasn't ready to admit that it was beginning to pound. He wanted to be a spinning numskull a little while longer before he slumped to a throbbing fool.

"Let me take your boots off for you," she said sweetly, so sweetly. *Take it all off*, he wanted to say, but she was having enough trouble with the boots. "Bending is hard on your back," she commiserated as she tugged.

He lifted his head, blinked, blinked again. Each time it was the same. She was mooning him, her sweet little ass peeking out from underneath her nightshirt. She got the first boot off, then straddled the other leg. He might have been drunk, but he had the presence of mind to add to her difficulties this time by arching his foot. She took a tighter grip, a tougher stance, a deep breath . . .

I don't know what you're sucking in, but please, please don't tuck that under.

"You do too much bending in your work," she was saying as the boot, sadly, slid away from his foot. His sock tagged along for the ride.

"I'm workin' on a new method, but so far they can't seem

to get the hang of it." He dropped his head back and laughed. "Hell, I keep tellin' 'em, if a dog can do it, a horse can do it. Tryin' to prick their pride, you know? Two simple commands. Even tried whispering. *Sit. Shake*."

She stared for a moment, then plopped on her butt, laughing.

"Yeah, see?" He propped himself up on his elbow, grinning. He could have sworn they were drifting on the high seas. She'd just rocked the boat. "See, they do the same thing. *Eee-hee-hee-hee*."

"Horses like to roll." She scooted across the floor and leaned against the sofa, primly adjusting her nightshirt. "Tell them to roll on their backs and put their feet up in the air."

"That could work. That could definitely work. Could you just demonstrate that for me once?"

"You're the one who's drunk, dear, not me." She patted her lap and beckoned him. "Come lay your head here."

He moved very quickly for a man who was half shot and sore all over.

"How do you feel?"

"Stupid." He closed his eyes when she began massaging his temples, making little circles. Felt like she was stirring his head around in a big bowl. "God, that's good. Can you stop the waves from rockin' our boat?"

"There's no boat and no waves. We're in Wyoming."

"Hills. Treetops. Rock-a-bye baby."

"I'll hold you, but I won't rock you. I don't want you to go to sleep for a while. Does your head hurt at all?"

"If I say yes, will you sleep with me?"

"I'll sit up with you." She stroked his forehead.

He imagined her plumping and shaping the big, dumb doughboy. *Ah, just put me in the oven and turn the heat up, honey.*

"You scared me, Clay."

"Didn't mean to."

"You shouldn't mix pills and booze."

"Didn't mean to." He opened his eyes slowly. She was close, so close. Having her in his life was all he'd ever wanted, and here she was, holding him, fussing over him, and filling his heart with hope. "You shouldn't lock yourself away."

"I don't . . ." She turned her face from him, leaving his gullible heart in the lurch. "I don't. Nothing's locked."

"Feels like it." He closed his eyes against the pain. "Feels like you're within my reach, but I can't . . . quite . . ."

"Don't sleep, Clay. Stay up with me."

"Can't touch you," he said, lifting his hand. "Let me touch you. Your face, okay? Just your face." She tried to drive him off with a simple frown, but he pressed out the crease with a blunt finger. "So sweet," he said. "So pretty and perfect."

She gave her head a quick shake, mouth crinkling, voice trembling as though he'd called her the worst name there was. "Not so, not so," she said.

"Only so-so? So-so, then."

She choked on a teary laugh, chanting, "So, so. So buttons."

"Does this hurt?" He continued to rub her forehead with his thumb, merely the return of a favor, but something was making her sad.

Again she shook her head quickly.

"Why are you crying, Savannah?"

"I'm not." Tight smile. Obvious lie. "I'm just so, so, *so* far from perfect."

"Tell me about it," he gibed gently. Then, seriously: "Tell me about it, Savannah. I'm sauced. Tomorrow I won't remember a thing." A lie, too, but he owed her one.

"It's no secret. I'm not all here." Her hand settled lightly between her breasts. "You're all set to party, and we're one jug short."

He groaned. "Can't believe you said that."

"You said to tell you, so I'm telling you. You're half shot. I'm half off."

"We're the perfect pair, then. Perfectly imperfect. Let me hold you while you tell me how imperfect we are." He tried to sit up, but she used the chance to scoot away. "I didn't say *party*; I said—"

"Turn over," she entreated, drawing his head back to her lap, but facedown. "Let me rub your imperfect back."

With his face between her perfect-in-his-eyes thighs? She would kill him yet with her tenderness. Maybe he should refuse. Maybe indifference was better.

And maybe motorcycles were better than horses.

"Only if I get to take my turn rubbing yours."

"We'll see," she said as she pressed her magic fingertips into his aching back.

But he fell asleep, she slipped away, and later they watched the coming of morning through their separate windows.

When Patty asked her to bring the bushel basket out to the garden, Savannah should have known her mother-in-law had more than produce-picking in mind. Patty was more interested in picking bones and brains than beans, but beans were handier.

"Bound to get a hard freeze this week," she muttered as she ambled around the perimeter, followed by Savannah with the big empty basket. "Tired of dragging the bed sheets back and forth to cover the plants, might as well save what's left. Could be my last garden. Never know."

"I guess we'll know by spring."

Patty stopped, turned, stared, finally smiled. "Somebody will, anyway."

"Somebody will," Savannah echoed as she tossed Patty the basket. "What are we picking?"

"Green tomatoes." Patty dropped the basket in the cultivated path between rows of leggy, late-season plants spilling over their tipping cages. "Now, what was all that ruckus about last night? Are you two hittin' it off that good in the bedroom, or is the honeymoon over?"

"I answered the first question last night," Savannah said. She thought for a moment, then shook her head for lack of a good comeback. "No, I think I'll just politely ignore the second one."

"Tryin' to show me up, huh?" Patty hooted when she laughed. "Aw, damn. Think I can learn by example? I'm 'fraid it's too late, honey. I'm too old to change my rude spots. All I can do is add to them." She stuck her scrawny, liver-spotted arm under Savannah's nose. "See these? They're like oil on water, all running together. Got any professional tips for me?"

"Stay out of the sun."

"That must be another example you've been setting for me by stickin' close to the house. I was hoping for one of them model's secrets, like they sell for three installments of nineteen ninety-nine on the infomercials, some magic elixir or something."

"Bleach. And then stay out of the sun."

"No can do, not this ol' country gal. I never was a beauty anyway. Good thing I was a banker's daughter. If it wasn't for my daddy's assets, I'd be an old maid." Patty leaned closer. "But don't tell Clayton. He doesn't know I'm homely." Savannah tried unsuccessfully to wedge a word in, but Patty wagged a warning finger. "Don't doubt me, either. He doesn't."

"I wasn't going to argue with you."

"Not at all?" Patty said, giving her one more chance.

Savannah smiled and shook her head.

"I guess my son knows I wasn't exactly the love of his daddy's life. Has he ever told you that?"

"No."

"How about Kole? He ever tell you—"

"No." She shouldn't discuss Kole with Patty, she reminded herself as she reached for a cluster of green tomatoes. But maybe for Claudia's sake . . . "I asked Kole once, and he said his parents were never married because Jonas Keogh wasn't man enough for his mother. He wouldn't elaborate. He didn't like to talk about either of them."

"His mother's name was Lana." Patty moved to the opposite side of the same plant, plucked one tomato, and handed it to Savannah for the basket. "I knew about her and her son when I married Jonas. But since she was an Indian woman, I thought, well, I've got nothing to worry about. Like the politicians say, youthful indiscretion. Obviously he couldn't marry her, probably never even considered it." She looked directly at Savannah. "I only saw her once. She was beautiful. Smaller than me, but striking and strong and self-possessed."

"You met her?"

"She brought Kole to live with us when he was about thirteen. She wasn't gonna take no for an answer, even though you could tell he didn't want to be here any more than we"—she lifted one shoulder to help her admission along—"than *I* wanted him to stay. But you should've seen Clayton turn himself inside out right there on the spot, trying to convince everybody, including Kole, that he should stay. 'We've got lots of room,' Clayton said. 'Do you like horses? We've got lots of horses.' " Patty laughed, a surprisingly lusty, loving laugh. "If that boy had his way, we'd be running a shelter for every—"

"Why did she give him up?"

Patty's wistful smile melted away. "She said she wanted him to have a better life, insisted that Jonas owed him that much. But you know damn well that wasn't it. She was involved with that Indian protest group. Same kinda stuff that got Kole into trouble later on."

"So she wanted him out of the way?"

"She wanted him out of harm's way. I don't know what happened to her, but I don't think she died of exposure like they said. And it wasn't until she died that I really understood how my husband felt about her." She sighed. "Kole was right. Jonas wasn't man enough for Lana Kills Crow. Just goes to show," she said as she bent to reach for more unripe fruit, "paper covers rock, but money tops looks."

"What about love?"

"It's widely reported to conquer all. Around here, I'd have to say that remains to be seen." Patty peered past shriveling leaves. "It sure hasn't conquered this ol' gal."

"I don't know if I buy that." Tomatoes rolled from Savannah's hand into the basket. "I saw you slip Claudia that extra cookie."

"You know what's funny? She has Kole's looks and Clay's ways. How in hell do you suppose that happened?"

"She has her own looks and her own personality. She's not like anyone else. Certainly not like her mother. We don't have to worry about that."

"I wasn't worried. I worry about her father, though. And I wonder when you're gonna tell her who he is so she doesn't find out some other way."

"She's just a little girl."

"Clayton was a little boy when Kole came to live with us, and I didn't want to tell him right away that they were brothers. I thought it would confuse him. I was worried about what he'd think of his father. Get real, huh?" Patty laughed. "How was that gonna change the way a nine-year-old felt about his father? The only person it bothered was me, so I didn't tell him.

"It was Kole who let the cat out of the bag one time when he was mad about something. Said Clayton was too stupid to be his brother. So I had to explain the whole thing. 'Course, I got into a lot more than the boy needed to know, so most of it went in one ear and out the other, thank God. All he cared about was the brother part. He had a brother.

The coolest guy on the face of the earth was his real, honest-to-God brother. Clayton was one happy little kid anytime Kole would just simply allow him to tag along. And he did. Grudgingly at first, but Clayton got under his skin after a while. Well, you know how he does."

Savannah nodded. "I think Kole would be pleased to know that Clay's going to help me raise his daughter. But with all the trouble he's had, he thinks Claudia is better off not knowing about him until she's older. He doesn't want any of that to touch her."

"But Kole was a novelty in Sunbonnet. People here haven't forgotten him."

"I know." Savannah braced her hands on her knees and watched a wispy cloud slide across the western sky. "It's funny how things turn out. You wait in line, climb the ladder, get to the top, and sit there for a minute so everyone can see you. Then you push off, and the slide takes you right back where you started. I didn't have anywhere else to go, or anyone else . . ."

"Yeah, well, here you are, and you've got yourself a protector," Patty said. "You're not the only woman in the world who's ever tried to hide something, so don't go thinking you're anything special. Hiding yourself away isn't even too original. Howard Hughes did it. Greta Garbo. Beautiful people, you know. Too beautiful for the rest of us. 'Course, if you wanna do it right, you gotta have money. Besides a good heart and a bad back, all Clayton has is this place. He ain't got nooo money, honey." She waited until she had Savannah's complete attention before she smiled, old blue eyes glinting in the sunlight. "Bet you didn't know that, did you?"

"Money only beats looks," Savannah quipped. "Love conquers all."

"Except truth," Patty said. "You can't hide from the truth, Savannah, whatever it is."

.

Chapter 14

Clay tossed the Sun-Bee *aside as he swung his boots off* his desk.

Without a puppy to housebreak, he didn't know why he subscribed to the thing. Nothing but old news. Last month's livestock prices and last year's faulty forecast for improvement this fall. The feeder calf market should have bottomed out and bounced back, according to the wizards and fortune-tellers who got paid to read the signs. When they were wrong, they'd claim they were only a little off. Next year for sure. Right now, prices were flat, but at least they weren't falling.

Falling, hell. The old wooden desk chair squawked as he swiveled. There wasn't any place to fall. *Flat* was an easy call to make, since the floor was a pretty damn flat place to be.

He'd turned down a lowball offer from a buyer in favor of taking his chances at auction, and now he dreaded rounding up the herd and trucking the calves to the sale barn. It wouldn't be so bad if he had only his mother and Uncle Mick to worry about. They'd been ranchers all their lives, and they knew nobody was in it for the money these days. They knew all about belt-tightening. Most ranchers' belts were notched all the way down to the buckle. But Clay had other people to provide for. Bringing that check home to Patty and Mick was no problem, but he couldn't bear to disappoint Savannah.

Of course, he wouldn't have to tell her, and she probably wouldn't ask, and she certainly wouldn't go along to the sale.

He wanted to buy her something before he took his calves to the sale. Now, before the returns were in. Today he could say, *Buy anything you like*. He could let Claudia pick something for her birthday, which was coming up. He'd have to get something for the other three kids, too, couldn't leave them out. Today, before the receipts were in and the bills came due, he could still play Santa Claus.

He worked it out with Claudia. They would make a day of it, get her mother into a store to shop for her little girl, which they would do, but they'd maneuver Savannah into the women's department as well. Claudia loved the idea. The trick was to get her mother to leave the ranch.

But when he broached the subject at the tail end of a lesson in feeding his senior equines, Savannah surprised him.

"Actually, I was going to talk to you about maybe taking a trip to the big city," she said shyly.

He didn't know which big city she had in mind, and he was afraid to ask. There weren't any in Wyoming.

"I was half thinking that I might try one of those group talk sessions," she said as she turned the last of the old horses out after it had polished off a ration of easy-to-gum pelleted feed.

Clay stood there with what he hoped was a blank look on his face. If she needed to go back to New York to find someone to talk to, he wasn't going to kick. If it would help her, he'd pay her way. And he'd try not to wonder whether she'd find her way back.

She smiled. "You know, women comparing notes on their ills. I've tried it before and failed miserably, but I thought—"

"You mean, like, group therapy? You don't get graded, do you?"

"More like a support group, and I guess I . . ." She hung the nylon halter on a hook next to the stall door. "I remember one woman—her name was Deborah, I think." She laughed. "I *know* it was Deborah. I couldn't *stand* Deborah. Such a cheerleader. *Positive attitude*, she kept saying. I had a positive attitude; I was positive I was going to die. But she seemed so unsinkable. And it was so disgusting."

"Sounds like . . ."

She gave him a go-ahead-and-say-it look, but he wouldn't, so she did. "Sounds like failure. Straight F's. Support-group drop-out."

"But you want to give it another try?"

"Maybe." She bent to pick up an empty feed bucket. "I called Dr. Mears, and she suggested one that meets in Jackson Hole. We could shop there, couldn't we?"

"Oh, yeah." He didn't know of any songs about Jackson Hole, but it sure sounded like music to his ears. It wasn't New York. "They've got shops."

"Maybe you've got work you could do there. Make it worth your while."

"It's already worth my while, and we haven't left yet. I don't have to work *all* the time. Some days I get to buy presents for my girls and take them out to eat and watch other people work. Don't I?"

"I don't know why not."

But he did, so he scheduled two shoe resets. He enjoyed the shopping, knowing that the resets would pay for it.

An unusual six-year-old, Claudia wasn't interested in finding a toy store. She shopped the store windows, passing up ski wear in favor of Annie's Fine Western Apparel. All she wanted for her birthday was cowboy boots, but Clay talked her into a hat to go with them. And they both talked Savannah into trying on "boot-cut" jeans, which meant she had to try them on with boots, and with those she really had to combine a broom-handle skirt and a cropped jacket. And a Pendleton blazer. And a couple of pairs of slacks, and one more skirt.

At first she tried to play the quick-change artist, calling out, "It fits," from the safety of her chosen cubicle.

But her family was having none of it.

"Show us, Mommy."

"We want to see what you mean by *fits*."

She peeked over the cubicle gate, made sure there were no curious bystanders other than her own two, who occupied the two "fashion advisor" chairs near the three-way mirror. She emerged cautiously in the slacks and blazer. " 'Fits' means *fits*."

"But how does it look? Step away from that . . ." Clay cupped his hand around his mouth and lowered his voice. "Step away from that door and put your hands behind your head."

Savannah glanced around again before picking up her cue. She assumed a chic version of "the position" and slowly sashayed toward the wood-floor runway that led to the mirrored bay.

Claudia was already giggling.

"Now walk a straight line," Clay ordered through his makeshift megaphone. "Turn. Keep turning. Not bad. Arms down, but don't try anything funny. I have to confer with my partner here."

At his signal, Claudia crawled into his lap. He leaned close to her ear. "What do you think? Is this the one?"

"I think she should keep trying."

"We're not convinced, ma'am," Clay announced. "We'd like to see the demonstration again. Only this time . . ." He whispered loudly to Claudia, "Which one?"

"The blue one. Blue is your best color, Mo—madam."

Savannah put more effort into it the next time out. She'd combed her hair and added some lipstick, which prompted her to smile more. Then she began to forget herself, and before she knew it, she was putting on a show, just for them. Her chin came up, shoulders dropped back, hips swayed, eyes flirted, and the clothes were suddenly splendid, every piece.

A private showing, and Clay was the buyer. He'd take them all. She could sell him flour sacks with that blue-gem smile in her eyes.

"Well, what'll it be?" he asked finally. She gave him a blank look. "Anything strike your fancy, or should we move on to another store?"

"My fancy?" She had the look of a bird that had just regained the use of its wings, just remembered its true nature, what it was supposed to be. But Clay's question reminded Savannah that she was there as a shopper. She turned toward the dressing room, pirouetted as though she were fluttering down to earth. "I guess I could use the boots."

"What else?"

Her voice softened more. "Well, the jeans if I'm going to ride."

"Mommy," Claudia said impatiently. "You have to get the blue jacket with that crinkly skirt."

"She's right. Everything you tried on looked pretty, but that outfit . . ." Clay gave his wife a knowing look. "You didn't really look in the mirror, did you?"

"I had you two."

"If it's up to us, we pick the blue outfit for sure," he said, glanced at Claudia, and extended his right thumb, then a finger at a time. "The boots, the jeans with that white shirt, huh?" Claudia nodded. "How about the pink number with the tan sort of . . ." Claudia nodded harder. "Yeah, with the belt."

"It's not *my* birthday," Savannah protested. "And I really don't need—"

"Lady, you should have the whole works," a strange man in a cowboy hat interrupted. He was standing with two women near a rack of Australian oilcloth dusters.

"You should be a model," one of the women said.

"You could easily be a model," the man agreed.

"In fact, you look familiar," said a store clerk.

Claudia piped up. "She used to—"

"—look a lot like some famous model when she was younger," Clay cut in, grinning at his wife. "See, honey, you've still got it." And to the store clerk: "We'll take everything."

"Clay, don't be—"

"And we'll find some more stuff for the birthday girl. Tell you what, Kitten, this is the best time of year to have a birthday." He turned to the couple still watching. "Harvest time, right?"

"Right," the man said with a snort. "If it's good for you, I'd sure like to know what you're raising besides kittens."

"Little of this, little of that." Clay slipped Claudia a wink. "But our kittens aren't for sale."

The Jackson Hole support group was one of half a dozen on the list Charlotte Mears had provided, but as long as Savannah was going to have to drive some distance to get to any of them, this was the one Dr. Mears had said might be the best "fit." Savannah wondered how doctors defined the word "fit." The building looked more like a ski chalet than a clinic. Niggling doubt followed her up the steps to the big blue doors. Maybe she really didn't need this.

In the street behind her, the pickup engine growled. She spun around in time to catch a parting wave from Claudia. They might be gone longer than the two hours scheduled for the group session, Clay had warned, but Savannah had said she'd be fine. Now she wondered whether she could run fast enough to catch up with him.

What was two hours? She could easily do two hours. Facilitator Cheryl Estes assured her that after she introduced herself to the eight women in the circle, she could get her bearings by listening. She didn't have to say anything if she didn't want to. No one seemed to recognize her. She gave her first name, briefly described her surgery, mentioned New York, her move, her recent marriage to her childhood sweetheart. Had she actually said "sweetheart"? For the next thirty minutes she had little desire to say more. She was the only newcomer to the group, and everyone else was able to pick up some thread left dangling from the last session.

The first one was phantom pain. Savannah hadn't experienced the phenomenon in several months. She stuck her neck out simply to mention that, and she was told by a large redhead named Barbara that she shouldn't have had it at all, since her body image hadn't changed. "You're grieving," the woman said. "Still trapped in the grief cycle. You have implants, right, Stella? And you had a *double*."

Stella said she did and hadn't experienced phantom pain. So did that mean Savannah wasn't allowed? Doing it wrong again?

"You're keeping that grief active, girl. You've got to stop reminding yourself of the loss," Barbara said. "We've all been there."

"I haven't had . . ." Savannah smiled and nodded, thinking that with an hour and a half to go, she'd pretend she hadn't heard the *we've-been-there* part. "I'm sure you're right. It must have been *imaginary* phantom pain."

"No, no, I didn't mean to minimize it. I mean, we've all been there."

Savannah nodded again. She looked at her watch. That was it; that was her attempt. Talk about grief she didn't need, this experience would definitely qualify.

Husbands were the next dangling thread. Not all the women had them, but those who did reported responses that ran the gamut from "my rock" to "more scared than I am" to "so far out in left field he might as well be playing for the other team."

Denise, who'd had a traditional mastectomy at the age of forty, described the look on her husband's face the first time he saw the results of her surgery. "We have an unspoken agreement now. He doesn't look, and we don't talk about it."

"Have you tried to talk about it?" the facilitator wanted to know.

"A little. I talked. He tried to find something to be looking at besides me while he . . . heard me out, I guess. So now we don't talk about it." Denise paused, shifting in her chair. "He never said anything mean, you understand. It was just the look on his face, like I was an amputee or something. Which I am, I guess, but . . . he always loved to look at me naked . . ." Her hand fluttered over her chest, which was dramatically draped with a beautiful silk scarf. "Here."

"Does he love you less?" Cheryl prompted.

"I don't know." Denise searched the ceiling for an answer. "Maybe not, but he doesn't find me as attractive as he used to. He's good to me, but he doesn't treat me the same. I think he's afraid of me, almost."

"Afraid to hurt you?"

"He's afraid to lose you," Barbara said. "Men show their fear differently, I think. He'll get over it. He'll see you're not going anywhere." She turned abruptly to Savannah. "Must be tough for newlyweds. Was your husband around for the exciting part?"

"No."

"*This* is the exciting part, Barbara," Stella put in. "Living to tell about it."

Barbara laughed, but she wasn't finished prying. "So how did he take it when he saw your scars? Did he—"

"He hasn't seen me. I don't intend for him to." Savannah

gave a tight smile. She couldn't believe she'd answered that question. "We haven't been married very long, and I don't want to scare him off."

Good God, where was this coming from?

"With a face like yours?" Stella grinned as she glanced around the room. "The rest of us are in serious trouble."

"I've never heard of a tram flap," Barbara said. "You say they scoop out the insides like they're making a melon boat and then squeeze your own stomach muscle up there? Kinda like a pastry-bag process?"

Savannah offered a cold stare. "What are you, a chef?"

"Just a housewife, but I'm trying to imagine it. I'll show you mine if you show me yours."

"Absolutely not."

"It's not a fair bargain, Barbara," a tiny blonde named Margo said. "Your lumpectomy didn't leave you with much of a scar."

"Yours, either."

"No, but I'm going back for more." Margo glanced at the facilitator, who encouraged her with a subtle nod. "They found something again. I go in Wednesday. They don't give you much time to think about it." She smiled as Stella, sitting next to her, reached for her hand. "I was glad we were meeting today, though. I haven't been coming the last few months. I really thought I was out of the woods."

"Do we ever get out of the woods?" Savannah heard herself asking quietly. All eyes turned to her, some silently questioning her choice of comment on the heels of Margo's news. But she'd said "we." And that made her one of them, which was strange but oddly comforting.

"We get to the edge," Margo said softly.

"I'm not a living-on-the-edge sort of person, though, not if I can help it," Stella remarked. "How about you, Savannah?"

"Not anymore. I want to come away from the edge. Lately

all I want to do is crawl into the middle of a very safe place and pull my daughter in with me."

"But I hate that fear," someone said, and Savannah realized that if she wasn't looking at faces, the voices sounded much the same. They had begun to blend. "I really hate it. I don't want to live in the shadows."

"Is it death?" Cheryl asked. "Is that what you want to hide from?"

"Sometimes I think I carry death inside me." Savannah couldn't look at Margo, and she didn't want to look at Barbara, so she studied her hands, tightly folded in her lap. "Maybe that's what I'm hiding. I don't want anyone to see that."

"News flash," Barbara quipped. "Everyone carries death inside. Everyone. It's part of being alive."

"But cancer has to be the ugliest, doesn't it?" Savannah mused. "Nobody wants to get near it. It's the worst news, the worst way to go. It really looks awful. It has a revolting face with black lips, green tongue, and pointy teeth that eat away at you."

"What kind of meds are you on?" Barbara teased.

Savannah shook her head. "Even if it's gone, at least for now, it still shows."

"So do blackheads and warts, but you never had to worry about those, did you?" Barbara replied lightly.

Margo turned in her chair. "I bet I know your husband."

Savannah questioned her with a look.

"I saw you drive up," Margo said. "Looked like my farrier's pickup. Clay?" Savannah nodded, and Margo smiled. "He's fabulous. You watch him work, and you think if he's that patient with horses, that gentle, that sensitive, what would it be like to be . . ." She laughed. "Sorry. I'm going back under the knife this week. I'm entitled. Anyway, I'm probably old enough to be his mother." Her smile became a bit too wistful. "He's a good man. He listens."

"I'm not here to discuss my husband."

"And I don't particularly want to talk about being eaten up by black lips and pointy teeth."

"I'm sorry." Savannah sighed. "See, I don't belong in these groups. I'm not a group person. I don't know why people always think it helps to talk about this crap. You can talk all you want, but it's still there."

"That's right, but so are you. Talking can help you get over yourself sometimes. You're no different from the rest of us, Savannah. No better off, no worse off. With us, you don't have to worry about being ugly."

"She worries about being beautiful," Barbara said.

"We all do," Margo told Savannah. "Believe it or not, we had as much to lose as you did. Whether you're an A-cup or a double D, whether you've nursed babies or lovers, whether you're a scientist or a secretary, rich or poor, fat or skinny, gay or straight, there's something about this part of a woman's body . . ." Margo laid her hand on her breast, and Savannah couldn't help wondering whether it was the one she was about to lose. "Something that identifies her as a female in her own head. *In her own head.*"

"Where are you living right now, Savannah?" Cheryl asked.

"In my husband's house."

"You went from New York to Wyoming, from your aunt's house to your husband's house, but you're afraid to go out," Margo said. "You're living in your own head."

"You gotta get over yourself, girl."

"We know you, Savannah. You're just like us."

"So show us what a tram flap looks like."

"Yeah, show us your boobs!"

"You don't have to," Cheryl assured her.

Savannah looked at Margo. "Do you think they'll take the whole breast this time?"

Margo nodded.

Savannah's hands went to the buttons on her blouse. "Well, this is another option."

It wasn't like getting undressed for an exam or standing in front of a mirror. It wasn't clinical. It wasn't critical. It was more like sharing secrets with friends at a slumber party, with all the innocence and none of the cattiness. She did have something in common with these women. They all had screwed-up breasts.

But that wasn't who they were.

Savannah wasn't ready for any group hugs, but she did find herself mopping up a few tears. After the session was over, Margo thanked her for her candor. "I'd like to talk to Clay about taking one of my horses," she added.

"He really doesn't need any more, and I don't think he can afford to buy—"

"I don't want to sell her. I want to retire her," Margo explained as they headed down the hall together. "With this surgery and more treatment coming up, I'm going to have to give up the horses, and I can sell most of them, but not Bronwyn. She's too old. She was one of my first horses, and she gave me so much pleasure. She taught me to ride. Clay's so good with her, and I've heard that he takes in older horses."

"He doesn't exactly—" Savannah groaned. "Yes, he does, he buys them sometimes, and he'd probably buy yours, but please don't ask him, because I don't know what he's going to do with them all."

"He doesn't have to do anything except give her a comfortable retirement, for which I'm prepared to pay the going rate and then some." Margo stopped when they reached the lobby, which had skylights and a huge glass window. She turned to Savannah. "I'm quite serious. I spend part of the winter in Florida, and I know there's a horse-retirement farm there. I'd hate to move her, though. I thought that was something Clay did."

"Not really."

"I'm going to miss the horses. They're good for the soul, you know? Especially wounded souls like ours."

Savannah glanced through the window and saw that Clay and Claudia were waiting for her. "Do you have a family?"

Margo was a petite, attractive woman, but the flood of sunlight betrayed her fatigue and her age. "I've been divorced for ten years. Two grown children. Good friends—I have lots of good friends."

"Clay's my best friend. We grew up together."

"How can he be your friend if you don't trust him?"

"I do trust him." Savannah glanced away. "We have an understanding."

"Oh. I thought you said you had a marriage. My exhusband and I have an understanding. We're friends, too, actually. He'll come to the hospital to see me. I'm sure he cares whether I live or die." She touched Savannah's arm. "I don't think I'll be showing him my scars, either. Mainly because he goes home to his bed and I go home to mine. We don't share things like scars anymore. Or moonbeams or morning coffee. We're no longer married."

Margo headed for the exit to the parking lot, leaving Savannah her card with the invitation to call her anytime. Savannah said she'd be thinking of her on Wednesday.

Thinking of her on Wednesday. How generous. What good was thinking of someone? Maybe, just *possibly*, she could call the woman. Or get her butt out of the house and visit her on Thursday. Or help her with her horse.

You're living in your own head.

Thinking of someone might have its merits, she thought as she headed for the front door. She remembered a schoolbook she'd had called *Think and Do*, a workbook. She greeted the man coming up the walk with a smile. Her hardworking man, clutching her daughter's hand. Neither of them had any trouble with *doing*, and they didn't go around offering to think of people. It was no big deal for them. Their heads weren't boxes full of quicksand.

A cartoonish mental picture of herself as a boxhead made her laugh aloud, which was Claudia's cue to hop, skip, run up the walk, and wrap herself around her mother's legs. Savannah admired her husband's powerful stride as she stroked her daughter's hair. Powerful legs, powerful hands, power in his handsome face. Time was, she'd thought Kole was the handsome one, the exciting and elusive one.

Time was, she'd been a kid.

Clay slipped his arm around her, said he hoped she hadn't been waiting long, then spoke of how helpful Claudia had been that day as he walked them to the pickup. Clay's power was more than physical. It was beyond handsome and exciting. To a woman—she was, after all, still a woman—it was deeply stirring.

Perhaps *finally* a woman was more accurate.

The drive home took them through the mountain passes of the Grand Tetons. Claudia said it felt like they were driving up to heaven, and Clay said he was pretty sure this was as close as a person could get to heaven on earth. They saw an elk, a family of mule deer, and a high-flying eagle. Clay laid on the horn when a mountain goat decided to cross the road in front of them. From her perch on the child safety seat Clay had installed in the backseat of the pickup's cab, Claudia chirped and chattered with delight. Savannah quietly enjoyed every sight and sound, even the horn, as she replayed the events of the day in her mind.

And Clay tuned right in. "I know these group things are confidential, but did it help?"

"It was good," she quipped cheerily. She wasn't sure how good she could manage to be when the quicksand started sucking at her again, but for now she was high on the experience. That was all she could say.

Which—she could tell from the way he brightened—would not be enough for Clay.

"Yeah? Is it a weekly thing? 'Cause I can sure take you any—"

"I don't think I need to go every week, or even . . ." A plan was like a promise, and she wasn't making any promises yet. "It's a long drive."

"We can always find something to do in Jackson. Right, Kitten? We ended up doing a couple of extra horses today."

"Yeah," Claudia enthused from the backseat. "Even though that one woman kept talking and talking and made us late getting to the next place."

"Really?" Savannah said, mildly curious.

"She showed us what she was feeding her racing horse and her new saddle and her new horse trailer with the little kitchen and bathroom and bedroom in it and all kinds of stuff."

"Really. A horse trailer with a place for the rider to sleep." Savannah glanced at Clay. "How handy."

"Yeah," Claudia said. "She goes to races. She even puts one on herself, and she wants us to go to it so in case her horse loses a shoe, we can fix it."

"*Real*-ly." Savannah's curiosity was heating up, mild to medium.

"Or any other horses," Claudia continued. "It lasts three days, and horses lose lots of shoes, so we could really make lots and lots of money."

"I do some fall events like endurance races if I can fit them in," Clay explained. "The money's good, but it takes time. I told her I probably couldn't make it this year." He glanced at Savannah. "Unless you wanted to go along. You might enjoy—"

"Sleeping in a horse trailer? I don't think I'd be very good at that."

"You're good around horses." His smile was utterly

charming. He was looking for plans and promises. "And you've got new boots."

"One day at a time," she said. "That's the name of the game."

"You're gettin' better at it," he said.

She nodded. She didn't want to jinx it.

Chapter 15

The muted colors of Indian summer draped the broad shoulders of the Lazy K foothills like a warm trade blanket. It was time to bring in the cattle, separate the calves, and truck them to the sale barn. In a good year, the event was cause for celebration. Even in an ordinary year, it was cause to socialize. Riders were required for a roundup, and a good meal was all they expected in return for long hours spent in the saddle.

Roxie's kids hitched a ride from town with Aunt Billie to lend a hand. Billie, who had closed the store for the day, came to ride. Clay had promised to keep the crew to a minimum of outsiders if Savannah would participate. She offered to cook. She told him that was just what she wanted to do, she wanted to cook. What she really wanted to do was ride, but not with any crew. One of her boobs didn't bounce as well as the other, and her abdominal muscles were operating at half strength. "I'll do the Lazy K chuck wagon proud," she promised.

And with a little help from her mother-in-law, she did. They put together a meal of barbecued beef—like all her best recipes, stolen from Heather—with every kind of starchy salad Savannah could think of, along with Aunt Billie's baked beans. But the only dessert she ever made was cookies. "I'll make pie," Patty said. "With *my* apples from the trees I raised from twigs."

"And lovely trees they are."

Patty's cool glance said she took the remark for sarcasm.

Savannah laughed. "I remember when you got after Clay and me for throwing green apples at each other. We didn't think they were any good."

"Good for pies," Patty said.

"At that point, I don't think I'd ever had pie made from fresh apples. I learned to cook from a friend in New York." Savannah offered a forkful of potato salad for Patty to sample. "You never asked me to stay for supper, so I never got a taste of your pie."

"Well, see, that's what you get for throwin' my apples." Patty smacked her lips over the potato salad. "It's good. It's good you learned something useful out East."

"It is," Savannah agreed. "Good food, good manners. I seldom throw things anymore." Her smile was saucy. "And if pie is all you can cook, it's good you learned to *grow* things."

"Wasn't a tree in this yard when I moved in." Patty acknowledged the touché with a glance, a little lopsided smile that reminded Savannah of Clay. "Can you picture that? It ain't easy growing apples out here. There's grapes I put in, too. You get winter kill, you just start all over. It ain't easy." The glance turned pointed. "If it was easy, the fruit wouldn't taste nearly as sweet."

"Sweet?"

"If it ain't sweet, you make it sweet. And those grapes would make good wine."

"You make your own wine?"

Patty shrugged. "Been meaning to."

Aunt Billie returned after a couple of hours' ride with a sunburned nose, stiff legs, and an estimated time of arrival for cows and cowboys. Dinner was ready and the kitchen was filled with the aroma of apple pie when the bawling herd spilled over the last hill and into the small pasture near the sorting pens. A couple of new faces had slipped into the crew somewhere along the way—a neighbor named Jim and a guy named Richard Frank, with whom, Savannah was reminded, she'd gone to school. "They came to help us separate the cows from the calves," Clay explained.

It was okay, Savannah realized. Jim said he'd seen her pictures, and Richard thought he might have one or two catalogs around the house somewhere. He said his wife had been wondering why any woman would want to give up a job like that. "It's pretty obvious, ain't it?" he said. "You wanna be in pictures, you gotta go to New York, California, places where they'll pay people to do just about anything. You name it, man—put on two pieces of lace and call it underwear, sell plain water in bottles, beat up your mother on a talk show, they'll pay you for it." Richard nodded at Clay. "But you want a man, you gotta come to Wyoming."

"Damn, Rich, you—"

"You're absolutely right, Richard. There comes a time in every woman's life when she needs a man to call her own. And where does she go?" Savannah smiled as she hooked her arm with her husband's. "To that hard-to-reach shelf where they keep all the good ones."

"Damn straight," Richard said, toasting the couple with his beer.

Later, on his way out the door, Clay quietly congratulated Savannah for giving Richard a nice story to spread around Sunbonnet.

"It *is* nice," she protested.

"That's what I said."

It took the rest of the day to separate the calves and load them into cattle trucks, which would take them to a livestock auction house where they would be sold the following day.

It was Clay's habit to follow the trucks, supervise the unloading, and stay in town overnight.

Patty hadn't been to an auction in years, and she wasn't going to miss this one.

Clay had his gear ready to go. "You can come along with Mick and me if you want to, Mom. But I want to be there when the trucks pull in, so we'll be headin' out pretty quick here."

"I don't need to race the trucks, long as I get there before they open the bidding," Patty said. "You should take your wife along with you, and Mick and me can go on our own."

Clay looked at his mother as though she'd just spit in the wind. "Jeez, Mom, Savannah doesn't want to go to a calf auction. I wouldn't spend my day in a stinky sale barn if I didn't have to."

"But you'll be gone overnight. You might as well have a night in a motel together. You could call it a honeymoon."

"Maybe I'm planning to take her someplace warm this winter. Someplace nice. I sure wouldn't insult her by trying to pass off a night in Riverton as a honeymoon."

"I wouldn't be insulted."

He turned his incredulous look on Savannah. "You wanna go?"

"Do you . . ." *Want me to?* Plainly he didn't, which was fine. "Actually, I was hoping to spend some time with Aunt Billie." She glanced at her aunt. "I thought we might check on a sick friend."

Aunt Billie did a double take. "You have a sick—"

"Friend. I do have friends."

"You look after your friend. We'll be back tomorrow night." Clay didn't question, didn't doubt or hesitate, had the pickup door open and his leg inside before anyone could alter his plan. "Mom, this bus is leaving in two minutes. C'mon, Mick."

*   *   *

It could have been worse. As Uncle Mick was fond of saying, they could have been sheep ranchers. Or pig farmers, or anybody else looking at worse prices than cattlemen. In a flat market, they'd done better than most of their neighbors. They would cover their most pressing bills and bank some operating capital, but not much. By spring they'd be back in the red. Without the horseshoeing business, the extras would be limited to groceries.

They'd had their ups and downs ever since Clay had come home to help his mother run the place—hell, Wyoming was made of ups and downs—but he figured they were overdue for an upturn. Now that Roxie no longer had access to the checkbook, an upturn might be funneled into some expansion. They could use about four hundred more head. He could use a break from the roller coaster.

Well, there was always next year.

Hell, he was tired of busting his ass for the promise of next year.

Last year he almost would have been pleased with the check he pocketed at the accounting window. But this wasn't last year. This was *this* year, and this year he'd wanted—*needed*—to do better for his family. And for the Lazy K, which he'd hoped to someday share with his brother. At the very least, he didn't want to let Kole's daughter down.

A loudspeaker carried the auctioneer's announcements to the livestock lot and the adjacent parking area. They were about to run a few horses through the ring.

"That's our cue to skedaddle," Patty said. She had her eye on the dusty white pickup and trailer parked near the loading dock, and she was on the move. Mick was already in the pickup.

But there was a horse trailer in Clay's path. A skinny old man with arthritic hands was cursing a stubborn latch.

"What are you trying to do?" Clay asked, coming to the

rescue. The poor guy could barely close his hand around the handle.

"Just trying to unload this horse, is all. Damn rusted-up trailer." He kicked the bottom of the door. The occupant on the other side kicked back. "I'm tryin'!"

"Let's see if I can help." Clay worked on the latch until it gave under the pressure and broke off, leaving him with a gash in his hand from the rusty metal.

"Now look what you done," the old man complained. "How am I gonna keep it shut now?"

"You wanted it open."

"Well, you done it now. I can prob'ly tie it up some way, good enough to get home once it's empty."

Clay added blood to the rust as he pulled the door open against the protest of squealing hinges. What he saw inside pinched his gut. Bile backed up in his throat. He was looking at the ass end of an emaciated paint. The hide formed what looked like a sagging field tent over the hip joints and spine. Clay knew if he lifted the tail he could drive a truck between the horse's thin flanks.

He whirled to face the old man.

"You're going to run him through the ring like this? Don't tell me he *summered* hard."

The man stepped back. "He's part Arab. To me they always look kinda ganted up."

"You know what they'll say to you in there?" Clay thrust a bloody finger toward the sale barn.

"I know he don't look the best. All he needs is better grass than what I've got. I'm grazed down to cactus and sand burrs. I put up a sign to sell him, but I can't get no takers, so I . . ." The old fellow doffed his cap and rubbed the shiny skin on top of his head. "I don't know what else to do."

Clay glanced over his shoulder at his mother, standing next to the open door of his pickup and looking back at him.

She lowered her gaze, wagged her white head. He blew a deep sigh, adjusted his hat.

I don't know what else to do.

The magic words.

Cold rain had followed them home, the intermittent peltings turning into an evening drizzle that seeped into the bones. Clay sent Mick into the house, saying he'd be along soon, which they both knew wasn't true. Clay couldn't go in the house until he took care of his new charge. It would be time for another feeding soon. If it weren't for the cold, he'd consider bunking in the big box stall with the poor beast.

The cold and the cows. They were still hanging close to the pens from which they'd last seen their calves, still calling to them. It was impossible to turn a deaf ear to those plaintive voices, and he knew he'd still hear it in the house, in the shower, in his sleep. He knew each cow by her looks and personality as well as her ear tag and production history, but her calf would recognize its mother's voice, just the way human babies did. They didn't give up easily, those bosses. They'd seen the pickup, the one that might mean food when the ground was covered with snow or a hole in the ice for water. They knew he was home. They wanted their calves back.

Well, the calves were gone, and that was that. "They'll have to look to the future, just like the rest of us," he told the scrawny paint as he dumped a wheelbarrow full of sawdust in the stall. Couldn't trust this poor guy with straw. "That's what the bulls are for."

He rubbed the paint's flaccid neck, scratched his dished back, wincing at the feel of protruding bone. A veterinarian had taught Clay to eyeball a horse for body condition by using a scoring system, and this horse was definitely on the low end of the scale.

"How're you doin', ol' boy? You've got problems, too, but

I don't hear you complaining." The horse snuffled his hand. "Soon," Clay promised. "Trust me, boy, I won't let you down. I've got you on a strict feeding schedule, and it's not quite time." He'd have to trek out there during the night for the first few days of the horse's rehabilitation. He'd done this before, and it took time and patience. You couldn't just pour the feed to a starving horse.

But you could sing to him, improvise a bit. "Git along, Ol' Paint, don't be stompin' on my foot."

" 'Cause you know the Lazy K's gon-na be yer new hooome," came the rejoinder from beyond the stall.

He was spreading the sawdust for bedding, but he looked up smiling when Savannah peeked over the stall door, wearing a yellow slicker he recognized as his. Singing with a voice he recognized as . . . hers. "I hope you dressed warm," he told her. "Ol' Paint and me, we're freezin' our asses off out here. You can see his is pretty puny."

She lifted a steaming mug above the stall gate. "I brought something to warm yours up."

"Thanks." The hot cup felt good in his bandaged hand. He let himself out of the stall, slurping noisily. She touched the bandage as he moved past her, and he assured her that his shots were up to date.

"Shots?" She hung the slicker on a large tack hook between two stalls. "Patty said you'd probably spend the night out here so you wouldn't get barked at, but she didn't say she'd already bit you."

"Bit me?" He chuckled. "Hell, it wasn't that bad. We did better than most."

"She didn't say anything about the sale. It's this paint purchase she's grumbling about." Savannah lapped her large wool shirt jacket around her and folded her arms. "Apparently we don't need the paint."

"I felt sorry for him. And for the crazy old guy who thought he was going to run him through the ring. I was all set to light into him for letting the horse get like this, and then I realized he didn't do it on purpose. Retired guy, doesn't have much . . ."

The whole scene was an embarrassment. Thinking back on it, he should've minded his own damn business and kept walking. He sighed. "An inspector would see this animal and slap a fine on the old fellow. So I asked him what he'd take for the paint. Thought he was gonna bust out cryin'. Just feed him for me, the guy said."

Savannah clucked softly. "He looks sick."

"I had a vet look him over just to make sure I wasn't bringing in anything contagious. He just hasn't been eatin' too good lately."

"Your typical understatement. Can you save him?"

"Oh, yeah. I've seen worse. Start by feeding him small amounts of leafy alfalfa every few hours, kinda like feeding a new baby. He'll pick up." He leaned his shoulder against the doorframe of the stall, cradling the mug in his hands. Had to admit, the poor animal was hard to look at. "This I can fix."

"You're a pretty good fixer."

"If I'd gone to veterinary school like you kept telling me to, I could fix a lot more. But I can worm him. You can tell by his coat he needs worming. I checked his teeth, which might be part of his problem, but I can fix that with a file." He sipped his coffee. It felt warm going down, like her compliment. "Did you know I can float teeth? I apprenticed with an old-time farrier. People think they need a vet to float the teeth. Depends on the state you're in and what the regulations are, but a good farrier with the right tools is probably more skilled with a file than most vets." He turned around again. The horse's eyes were at half-mast. "I can take care of this guy. This is something I can't turn my back on, you know?"

"I'm beginning to."

"Mom didn't say anything the whole way home. Neither

did Mick. I don't think it was because of the horse, although that's not goin' down too good, either." He studied the horse, mentally adding a couple hundred pounds of flesh. With his tobiano markings, he'd be worth more per pound than the calves they'd sold were worth. "It wasn't as bad as I feared, not as good as I hoped."

"The sale?" she asked, and he grunted, hoping she'd be satisfied with that. "Was it enough?"

"Enough to get us by." He smiled. "But the good news is that while cattlemen are a dime a dozen, you can name your price for a farrier right now. Got yourself a rare breed on that score. I'll do better than get us by."

She touched the sleeve of his denim jacket. "Clay, you work so hard."

"I don't mind that. It's what I know, what I'm good for." He studied the bandage, turned his hand palm up, and made a fist around the white tape. "There's so much of it that's out of my hands." Which was hard to admit, especially now, especially to her.

"I used to hear people who came into the store talk about livestock prices. I didn't think it affected me, so it wasn't that important. Only mildly interesting."

"It's not just the price of beef. It's getting so this land is worth more to developers than guys like us can come up with."

"But your family's been here for a long time."

"That doesn't count for much anymore. The Indians were here a long time before that. When people with money and power start looking at an area like this and licking their chops, they can make it tough to hold on."

"Maybe another source of income would make it a little easier," she suggested.

"That's what the horseshoeing is, a second income. The cattle business supports the land. The shoeing supports the household."

"You and Uncle Mick can't—"

"We've been hiring a haying crew, and I bring in a custom combiner to free me up in the summer. I don't do much horseshoeing in the winter, been turning down a lot of jobs in the spring when we're calving."

"I'll help you," she said, her blue eyes childlike with her eagerness, her arms folded around the big wool jacket like a drawstring, as though she clutched a sack full of surprises for him. She searched his eyes. "You don't believe me," she somehow concluded.

"Of course I do." He said it too quickly. She was still searching, needing something from him. Recognition, maybe. "You've taken a shine to these old horses, and I don't know when I've eaten this good."

"I met a woman in the survivor support group, or whatever it's called, who says she knows you. I guess I'm not supposed to divulge identities, but you shoe her horses, and she seems to have a lot of—"

"Margo Ross?" He drained the coffee mug and set it aside. "I saw her car. She's told me about her problems. You're not divulging anything."

"Do they all tell you their problems?"

"Some do. I'm a captive audience while they've got me underneath their horse."

"Even when you're not under the horse, these horse-women seem to have things to show and tell." She took his bandaged hand between hers, lowered her head over the sandwich she'd made, and opened her mouth as though she would have a bite. But she only meant to warm his injured hand with her breath.

He trembled inside.

She raised her head and smiled. "Do they whisper their secrets? There seems to be a lot of whispering in this horse business."

"I'm not the whispering kind."

"But you're the listening kind."

"I guess I appear to be when I'm workin' and they're talkin'." With his free hand he lifted the hair at her temple, touched her smooth forehead with his thumb. "I wouldn't have taken you for the jealous kind."

"I'm not," she protested adamantly.

"That's good. I already had one of those, and I never did figure out how to handle a problem when it's all in somebody else's head."

"I got the impression Roxie was the one with the roving eye. If that was the case, then nobody could blame you for doing a little roving of your—"

"I didn't." He held her gaze with his. "The marriage didn't work. It was like a dying animal that couldn't be helped, so we put it out of its misery. Simple as that. Getting jealous seems like wasted energy."

"It is. That's why I don't." She backed away. "I'm not."

"You want me to whisper?" He smiled and reached for her. "Come here. Let me tell you a secret."

"I have an idea," she said.

"Okay, yours first." He drew her closer. "Come whisper it to me."

"It's an *idea*. And it might be a good one, so I want you to hear it."

"If it's a good one, we want to keep it quiet so nobody steals it from us."

"I'm serious."

"Me, too." He lowered his head, traced her temple with the tip of his nose, and felt her shiver. Cold nose. He exchanged nose for lips, filled her ear with his warm breath, and whispered, "I've never been more serious."

She closed her eyes and lifted her chin to let the shivers run their course. Cold on warm, warm on cold, the mixture made shiver-beads that rolled down the side of her neck and played her vertebrae like a xylophone. She sucked a breath of air that was sweet with him, all rain-damp and earthy. It made her feel a little light-headed, and she didn't want to lose her train of thought, which might be worth something to him if he'd listen and consider it.

She leaned back. "Margo said she wanted to talk to you about retiring an old horse of hers."

"Retiring?" He scowled. "Putting him down? I do hooves and sometimes teeth, but that's one job I'll leave to the vets."

"She wants you to board it, and she expects to pay you handsomely." His scowl deepened, as if she were suddenly speaking in tongues. "Clay, you're taking these horses in for nothing. People who love their horses want to be able to put them out to pasture when retirement time comes."

He laughed. "None of these horses came with retirement plans. Their former owners don't have retirement plans for themselves, never mind horses. They plan to work till they die, which is when they finally get put out to pasture, if there's any pasture left. The only retirement plan for a rancher is to sell out."

"I'm not talking about ranchers. I'm talking about Margo." She grabbed handfuls of his damp jacket sleeves. "Maybe you're taking in the wrong horses."

He glanced over his shoulder at the sorry creature in the stall. "These are the ones that needed taking in."

"But you *bought* them, or else you adopted them. If you boarded them, you'd make money."

"Board? Honey . . ." He shook his head, chuckling. "This ain't New York. Nobody's gonna want to board horses out here."

"*Margo does.*" She tugged on his sleeves, trying to shake him, to get him to listen. He listened to everyone else, didn't he? "She's not looking for a place to board and ride. She wants to retire her dear old horse, and she trusts *you*. Clay, this could be a good sideline."

He stared at her for a long moment, as though suddenly he couldn't figure out where she'd come from.

"You know, I don't do this to make money. I raise cattle to make money. I shoe horses for a second income. I might take on a horse like that if I see a need, but if I tried to turn it into an enterprise . . ." He glanced over his shoulder again. "It wouldn't seem right."

"Why not?"

"I don't know." With an exasperated sigh, he stepped back. "I don't wanna go around looking for rich old horses, for one thing."

"Maybe that's how I could help."

His eyes narrowed. A hint of suspicion, maybe curiosity. "How would you go about it?"

"I'd start with Margo."

"What would you charge her?"

"Well, we talked about that. We . . ." Arms folded tightly, she braced her back against the stall door. "Aunt Billie and I went to the hospital to see her."

"There *was* a sick friend?" Amazement turned to near de-light. "You really went somewhere to see somebody?"

What had he thought?

"A medal isn't necessary, though I'll take a little pat on the back." But she kept her back to the stall door, didn't give him access. "Margo was in the hospital. She just had more surgery. She's doing very well, thank you, considering how scary it is to have it come back. We talked a lot about horses, which is better than talking about cancer, even when the topic is retirement. She talked about what it would be worth to her to know that her old horse was well cared-for."

Savannah shrugged, a little uncomfortable with how Clay was looking at her. "Money isn't a problem for her, so I guess I'd charge her as much as I could get her to pay. And then I'd get her to spread the word to her rich, horse-loving friends, which I think she'd gladly do. How much room do you have?"

"There's room for Margo's horse."

"No more?"

"That's what I keep saying. This is the last one. But I always seem to find room for the next hard-luck horse that comes along, and if Margo's sick again . . ."

"That's not the point, Clay, she's not asking us to do her a favor. This won't be about favors. This will be different," she promised. And, oh, the enthusiasm felt fine and toasty, like a sip of warm brandy making its way to her belly.

She could help *him.*

"We'll have a contract, so we're agreeing to provide only certain care. The owner will be responsible for extras, like veterinary bills. Starting with Margo. We could just try it and see how it goes."

"I like that *we* part, but I don't know about the rest."

"This is going to be my responsibility. Would be," she amended quickly. "If we decided to do it. Of course, I don't know that much about horses, so that's where the *we* comes in. You're the expert."

He smiled. "Does that mean my name goes on the contract?"

"It could be *our* names. You're the one they'd come for. I'd be the lackey."

"What's a lackey?"

"A stable girl."

"Woman," he corrected. "This is what it'll take to make you a stable woman?"

She laughed and punched overhead with a fist. "Finally!"

"Pretty soon people will be saying, 'Look what those crazy Keoghs are up to.' And you'll be the stable one, so I'm the one they'll be coming for."

"Not that way," she said with a laugh.

"What way, then?" He reached for her, filled his big hands with the lapels of her wool jacket. His eyes sparkled with mischief. "How about you coming for me? I'll make you feel like the luckiest lackey in Wyoming."

"How many are there?"

"We don't go in for lackeys much. You're the only one I know." He took her face in his hands. "The only one I want to know."

His kiss was breathtaking. At first she didn't know anything but that this felt good; it felt right. She lifted her arms to his shoulders, fastening herself to him, fingers in his damp hair, mouth greeting mouth, tongue touching tongue. He was all goodness and strength, all wonder and delight. She reached and held and hoped to absorb it all, directly through her pores. Pure essence of Clay sluicing through her body, lighting her dark corners, mending her broken parts.

Ah, the pleasure, the pleasure. The tickle of his bandage, the abrasion of his calluses, the comfort of his caring fingers, of his skin touching hers, caressing her back, pressing the swell of her hips, the vale of her spine—he was gathering her to him. Power radiated from the places he touched. Power surged from deep in her belly, power rushing to meet power. His touch restored her.

Until it strayed to her breasts. If he hadn't touched them both, she might have forgotten the difference. But one welcomed him, and the other didn't. It hung there, rude and stupid, unnatural, lacking feeling, lacking joy. A little piece of death.

She jumped away from him as though she'd touched too much fire.

Dazed, he stared down at his empty hands as though he didn't know what to make of them, or of this . . . or of her as he lifted his gaze.

"I'm sorry, honey, did I hurt you?"

"No," she said quickly. He looked a little scared. Maybe she should let him think it hurt so he wouldn't try it again. She glanced at the bandage on the hand he'd withdrawn, then shook her head. "No, I don't feel anything . . . much."

"What do you mean?"

"It's not . . . it doesn't hurt. I just don't want you to touch me like that, because I'm not . . ."

"Not what?" Staring at her chest, he frowned as if he were trying hard to see through her coat. "If that's not your breast, it sure is a good imitation."

She nodded. It ought to be good. She'd paid dearly. "I don't want you to touch me like that." Her voice had gone all raspy.

"All right! I'm sorry." He tried to touch her cheek, but she turned it away from him. He groaned. "Don't look at me like that. *I'm sorry*."

"You caught me off guard."

"What are you guarding, Savannah? I would never hurt you. All you have to do is clue me in a little."

"I did. I *did* clue you in." It was true, but it was also true that since she'd clued him, she'd kissed him, and that was a clue as well. He watched her, and she knew that the more he watched, the more clues he'd see. This was her body. These were her terms.

She shifted her stance and declared, "If you want to fuck, we'll fuck." The hell with her silly ideas.

"Jesus, that's not . . ."

She wasn't looking at him now, but she knew he'd swallowed hard. She could hear it. His pride, perhaps? Of course he wanted to fuck. They both did. How bad did he want it? How bad could she make it?

But he wasn't interested in how. He wanted to know—"*Why*, Savannah? Why do you say it like that?"

"Oh, stop being such a saint. It's a perfectly good word. We're married, Clay. We can say it; we can do it." She unzipped her jeans as she whirled on her bootheels. "Where should we do it? Outside? Inside? Where could you sit? You're a big guy. It's easier if I straddle you. You can . . ." She whirled again at the sound of his footsteps. "Where are you going?"

"To get this guy something to eat. I know what his problem is, and I know how to handle it."

"It *is* a good imitation," she shouted at his back.

He stopped in his tracks, but he did not turn. He waited. He was fresh out of clues.

"I had a mastectomy," she began quietly, her voice a bit shaky, but not from anything so silly as tears. From shouting. She nodded and steadied her whole self. "They took what was inside and left the shell. Basically, the skin. Then they rebuilt the breast from my own tissue. The miracle of plastic surgery. And it *is*, it's remarkable." She lowered her head as she slipped her hand inside her coat. "I can't feel much here. I don't have a real nipple—I have a tattooed bump." She looked up at him finally, offered what smile she could muster. "So that's it, that's what's underneath my bra. And that's what I'm guarding."

"Savannah . . ." He came back to her, moving cautiously. She watched him, anticipating what he would say, the next questions he would ask. "This operation saved your life, didn't it?"

Not one of the questions on her list.

She nodded briefly. "For the time being."

"Then who cares how it looks?"

"I do. I care." But suddenly not so much about the look of a battered breast as about a new feel of it from the inside out, a new awareness that it guarded the deeper secret of her racing heart.

"Okay," he allowed, carefully cupping his hand around her face. "Okay, I care. I care that it hurt you before, and I care that it worries you now, that it makes you sad and shy and scared. But I care more that it kept you alive."

"I want us to—" She tipped her head back and closed her eyes. "To have sex. It's always been good with you. I mean, you've always been very considerate. Attentive. You've always made sure . . ."

"I haven't always known what I was doing. I do now. I

gotta tell you a secret." He traced the contours of her face with two fingers as he spoke. "When we were kids, I had to be attentive because I was hoping you'd give me some hint about what the hell I was supposed do. All guys know for sure is that somehow you gotta get in there and pump like crazy. I always wondered how you knew so much."

"I read women's magazines. And I knew what felt good when you—when you did it. And there was nothing wrong with me then. I was perfectly—" She put her arms around him and buried her face against his neck. "We're not kids, and I want us to have sex, and so do you. I just don't want you to . . . can't we just . . ."

"I need you to trust me, Savannah. I want you to forget yourself and become part of me, while I do the same, trusting you. I want us to fall asleep together and wake up together. I want to make it last."

"You were always good at that."

"I'm talkin' a lifetime."

Chapter 16

Clay left the house before daybreak the next morning.

Between the bawling cows and the hungry horse in the barn, not to mention the all-over ache his wife had left him with, he hadn't gotten much sleep. He'd gone over emaciated Ol' Paint's feeding schedule with Uncle Mick and discussed other chores. Before the winter chores started, Clay had decided to take on all the horseshoeing he could fit into his day. Weekends, too—might as well shoe at a couple of those three-day events he'd been offered. If he didn't, they might stop calling. Charlotte had been warning him to cut back or he'd soon be walking like an old man, but fall was a good time for horsing around. Lots of shows and events, lots of work. Except for some pain once in a while, he had no real call to slow down. Plenty of call to work harder.

He stopped at a diner for breakfast, something he normally didn't do. Not when he was traveling alone, which was the way he normally traveled. He took a stool at the counter—table for loners—and ordered the "Big Man's Breakfast," complete with eggs, flapjacks, bacon, sausage, a pile of toast, jelly in a pouch, juice, and coffee. He ate the bacon, drank the coffee, finally walked away from the rest, feeling no more satisfied than he had when he'd walked in.

Outside the diner, he glanced through the window at the row of backs hunched over the counter. Truckers, some of them. Old ranchers, one hitchhiker—now, that was something you didn't see much anymore. Clay had offered him a ride east, but the kid was headed west. Everybody was hungry for something, and each one was trying to fill up on eggs.

Clay pointed his pickup east, toward Haroldson's place, where he would pull a bunch of shoes, trim up the feet, and leave them bare until spring. He had plenty of work to do, and he wasn't hungry for anything. Had everything he'd ever wanted at home. Didn't matter whether she wanted him or not, as long as she needed him. A person could do without what he wanted, but needs were different. Certain needs had to be taken care of.

Being needed was a good thing. A man with skilled hands and a strong back was sorely needed just about any place you looked these days. Clay had all kinds of work to do.

Claudia was busy getting dressed for school. She'd told her mother she wouldn't need her until it was time for her hair. Savannah smiled to herself as she knocked on the door between the bathroom and the den. It was early. Surely Clay had time for breakfast. She wanted to apologize, to explain, to somehow expunge that awful moment from the record of last night.

She'd loved the sweet way he'd touched her face, loved the kissing, loved feeling safe and warm in his arms. She'd loved feeling loved. But she'd acted like a shrew, shrinking away from his touch, making him feel at fault for a problem that wasn't his. She wanted him to understand that. Her flaws and foolishness had nothing to do with him, even though he had to do with her. He was hers, her husband, and she was his wife, but there were parts of her he didn't need, wouldn't want. They were only for looks. He should just—

No answer. No breakfast. He'd left ungodly early.

Claudia asked for Froot Loops and raisin toast with peanut butter. There weren't any Fruit Loops. She wanted cookies, then. She couldn't have cookies. Then she didn't want anything else. It would be a long wait for lunch, Savannah said. Half a piece of toast, orange juice, and a chewable vitamin weren't much thinking fuel. Claudia thought she'd said *thinking fool,* which sounded silly enough to get her to finish the toast.

On the way to the bus stop Savannah ground the pickup gears only once, which got her mind completely off apologies and onto the progress she was making. Clay had let her try driving Uncle Mick's pickup when they were kids, but he'd taken over after some major grinding on the gears. She'd said she was never going to drive a stupid stick shift again. She wouldn't need to. She'd buy *good* cars and hire people to drive them. But she was back to driving Uncle Mick's pickup, and she was getting the hang of it, driving her daughter to the bus stop. She'd charged forward and rolled backward with and without style over the intervening years, but she and Claudia were getting themselves to the bus stop now. This was progress.

Afterward, she went to the barn to do the morning chores she'd lately claimed as her own. This, too, was progress. A new routine, something she could handle, which gave her ideas about doing more.

Uncle Mick was measuring out the new horse's ration of hay. "I don't know what that boy's thinking," he complained as Savannah approached. "It's like having a baby you have to feed every four hours. I had me a feelin' when I saw that ol' man and his damn horse trailer."

"And now you're stuck doing the work."

"Ain't hardly no work to it. You just have to be here, is all." He turned to her, smiling, rocking his cap by the brim as though he were tipping it to her. "But where else would I be? I don't mind doin' it, long as I don't forget. That'd be awful if I forgot."

"I'll help, and we'll remind each other. I'm here all day, too."

"You can take my ol' pickup anytime you like, you know."

"Thanks, Uncle Mick. I'm doing better with it. Slipped around in the mud a little bit this morning, but I didn't panic, and we didn't get stuck."

"Good girl." He turned to the wheelbarrow filled with dry, gray-green alfalfa hay and peeled a chunk off the partial bale. "This is how much he gets, about a pound. But we can't be overfeeding."

"Let's tack up a schedule next to the stall and tie a pencil up there with it so we can check off when we feed. That should help us remember."

Uncle Mick was so taken with the idea that he rounded up paper, pencil, string, and staple gun, which he said "oughta fix 'er down." He helped Savannah feed the rest of the horses, and they talked about an idea he'd been toying with for a new system of feeding troughs that he thought he could make himself. He wanted to use cement, but he knew that would be a major project. It pleased him when Savannah asked how major it would be. He showed her a plan he'd sketched out some time ago. She thought it a wonderful design. He shuffled his papers and beamed.

"But we'd have to rent one of them mixers," he said.

"Are they expensive?"

"Never rented one."

"I could call and check."

The old man shrugged. "I'm always thinkin' up stuff like this and sketchin' it out. I don't ever show nobody. I don't know what it would cost."

"But it's a good idea, and it would cut the time it takes for feeding."

"Some of the horses you gotta bring in and feed in the stalls or they don't get their share."

"But not all of them, and not all the time. Is it the cost? Patty says there isn't any money."

"We've always had all we needed." He nodded toward the stall where Old Paint was still noisily grinding hay. "He don't need money. Regular water and grass don't cost nuthin', and that's all he needs. Water and grass."

"Grain, too."

"That's a luxury, grain is. Like a chunk of meat with your potatoes."

"You can't live on nothing but potatoes."

"My grandparents did." Mick laid his plans on the top of a wooden grain box, shoved his hands into his pockets, and moved back a few steps, as though distancing himself from a dream. "I don't need much money. Been drivin' the same pickup for thirty years, and I plan to keep it going another thirty. I earn my keep around here. Least I think I do. My brother got all the brains in the family, but I ain't afraid to work. Got good hands." He nodded toward the stall. "Now that we got this schedule up, I won't forget. Every time I walk into the barn, I'll see this poor scarecrow. I just, you know, like to think things up."

"Me, too." She eyed the horse. "Scarecrow was the one Dorothy loved best. Good name." She touched Uncle Mick's arm. "I might take you up on your offer to use your pickup. Wouldn't Clay be surprised if I got my driver's license?"

Mick laughed. "Wouldn't he be surprised if you drove home in a cement mixer?"

After she left the barn, she drew herself up to her full height, full breadth, full strength, and called Heather in New York. Heather was more than she could handle at times—no one could pump her up or deflate her faster—but they were important to each other. Had been since the first day they met. Heather was important to Savannah, anyway. Her opinion was important, her approval, her mere notice. After she'd left Wyoming, there had been few real friends.

Heather was genuinely glad to hear from her, but skeptical. Especially when Savannah told her that she needed her advice about something.

"My advice? Savannah, why do you always call me for advice *after*, waaay after—"

"No, this is serious. I've been thinking about you a lot, about things you've said, things you've written. Inspirational, really, the way you're always writing about people who champion causes."

"Savannah, what's wrong?"

"Nothing's wrong."

"Is the cowboy treating you all right? If he's giving you any cause to regret jumping into . . . Do you need any help, Savannah?"

"I need some advice."

"It's too late for a prenuptial agreement."

"*He's* not looking for advice, dear, I am." Savannah took a deep breath. "How do you start a cause?"

"Start a *cause*? Seriously, Savannah, if you and Claudia need help, I'm there. You said you wanted to go home, that's what you told me before you left, you said that was where you really really wanted to be. But if that's not working out—"

"A cause other than myself, Heather. I'm . . ." There were times when she hated Heather's helpfulness. It made her feel weak. She was already looking for a chair. "I joined a cancer survivors' group. Well, not really joined—so far I've attended one session. And I participated. I talked a little bit. I'm . . ." She propped her elbows on the kitchen counter, bumped a stool aside with her hip. "I want to do something, Heather."

"You're getting some counseling."

"As I said, I've only been once."

"It's not the thought that counts, Savannah, it's taking the first step, getting out and getting started and getting involved. Oh, Savannah, I'm so glad! This is just what you need. A cause. A march against breast cancer. What a marvelous spokesman you'll be, too. I mean, everyone knows that fabulous face of yours, and when you come out of that closet you call Wyoming and tell your story—when you remind people how important it is to get those mammograms . . ."

A breath? Was she stopping for air? Not the way she blew it out.

"Heather, what are you doing?" Savannah asked.

"I just had one myself, and I'm not even old enough, but I insisted. And told the technician my best friend—"

"That's not the cause. Heather, are you—"

"Affordable health care?"

"Good cause, but no."

"Single-parent adoption?"

"Are you smoking again?"

"Not every day. What's the cause?"

"I want to start a retirement home for horses."

There was a long pause.

"Are you still there, Heather?"

"I'm finishing my cigarette while I wait politely for the punch line."

"Does it sound stupid? Maybe I should call it something else. But if I use words like 'rescue' or 'shelter,' people will get the wrong idea. 'Retirement' sounds more dignified, and if you could see the horses, you wouldn't think it was such a stupid idea. People are always ready to help animals, Heather. What happens to a horse when he can't carry a rider or pull a cart anymore?"

"They shoot them, don't they?"

Savannah wasn't laughing.

"Okay, sorry. Playing a little devil's advocate here. Seriously, what happens to a horse when he can't work anymore?"

"My husband takes him in if he's within a thousand-mile radius of the Lazy K."

"The Lazy K," Heather echoed, stretching each syllable until it sagged. "That sounds like a cause in itself. Maybe your husband needs a support group."

"Do you see why I stopped calling you when I started running out of options and couldn't pay the bills?"

"You didn't tell me you were in such—"

"Because it drives me crazy when you have all the answers except the one for the question I'm asking, which you think is a joke."

"No, I don't." Pause. "You're serious, aren't you?"

Savannah let silence be her answer.

"I'm not laughing, Savannah. I love animals. I just don't happen to know much about horses or cowboys, and neither strikes me as the kind of cause . . . But they've grabbed you."

"Yes."

"Grabbed you by the heart."

"That's right."

"This cowboy you've known since high school."

"Technically, I've known him longer than that, but I've never really . . ." *Known* him. Never made her heart available for knowing him. Until now?

She'd married him. She'd damn well better know him.

"That's right, Heather, he's grabbed me by the heart, but that's not the cause. What I'm asking you is—"

"Oh, yes, it is, my friend. If it's a good cause, it grabs the heart that feeds the hand that writes the check. And I'll believe it's a good cause if you say so." Another puff on that infernal cigarette. "If I could see you, you wouldn't even have to say so. You've got such an honest face."

"It's an *idea*. I'm trying to propose an idea, if you'd just listen. And *then* I want your advice. I'm not getting all sentimental over this, Heather. I'm the practical one in this family."

"Which family?"

"*My* family. I'm back home now, and I—I have a family. And I have an idea, so, just listen. There *are* retirement homes for horses. They do exist."

"Where?"

"I know of one in Florida."

"And?"

"Well, that's the only one I know of, but I'm just getting into this. Now hear me out. You're the one with all the lofty ideals, Heather. This should be right up your alley."

"Not *my* alley. I've never had a horse in my alley."

"No, but you've got Indians in your cupboard."

"My bookcase," Heather said with a laugh. "Yes, dear girl, that's my idea of a cause. Now, what's your idea?"

"Well, I know there are horse people out there who would love to retire their geriatric horses at a beautiful refuge in the mountains of Wyoming. People who would pay well for the privilege. I just have to find them. But what about the underprivileged horse? What about the poor old guy who can no longer afford to feed his poor old horse that nobody wants?"

"He calls The Humane Society?"

"Animal shelters are burgeoning with dogs and cats. Animal lovers are coming up with all kinds of programs—foster care for dogs, Adopt-a-Wolf, Save the Whale. I want to help the ranchers like my husband who are willing to put homeless horses out to pasture."

"How about Sponsor-a-Nag?"

"Heather!"

"Pull-a-Plug?"

"Now, that's catchy, but I doubt if I can use it to sell this cause."

"Your face will sell the cause, Savannah. Just the way it sold underwear."

"It wasn't my face that sold underwear."

"It sure wasn't your boobs. Is that what you thought? Think again." Puff again. Oh, how Savannah wished her friend would stop— "When I ordered a bra from that catalog, my only thought was, This woman looks friendly and relaxed, not to mention beautiful. That must be some bra. Gotta get one.

"Now, that's some face, Savannah. You put that face together with a needy horse, people are gonna think, Don't I know her from somewhere? What's up with this beautiful woman and this pathetic beast? And wham!" Across the miles, Savannah could hear Heather slap her desk. "You've got 'em hooked."

"I wasn't planning to do any sort of personal campaigning," Savannah hedged. There was only one way to put her face on a campaign, and that would involve a camera. "I was thinking you might have some connections."

"Maybe we could trade connections."

Savannah groaned.

Heather laughed. "You sound good, Savannah. You know I'll help you any way I can. But if you want to sell a cause, use your face."

Once a month, the highway patrol gave road tests in Sunbonnet.

Savannah had been told that if she showed up, even without an appointment, the trooper could probably work her in. She took a chance, got Aunt Billie to go with her, but she was determined to pass the test on Uncle Mick's pickup. She was the only tester to show up.

She was a little rusty, but the trooper took pity on her when she explained that she'd been living in New York City, where sane people didn't drive. At least, that appeared to be the deciding moment. He was pretty sympathetic when she stalled trying to parallel-park. He allowed that she just needed a little time to get used to a standard transmission, and she promised to practice. She could tell he liked her smile. She wondered how much she could sell him with it, and she almost asked him how he felt about geriatric horses. But when he added up her test score and marked her "passed," she decided not to push her luck.

After she dropped Aunt Billie off at the store, Savannah decided to stop at school and surprise Claudia. She had surprises for everyone, surprises up both sleeves. The first surprise was on her, though. School wasn't out yet. But Mary Larpenter was glad she'd stopped in, glad to see her up and about, hoped she'd kicked that old whatever-it-was she'd been having such problems with, had no problem with Claudia leaving school a few minutes early.

And, once summoned, Claudia vacated her seat like a princess whose carriage had come for her.

On the way back to the pickup Savannah glimpsed a familiar mop of straw-colored hair cutting across the street. Cheyenne was alone. Savannah waved her down with the yellow sheet of paper the state trooper had given her. "I just passed my driver's test," she shouted.

Cheyenne almost smiled. "Cool."

"School's not out yet, is it?" Savannah asked as they all fell into step together. The pickup was parked in the shade across the street from the school.

"I have a study hall the last period, so I said I had cramps and my mom said I could go home."

"How much of that is true?"

"I have a study hall the last period."

"Well, I'm celebrating," Savannah proclaimed, arms forming a high, wide V. "We were talking about hairstyles when you came out to the ranch, and I was thinking we could all go over to the Tip Top Shop and get ourselves fixed up."

"Get our hair done?"

"I'm buying. Haircuts all around."

Claudia grabbed her late-in-the-day ponytail protectively. "I'm not getting my hair cut."

"Or nails," Savannah added. "Leanne offered me a free set."

"How about a dye job?" Cheyenne asked, warming to the proposal. "Would she dye my hair black?"

"I think she'd have to get parental permission for that. I think there's a law." Savannah laughed as she took Cheyenne by the arm. "Come on. I know she's got a Coke machine. You can call your mother when we get there and let her know where you are."

"Yeah, maybe show her how that's done."

"She's not home?" Savannah opened the pickup door and gestured for Claudia to climb over the driver's seat. "What about Dallas?"

"He went home with Reno. Mom's working today. She does the books for the grain elevator and Grumpy's. She says she's really good at it when it's not her money." Cheyenne peeked at herself in the mirror on the driver's side door. "Don't you think black hair makes a person look more mature?"

"Let's see what Leanne has to say about styling your hair. She's really good at it when it's not her hair." Savannah wagged a finger at Cheyenne. "Don't you dare quote me."

Leanne welcomed the trio with an offer of drinks while she moved magazines off the two waiting chairs. The Tip Top was a one-person operation, but there was a shampoo chair, a manicure station, and a styling chair—"very uptown." Leanne said she wanted a second styling chair—"But they're real spendy"—so that her customers wouldn't have to play musical chairs when she worked more than one in at a time. "Some people said this town wouldn't support a beauty shop, but I've paid off almost all my loans."

She had just finished putting a rinse in Mrs. Ellertson's white hair. Claudia frowned as she watched her fluff the sparse hair with a plastic pick. "It looks blue," she said. "Did you want it to be blue?"

"I don't want it to be dull," the old woman said. "I hate dull."

"Me, too. I hate dull." Claudia's reflection joined Mrs. Ellertson's in the mirror behind the styling chair. "Is black dull?"

"Not at all," the old woman said. "Your hair is beautiful. I had a friend with beautiful black hair that was just as beautiful when she went gray. Salt and pepper, you know. She never had to do anything to it. She was lucky."

"Well, personally, I love dull hair," Leanne said as she offered Mrs. Ellertson a hand mirror, then spun the chair. "It brings me the most interesting customers."

"I'd come to see you anyway, dear. How else would I keep up on the latest news? Old people only tell you who died." She searched the hand mirror for a glimpse of the side of herself she seldom saw. "I want to know who got born, who got married. People get together and split up so fast around here, you need a score card to keep track."

"Why do you need to keep track?" Savannah wondered idly. She thought she remembered the woman coming into the store occasionally, somebody's grandmother; she didn't remember whose.

If the woman knew who Savannah was, she didn't say. Nor did she smile. She simply set the mirror down and reached for her purse. "I need some kind of amusement. I gave my television set away when my eyes started going bad. I listen to books on tape, and I come to the beauty shop."

Claudia peered up at her. "Maybe you need new glasses."

The old woman laughed. "If they get any thicker, I'll be walking around with my nose to the ground."

After Mrs. Ellertson left, Savannah ordered three haircuts. Leanne started with Claudia, who needed fresh ends, while Cheyenne and Savannah paged through style books. "Radical" was Cheyenne's word for the styles that caught her eye, and radical they were. Savannah kept steering for the middle of the road, and in the end they found a compromise: an easy style jazzed up with some color highlights. "Subtle," Savannah advised. "The kind that have people saying, 'Your hair looks great. What have you done to it?' Not, 'Ohhh, my Gaawd, what have you done!' "

"Yeah," Claudia said. "Don't make it blue. Blue hair looks funny."

"Don't tell Mrs. Ellertson," Leanne said. "She's my best customer. So tell me, what's going on at the Lazy K these days, Claudia Ann?"

"We have another new horse, but I haven't seen it yet."

"He's a special-needs horse," Savannah said. "He has some special needs. Like food."

"Clay has a soft spot for the sad cases, doesn't he?"

"His mother would say it's in his head."

"But you know better. The only thing soft about that man is his heart." Leanne slid Savannah a playful smile. " 'Course, I'm only guessing."

"Well, I'm developing a theory about soft hearts. They're incurable, so you might as well work with them. How does a retirement home for horses strike you? The next Lazy K sideline."

"Strikes me your husband must have gone off the deep end."

"No way, Leanne. The correct answer is that it strikes you as a bolt of visionary genius."

"Your idea?"

Savannah nodded, smiling.

"Obviously, you two were made for each other."

Leanne worked on Cheyenne next. While her color was "processing," Cheyenne painted Claudia's nails and Savannah took the focal chair. Leanne confessed to being a little nervous about cutting a famous model's hair.

"You should have seen me when I was on chemo," Savannah said. She almost wished she had pictures. It occurred to her that if she had some, she'd have no problem slapping them on the counter. The image of such daring made her laugh. "Don't think of me as a model, Leanne. Think of me as a visionary genius."

Later, the bell on the shop door tinkled, and Clay ducked inside, looking exactly like the proverbial bull entering the china shop. "Saw Uncle Mick's pickup outside. Had to see for myself if he was getting his first real professional haircut." He glanced at the girls, whose heads were now bent over Cheyenne's nails on the manicure table. "I see everybody else is."

"Not me!" Claudia protested. "I just got a little bit trimmed, hardly any. I'm never getting my hair cut off. But look at my fingernails." Proudly she displayed her pink-tipped hands. "Cheyenne painted them for me."

"Very pretty." Clay's smile was quick and tight. "I went to pick you up at school. Had me worried there for a bit."

"Mommy came and got me early 'cause we're celebrating."

He glanced at Savannah. "What are we celebrating?"

"Mommy passed her . . ."

"Muffin, that's my surprise," Savannah admonished. Her eyes met Clay's. Hers shone, urging his to share the light. *I'm sorry about the worry, but . . .* "I passed my driver's test."

"Great." His tone was uncharacteristically flat. "I didn't know you were thinking of taking it."

"I didn't really think about it. I just did it."

"And Mommy's going to start up—"

"Claudia," Savannah warned. "Mommy's not going to start up anything. We were just talking about all kinds of wild things while Leanne worked on us. What do you think, Clay?"

"Everybody looks great. I, uh . . ." He shoved his hands in

his pockets. "You all look beautiful. You do good work, Leanne."

Cheyenne blew on her purple-glitter nails. "I wanted to dye my hair black, but Savannah said we should use highlights. Can you tell the difference?"

"Oh, yeah. It shines on its own, like it's full of sunlight."

The girl beamed, basking in the compliment. "Really?"

"You know what?" Clay clapped his hands to his denim shirt pockets, slid them down his torso as though he were wiping them off, checking for cigarettes, floundering somehow. "I've been working all day, and I feel like the pig in the powder room. If nobody needs a lift, I'll head home and clean up for supper."

Savannah followed him out the door. "Clay?" She missed the last porch step in her rush to catch him, bobbled but caught herself. She was surprised to find that it was already getting dark. Where had the time gone? "I didn't mean to stay in town this long. I think there's plenty of leftovers in the refrigerator for tonight."

"You know what I think?" He closed the door to the pickup and retraced his steps, obviously choosing his words, tempering his tone. "I think you oughta let me know if you're gonna pick Claudia up."

"I wasn't planning—"

"Because I told her I'd be there to pick her up today, which I've been doing as often as I can so she doesn't have to ride the bus every day. Because the way I remember it, riding the bus both ways makes a long day for a little kid. So I sat in front of the school and watched the doors until the stream of kids slowed to a trickle. Then I went looking for her in her classroom; there was nobody around. I called home, stopped over to Roxie's, nobody knew anything."

"I'm sorry. Uncle Mick—"

"I didn't talk to him. Didn't see him, didn't expect him to know. My mother—you know how she is—said you weren't around, figured you were messin' around out to the barn or maybe, you know . . . gone."

"Gone?"

He swallowed hard, his eyes glittering. "Or something. What am I supposed to think, Savannah? Couple weeks ago you wouldn't hardly leave the house."

"I wanted to surprise you."

"You scared the livin' shit . . ." He shook his head to clear it, or the air. "You had me worried. I was worried about both of you."

"I'm sorry. I called to find out about taking the driver's test, and one step led to another, and I found myself actually taking steps." Softly, wishfully, she added, "I thought you'd be pleased."

"I'm glad you got your license." He lifted his hand to her hair but drew it back without touching, as though he didn't want to mess it up. "Looks real nice. You look like . . ." He gave a mirthless chuckle. "You oughta be in pictures."

"We'll be home soon," she said to his back as he headed for his pickup.

Patty and Mick were sitting at the kitchen table eating leftover stew when Savannah herded Claudia through the back door. "I'm sorry about the leftovers." She whispered to Claudia to sit by Uncle Mick, then took a bowl down from the cupboard. "I didn't plan this very well."

"Plan what?" Patty asked, as though she still thought they'd been out to the barn all this time.

"I borrowed Uncle Mick's truck so I could . . ." Savannah turned to Mick. She needed somebody to appreciate her accomplishment. "I passed. I got my license."

"Good for you, Savannah Banana. Tell you what, this tastes even better than it did last night. Nothin' wrong with leftovers."

"Where's Clay?" she asked as she set a bowl of stew in front of Claudia. "Has he eaten already?"

Patty shrugged between bites. "Probably messin' around out to the barn."

Savannah went upstairs to change her clothes. She would go out to the barn and ask him to have supper with her if he hadn't already eaten. Just the two of them. Maybe she'd find some candles. She had a new hairdo and a new driver's license. Growing confidence, shrinking fear. She felt alive; she was beginning to think she was actually going to be around for a while. She wished she'd thought of picking up a bottle of wine. She opened a drawer, looking for her new jeans. She hadn't even taken the tags off them yet. Where had she left those fingernail clippers?

She opened the bathroom door, automatically reaching for the light switch even as brightness of the light registered, the trickle of water, the steam. His presence suddenly rolled over her like a wave of heat.

He was soaking in the tub. Head resting against the tile wall, eyes closed, steam rising from his bath like autumn mist. His hair was slick, his stubbled face beaded with moisture, defining its strong angles with a soft sheen. He looked like a perfect piece of sculpture, a god in repose.

He didn't stir right away, even though he must have heard her come in. But neither did she. His physicality was stunning. There was so much of him, and it was all so long and sleek and sturdy and touchingly exposed. It was almost like looking at a photograph of a guileless boy in the bath. Ninety-nine and forty-four one-hundredths percent pure. In the small room with the walls so close, he seemed so much bigger than life.

Then he moved. Skin rubbing porcelain caused a squeal. Slowly, languidly, he lifted shoulders, lowered knees, sloshed water, which lapped his chest and swirled around his fully erect penis. Long, sleek, sturdy.

"I was just thinking about you," he said.

She had not seen him open his eyes, but they were open now, and they were taunting her.

She stepped back and closed the door, then spoke to it, through it. "Excuse me." She cleared her gorged throat. "They told me you were out in the barn."

"Like they say, the barn door's open and the horse got out."

She laughed, or tried to. "Looks like it."

"What do you need, Savannah?"

She pressed her forehead against the door, closed her eyes, the fabulous phallic image of him floating in her mind. One hand squeezed the doorknob, the other touched the door tenderly, as though it were flesh instead of wood.

You. I need you.

"Nothing, just . . . I'm sorry."

"No problem."

"I mean about today."

"No problem." Another trickle, a small splash. "You wanna come in?"

"No hurry." Yes, she did. God, yes, she did. "We . . . we could have supper together when you're finished."

An interminable, steamy moment passed.

"You go ahead," he said finally. "I've had enough."

Chapter 17

The night had begun to fade.

Finally. It had been cloudy, moonless, fiercely dark.

Savannah had waited through it, and for what? She might have gone to him. He slept only a few steps away. But she had lain in his bed hoping he would come to her, thought she heard the door a couple of times—or dreamed she had—but no one moved. Nothing happened.

He'd left it to her. His invitation hung in the air—*Come in*—and the want, the word, the way she'd nearly answered him hung there, too, listing toward the bathroom door. It was a scary combination, a formula for fiasco. He wanted her; that much was fine. He was supposed to want her. But she was not supposed to want him, or picture exposing herself as easily as he did, or imagine him still admiring what he saw once he had seen it all.

Because she was not as beautiful as he was.

Because she was not as good as he was. She never had been. Look what she'd done to him yesterday.

He was in the kitchen when she went downstairs, early enough, she hoped, to make him some breakfast, thinking she could do that much for him without acting like a nutcase. When had he gotten up? She'd heard nothing. The silly fuss in her own head had a way of blocking everything else out.

You're living in your head.

It was a small world after all. The thought made her smile, but only a little.

He'd made coffee, and he was already pouring some for her. It felt like the makings of an intimacy, sharing this soft-light time of day, but neither said good morning or asked how the other had slept. Too personal a question, perhaps, or too painful. No moonbeams shared. But there was the morning coffee.

"I've fed Ol' Paint, but he'll need another pound or so of alfalfa the same time the others get their grain and then—"

"Four hours after that," she finished for him. "Uncle Mick explained. I'd like to take care of that for you."

He handed her the coffee with a pointed look. "You'd have to be here."

"Not forever," she said, then sipped. "After three days, you gradually increase the intervals and the amount of feed. The four-hour feedings don't go on forever."

"Well, Mick's here, anyway."

"So am I." She gave his pointed look back to him. "I went into the school yesterday to get Claudia. I didn't really think about it. I just did it. I spoke to Mary Wheeler. *Mrs. Larpenter.* She was busy, of course, so there was no time for any sort of an interview, but I was okay. I didn't feel panicky. Not much, anyway, nothing I couldn't handle. Mary told me how much she enjoys having Claudia in class."

"She was really happy last night." He sat on one of the tall stools at the counter. *Half* sat, one leg up, the other ready to push off. Half willing to give her a break, for Claudia's sake. "I went in and told her good night, told her I wouldn't be able to pick her up at school today. She didn't seem to mind. She said her mom could drive now. She's talking about having more horses than anyone else at school and never cutting her hair and how Cheyenne wanted black hair like hers. And how she heard one of the kids whispering about you when you were talking to her teacher."

"Whispering?"

"About how pretty you are." Hands at the edge of the counter, he straightened his arms, launching the push. "I'm going up north today. Taking on a couple of new clients."

She nodded. "Would you like some breakfast?"

"I had something already."

He couldn't even tell her what? "New clients," she said. "I thought this was supposed to be winding down for the winter, this horseshoeing."

"I'm already pulling a lot of shoes off for the winter, but there are still some fall events yet. Couple of women up north who compete. I can handle a few more."

"So you'll be late getting home?"

"Not so's you'd notice," he said, reaching for the coffeepot to top off his travel cup.

"Yes, I do—I notice. I thought ranchers stayed home more."

"Ranchers do what they have to do to pay the bills." He fixed the lid on the insulated cup. "We've got three pickups around here, but no car. If you'd rather have a car, we can—"

"I don't need a car. Patty never drives, and I really don't have too many excuses to go anywhere, except maybe to drop in on that group thing in Jackson Hole, but that doesn't have to be—"

"Yes, it does. Anytime you want to go, feel free. You know those mountain roads as well as I do."

"I don't think I could handle a stick shift on those roads."

"I think you're on the road to handling anything and anybody, just like you used to." He moved to the table, where he'd left his cap and his keys. "Like I say, if we don't have a vehicle that suits you, we'll get you one."

He didn't seem to have time to look at her, but she

watched his every move, the way he adjusted his cap, smoothing it over his hair in back, pulling it low in front. She liked him better in a cowboy hat.

She liked him better when he wasn't dismissing her out of hand.

"I thought we could go to Jackson together," she said softly.

"Why? Has the fire gone out already?" He laughed. When she didn't, he shrugged. "A little joke. Remember that song? No, that's right, you're more rock 'n' roll. I'm the one who's country." He reached for his travel cup. "When's the next meeting? You want me to take you, just let me know. A little advance warning, that's all I ask."

"No surprises, ever?" Without thinking, she closed in on him, stalking. "No hasty decisions, no rash moves?"

"If it wasn't for hasty decisions and rash moves, you wouldn't be here, right?"

"I don't know about you, but I did, Clay. I got married in one hell of a fever."

"You weren't yourself, were you? You were sick and scared." Pain flashed in his eyes as he touched her cheek with one careful finger. "You're all I've ever wanted. You know that, don't you? I thought it would be enough just to have you here, this close, where I could see you every day."

She shut her eyes and willed him to step closer, press his palm to her cheek, and touch her more fully. "Some days I hardly see you."

"Yeah, well, last night you saw all there is to see," he said, irony replacing regret. Her eyes flew open. His gaze immediately claimed hers. "But seeing is such a small part of knowing. When you say you're *seeing* someone, it's only the beginning, just skimming the surface."

"And when you say you're sleeping with someone, what is that?"

"Marriage," he said, stepping away. "Should be, anyway."

"You're so old-fashioned."

"Yep." He touched the bill of his cap. "But we'll go to Jackson whenever you say."

"Clay?"

He turned at her touch, looked at her over his shoulder, his eyes receptive, hopeful. Hopeful of what? A reprieve? A blessing? She'd apologized, hadn't she? She'd made it pretty clear that she hated to see him go.

But they were adults, and he had work to do.

"Old-fashioned is nice," she said. And he laughed.

Maybe it was time he stopped being so damned nice.

His name rang in his ears all day. The way she'd said it, like she hated to see him go. The way she'd stopped him, turned him, pulled on him as though she had his heart on a string. All she had to do was ask him to stay. The hell with more clients, what he needed was more sex.

What he needed was to get off his high horse and take what he was offered. *If you want to fuck, we'll fuck.*

"What happened?" a female voice asked, interfering with his thoughts.

He looked up from the hoof he was hot-shoeing. He'd forgotten the woman was watching. He'd forgotten her name, and he'd forgotten his manners. Hadn't meant to let the word slip. It wasn't his kind of cuss word.

"Did you poke yourself?"

"Almost." He had to pluck the nail from his mouth before he swallowed it. "Sorry."

"If you're not available, it would be just my luck to throw a shoe during the race."

She'd been nagging about this race the whole time he'd been working on her horse, kept telling him how relieved she was to find a farrier who could custom-build the kind of shoes she'd been able to get where she lived before. Wherever that was.

"I'll check my schedule. Check . . . with my wife." Sounded good, anyway.

The woman gave him an odd look, as though she could read trouble on his mind. He noticed for the first time that she wasn't bad-looking. Reddish-brown hair, strong features, smiling eyes. She had a rider's thighs.

He got his head back down under her horse. What the hell was he doing, noticing thighs?

"It would tie you up for a weekend," she was saying, "but it would be worth your while. It's next to impossible to find anybody who'll do good, old-fashioned hot shoeing anymore, and with his hooves, the way they crack . . ."

Clay nodded every once in a while, let her go on thinking she knew what she was talking about, but he only heard pieces. *Good, old-fashioned hot shoeing.* Good, old-fashioned hots was what he saw in her eyes. Muscles on her thighs, hots in her eyes. He wasn't looking past the toes of her boots anymore, but he had this verse thing going in his head now, driving him crazy. Muscles on her thighs, hots in her eyes. The hots for good, old-fashioned, plain-as-mud Clay. They sure had named him right. He wanted to laugh. He wanted to straighten up for a minute, unkink his back. But then he'd have to look at her, and he *would* laugh.

Hell, he'd mentioned his wife. Had he forgotten to mention that he was married to the most beautiful woman in the world? A heavenly beauty hastily married to earthbound Clay during a temporary downturn in her fortunes. But she was getting her feet back under her. Once she got those angel wings flapping, Earth would just be a place to push off from.

". . . so I just moved out here, put all that insanity behind me. As far as I'm concerned, they can keep California. Except during the winter. When the roads start closing around here, I'm gone." She took a breath, but she wasn't done. "Have you been married long?"

"Not too long."

"Ah."

What was that supposed to mean? *Ah*. Add a *d*, he thought, and sum up this entire conversation. *Odd*.

"You'll know when it's been too long," she said, and before he could think of a way to change the subject, she said something even odder. "Do you board?"

Bored? "You don't know my wife."

She laughed. "Horses. She's not threatened by horses, is she?"

He glanced up, about to ask her what she meant by "threatened," but one look at those eyes, that knowing smile, and he didn't have to ask. She must've smelled trouble. He might as well just pin a damn sign to his back. *My beautiful wife won't sleep with me.*

"I'd like a place to board a couple of horses while I'm gone this winter," she said.

Board. He chuckled. "I'm way over my head here. Over my limit on horses and women at home, both. Right about now, I could use a couple of hours of mind-numbing, smoke-filled boredom."

"Could you use a beer to start with?"

He had been gone all night.

She had waited, listened for him, peeked out the window at the moon-washed driveway and the empty place near the clothesline where his pickup should have been. When she thought she might have dozed off for a time and missed something, she slipped out of bed, crept down the hall, and tortured herself by peering into the den. Its emptiness made her throat burn. She went out to the barn to feed the paint, told the horse she wondered where Clay was at two in the morning. Then, as she combed the sorry horse's mane and listened to him grind his precious food, she heard herself whisper, "I don't care where he is or what he's doing. I just hope he's all right."   •

And her throat burned again.

Back in the house, she lurked downstairs in the dark, wrapped herself in a lap robe, tucked herself in the window seat in the living room for a while, feeling mystified and helpless, half hoping that Patty would come out and tell her that there was nothing to worry about.

But Cheyenne called early in the morning to tell her there was a little something, if she was of a mind to worry. Savannah's husband was sleeping on the sofa at his ex-wife's house. "Asleep or passed out, one of the two. He's not in the way or anything. I just thought you might be looking for him."

There it was, thank God. Mystery solved. Now for the helplessness.

"Where's your mother?"

"Well, she's not on the sofa."

Savannah hung up the phone, head all a-muddle. He was safe, then. The night's worst fears dissipated like a cloud of smoke. She tried to tell herself that under the circumstances, this was all she was supposed to feel, all she was allowed to feel. Relieved for his safety. Not angry. She had no business being angry.

While Claudia was getting dressed for school, Savannah dashed back to the barn for the paint's six o'clock feeding. She wasn't feeling anything except responsible. She had duties, important things to take care of. Living things.

"Hello, you sweet Scarecrow," she said, very cheerfully. Exceedingly upbeat as she piled exactly a pound of alfalfa into the corner manger of a clean stall. She slipped a halter over the horse's ears. "It's just me again. He's still not back, but I know the routine. I guess I don't know his routine as well as I thought I did, but I know yours, which is new for you, isn't it?" she chattered as she led him to his food. "Yeah, getting fed regularly. Pretty good, huh?" She watched the horse lower his mist-making nose into the hay, and she said, "Good boy. You'll be good for me now, won't you? You won't run off on me?"

Of course not. You're gorgeous, and you give good hay.

"So I'm going to clean out your bedroom while you finish that up. Aren't you lucky?" She maneuvered the wheelbarrow into place and went to work with the manure fork, still chattering, her breath making its own morning mist. "Routine is good. It's therapeutic. We're all trying to adjust to new—"

The side door creaked, then swatted shut. Savannah stood up quickly, gripping the long-handled tool. Her heart pounded, and her mind raced with things to say. *You're home, thank God. I see you're all right. You know you've been out all night, don't you? I'm sure there's some perfectly good reason, involving . . . who? What, where, why, why,* why?

Why plagued her with the most urgency; she would have to ask why, even though she certainly knew the answer. Certainly *she* was why.

But she was wrong about *who*.

Her heart fell when she turned and saw that it was only Uncle Mick.

Only? God, she was cold. She tried to smile for the dear old man, struggled to keep her coldness to herself. "Scarecrow's doing well, don't you think?"

"He's lookin' a lot better. Did the boy leave already? I thought he was gonna take time out to move some stock around today."

"All he does is work." She dumped the last forkful of horse manure into the wheelbarrow. "Maybe I could help after I get Claudia off to school."

"We can always use another good hand." Uncle Mick wasn't fooled. He had that look in his eyes. "But not one that's dead on her feet. Me and the boy'll get 'er done."

"Clay went up north yesterday. Way up north." She laid

the fork over the load and grasped the wheelbarrow handles. "New clients."

"Montana?" He took over on the wheelbarrow. She moved away with a shrug, realizing that Clay hadn't really said how far north he was going. "He ain't back yet?"

"He got as far as Sunbonnet."

"Pickup trouble? Does he need . . ." Mick started toward the side door, then stopped, looked at her, hiked a wiry eyebrow. "Or did he tie one on?"

"One what? If that's all it is, that's no problem." Booze she could handle. Another woman was something else. He did seem to drink more than he used to, but the pills complicated that matter. If his only problem was a little too much liquor once in a while . . . "It's not a problem, is it?"

"His problem is he works too hard." Mick let her mull that over while he pushed the wheelbarrow down the aisle and out the door. He returned elaborating. "*My* problem was not workin' hard enough. Either way, when a man don't come home and his wife stays up all night frettin' over him, there's a problem. I can tell you that from experience."

It took her a moment to shift gears. She'd been thinking about herself and about Clay, thinking maybe her infamous boob wasn't the only thing she had to be concerned about.

Uncle Mick? Uncle Mick had a problem?

"I don't remember a time when you weren't right here taking care of all the Lazy K's nuts and bolts, Uncle Mick."

"Well, I'm glad you don't. I'm sure glad you don't." He sat down on a small pyramid of alfalfa bales, gnarled hands braced on bony knees. "But I had a different life before I came home to work for my brother. I was married for a little while, did a hitch in the army, went to Korea. Came back, couldn't do nothin' right for a time. I was a good mechanic, but I couldn't hang onto a job. Drove my wife off with my drinkin'.

"I came back to the Lazy K when there was no place else

to go, and I stayed on, and I don't hardly never leave, except maybe for a calf sale or maybe to help out a neighbor or something. I just don't . . ." He smacked one knee. "As long as I'm right here, I know what I'm doing. I know how to handle just this much. I can fix a broken engine or a fence, doctor up a cow with pinkeye or a frostbit calf. I don't need much money. Don't even want much, don't want to think about what it might buy." He gave a dry chuckle. "I know somebody has to, but I know it ain't gonna be me."

"I'm not very good with money, either," Savannah confessed. "I had a lot of it for a while, but then I . . ." She brushed alfalfa leaves off her jacket sleeve. "Well, I lost my job, too. Or quit. Took some time off. Got sick, and I wasn't prepared for that. Turned out I needed a lot of money then." She looked at the old man through the mist of her breath. "You don't think Clay's sick, do you?"

"I think he's human. I think he works too hard. And I think he spends a lot of time thinkin' about what other people need 'cause he's scared to think about needin' anything for himself."

"Scared?"

"It don't make no sense to me neither. He don't mind being needed. Now, that's what scares me—thinkin' somebody's dependin' on me. But Clay, he goes lookin' for it; he loves it. He'll work himself into the ground for it. For you and that little girl. But he can't be needin' anything from you. That ain't his way."

After she finished getting Claudia ready for school, she discovered the old black pickup waiting for them like a chariot, all scraped and warmed and delivered by a shy footman for their drive to the bus stop. Everything else in the yard was sugared with frost. The dapple-white pastures were hushed, still, bright. Overnight, the bristly foxtail barley had become a roadside crop of fine white feathers. Frost softened the barbed-wire fences and turned a willow into a crystal chandelier.

Savannah's outlook brightened.

"How about if I take you to school today?"

"And Clay picks me up?"

"I'll probably pick you up, too, muffin. Uncle Mick needs Clay to help him with the cows today."

"If Clay needs me to help, I could." Claudia folded her arms around her Winnie the Pooh backpack. "Clay's mom told me I could call her Grandma."

"She did?"

"And there's *Uncle* Mick and *Aunt* Billie . . ." She rested her cheek against the backpack, throwing her mother an oddly challenging stare. "I don't call Clay anything."

"You call him Clay."

"I want to call him something else. Can I?"

"That's between you two, sweetheart."

Claudia was quiet during the rest of the drive. When they reached the school, she kissed Savannah, then drew back with that look still burning in her eyes. "I want him to be my dad," she said firmly, "and I don't want my dad to be an Indian."

"Oh."

Savannah watched her daughter run up the sidewalk to the building where all these notions had undoubtedly originated. Now what? She'd been so careful with these tender topics—hadn't she been careful? Now, suddenly, Claudia had fiercely staked her own claim.

And where was her chosen father?

Sleeping—or passed out, one of the two—on his ex-wife's sofa.

Savannah wasn't even sure where Roxie and her brood lived. She meant to head straight for Main Street, maybe stop at the Mercantile. But then again, she didn't want to discuss any of this with anyone right now. So she *meant* to get out of Dodge and head straight for her new home, her room, and her bed. Clay's bed, the bed he'd given her.

But she took a couple of unnecessary turns. Without meaning to, she spotted the white pickup parked in front of a little shotgun house. And once she'd seen the vehicle, she had to stop and see the rest—whatever there was to see—for herself.

Roxie answered the door. She was wearing jeans and a sweatshirt, and her bloody-looking hair was combed. She had her shoes on. Reeboks. Savannah's indignant rap-rap-rap obviously hadn't gotten her out of bed.

"Is Clay here?"

Roxie glanced past her, as though checking to see who else she'd brought. "I suppose I could try to convince you that I borrowed his pickup."

"Don't bother. Cheyenne called me."

"Well, that little weasel." Roxie rolled her hand in what might have passed for a welcoming gesture. "Come on in. Nobody's tryin' to hide nothin'. Your husband's in the bathroom. He ain't feelin' too good, so if you're here to cuss him out, have a heart and keep your voice down."

The floor beneath the shag carpet creaked as Savannah entered the small front room of the modest house. She could smell coffee and steam heat, could tell that someone might, indeed, have slept on the slipcovered sofa. There was a small, round pillow jammed against one overstuffed arm and an old crocheted afghan tossed over the other. Between those two clues she thought she detected a big body print.

There was also a witness. "Cheyenne was just trying to help," she told Roxie. "She thought I might be worried."

"About what?"

"About whether he was all right. I was glad she called, relieved to know . . ."

"That he's right here, safe with me?" Roxie laughed.

"Right. I'd love to have been a fly on your wall when you got that call, honey."

Savannah's face flamed. Her throat suddenly started stinging again. If she opened her mouth just then, she knew she'd cry.

"I wouldn't say he was all right," Roxie continued, far too eagerly. "The man got himself totally wasted. Looked like he'd already had a few when he stopped in the Naughty Pines. We closed the place down, and there was no way he was gonna drive home."

Savannah wanted to sit down, but not in Roxie's presence. She swallowed, swallowed again, then quietly said, "I would've appreciated a call last night."

"Unlike my daughter, I'm not a snitch."

"She's a good girl," said a deep voice toward the back of the house. Clay appeared in the doorway between the kitchen and the dining table. His hair was damp and slicked back, his face stubbly and ashen, his eyes spiritless. "Cheyenne did the right thing," he said flatly. "It's a worry when you don't know where somebody is. People need to let other people know when something comes up. Celebrating is no excuse."

"Were we celebrating?" Roxie wondered. "Sure coulda fooled me."

"Weren't we? Or was I cryin' in my beer?"

"Don't you remember? It was Jim Beam, and if you don't remember, have I got a tale to tell. It'll cost you to keep me quiet." Roxie flashed Savannah an insolent wink. "He's so much fun when you're not married to him."

"Thanks, Roxie," Clay grumbled from the kitchen. He was helping himself to coffee. "You're a real pal."

"Just like always, huh?" Roxie laughed again, freely, as though nothing was wrong. "I'm gonna do everybody a big favor and head off to work before the fireworks start. Or waterworks. Which sign are you, Savannah, fire or water? By the way, I owe you for Cheyenne's hair."

"Leanne wouldn't take any money this time."

"Well, her hair looks nice. I owe you for that. So that's why I kept my horny hands off our boy here." She caught some kind of look or signal from Clay as he trudged past her. "*Hers*. You're all hers. Except for this—" She plucked at his sleeve, then examined her thumb and forefinger like a mime, changing the angles, angling for light. "This one long hair. Oops, it's red." She grinned at Savannah as she brandished her invisible trophy. "This part's mine."

The sound of the door shutting behind Roxie reverberated in the silence that followed. He would speak first, Savannah decided. She wasn't sure which of her feelings would rise above the tumult, but if he spoke first, she could simply respond. One word. Two words. No gush from the gut.

"Would you like some coffee?"

She shook her head. That didn't count. She wasn't opening up for coffee. Besides, it was Roxie's coffee. It wasn't his to offer. He didn't belong here.

"I slept on the sofa," he said, far too calmly. And he sat down on that very sofa, as if by sleeping there he'd staked out the territory. "One sofa's as good as another."

"You have an extra bedroom at—" *Home*. She wouldn't profane the word by using it now, here.

"I like sleeping on the sofa. It feels temporary."

"Were you taking those pills again?"

He shrugged noncommittally.

"You can't do that anymore, Clay." She felt a little awkward, standing over him like a teacher who'd caught him cheating on a test. Awkward, but somewhat superior. For the moment, the high ground was hers. "You can't mix booze and painkillers. Believe me, I know."

"You've tried it?"

"Once, when I thought I was going to die anyway, so what the hell."

"I could be goin' that way myself," he muttered, face in his hands. "I feel like shit."

"I know." Without thinking, she sat down beside him. Without meaning to, she laid her hand on his broad back.

He lifted his head. "You look as worn out as I feel."

"I was up during the night feeding Scarecrow. That's what I named the paint. Scarecrow." Her fingertips curled into the hair at his nape. He smelled of smoke and stale beer, but the look in his eyes was artlessly forlorn. "You know, skinny body, intelligent face."

"You're thinkin' of my brother again."

"I'm thinking of best friends."

He closed his eyes, tipped his head back until her fingers brushed his scalp. Then he sat up quickly. "I've gotta get rid of some horses, so don't be gettin' too attached."

Her hand slid down his back.

"I called a friend of mine who's very knowledgeable about getting support for all kinds of causes—animals, children, minorities, women, you name it—and I was telling her about the horses and this idea we had for starting some sort of retirement program, and she said—"

"Idea *we* had? You mean that boarding scheme you and Margo Ross hatched? I'll take her horse, but that's it. No more. I don't have time. I agreed to go to a three-day endurance race in, uh . . ." He leaned back with a sigh. "Jesus, I can't even remember where. That was between the first two beers. All I know is the money's too good to pass up."

"Heather thinks we could get people to sponsor some of the neglected horses you take in."

He grunted, his eyes drifting shut again. "Who's Heather?"

"She was my roommate for a while in New York. She's a journalist, and she's written lots of stories about programs like this. People like Margo would pay for retirement for their horses, but for a horse like Scarecrow, we'd get people to contribute to a nonprofit—"

"Like a charity?" He rolled his head far enough to shoot her an incredulous glance. "Charity is for homeless people and hungry kids and disaster victims. The Lazy K isn't a charity."

"I'm talking about the horses, not the—"

"They're my horses. They don't need charity." He hauled himself to his feet, trying to escape. "I'm looking after them."

"*We* are." Saggy springs sighed as she ejected herself from the sofa. "I'm helping you now. And I have a good, solid idea that might turn this little weakness of yours into—"

"It's not a weakness. I like horses. I feel like we've been using these animals for all these centuries, maybe we owe them a decent . . ." His hand dropped from an expansive gesture. "But I'm not interested in taking up a collection."

"I didn't mean weakness. Compassion." She touched his arm. "It's not such a crazy idea, Clay. At one time or another, every kid dreams of having a horse. Every adult harbors that latent wish. People would love to help you give horses like Scarecrow—"

"I'm gonna fatten him up and sell him, Savannah."

"To a canner?"

"I never sell to canners. I sell saddle horses."

They were nose to nose now, one above the other.

"When was the last time you sold a horse?"

"Last spring."

"Out of the geriatric bunch?"

"No, but I can sell that paint, once I get him in shape. Horse people are looking for color nowadays."

She folded her arms. "Your mother says you're horse-poor."

"Since when did you start quoting the wisdom of Patty Keogh?"

"Margo thinks it's a good idea. Aunt Billie thinks it can work. I know I can get Uncle Mick on my side. Heather said she'd check around with animal-relief organizations and see what's already in place."

"It doesn't matter what's already in place or who's on your side. I ain't runnin' no charity for—"

"Remember what you said about singing with my face? I asked Heather how I could sell this as a cause, and she said I should use my face. Like a celebrity or something. I can't imagine people are going to remember me." She looked to him for a hint of protest, but he offered only a cool stare, which she tried to shrug off. "Although people might think I look familiar."

"Just take off your shirt."

"Now, you see, that's what I said. It wasn't my face that sold the underwear." She quickly realized how different it felt, saying it to him.

But you said it was. You said I could sing with my face.

She could really use that protest from him now.

"Yeah, well, we sell calves, not causes." He stepped back, eyeing the right side pocket on her oversized wool shirt jacket. "I didn't hear you offering to put your picture on our auction flier. You missed a great chance to jump-start your modeling comeback in Wyoming."

"I'm not interested in making a comeback. I'm interested in doing something that I thought . . . *might* . . . help."

"Charity's kind of a cuss word around here. You know that. I don't need any help." A deep breath softened his tone. "What I need to do is swear off the Jim Beam and leave the damn stock trailer at home so I can't pick up any more horses. That should do it, huh?" He shoved his hair back with an unsteady hand. "Aspirin won't help, will it?"

"Try going home," she suggested, putting a lid on her sympathy. But she'd said it. The word had slipped out. "That helps."

"I know this didn't look too good." With a nod he indi-cated the sofa.

"I didn't come to look. I brought Claudia to school."

"You didn't say anything about . . ."

"When she was telling me she wants to call you Dad? No, I didn't say anything about you sleeping on your ex-wife's sofa."

His eyes cooled toward her again. "Like I said, one sofa's pretty much the same as another."

Chapter 18

Autumn was a season of majesty in Wyoming.

The Grand Teton Mountains wore the coming of winter in fierce glory, like a legion of emperors. Shy quaking aspens donned yellow for the occasion, dressing up the red road cuts, the black-green stands of pine, and the striations of granite and snow touching the heavens. Soon the passes would be closed as often as not, but for now, the way was clear. Savannah attended another group meeting in Jackson Hole, taking Aunt Billie with her as a guest.

Aunt Billie took a seat outside the circle, and for a while she listened quietly, but the mention of sisters prompted her to contribute a comment about being the sister left behind. Chairs shifted, and the circle became an egg. Savannah had never heard her aunt express her own feelings about the death of her younger sister, Savannah's mother.

"I always felt like my mother had me first so I could be Caroline's guardian," Aunt Billie said. "She was such a frivolous little thing so much of the time, with so many high-flyin' notions, and I was always trying to tackle her by the ankles, make her keep her shoes and socks on. I figured if she happened to come down to earth once in a while, at least she wouldn't be barefoot.

318

"I was her lead weight," she told the group. "All of a sudden, she just took off. I couldn't do anything to stop her. I kept thinking it wouldn't happen, but it did. She's gone, and I miss her, and I'm still here. Still a lead weight."

Aunt Billie didn't cry, but Savannah did. She'd thought *she* was her mother's lead weight. The baby nobody was ready for. The little girl who had drained off her mother's youthful beauty. *Better put that beauty to good use.*

"What I remember most about my mother is her exquisite eyes," Savannah told her aunt. "Beautiful and distant. Even when she was close, she always seemed far away, and I always felt desperate to get to her. If I won the next contest, I'd get to her. If I got a cover, I'd get to her."

"If you die the way she did, you'll get to her?" someone asked quietly.

Savannah couldn't see who it was. Her eyes were burning with tears.

She shook her head. "If I really live while I'm alive and teach my daughter to do the same . . ." Barbara passed the tissue box. Savannah snatched one, mopped her face, laughed. "I guess we'll get to her sooner or later, won't we, Aunt Billie?"

"If that's the way it works."

"Right now, it's good to be home with the Larsen sister who raised me." Savannah managed a teary smile. "You said you'd never been to a support group, Aunt Billie. You're good at this."

"I thought maybe there was some special trick to it. What do you think we do at the Thursday-night book group? We solve everybody's problems, but with the added benefit that I sell six copies of a different book every month." She looked directly at facilitator Cheryl Estes. "If you're not selling a book to these folks, you're missing a prime opportunity."

*   *   *

The day that Margo brought her old horse to leave with Savannah, she brought a friend with her. Margo wasn't up to driving, and her friend, Carol, was also looking for a place to retire two old horses. Savannah showed the women around, then brought Angel and Sugarfoot into the barn to meet Bronwyn and enjoy some therapeutic grooming. "It's therapy for us," Savannah told the women as she handing out the currycombs.

"It's nice to have something to comb," Margo said. She was wearing a soft knit cloche. "I'm already going bald, but it'll grow back after I finish the chemo. It did before. But now, hairless and breastless, my female pride goes down the tubes."

"You look beautiful," Savannah said.

"You're a very poor liar."

"You *are* beautiful."

"That I'll buy." Margo slipped an arm around the mare's neck, kissed her hairy cheek. "Along with all the creature comforts available to me and this sweet old gal. You know what you need to do . . ."

Margo had ideas. More partitions in the pasture. More stalls. Another loafing shed. She liked Uncle Mick's plan for a new system of feeding troughs. She was impressed with the quality of the hay and with Clay's grain recipes. "It must be costing him a fortune to keep these horses like this. What's the matter with him? He could be doing it for profit."

"We'll keep yours for profit," Savannah said as she introduced Scarecrow, who had already picked up enough weight to be taken off the endangered list. "Guys like this are the ones Clay can't walk away from, and I have a feeling that's what's costing him."

"I'll get you some supporters," Carol said as she rubbed Scarecrow's mainly white face. "It's part of being a horseman, just like supporting Ducks Unlimited is part of being a hunter. If you enjoy it as a sport, you give something back.

We've got more horses in this country now than we've had since they were pulling plows. But they're more like pets now. You don't turn a beloved old pet into a can of dog food. And this —there's no excuse for this."

"Clay said the man who owned him simply didn't have the means to care for him anymore. They're not like dogs and cats. And when the pasture's gone, they can get run-down so fast."

"*We'll* get you supporters," Margo promised. "I've gotta get my body someplace warm, but my heart stays here. I love this country, and so does Bronwyn. Right, girl? If we die here, we'll die happy." She traded brushes with Savannah, who was hogging the one with dark bristles and not doing much with it. "Which means I'll be back. But I'm going to be talking your program up. It's a good idea, and it'll keep my mind off the boobs . . . which my mind thinks are still there."

"Ah, the spectral tits." Savannah put her arm around the woman's slight shoulders, tipped her head to the side, and nestled her face in the soft cloche. "There is life after boobs," she said. "Let's call it our LAB—Life After Boobs."

"I love it!" Margo shrieked. "Ladies, we're now in our LAB, and we are stirring up a whole new brew."

"Sounds like a recipe for toil and trouble," Patty predicted as she approached.

Savannah introduced her friends to her mother-in-law. "We've worked out the details," she told Patty. "Margo's paying us five hundred dollars a month to retire Bronwyn with us."

"Five hun—"

"I realize that's an introductory rate," Margo trumpeted. "I have friends back East who pay a thousand to board, so I'm willing to go higher."

"A thou—"

Savannah laughed. She'd never seen Patty's eyes achieve

perfect roundness. "But, of course, that includes a whole catalog of amenities," she said.

"Rich people are crazy."

"That's true, but some are bad crazy and others are good crazy," Carol said. "And some are horse crazy."

"I've got a son who's horse crazy, and he ain't rich."

"If you can retire my horses at your introductory rate, I'd say you're in business."

"Clay agreed to take Margo's horse, but I haven't asked him about Carol's," Savannah told her mother-in-law.

"Ask *me*," Patty suggested. "You people with all your money, you're changing things out here. I don't know what's gonna happen when we can't afford to raise beef anymore. Who's gonna put meat on your plate when we're nursing your retired show horses?"

"Why can't we do both?" Savannah wanted to know.

"If they're willing to pay, hell, I'm all for it. If you can't beat 'em, take their money." Patty patted Bronwyn's rump. "For the right price, we'll treat this lady like a queen."

"You're going to help me?" Savannah asked.

"Pitching hay?"

"Pitching the plan to Clay."

"Oh, hell's bells and fast balls, girl, you tellin' me you don't know how to pitch to your own big Babe?" Patty snorted as she fished a cigarette from her jacket pocket. "Selling Clayton on horses is like talking a wino into letting you open a package store in the front room. And here, the rest of us look at you, Miss Savannah, and we think if we'da been born with a face like that, we'da ruled in his world and rocked in our own." She gave Carol the high sign. "As far as I'm concerned, you're in."

"Colorful," Margo muttered as they watched Patty head outside to have her smoke.

"She is that." But so was Margo, whose lips were turning blue. Again Savannah put her arm around the smaller woman. "Let's get you in the kitchen for some hot tea and all the sympathy you can stomach."

Clay could feel Savannah watching him as he rode down the gravel road on horseback with Claudia and Dallas. He'd brought them home from school with the promise of a ride, and Mick had mentioned the probability of a busted fence somewhere along the approach. One of the horses had shown up for supper on the wrong side of the fence. Then Savannah had said she wanted to talk, and he'd said, "Later," and herded the kids out the door.

He didn't want to get into it with her about Margo's old horse or Margo's friend or her going off somewhere to get involved with something in which he would ultimately have no role. Partly he didn't want to get into it because the kids needed his attention now, and partly because Savannah wanted his approval, and he didn't much like himself for holding out on her. She was looking, feeling, acting healthier all the time, and he was glad about that; he wanted her healthy. He just didn't want her gone.

"My foot's loose," Claudia said, and Clay turned from his thoughts to see what she was talking about. She was looking at him expectantly, as though she wanted to show him something but had to make sure he was ready. "Daddy, my—my foot came loose."

His heart surged in his chest. He dismounted slowly, giving himself time to get properly collected. She'd just told him who he was in her eyes, the only eyes that counted now, this minute. It was all right, he told himself. He could be what she was calling him. She knew no other father.

For now, he banished Kole to one corner of his mind, put Savannah in another. He bit the tip of the middle finger of his rawhide glove, pulling it off as he carefully moved Claudia's leg aside to make an adjustment in the length of her stirrup. Slowly, deliberately, he took her small foot in his big hand and fit it into the stirrup. Only then did he, her humble footman, look up and smile into her eyes.

"How's that?"

"Good. Thank you, Daddy." Smoother, more natural this time.

"It's right, then." He patted her knee. "Just right."

Dallas was eager to be moving. As soon as Clay swung back into the saddle, the boy clucked and pressed for speed. A trot, at least. Clay told him to hold up.

The response was: "So how come she gets to call you Dad?"

"Because I'm his little girl now," Claudia said.

Suddenly it was between the two kids. Clay was out of it.

"He was married to my mom, too, but I always call him Clay."

"Well, you have a dad in Dallas. I don't. My mom adopted me when I was a baby, and she didn't have a husband, so I didn't have a dad. But now she has a husband, so I have a dad."

"Your dad's an Indian. You already said that."

"He isn't anymore. Are you, Clay? I mean, Daddy."

"You know what, you guys? I'd be pleased to have you both call me Dad, but you'll have to promise me one thing." He'd circled Dallas's sorrel gelding and cut in between them. "When you talk about me behind my back, you won't be calling me 'the old man.' "

"You're not old," Claudia protested.

"I will be." He pointed at the fence line up ahead with a gloved hand. "There it is, right there. That's where that horse got out." He left them in the road while he cut through the grassy ditch to inspect the fallen wire. He was going to have to replace a post, which he couldn't do right now, but he wanted to bind the loose wire to keep the stock from getting wire-cut. "Dallas, I need your help. You got those cutters?"

Dallas, the designated tool carrier, leaped to the call. He

responded so eagerly that he accidentally kicked Angel on the dismount. Startled, the mare jerked to one side, tumbling Claudia off the other.

Clay saw it coming, but he couldn't get there in time to prevent it. She landed in the grassy ditch and rolled like a tumbleweed, just that weightless and soundless. Nothing but a swish through the grass. It terrified him.

He knelt beside her. She stared, wide-eyed. They blinked at each other, each waiting for a signal. He expected her to cry, but she only looked surprised. "Don't move if it hurts," he said. "Does it hurt anywhere?"

She sat up and shook her head.

"You sure, Kitten?" He held his hand out to her. She grabbed it like a lifeline, and he towed her into his arms. "Tell me where you bumped," he invited quietly, close to her ear. She held onto his shoulder, saying nothing as he stood up.

"You ready to get back on?"

She shook her head again, then whispered into his ear, "Just my hand."

"Let me see." He examined it first, then kissed the scraped palm. "We'll fix it," he said, grateful for something to tend to that was easily fixable. "It'll be okay. It was a soft fall. Did you see the way Angel moved over? She didn't want to step on you. She's a good little horse, and you're a good rider because you fell nice and relaxed. We'll go home now. Can you show Angel you're okay?"

Dallas stood there, chagrined, holding both horses' reins. "It's okay, son," Clay said as he took the reins and gestured for the boy to retrieve his own mount, who stood where Clay had left him, ground-tied the way he'd been trained.

"Can you get back on?"

Claudia shook her head. Finally her face crumpled, and the silent tears started to roll.

"It's okay, sweetheart. You can ride with me, but I want

you to tell Angel everything's okay so she won't be scared. Pet her a little." He guided her hand. "Let her sniff your hand. See, Angel? See what a good rider this girl is?"

"Tickles," Claudia said, sniffling, crying, and laughing, a measure of each.

Clay turned toward the hand tapping on his arm. Dallas shyly offered up Claudia's new cowboy hat.

"Thanks, partner. Can you handle both horses?"

"It's okay," Claudia said. "I guess I can ride her myself."

Savannah stood in the yard, clutching her big wool jacket closed in front while the wind toyed with her bright hair and her dark skirt. She couldn't have seen the spill from the house, but she must have been keeping an eye out for her daughter, who was eager to jump to the ground and tell of her adventures.

"Mommy, I got bucked off my horse, but I got back on." She lifted her palm for Savannah's inspection. "See? It's hardly scraped up at all."

"Bucked off?" Savannah shot an accusing look at Clay.

"The mare spooked a little bit. Nothing we couldn't handle."

"She's not ready to be racing around with—"

"There was no racing," he told her. "Nobody was trying to race."

"Dallas was going a little bit too fast, though."

"Can I go home now?" Dallas asked quietly.

"Not until we unsaddle the horses, you and me." Clay tapped the boy's shoulder with a gloved hand. "You and me, partner. And on the way out, maybe you'd still want to help me with that fence."

"Sure," Dallas muttered.

"I can unsaddle, too!" Claudia exclaimed.

"You hurt your hand," Dallas shot back. "You'd better get a Band-Aid or somethin'."

"Better get a bath," Savannah said, then led her daughter away, but not before sparing Clay one more glance containing some personal message. He wasn't sure what, but he could just about guess.

Clay had missed supper, though not for any diversionary reasons. He and Dallas had taken care of some business. They'd taken care of the horses, fed the paint and cleaned his stall, then restocked Clay's pickup with shoeing supplies, all the while shootin' the bull about school starting and the new football program for elementary school and some kid who had a new video contraption he could hook up to his TV. They hadn't completely fixed the fence, but they'd taken care of the loose wire.

Then, since Savannah hadn't offered, Clay had decided to treat Dallas to a burger at Grumpy's before he dropped the boy off at home. Dallas didn't show it, but he was feeling pretty shook up over Claudia's fall. He was also feeling like the kid not chosen, or maybe the youngest, whose place had been usurped.

Clay parked his pickup near the clothesline and headed across the yard. Bedside lamps burned in two windows—his mother's on the first floor and his wife's on the second. He wondered which of them had left the porch light on for him.

The house cat rubbed against his legs as he peeled off his jacket in the dark and hung it on his hook near the back door. He upended his Stetson and stowed it on the shelf above the hooks. He didn't need light. If he lost his sight someday, he'd have no trouble finding his way around this house. Except for his hitch in the army, he'd never lived anywhere else. This was his rightful place.

He peeked into Claudia's room. A small light with a cover the shape of a seashell was plugged into the wall near the bathroom door. It cast a soft glow over the stillness in the room. He turned to leave.

"Clay?" said a small voice. "Dad, I mean. Daddy."

Oh, how he liked the sound of that. He moved a wicker

chair closer to the bed, sat down just as she sat up, extending her wounded hand to him. He kissed it again, then
smiled at her. God, how she reminded him of Kole. Maybe
it wasn't really right to let her call him Dad, but he sure liked
the sound of it.

"Angel didn't make me fall," she whispered. "I got too far
over to one side, and then Dallas wasn't watching what he
was doing, and he scared Angel."

"Things like that happen sometimes, but you did fine. I
sure admire the way you got right back on and rode home.
You didn't have to, but you did. You're going to be a fine
horsewoman."

"Are you really gonna let Dallas call you Dad?"

"It's funny. He never asked to before. None of them did."
Clay adjusted the fluffly comforter over her shoulder. "But I
tried to look after them like their father would, so I don't
mind him calling me that. Is that okay with you?"

"I guess." She scooted closer to the edge of the bed. Closer
to him. "But they don't live here like your kids would."

"No, they don't. But I still help them out when I can. They
kinda need some lookin' after sometimes."

"Dallas says his mom says my real dad used to live here.
Is that true?"

Clay drew a deep breath. *Man, this topic sure peeked out
of the closet a lot.*

"It is."

"Did you know him?"

"I do, Kitten. He's my brother." The words rolled easily
off his tongue, partly because he'd thought about it, and he'd
already decided that when she asked—which was bound to
happen, knowing Sunbonnet and knowing Claudia—he
wasn't going to lie or even hedge. And partly because he
would never deny Kole. Never. "I haven't seen him in a long,
long time, and I miss him a lot."

Her little arm shot out from beneath the covers, and he

thought for a moment that she might want to wallop him, just because kids did crazy things when they got confused. Kole had slammed him in the gut once for something he'd said, some expression he'd used referring to Indians. *'Skins*, maybe. Clay was trying to learn how to be a cocky teenager, and Kole was his role model. Kole's disapproval had hurt more than his punch, which was no love tap.

But Claudia's pat on his arm was just that; a love tap. Comforting him because he missed his brother.

"Are you an Indian, too?"

"No. His mother was an Indian. Him and me, we had the same dad. It's a little complicated, but . . ." He reached out to brush a wisp of dark hair back from her sweet face. "Anybody ever says anything to you about him, you come to me. I'll always tell you the truth. Okay?"

She nodded. "If Dallas calls you Dad, that means he has two dads—one in Dallas and one here."

He smiled. "More than most people, huh?"

"Where's my other dad?"

"I don't know. I haven't seen him in a long time. Wherever he is, he knows you're happy. He gave you to your mom because he knew what a good mom she'd be." How could he make the truth sound fine enough for one so dear as this child, *his* child?

"People . . . sometimes they can't do for their babies themselves, so they find the best parents they can. My brother picked your mom because he knew how much she would love you. He didn't necessarily pick me to be your dad, but . . ."

"Mommy picked you." Claudia patted his arm again. "I think she made a good pick."

"Thanks." Clay leaned over to kiss her above her eyebrow. "Good night, Kitten."

"I love you, Daddy."

"I love you, too, sweetheart. More than I can say."

"Can you sing to me now? Sing that walks-with-me, talks-with-me song."

He did. He sang from his heart, very softly.

The house was quiet, but there was no way he was going to be able to sleep. He felt all warmed up inside. He went downstairs, built a fire in the big stone fireplace, and poured himself a drink to keep the warm feeling going strong. He was half elated, half running scared. He shouldn't have been the one to tell her. If he was going to do it, he should've asked first. It should have been both of them together, him and Savannah. It shouldn't have happened the way it did.

But he'd handled it pretty good, he thought. Hadn't given her any more than she'd asked for, which was probably all she thought she could handle. Kids were pretty resilient. He'd learned that from Roxie's kids. Adults could screw them up, sure, but they could still learn enough to get un-screwed. You just had to be willing to hang in there with them. You couldn't lie to them, that was the main thing. You didn't have to tell them every detail, but when they asked you about things, you had to be straight with them. He knew that much.

Just like you had to be straight with your wife when you screwed up and got loaded and landed on your old shoe's saggy-springed sofa. And then you expected your wife to be straight with you and tell you to go straight to hell. When she didn't say anything of the kind, you had to face the fact that she didn't give a damn where you slept, as long as it wasn't with her. But you also had to remember that she'd never lied to you about that. She'd told you right off you wouldn't be sleeping with her. You knew from the day you said, "I do," that she didn't much care whether you did or didn't. This wasn't a regular marriage. He'd never had a reg-ular marriage.

Had he ever seen a regular marriage?

What the hell *was* a regular marriage?

He had kids calling him Dad, and he wasn't a regular father.

I love you, Daddy.

Damn, that sure sounded regular.

He just hoped he'd said the right things. He was having a second drink, replaying the whole event in his mind, watching the flames dance and feeling considerably mellower, when he heard footsteps on the stairs. Not little footsteps. Long, beautiful, supple feet stepping quietly, letting him know that she was coming. A small blanket fluttered around her shoulders as she drifted across the floor, which hardly even creaked beneath her. She settled on the big hassock between him and the fire. With her new hair slicked back, sticking up a little on top, his witnessing her entrance was like watching a crested titmouse light on a tree stump.

"I heard you singing to Claudia." She touched his knee with tentative fingertips, the overture to a firelit smile. "You sound so good, it makes me shiver. I haven't sung to her since she was a baby."

"You read to her now. That's better."

"She needs both. I don't sing anymore, now that she's old enough to know how bad I sound."

He chuckled. "You think she cares?"

"She knows how good you are. She told me. And I don't hear you objecting about the quality of my singing voice."

"What do I know? You haven't sung to me since I was . . ." He lifted one shoulder. "Okay, old enough to know you were flat. But just like Claudia, I was too lovesick to care. Would you like a drink?"

"No, thanks."

"You sure?" She nodded, closing that topic, leaving him to teeter on the threshold of confession time. He sipped his drink. "You didn't happen to hear us talking before we had the lullabye?"

"You know I wouldn't eavesdrop. Was she still shook up over getting 'bucked off'?"

"She didn't get bucked off, but I gotta tell you, I was pretty . . ." Savannah was looking at him a little strangely, as if to say, *Your point?* "She asked me if I knew her father."

He searched her eyes for censure, even though he hadn't said anything censurable yet. So far, the rebuke wasn't there. She simply waited.

He stared into the glass in his hand. "The kids had told her he used to live here. She asked me flat out if I knew him."

"What did you tell her?"

"No more than what she asked for, Savannah, but I had to be straight with her. She wants to call me Dad. I don't know how Kole would feel about that, but the important thing is how she feels. I want her to know, right from the start, that I won't lie to her."

"And I will?"

"No, I'm not saying that. I don't know what you've told her."

"That's right, you don't. But you took it upon yourself—"

"Honey, she's in school now. Kids say all kinds of stuff. She's living in our hometown. You can't control what she hears. Everybody knows all about the Keoghs and Kole Kills Crow and Savannah Stephens."

"They don't know anything."

"They know that you and Kole are the two most fascinating products of Sunbonnet, Wyoming. They know you both went off to live unimaginable lives in all kinds of strange places, and now you're back home, and we're married, and your little girl looks just like . . ." He gestured, the answer in his hand. "They know she's Kole's daughter, Savannah. She deserves straight answers to her questions so she'll know there's nothing wrong with who she is and where she comes from. I'm not gonna act like there is by lying about it. I told her that her father is my brother. Obviously, that means I know him."

"I haven't lied to her, either. She's never asked me who her father was. Where, yes, and I said I didn't know, and that's true. You should have told her to ask me."

"She asked me if I knew him. I should have told her to ask *you* if I knew him?"

"You could have said, 'Wait a minute. Let's get Mommy.' "

"Is that how it's gonna be? She can't talk to me directly—it's gotta be through you?"

"This was too important for you to just blurt it out. I was right down the hall."

"Well, I guess I just didn't think about calling a time-out."

Fire danced in her eyes, but her tone turned cold. "It's not a game."

"No, it isn't. It's real life, and it's a hell of a challenge, and I'm doin' the best I know how."

She dropped her gaze to her hands, which rested on her thighs like played-out puppies. "What does she think?" she asked quietly.

"She thinks you were picked to be her mother. She thinks you're the most beautiful woman in the world—she told me that the first time I saw her." He lifted Savannah's chin with the tips of his fingers. When her eyes met his, he gave her the big news. "She thinks you picked me to be her dad."

"What does she think about Kole?"

"She doesn't know Kole," he reminded her, wishing he could shake her and demand what the hell kind of a response that was to what he'd just said. *God, she could be dense sometimes.* "She knows us. She knows you're her mother and that you love her." And the way Savannah was looking at Clay, deep into his eyes and still missing the point, made him ache inside. "She knows I do, too."

* * *

The next morning Claudia brought her hairbrush in early and asked Savannah to French-braid her hair. Savannah almost said there wasn't time, but she caught herself. She wouldn't lie, either. How could there not be time?

Claudia sat on the bed, her stockinged feet tucked under her butt, toying with the covered hair band that would eventually tie the project off, while Savannah stood behind her and plaited her long black hair into a single thick strand. She could almost hear the thoughts clicking in the child's mind. She knew how that precocious mind worked, how it conjured questions and dreamed up satisfactory explanations without asking for mundane answers. But Claudia had asked Clay.

And now all her questions were about Clay.

"If my real dad is Clay's brother, what is Clay really to me?"

"He's really your uncle."

"But I don't have to call him that, do I? Because I decided to call him Dad."

"I think he's very pleased that you did." Running out of hair, Savannah held her hand out for the elastic binder. "Since he and I are married, he'll be like your dad, even though he's really your—"

"Let's not say 'uncle,'" Claudia determined. "I was thinking they could just trade, and if my real dad ever comes to see us, he could be my uncle. Wouldn't that be good?"

"That would be very good." Clay had appeared in the doorway. He wanted to take his child to school this morning as Kole might have done, tearing down the gravel road, leaving a billowing dust wake that could be seen for miles. A flag to proclaim their presence. "But you know what?" he said. "Some people even have two dads."

"Some people don't have any. I guess I don't mind having two, but . . ." Claudia hopped off the bed and grabbed her shoes. "I'm glad we live with you."

"I am, too."

"And if the other kids wanna move back in, they can, but I don't know if I trust Dallas to ride Angel, because he scared her yesterday. She doesn't like it when people act loud. And he better not be telling people I got bucked off." She stood at Clay's feet, her head tipped back. "Can I tell you a secret?"

"Sure." He hunkered down, sitting on the heels of his boots to get to her eye level. But his eyes sought Savannah's. She stood across the room, watching, her eyes meeting his. She seemed separate, farther away than she had been a moment ago.

Claudia cupped her hands around his ear, whispered, "Remember, I still love you," and kissed his cheek. He was so stunned, he neglected to return the favor before she ran to get her coat.

"What did she say?" Savannah asked distantly.

"You heard her. It's a secret." He smiled, oddly willing to torture her a bit. "When you love someone, you trust him with your secrets."

Chapter 19

Clay's pickup was parked outside the barn the next morning.

The light was on when Savannah walked in, the wheelbarrow contained evidence that a stall-cleaning had been committed, and somebody with big teeth was contentedly chewing. Which meant somebody else had done her job.

"Ol' straw-bones here is looking less scary," Clay called out from the stall as she approached, carrying her morning coffee. "We can start increasing the amount of alfalfa and decreasing the frequency of the meals," he told her without looking up. "Gradually. The trick is not to push."

"I'll remember that," she said to his back. When he finally turned, she handed him the coffee, as though she'd brought it for him. "Good morning."

"Thanks." He sipped noisily. "Does this mean you forgive me?"

"For spilling my beans?" She leaned against the frame of the open stall door. "She doesn't seem to be too traumatized."

"And they're not all your beans."

He sipped again. Over the rim of the cup, his eyes challenged her to disagree. She declined with a shrug. For a moment they stood there listening to the grinding of horse teeth, watching the feeding as though they were fascinated.

"I'll be gone this weekend," Clay said. He seemed to think the horse might be the only one interested. "All weekend. I agreed to work an endurance event they're having in the Bighorns." He scratched Scarecrow's ears, suggesting quietly, "Maybe you'd like to go along."

"Me?" She heard herself sounding pop-eyed. She hadn't meant to. "What would I . . . what do you do?"

"Camp. Set up shop. Replace shoes. It's not like going to the racetrack. There's a lot of time spent waiting, so if you went along, we could take our own horses and maybe relax a little bit. Ride the trails and roast marshmallows."

"Isn't it getting a little too cold for that? Claudia's already got the sniffles. I'll bet Reno would go with you."

"He would if I asked him, but I'm asking you. Claudia wouldn't have to go this time." He gave her a guarded look. "It could be just you and me. It's the kind of thing we used to do when we were kids." He glanced away. "Back when we did things kinda normally."

"Define *normal*." She gave a quick laugh, as she pushed away from the door frame, reaching in her jacket pocket for a diversion. "Did I show you the plan Uncle Mick drew up for the barn?"

"No."

"I didn't even ask him to, Clay. This was all his idea. Look." She unfolded the drawing, penciled on the back of a flyer advertising bull semen. "He says we can easily add four more stalls here. And we can have a wash rack here."

"A *wash rack*?" Clay barely glanced at the paper she'd shoved under his nose. "This ain't no goddamn show barn."

"He says it wouldn't cost anything to put it in, and we could use it for lots of things."

"What? Maybe a car wash as another sideline? Maybe we could set up a vegetable stand while we're at it. Put up a sign on the highway. 'SUDS 'N' SPUDS. Support Our Poor Old Horses.' "

"Oh, Clay."

"That's right, they're not all poor."

"Why can't you just admit that this is beginning to look feasible? You of all people, Clay, this should appeal to your sense of—"

"It doesn't appeal to any sense of mine. None whatsoever. I don't know why I let it go this far. You don't need to be takin' care of somebody else's broken-down horses."

"But you were already doing it."

"Those are *my own* broken-down horses." He spared Scarecrow a custodial pat on the shoulder. "I'll get you a good horse, Savannah. I'll get you lots of good horses. All you want. I'll build you more stalls. I'll . . ."

"I had a call from another woman who wants to place a horse with us. I haven't advertised anything, Clay. This is all word-of-mouth." She was getting into it now, eagerly flapping Uncle Mick's drawing, the little trip to the Bighorns all but forgotten. "Two thousand dollars a month. Can you imagine?"

"No, I can't." He took the paper from her hand, just to get it out from under his nose. "How do some people end up with more money than brains?"

"You won't have to work so hard."

"I don't know how you figure that."

"Your back hurts all the time, but you're still taking on new clients. Horseshoeing is so hard on you."

"Cattle prices are down. When they go back up, I'll cut back on the clients. Right now, farriers are scarce around here, so I can make—"

"Good money, I know. I can, too. Especially if I can put the retirement idea together with this other program."

"Do what you want," he said as he stepped around her and out of the stall. "You're used to runnin' with a different crowd, and they like to get stuff going. I'll clean out the pole barn and you can have a charity dance if you want."

"I can think of nothing more terrifying, and that's not the kind of program I'm . . ." She stepped out behind him and closed the door, muttering, "There are ways to do what you do without going broke."

"We're not going broke!" He whirled so quickly, he spilled the coffee he'd forgotten he carried, splashing his jacket. "Shit."

"I didn't mean—"

"So your answer is no."

"The trick is not to push." She turned to close the stall door.

"Do what you want, Savannah." He tossed the rest of the coffee. The stream arced in the air, then hit the floor with a satisfying splat. "We've got more'n thirty thousand acres here. We won't get in each other's way too much."

"I won't do anything you don't want me to do."

"Sorry, but that's my line." He laughed. "That's the high ground. I'm already staked out up there."

"I don't see what's so high about it," she snapped, spinning on the heel of her new boot.

He didn't, either. He felt pretty low as he watched her walk away. She needed something to do, something more exciting than cooking for the Lazy K or camping in the Bighorns. He knew damn well it was only a matter of time before she got her confidence tucked back into her craw and took off for the kind of place where they didn't use a barn for a ballroom.

What was he going to do about it?

He looked down at his working-man's hands, holding an empty coffee cup and a piece of paper. Stuff she'd tried to appease him with. He pitched and broke one, crumpled and pitched the other. Changed nothing, but felt good. He'd gouged a nice little notch in the wall. Hell, distress was good for barn wood. He kicked the broken pottery aside, but the ball of paper wouldn't let him pass. He squatted to retrieve it, bounced it from hand to hand a couple of times, finally straightened it out and gave it another look.

He compared the drawing with the structure around him. Mick's plan claimed space that was used for storage, but most of what was being stored was junk. Clay checked the measurements in the sketch, imagined tying into the beams and adding a structure to the outside. Wouldn't take much.

He laughed aloud when he realized where his thinking was headed. He'd add polished wood floors and mirrors to the place if she wanted them. *Goddamn, he was one sorry, lovesick fool.*

She was getting ready to take Claudia to the bus stop when he came back to the house. "I'll build your stalls," he told her.

She raised her brow, surprised.

"You want four more?"

"The four stalls were Uncle Mick's idea."

"I can put in four pretty easy." He glanced at the coffeepot. Still some left, but the light was off. Probably cold, but he could nuke it in the microwave. "Tell you what, though. If your rich friends start agitating for heat, that's where I draw the line."

She opened a cupboard and handed him a cup. "If they want heat, they can go to Florida."

"That's what I say."

Savannah sat on the floor in the dark, her back braced against the side of the bed, hugging her knees, contemplating the night sky through the tall bedroom window. She wiggled her toes in the thick pile of the bedside rug as she mentally recounted all the normal things she'd done that day. She'd taken her daughter to school, stopped at the Mercantile for groceries and a visit with her aunt, groomed four horses, washed clothes, fricasseed a chicken, groomed two more horses, read about the adventures of Paddington Bear—so normal! And her husband, who had presumably worked his normal fourteen-hour day, was now soaking in the bathtub.

It was late. The house was quiet. If she listened closely, she could actually hear him lather his hair. She could feel the water trickle down the back of his neck. She could imagine which lovely part of him was moving by the plunk and dribble it caused in the water.

Or she could go look for herself.

She'd done it before, hadn't she? Accidentally. Recalling the glorious sight of him, every inch of him, she tucked her right hand between her thighs and chest and tested the feel of her breasts. Once they had been twins, one as sensitive and responsive as the other. Now they were barely sisters. They had all they could do to keep up appearances, to play a role.

Which was all Savannah wanted, really. A role, some worthwhile role to play. With Clay. To play. To play with Clay . . .

Darkness bolstered her impulse. She crept across the room, rapped softly on the door. "May I come in?"

It took him a moment to answer. "Depends on your intentions. Are you a serious buyer, or just window-shopping this evening?"

She cracked open the door. She might have seen him in the mirror, but she didn't look. "My intentions are honorable."

"Then don't bring them in here," he said quietly. "You wanna look without touching, go find a picture."

She reached through the crack and slid her hand over the switch, dousing the light. "That settles the looking question."

He laughed in the dark. "Now you really have me at a disadvantage."

"I was hoping to catch you taking a break from the high ground." The hinges creaked as she slipped past the door and knelt on the mat beside the tub. Feeling deliciously mischievous, she whispered, "How about if I touch without looking?"

"Sounds like a woman thing."

"Maybe. But I want to touch man things." She lowered her hand, found water, then smooth hip, then muscular thigh. "How does the term 'touching base' strike you?"

"Is that a military thing? Nautical, maybe?" He laid his wet hand over hers, rocked it back and forth so that the sparse hairs on his thigh tickled her palm. "Try touching it stem to stern."

"I love to touch." Her hand escaped, skated over his hip, and slid home to his hard belly. His penis brushed the back of her hand. She caressed him under the water, her little finger the first to tangle in the bog that grounded his erection. He caught his breath when she found the soft eggs in that nest, and she smiled, delighted in the dark. "I never used to do much of the touching, remember?" she whispered. "I wanted to be on the receiving end. But now touching brings me pleasure."

"That makes two of us."

"I love to listen to you bathe," she said.

"You listen?"

"It's so much more interesting than listening to the shower run."

"I won't ask where it ranks with watching grass . . . ahh . . . grow."

"Grow, yes," she whispered, encouraging him. "You may have a bad back, but you surely put up a good front."

"It's a warning," he said, causing a slosh as he shifted his body. "Dangerous waters."

"I don't think so. I'd love it if you would touch your stem with my stern, but I know you wouldn't be—"

He cut her off with a kiss. When she balanced herself against him, hands near his waist, pulling her into the water on top of him became a matter of course, as did kissing her through the little she struggled, kissing her breathless. And when she was thoroughly kissed and thoroughly wet and thoroughly seated in his lap, he asked, "Wouldn't be what, Savannah?"

She laughed, caressing his silky-wet skin. "We're getting water all over the . . ."

"It's just water." He gathered the tail of her sopping night-shirt. "Take this off and let me—"

"No!" She pushed his hands away, knowing full well her response made no sense.

He growled, gripping her buttocks. "Fuck me, then."

The word, coming out of Clay's mouth, infuriated her. She tried to push away, but he was her only purchase, and they were both slick as seals. She slid against him, his huge, hard penis parting her like a letter opener, nicking the delicate contents with a blunt tip. The sweet shock of it made her gasp. *Did I hurt you?* she was sure he would say, but if he did, she didn't hear him. She rocked and rubbed. He shifted, sloshed more water, teased her within the puddle that had become their joint lap, his penis finding her clitoris as skillfully as a finger. He kissed her mouth, his tongue tangling with hers, and she opened up to him, wrapping herself in him, rocking her hips for that silky touch in the puddle.

He lifted her, set her on edge at the foot of the tub, cold porcelain beneath her bottom, warm, wet hands parting her thighs. She felt his face touch her belly. She pressed her hand over her abdominal scar, but he took it away, trapped her hands, one on the outside of each thigh as he cooled her wet skin with his breath.

But his tongue was no coolant. It was a tickler, a taster, a mover and shaker. It opened her more surely than his hands did, made her legs go limp without touching them, made her hands grip his, made her toes curl, her toneless voice discover C sharp. She came with a shuddering vengeance.

"*Now* fuck me," he exhorted, and she slithered, fell, dove into his arms, braced herself on his shoulders, lifted and located and lowered, a long, long slide, terribly long, exquisitely deep, until he fully filled her needy, raw-edged inside pocket. He was almost too much, soon would be, would overflow. They would both overflow. His breath quickened, sounded so bold and delicious that she wanted it for herself—his breath, blood, voice, energy, all bursting inside her.

And this, all this, he gave generously.

Later, when all tremors had passed and cooling water invited cooler awareness, they separated. She stood. He followed. As they stepped out of the tub she asked him not to turn the light on. "Darkness is kinder," she said. "Light can be so rude."

He said nothing. She started to hand him a towel, but it met with his chest, so she began blotting his chest, his shoulders, which, like a statue, he permitted. She would have leaned against him but for her wet nightshirt. She might have kissed the parts of him she'd dried, but he suddenly took the towel from her and wrapped it around his waist.

"Wouldn't wanna be rude," he said. "Will there be anything else tonight, ma'am?"

"Wasn't that . . ."

"Good for me?" He chuckled as he cupped her cheek in his hand, but she sensed no humor in him. "You're an adventure, Savannah. I'll say that."

She grabbed his hand before he could draw it away, turned her lips to his palm. An adventure, yes. Cryptic and kinky. Not quite all there. That awful prickling plagued her throat. How rude she was, too, rude as a flashlight.

"Anything else?" he whispered.

Come to bed with me, she might have said, had she been normal. But she shook her head.

And so, because he was kinder, he continued to let her have his bed to herself.

He left for the weekend without saying much except that she wouldn't be missing anything since the weather didn't look promising. But he was wrong about that. She was already missing him before his pickup disappeared over the first dip in the road to the Lazy K. She went about her chores missing him, and she began to wish she had agreed to go along with him. When it started raining, she wished it all the more. Not that she wished to be camping in the rain, but she wished to be with Clay when the rain came, muddying up the horses' hooves, soaking the legs of his jeans, chilling him to the bone.

It was a soft rain, unusual for Wyoming, quiet and gray. Was it raining like this in the Bighorns? Was her husband wet and shivering in the cold, trying to get some hot-blooded horse to hold still while he repaired a shoe? Or was he sitting in the pickup waiting for the rain to let up, heater running, radio soothing him with the strains of a sad, slow country song? And was he alone?

She could have gone with him. Claudia could have stayed with Aunt Billie. The child would have been fine. They both would have been fine, and she would have been with Clay. She might have been a help to him. She could be handing him nails. He might have let her dry him, warm him, cheer him, hold him while the rain pelted the pickup roof. She imagined these things all morning while she tended his horses.

Heather called with information about an organization called the Alliance for Animals, which appeared to be the perfect connection for Savannah's program, if the idea were to become a program. There were chapters all over the country, and one of their missions was to rescue animals. Another was to provide sanctuary. They were interested in having an ally in Wyoming, especially a horse rescuer with a well-known face.

Savannah fervently credited Clay with being the rescuer, but Heather reminded her that she had the face and urged her to come to New York and meet the president of the organization. Savannah laughed, said she couldn't afford the time or the ticket. But the thought didn't terrify her. She could see herself dressing up in the Western-style skirt Clay and Claudia had picked out for her and hopping in a cab with Heather for a go-see. She would be going to see about something other than herself or her body, healthy or sick. She could really do that, she thought. Amazing.

She felt tingly when she hung up the phone, like someone with sleeping limbs whose blood had just begun to stir. She couldn't wait to tell Clay.

Then Patty appeared in the kitchen doorway. "What does Clayton think of all this?"

Savannah looked at her, raised an eyebrow.

"I couldn't help but overhear." Patty pulled a stool up to the counter and sat down. "Okay, maybe I could've, but I didn't try. It sounds like you're wantin' to hook up with some left-wing, liberal, welfare-checks-for-all-God's-creatures kind of outfit."

"Horses only. No donkeys or elephants allowed."

"I repeat, what does Clayton think of all this?"

"He's skeptical." Savannah took two cups from a cupboard. She and Patty had begun regularly sharing a mid-morning cup of coffee. "I'm just doing a little research, Patty. It might not even be an option. You like the retirement plan so far, don't you?"

"I like soakin' those crazy Californians, but this sounds a

little different. Where's that girl from, the one you were just talkin' to?"

"New York."

"*Way* different. We don't wanna mess with that bunch. Those folks don't soak so easy."

"How do you know?"

"I watch TV," she said, and they both laughed.

"Clay said he'd build some more stalls in the barn."

Patty nodded, obviously not surprised. "For you. Not for your idea."

"It's a good idea, though. Isn't it?"

"You're thinking of going back to New York?"

"Oh, that was just Heather's idea. Some people she thinks I should meet. If you know the right people, it's amazing what avenues you can find . . ." Savannah set coffee on the counter in front of Patty. "Clay's working so hard to keep this place going."

"You're right about that." Patty sipped, then gestured with the cup. "You go easy on him with this, Savannah. You were always about one handful more than he knew what to do with."

"I've had the other handful surgically removed." She grinned. Then, earnestly: "I just want to help him."

"And he wants to help you." Patty glanced out the window. The slate clouds seemed to settle in her eyes. "Sometimes you can be too helpful. I was real helpful to Jonas. I knew I wasn't pretty, and I'm sure as hell not very lovable, so I made myself indispensable. Be sure and carve this on my tombstone." With a weathered hand, she sketched two lines in the air: "Patty Keogh— Dispensable At Last."

"Whatever you say." Savannah smiled. "But who says you're not lovable?"

"Nobody. They don't dare." Patty smiled back. "Maybe you should just try loving each other, Savannah. And if you don't, if you can't, then . . ." She shook her head sadly. "Don't bother trying to be helpful."

The Bighorns were shrouded in clouds, drenched in cold rain. Clay was glad Savannah had had the good sense to stay home and keep dry.

They ran the race through Saturday's drizzle, but by Sunday the veterinarians who checked the horses for soundness started pulling competitors. The riders were generally stubborn enough to continue if they could, but conditions were becoming hard on the horses. Clay prided himself on seeing a job through, but conditions were nearly as hard on him, mud being a frequent claimer of horseshoes when the hooves soaked up the moisture and expanded, working the nails loose.

They finally wrapped it up, the crazy bastards, riding through rain and sleet. True to its name, the race went to those who endured. Clay, too, had endured, and he had made good money, though he'd paid his own price. The damp cold permeated every bone in his body, he was exhausted, and his back was killing him. Medication wouldn't touch the pain that kept shooting down his legs. He needed a tub full of hot water in the worst way. Or Savannah's warm hands, in the best way.

He was almost home, but the desolate road still seemed endless. He didn't know what time it was, figured it had to be pretty late. He wasn't getting anything but static on the radio, leaving him to wish for the umpteenth time for a tape player. Something frivolous for himself. How bad could that be?

The pain was so bad he thought about stopping somewhere, pulling off the road and toughing it out until either the pain or the rain let up. He could handle one or the other. The combination was getting to him. Yet he kept going, kept thinking about that hot water, those magic hands taking the pain away. She'd do that for him. The closer he got to home, the harder it became to bear the pain, and he realized that it was more than his back. The pull of home caused him pain, growing sharper as he drew closer, so close he could see but not quite touch. Seeing was believing, and believing was deceiving.

Then, suddenly, he could no longer see. The pull of home and the pain of home conspired with physical pain and driving rain to take his power, his iron control. He couldn't see the road or the curve or the moving body in his path. He felt the jolt, heard the shrill cry, tasted the terror, saw the gravel turn to grass, the world tilt, shudder, and at last go still.

Thank God for stillness. Heart pounding wildly, he sat motionless and stared at the rain slanting through the cock-eyed light that speared the night. Then he heard that cry again, and he knew he'd caused unspeakable pain. He put his own aside, released his seat belt, and launched himself out of the pickup, into the night, looking for a buck, maybe, even a cow. Anything but what he feared.

He didn't have to go far. The animal he'd hit lay on its side, struggling against the odds of wet clay and shattered bones. It was so dark that all Clay could see at first was a bobbing hulk, trying in vain to right itself. But he knew what he'd done. He knew the terrorized cry and the agile action of its body, even in pain.

Clay's whole being went numb.

The icy rain drove him back to the pickup, to grab the keys, unlock the glove box, find the .22, load it, grab a flashlight, every move quick and precise despite his churning stomach. He could feel nothing else, no pain, no fear, nothing but the sickness he had to fight to hold down while he took steps. One foot in front of the other.

Goddamn his useless eyes, he'd hit a horse.

He followed the beam of the flashlight, retraced his steps, found blood but no animal. *Gone.*

Then he heard the shivering whinny, saw the staggering shadow, knew that the suffering creature had somehow gotten itself up and set its sights on the hills. It would flee until it dropped.

And Clay would be there with the horse when it did.

Chapter 20

Savannah had just gotten Claudia up for school when the phone rang.

"Savannah? It's Roxie."

Savannah said nothing. She'd already looked out the window, saw the big emptiness all around the clothesline. She was getting the phone call she had so primly and properly claimed she would have appreciated last time.

Just listen, then deliver a cool thanks for calling.

"It's early, I know, but I was out kinda late last night, couldn't get home until the rain let up some, you know? Actually, I just got in. But the thing is, I saw the pickup on the way home. It looks pretty bad. I'm not being nosy now. I just wanted to make sure everybody was okay."

The train of Savannah's thoughts abruptly jumped the track.

"Clay's pickup?"

"Out by the Sherwood cutoff. I stopped, but no one was around. What did he hit? A cow or something? Had to be bigger than a deer."

"He, uh . . ."

"He told Reno he was going up to the Bighorns for one of those horse deals over the weekend. So when I saw the pickup, what with the weather and all, I figured it musta just happened."

"Last night he . . ." She didn't know, couldn't think. He hadn't called, and her thoughts had hopped from regret to worry to anger to The hell with him. The Sherwood cutoff? *What did he hit?* "He came back last night," she said, guessing. Be damned if she would tell Roxie otherwise.

"Well, I'm glad he's okay, then. Sorry to bother you. The kids think of him like he's . . ." There was a pause, an indelicate snort. "Clay's a rock, you know? Kinda shook me up when I saw that pickup."

But she'd said he wasn't in the pickup, which meant he'd gotten out, which meant he must be okay. Had to be.

"I'll let him know you called, Roxie."

"You do that. Make him take it easy."

Savannah wasn't going to let anyone know anything until she found out for herself what was going on. She checked every room in the house. "Can you get yourself some cereal, muffin?" she asked when she stuck her head into Claudia's room. "I have to run out to the barn."

"Cereal muffin? How about muffin cereal?" Claudia giggled as she popped her head through a red turtleneck. "You put cereal in muffins sometimes. I think there should be muffin cereal."

"We'll work on it. Turn your shirt around, muffin, you've got the flower . . ." Savannah made a turn-around gesture with one hand while she closed the door with the other.

She pulled tall rubber paddock boots over thick wool socks. It had stopped raining, and the world felt cold, wet, abysmally dark. Her warm breath misted in quick puffs as she darted around puddles thinly crusted with ice. Her heart beat a tattoo for her worries: where-is-that-man, where-is-that-man.

She ran into Uncle Mick stacking square bales in the barn. "Have you seen Clay this morning?" she asked him.

"His pickup ain't here. Likely pulled into a motel last night. He wouldn't chance it in that storm." He gave an old man's knowing look. "Don't you worry, he'll call soon as he wakes up. Likely he's pure worn out."

Uncle Mick's explanation sounded so sensible, she told herself Roxie could have been mistaken about the pickup. It could have been someone else's. But if her hunch was right and he was still out there, probably at the Sherwood shack, he had to be cold and wet. She stuffed some of his clothes into a backpack, put Claudia on the bus, then drove to the cutoff.

Her heart leaped into her throat at the sight of Clay's pickup in the ditch. The front was crumpled, one headlight smashed. Spiderweb cracks in the windshield refracted the first rays of the morning sun. She checked the cab. No blood, but there was an open box of bullets sitting on the glove compartment door. Clearly he had gone after the wounded animal.

She drove as far as she could on the cutoff, abandoning the pickup where gravel turned to mud. From there she walked toward the foothills. The discovery of the dead horse left her heartsick, both for the animal and for Clay. It was covered with mud, stiff legs jutting at odd angles from the bloated belly. She couldn't tell whether he'd had to shoot it, but she didn't venture close enough to the rise where it lay to find out.

She expected to find him at the base of the hills in the old three-room shack, where they'd met with their friends in the green-gold days of their adolescence when a six-pack made a party. But whatever scurried across the floor when she opened the door was not Clay.

She looked to the hills. If this had happened to her, she knew where she would be now. She knew him. She knew how he felt about the death of that horse. She knew exactly where he was. She wished she'd worn her other boots and a lighter-weight jacket, but she adjusted the straps on the backpack and began her climb.

A thin trail of white smoke curled above Artemis's Castle. As soon as she saw it, the enormous weight she'd been carrying withdrew, dissipated, joined the smoke. A mere backpack and bulky jacket were nothing. After a long climb, she ran the final yards on the burst of energy that was her joy's gift. The sight of him—shirtless, hunkering close to a small fire beneath the rocky overhang of their old hideout—redoubled that joy. She called out to him as she made her stumbling, lead-foot run.

He stood slowly. Ah, she'd surprised him. He staggered when she flew at him, leaving him no choice but to catch her in his arms and permit her examination of his body.

She found the gash on his forehead, crusted with blood. "If the pickup's totaled, the next one will be new enough to have air bags," he said, flinching at her touch. "What are you . . . *how* did you know? How did you come?"

"You didn't know I was a tracker, did you?" Gingerly she touched a purpling bruise on his chest. "I drove as far as I could, then walked. Thank God you're all right. You are, aren't you?"

"I was trying to get home."

"The storm was terrible." She tugged at the straps of the backpack. "I saw the pickup. It looks . . . You're not hurt, are you? You must be freezing."

"No, I'm . . ." He shook his head, rubbed his hands over his arms. He seemed dazed, watching her tear into the backpack. "You saw what I did."

"I saw what happened." Her eyes sought his as she squatted with the backpack, the better to find what he needed, busy her hands, and do for him. But her heart went out to him, to the confusion and sadness in his eyes. "I'm so sorry, Clay."

"I should have stopped somewhere, but I . . ."

"There aren't that many places to stop out here, and you were almost home." She found the thermal pullover, then the socks, glad she'd thought of these things, glad she'd made the hike. She felt like Superwoman. "I brought you some clothes," she muttered into the open pack. "Dry clothes. I'll bet you're chilled to the bone. Where did you find dry wood?"

"I was close. I was so damn close, Savannah." He squatted next to her, his eyes searching hers as though she might have an explanation for him, maybe some kind of exoneration. But all she knew was that he was shivering, and for that she had a shirt. "There's no excuse," he said as she brought the white garment down on his head.

When his head reappeared, he was still looking at her, as though the contact hadn't been disturbed. "It's been raining off and on the whole miserable weekend," he reported, finally plunging his arms into the sleeves.

She smiled, remembering Claudia and her backward turtleneck and comparing the shape of their chins and eyes and thinking how good it was to have him safe.

But he had no idea what inspired her to smile, and he shook his head. "I knew better. I wasn't drinking or doing anything stupid, just trying to get home. I should've pulled over and waited it out."

"It's over now," she said, handing him a plaid wool shirt with a quilted lining. "One of those things that's done and can't be undone, and you thank God no one's—"

"Hurt? The horse is dead. I know where she got out, too. I never finished fixing that fence. I got too busy, or let my head get too . . ."

"Which one?" That the animal had an identity had not occurred to her, but suddenly it was one of theirs, a mare. "I didn't . . . I only got close enough to see that it was a horse."

"Sugarfoot."

Savannah shook her head. Couldn't be. "I'm pretty sure

she was there yesterday. The weather was so bad, I didn't take a head count or anything when I fed them." Part of the responsibility now rested with her. They were her charges. And that horse, that sweet, friendly, irreparably damaged— "Oh, Sugarfoot, I'm so sorry."

Clay hung his head. "At least it wasn't one of your boarders."

"It was an accident." She touched his cheek, but he backed away, recoiling from her sympathy. "Oh, Clay, you look so tired," she whispered anyway. "I should have gone with you. I could have helped."

"No, you were smart. I've been sitting up here thinking, Oh, God, it could have been a lot worse. Savannah could have been in the pickup with me." He sat staring into the fire now, arms draped over his knees. "It was raining pretty hard, so dark, she came out of nowhere. I didn't see . . ."

Savannah slid closer to him. "You're so tired."

He didn't seem to hear her. "I'm pretty much used to nowhere, coming from there myself. I know better."

"You were trying to get home." She wanted him to look into her eyes again and listen to what she was saying. "I was waiting for you at home."

"I know better." Clay gave a small, sad laugh. "You came from nowhere, too, but you're not the waiting kind. You're the charge-ahead kind, like Sugarfoot. Just as soon as you get those beautiful legs back underneath you, honey, you'll be waiting for no man. And that's good, Savannah; you should charge ahead. You got hit hard, but now you . . ." Finally Clay looked at her, his eyes full of guilt and pain. "I want you to be well, in your body and your mind both. I swear I do."

He seemed eager to convince her of something she did not doubt. "I think I'm almost there," she assured him quietly.

"I know you are."

"And I really want to charge ahead." Her gift to him, because he had helped her get strong enough to think straight, to emerge, to hope, to plan. "Carefully. Is it possible to charge cautiously? I want to try to make something of this idea with the horses. It fits so well with the way you—"

"I just killed one, Savannah. I just . . ." Such hurt filled his eyes that he turned from her again and stared into the fire. "They're old, you know, most of them. Old horses don't just fade away. They die. The place could be littered with corpses. You don't want that. I had to put a bullet in that mare's brain because she wouldn't quit running, dragging . . ." He glanced at her, shook his head, eyes back to the fire. "Because she was dying."

"She was running scared, Clay. I know how that is, how far it can take you." She laid her hand on his arm. "Maybe I'm dying, too."

He gave her a surprisingly defiant look.

"But I'm not hiding anymore," she added quickly as she turned away from that look. She took a pair of wool socks from the bag. "I'll bet your socks are wet. They say—"

"Hiding from what?" he barked as he pulled off one of his boots.

"I'm not running scared, thanks to you. I just don't feel like dying right now, frankly, so I haven't been thinking about it that much lately. I've been busy learning about the opposite of dying."

"Which is living." He grunted as he jerked on the other boot, and she heard the pain, knew it must be his back, regretted her thoughtlessness. She might have done him the service of removing his boots.

"And then some. For a while there, I was walking, talking, breathing, and all that, but I was going dead inside. I think it's loving. I'm learning about loving. All kinds of loving, some that I've taken for granted, some I've shunned, some I've belittled." She took his foot into her lap, keeping it near the crackling fire, and began peeling the wet sock as if she were unwrapping something she treasured. "I've always loved you, Clay."

"I know."

She looked up, smiling, rubbing his cold toes between her palms. "How can you know so many things about me that I don't know?"

"I've always loved you." But he didn't smile back. "There's all kinds of love, isn't there? You feel love for a child, a mother, a friend. It's a little different with each one."

"I've never loved a man as a husband before. Maybe I've never really loved a man before, although I've always thought of you as the man I most . . ." She slipped the dry sock on his big foot. "But not this way, not as a husband. I'm just learning."

"It's supposed to just happen, isn't it? Like lightning." His two-fingered fork speared the air. "*Zap*. Gotta have that man."

She smiled. "Like that first night I came up here?"

"Sha*zaam*," he said with a throaty chuckle.

"We've never had a shortage of lust between us, have we? I think that's different. Like you said, different ways of loving."

"Maybe it's the trust we're short on. I keep thinking that if she starts to trust me, maybe she'll learn to love me, let me love her."

"But I do—"

"You don't know how I could love you, Savannah. If you'd just take the wall down—that's the part I can't do."

She grabbed his other foot. She had to laugh. He'd nearly gotten himself killed, was still trying to get pneumonia, and all he could think about was taking her clothes off.

"When you love . . ." He leaned closer, his entreaty softer than the crackle of the fire. "You reveal all your secrets. Even the ones you hate the most, the ones that scare you the most."

"And the one who loves you doesn't turn away," she said without looking up.

"Maybe that's one sure way you can tell."

She pulled her bulky jacket closed in front, drew a deep breath. He was right. The surgical scars felt like thin cords strapped around her, holding her together. She felt every inch of the skin stretched over her two breasts, pushing against her bra, pressing for acceptance. Not his acceptance. Hers.

She felt foolish.

Why should *she* feel foolish when *he* was the one who didn't have the sense to come in out of the rain? He was the one who collided with the horse. This time he was the one wandering in the night. The rock was on a roll, poor guy, and he was . . .

Definitely the one.

"I don't know what I expect." She fingered the front of her jacket. "It seems so much safer to keep it a little mysterious, you know?"

"Which keeps us apart."

"What if you're disgusted, and I see that you're disgusted? What if I'm disgusted? What if it's even uglier than I thought?" She searched his eyes for answers, but all she saw was a dare. *Get it over with. Find out.* "You told me that I was all you ever wanted. This body is all I ever had, you see. All that you've ever wanted isn't all there anymore."

"You believe that?"

"No. In my head I don't. But I'm still scared."

"Me, too."

"Really?" She laughed. "What scares you the most?"

"I'm scared that nothing I do is gonna change the fact that pretty soon you won't need me."

"Any more than you need me?" Ah, yes, he had his blind spot, too. "You're a loving man, a generous man. You're adamant about looking after those you love. But no one is allowed to look after you." She slipped her jacket off, leaving her with a cardigan, a blouse, a bra. A step. Another challenge. "Try again. What scares you the most?"

"Doing what I did last night, maybe. I don't know. Dropping the baby on its head." He studied the buttons on her blouse, and she wondered whether they scared him, too. "What's the big deal about sleeping together anyway, right? People fuck all the time without—"

"You're right, Clay, that's not enough for us." She reached for his hand, drew it to her right breast, laid it over her blouse. "I never thought I'd show anyone. I used to have no problem baring it all, you know, because people loved it. *It*. Me. They loved me. They thought I was beautiful. Perfect. Well, I'm no longer . . ." She undid a button. "I showed it to the women in my support group. They're not perfect, either."

"Neither am I."

"No breasts, that's true, but you don't miss what you never had." Another button. Another. "And you've always been beautiful, and I've always loved you. No other man was ever good enough. And when you love"—she released the clasp between her breasts—" you reveal the secrets that scare you the most."

He lifted his hand instinctively, but he stopped, raised his eyes to hers, asking permission. She nodded. He had no problem looking, no problem touching, tracing the line of a scar. Loving, healing hands. She drew a slow, deep breath, breasts on the rise, heart on the rise, her whole being gone a-shiver.

"Are my hands cold?" His smile was so tender it nearly broke her heart. "Guess I never worried about that before, huh?"

"I don't have much feeling on that side. A little, not much. The nipple is just for show." Her laughter was as light as a child's. "Maybe what's showing is my vanity."

"I don't see that."

"What do you see?"

"I don't see . . ." He moved the dangling cups aside.

She watched, noticed the plainness of the bra, flesh-colored, padded for protection. No style. Lady Elizabeth would be mortified.

"It's hard to believe you had a breast removed," he said.

"Dr. Frankenstein has refined his technique." She leaned back, unsnapped her jeans, unveiled the scars on her abdomen. "This is where the insides came from."

He touched her tummy, slid his hand over her rib cage to her right breast, the journey itself a wonder to him. "You said they took and put it up here? Jesus, that is so cool."

She laughed. "You're such a male."

"There's no cure for that, I'm afraid. Even so, I see where they cut into you, where it must have hurt, maybe still hurts. And I'm thinking, How can I help her? How can I make it stop hurting?"

"Well, I guess you could shoot me."

He looked up, horrified.

She hugged him quickly. "I'm sorry. New York humor." Then, looking into his eyes again, she said, "There was a time when I would have been serious. I might have asked you to show me the same mercy you showed Sugarfoot, because I hurt so bad, and I'm so screwed up, and I don't know how to . . ." Bright idea. "What if you lost one of your balls?"

"I don't think I'd want to be shot."

"But you don't know for sure, do you? Would you mind if I . . ." Chattering now, full of herself with the import of her analogy, she started to unbuckle his belt. "Pretend something's missing down here, and I'm trying to get into your pants. And I probably wouldn't know the difference, because I'm not into counting balls, but I do enjoy touching you, and you know that's what I want to do."

"And I'd think you were counting and I'd be coming up short."

"Short? Now, *that* I might notice." He chuckled as she gripped his belt buckle, pressed her fist into his belly. "The thing is, you can't make it stop hurting. You end up hurting with me, is all, so why get messed up in it? I mean, if I take that fantasy one step further and imagine you losing that part or any part of you to cancer, that's a hurt that . . ."

"We'd share."

"You know what?" She stared at his crotch. "It just occurred to me that I'd gladly sacrifice the other breast to keep these balls right where they are."

He laughed.

She scowled at him. "No, I would. I really would."

"I'd never—"

"I know you wouldn't, but I would. Because, yeah, I'm scared of having it show up again, but I know I'm a lot tougher than I used to be, maybe even tougher than you. And I'm more scared of you hurting than me hurting." She thrust her chest out. "So go ahead and look all you want. I've just thought of something that scares me more than disappointing you."

"You disappoint me? When have I ever—"

"Seen anything quite like this?"

"Never." He cupped his hand beneath her battered breast, closed his eyes, eased back, stretching out, muttering, "Never been disappointed. Except a couple of those pictures. I didn't like the way some of those panties were cut. Come let me hold you a while." He cast a glance at the backpack. "What else did you bring?"

"I forgot the underwear."

"I forgot the pills. I've gotta lie down for a minute."

In all her revelation and speculation, she'd forgotten his pain. Real pain, not phantom pain. She tucked her jacket beneath his head, added pine fuel to the fire, then offered a massage.

"I want to hold you, Savannah." He reached for her. "Do

you still have those skimpy panties? They didn't look too comfortable, frankly."

"Those days are over," she told him, cuddling against his shoulder. "That body doesn't exist anymore. I don't know if it ever did."

"But this one does, full of more wonders than ever. Full of miracles. Full of you." He slid his hand over her breast, stroking. "Can you feel where my fingers are?"

"I know where they are."

"But can you feel them?"

"I feel the warmth," she said. "I feel warm all over."

"I don't remember a time when I didn't love you, but it's different now. One look, one word from you, and my life is yours."

"That's not fair. I can't match that with anything but poor odds."

"Whatever they are, I'll take 'em. But I'll tell you right now, if you don't outlive me, I'll be very disappointed in you."

"I don't want to outlive you. But then, I don't want to disappoint you, either." She propped herself up, looked him in the eye. "All right, you can go first, and I'll throw myself on your funeral pyre. Top that, big guy."

"If you go first, I'll stay. I'll keep your flame alive." He tapped his chest, where she would reside.

"Thank you." She closed her hand over his, hanging on, counting the reasons she had for doing so, no matter what. "After this weekend, we're lucky if we have one healthy chest between us."

"All I need is a little sleep."

"That's not all you need, but it's a start."

"After I fix the fence and round up anything else that got out."

"Uncle Mick and I can handle that. I got as close as I could with Uncle Mick's pickup, but we have a walk ahead of us."

Clay groaned.

"After I rub your back."

"Mmmm. I might fall asleep."

"Good." Savannah helped him turn over. "I'll be right here when you wake up."

Epilogue

After all he'd said about trust, Clay had trouble with Sa-
vannah's trip to New York before Christmas. Everyone had
tried to talk him into going with her—his mother, Aunt Billie, Uncle Mick, even Roxie. Not Claudia, though. He'd said
Savannah ought to take Claudia instead, and Claudia quite
agreed. She wanted to tell everybody she knew that she'd
skipped first grade. But maybe she was thinking the same
thing Clay was thinking.

What if Savannah didn't want to come back?

In that case, he'd be stuck with an extra job, taking care of
a few extra, useless horses, and with a bunch of extra Christmas presents. Not to mention some extra heartache. But he
was prepared. She'd looked glorious when he put her on the
plane. The old Savannah had been back in the saddle, her
beauty nearly unbearable. Kissing her good-bye had been a
thirty-second roller-coaster ride. He hadn't wanted it to end.

The tiny Jackson Hole Airport was quiet most of the day,
the occasional arrival or departure causing a flurry of activity. When the arrival of Savannah's flight was announced,
Clay kept his seat, kept his cool, and watched the disem-
barking passengers greet the folks who had come to pick
them up. He wasn't about to stand there, hat in hand. If she

365

didn't show, he figured he'd sit there until the waiting area cleared out.

But she did show, and he cursed himself for being surprised as he rose from the chair.

"There's Daddy! See, Mommy, the roads are *too* open." Claudia dropped her small bag and dove at his legs. He lifted her into his arms for a noisy kiss. "We had a bumpy ride on that little plane, and Mommy said the roads might not be open and you might not be able to come pick us up."

"I would have plowed them open myself to get here to pick you up." He glanced to one side, found Savannah. "I missed you."

"I missed you, too, Daddy. New York is kinda fun, but it's better living in Wyoming. I brought you a postcard of a policeman on a horse. It was the only horse postcard I could find. I was gonna mail it, but Mommy said we'd be home be-fore—"

"Claudia," Savannah enjoined. "I'd like one of those kisses, too."

He put his daughter down, took his wife in his arms, and had another one of those mouth-to-mouth roller-coaster rides, giving her more tongue than an airport greeting generally called for.

"I'm so glad to see you," she said when he let her breathe again.

"Same here."

"No kidding," Claudia said. "Everybody's looking."

"Let 'em look," Clay said as he took Claudia's hand and guided them both toward the sign directing them to baggage claim.

"No, don't let them." Savannah put her arm around his back as they walked. "I'm out of the have-a-look business. My new motto is: have a heart."

"And where are we putting this motto?"

"On our mirror. Would you be disappointed if the horse retirement program didn't work out?"

He glanced askance, eyebrows raised.

She returned a speculative look. "Would you be disappointed if it *did*?"

"Our favorite topic," he grumbled. "How do I disappoint thee? How about, would you be disappointed if I told you I haven't shown a profit in the cattle business in four years?"

"Not if you wouldn't be disappointed about a photo shoot I did while I was in New York." Another look was exchanged as they reached their destination. "Fully clothed, and for a good cause."

He eyed the array of bags. She was getting back into it. He shrugged. "I'd say your livelihood is a good cause."

"*Our* livelihood. I want to be your partner, Clay. The genuine article."

"Will you be going back for more pictures? Flying in and out of here in the winter can get dicey, so you might want to . . ."

"If we do more pictures, they'll be taken at the Lazy K. So far, all I've done is listen and learn and pose for an ad campaign that they're doing. The pictures weren't about me or about clothes or makeup. They were about caring for animals. And all I could talk about was what a big softy my husband is."

"Softy, huh?" He stared at her, swallowed hard. God, she looked good, her face radiant, her eyes alive with enthusiasm. Yeah, he was a softy; he was getting all choked up. "I wasn't sure you'd come back."

"I think I handled it well, Clay. I'm a lot stronger now, and I—" She drew a quick frown. "You thought I'd stay there?"

He suddenly felt exposed. He didn't know what to think, never did around Savannah. He was grateful for the chance to act when she recognized a black suitcase that looked to him like all the rest.

She got to it first, but he interceded. "Let me carry that."

"Okay." She smiled. "I could carry it myself, but it's nice that I don't have to." She glanced at Claudia, still holding Clay's hand. "It was a nice trip, too, but I was ready to leave when the time came. It's good to be home."

"We've still got a ways to go."

"I know we do. One step at a time. I think I took the first few standing on your feet, but now—"

"Now you've got new boots, and they're made for walking."

"Are you kidding?" She lifted one foot for his inspection, and he realized that she was dressed Western. Not New York. "These are riding boots. They're made for chasing you all over those thirty thousand Lazy K acres. And into Sunbonnet. And up to Artemis's Castle and over to the Bighorns for the next race. I know what I want now, too, and I'm not standing on your feet, but if you step out of line, I might have to step on your toes."

"One step at a time?"

She looped her arm through his as they headed for the exit. "Let's try a two-step. You and me, shoulder to shoulder, or as close as I can get to that height." The clown, she was walking on tiptoe. "I've thought of nothing else all day except that today we'd be home. We'd bring a little New York glamour back to Sunbonnet. We brought you some presents."

"I don't need glamour. All I need . . ."

"Yes?" She gave him a silly, expectant look. "I don't need fortune or fame, either. All I need is . . ." She was walking backward in front of him now, rolling her hand. "Sing it out, now."

"Love?" He laughed. Yeah, she was back in the saddle, full of games. He loved her games. "I've told you, you're all I've ever wanted."

"All I need is . . ."

"All I need is you."

"Yes! And my help." She poked a pretty finger at him. "You do. You need my help. Say it."

"Okay, I need your help." He jerked his chin, trying to tell her not to back through the glass. "Get the door."

She obliged. "And?"

"And since you've been gone, I realized how much you've taken on, so you about doubled my load by going away. And we got a call from another crazy, rich woman asking about the horse retirement program. I told her to bring ol' Skywalker on out. And now Charlotte's getting in on the act with some wild scheme for bringing a busload of people over for horse therapy, whatever the hell that is."

"Being around horses is therapeutic. I can attest to that. It's done wonders for you."

"Yeah, right. Now all I need is—"

"Hey, you guys," Claudia demanded as she tugged on Clay's hand. "Remember me? All I need right now is one little McDonald's Happy Meal."

Savannah had a surprise for him, she said, and she made him wait in the bedroom while she went behind the bathroom door and did some mysterious thing that produced only small sounds—a little running water, click, clack, brush, swish—door open, light off, and out she came, dressed as an angel. He sat up slowly. She glided across the room, yards of white gossamer floating from her shoulders, swirling around her legs.

"I didn't have a wedding dress."

"I offered to buy—"

"The groom doesn't buy the wedding dress." She did a runway turn, then gave him her best take-this-one look. "I decided it was time for a real wedding night. This is a wedding-night dress."

"What a waste."

"You don't like it?"

"Doesn't matter. If I have anything to say, you won't be wearing it for long."

"You have everything to say." She turned on the alarm-clock radio next to their bed and spun the dial until she found what she was looking for. A cowboy two-step. "Half of everything, anyway. The dress stays on until after the wedding dance."

Grinning, he took her in his arms, but then he backed off, eyeing his boots and her bare toes.

"It's all right, Clay." She pressed her hips against his and urged him to step with her to the rhythm they'd learned as children, long ago. "I trust you completely."

Acknowledgments

I could not have written this book without the help of my sister, Jill Pierson Boulrice, whose courage in the face of the terrible threat of breast cancer inspired me more surely and more deeply than I have ever been able to tell her. She's taught me about hanging in there, putting one foot in front of the other, keeping the faith. These are not clichés when a strong woman shows the rest of us how it's done. Thank you, Jill. I love you.

My sister was only forty years old when she discovered a lump in her breast. She thought it was a cyst at first—she'd had cysts for years. She was the mother of a four-year-old, and she thought she was too young, too healthy, it was much too soon for anything like cancer, which is what claimed our mother's life. But Jill went in for a mammogram, and we're so glad she did.

My sister is a breast-cancer survivor, and she happily joins me in encouraging readers to take care of themselves by getting regular checkups. The happy endings are beating out the sad ones these days. Just ask Jill's daughter, Abby!

Support breast-cancer research, for the sake of all our daughters.

"I need to get away from it all!"
❦

How many times have you cried out these words? The chance to change your life and maybe even be swept away by romance is so tempting . . . And as everyone knows, there's nothing like a good vacation . . .

The Avon Romance Superleaders are your passports to passion. As you enter the world created in each book, you have the chance to experience passion you've only dreamed of. Each destination is different—you might be whisked into Regency London, or perhaps to a secluded mountain cabin. But at each stop along the way, an unforgettable hero awaits to take your hand and guide you on a journey into love.

Imagine long, lazy summers in the country—the sun caresses your skin by day as you bask in its warmth in your favorite hammock . . . and each evening you curl up by the fire as contented as a cat. But something—or someone—is missing . . .

Then a compelling stranger comes striding into your life. And suddenly, a fire of a different sort begins to keep your nights hot. He's all-male, he's all-trouble . . . and he's got you . . .

All Shook Up

COMING JANUARY 2001

by Susan Andersen

"Are you planning on stalking me around my office?" Dru asked, Then she lost it. "Who taught you your manners, anyway? It certainly couldn't have been Great-aunt Edwina."

A muscle ticked in his jaw. "No, the lesson I learned from Edwina was that talk is cheap, and in the end there's only one person I can depend on—myself."

"Indeed? You'll have to excuse me if I don't cry big, sloppy tears over how misused you were. Because it seems to me that Edwina's talk wasn't all that cheap—for here you are, aren't you? Half owner in our lodge."

He took another step closer. "And that bothers you, doesn't it, sweetheart?"

She deliberately chose to misunderstand. "That you're bad-mouthing the woman who made it possible?" She ignored her reaction to his proximity this time and thrust her chin up. "Yes, I can honestly say I find that rather tacky."

For a moment his eyes went hot with some emotion Dru couldn't pin down, and she felt a burst of triumph that she'd managed to push one of his buttons. It was only fair, considering he seemed to have a natural facility for pushing all of hers.

Then his eyes went cool and distant. "Well, see, that's the thing about us lowlife types," he growled, stepping forward again. "Tacky is mother's milk to us, and we live for the opportunity to get something for nothing." He ran a rough-skinned fingertip down her cheek, leaving a streak of heat in its wake.

Dru jerked her head back, but he just moved in closer. "And we don't particularly care who we have to step on to get it either," he said in a low voice. "You might want to keep that in mind." His thumb rubbed her lower lip open, but he drew his hand back before she could slap it away. Giving her a slow once-over, he smiled insolently, and she saw that he didn't have bad teeth at all. They were maybe the slightest bit crooked—but very white and strong-looking.

The moment she dragged her gaze back to his eyes, he lifted an eyebrow. "The books?"

Blood thumping furiously in all her pulse points, Dru stalked over to the cabinet and pulled out the ledgers. A moment later she slapped them in his hands. "Here. These cover the past three years. Don't spill food on them and don't lose them."

"Guess that means I'd better not eat my peas with my knife again, huh?"

Embarrassed by her own snide rudeness, she resumed her seat, snatched up a pencil, and tapped it impatiently against the desktop, hoping to give the impression of a woman too busy for this nonsense. "Just be careful with them."

"Yes, ma'am." He gave her a bumptious salute and, with surprising grace for someone wearing several pounds of boot leather on each foot, strode out of the office.

Dru remained fuming at her desk long after he had gone. Things between her and J.D. were shaping up like Trouble with a capital *T*, but she had a bad, bad feeling that his being aggravating as all get-out was the *least* of her problems. She was more worried about the way she felt every time he was near.

*Oh to be a Regency debutante . . . to wear beautiful gowns
and to waltz (with permission, of course!) with a handsome
nobleman, hoping he'll steal a kiss—and more—once the
ball is over . . .*

*But what if your London season doesn't end in a spectacu-
lar match? Would you take the chance of traveling to the romantic Scottish Highlands and marrying a man you've
never met? Who would want to be someone's poor relation
anyway? After all, every woman needs a husband, and that's
reason enough to sign . . .*

The Marriage Contract

COMING FEBRUARY 2001

by Cathy Maxwell

"That is a wedding ring on your finger, isn't it?"

Anne had an unreasonable desire to hide her hand in the
folds of her skirts. She clenched her fist. She wasn't ready
for the confession, not ready at all.

He misinterpreted her fears, his gaze softened. "Your husband will be happy to know you are safe after such a bad accident."

"I hope he will," she managed to say. *Tell him,* her inner
voice urged. *Now.*

Her husband looked down at the way he was dressed and laughed in agreement. He had a melodic, carefree laugh, for such a large man. Anne knew he would have a fine singing voice, too. And he didn't sound mad at all.

"It's a ritual I have," he explained with a touch of sheepishness over his peculiar dress. "Based on Celt customs. Well, actually, they are customs of our own. They make the sport more enjoyable. Adds to the game of the chase."

"Game?"

"Aye, a little danger is a healthy thing." He shrugged with a rueful grin, like an overgrown boy who couldn't help himself from pulling a prank.

Relief teetered inside her. Her husband didn't sound *raving* mad—just unconventional. He had a reason for being blue. Of course, she didn't know what to make of a man who considered it a game to fight a wildcat with his bare hands, a man who *enjoyed* danger—but then, this was Scotland.

And as long as he wasn't howling at the moon, her marriage might work.

Heat rose in her own cheeks. She attempted to make her interest a purely medical one. "Perhaps someone should put a salve no your scratches."

"They can wait." He abruptly changed the subject. "I'm sorry, I don't know your name."

She had to tell him before courage deserted her. This imposing man, clad only in a kilt, could overpower her merely by his presence. And they were alone together in the beautiful, but desolate Highlands, where no one could protect her. Still, she had to tell him . . .

"My name is Anne. I've come from London, sent by your sister. And I am your wife."

Most women would do anything to get out of wearing a hideous bridesmaid dress. Of course, leaving town is one thing— but leaving this century is quite another! But that's just what Kelly Brennan does . . .

And she ends up in sultry, steamy New Orleans, landing in the arms of a dashing, wealthy, and tantalizing man, who woos her like a lady by day . . . and someone quite different by night. But is it too extreme to marry someone from another era, even if he proves that he loves you? . . .

Time After Time

by Constance O'Day-Flannery

"Mr. Gilmore! Please."

Kelly heard him breathing heavily and, even through the darkness, she could see his shocked expression.

"Oh my god! I beg your pardon, Miss Brennan. I . . . I am mortified by my own actions."

Kelly pushed her hair back from her face. What could she say? She couldn't condone what had just happened, yet she was still reeling from the kiss, the first kiss in many years that felt as though it had awakened something in her she thought had died when she was twenty-three.

"I . . . I saw you standing there in that nightgown, and for a moment I thought . . . well, I thought you were someone else." He took a deep, steadying breath.

Kelly knew he meant his wife, his dead wife. This was becoming too uncanny, for in the darkness, he again reminded her of Michael. She couldn't help it. She giggled in nervousness. "You certainly surprised me. Mr. Gilmore."

"Please call me Daniel. And again, I implore your forgiveness. I most certainly am not the type of man who accosts his houseguests in the middle of the night."

"I didn't think you were." Now, why in the world did she want him to take her back into his strong arms? Craziness. Would it never end?

"I guess I shouldn't have been wandering around your home in the dark." She was rambling now, but who could blame her?

He'd kissed her! Just like that. *Kissed her and she'd liked it!*

"This is a most awkward situation, Miss Brennan."

"Call me Kelly," she whispered. "My husband died when I was much younger. I sympathize with your loss."

"You were married?"

"Yes. He died when I was twenty-three. Honestly, I don't know that I've ever really gotten over it."

"Was it the war?"

"The war . . . No, it was an accident. Something that never should have happened. Well . . . I guess I should say good night."

"Good night, Kelly."

He said her name . . . and she loved how it sounded coming from his lips. Lips that had felt so inviting, so impassioned . . . what was wrong with her?

"Good night," she whispered again and quickly opened the door to her bedroom.

Closing it behind her Kelly leaned against it and sighed heavily. She looked around and sensed a familiarity she hadn't felt before. How could she possibly know this place . . . this house and, somehow, him?

If a proper young English lady finds herself having the ill fortune to be confined with a stranger in a public conveyance, she must take special care not to engage this person in any way— either by speaking or staring.

It is true that a carriage can be rather small, making it difficult to avoid speaking to a handsome stranger—even if he might not be a gentleman. But as everyone knows, conversation can lead to so much more. And a woman can be ruined if it's known she's committed . . .

The Indiscretion

COMING APRIL 2001

by Judith Ivory

She stared at his black hat tipped over most of his face. If he ever should play in a Wild West show, he'd be a stage-coach robber, she decided. Or a gunfighter, with a "quick temper and a quicker trigger finger," which was a line out of one of her brother Clive's Buffalo Bill novels. She entertained this fantasy for a few minutes, smiling over it. Yes, something about him, a leanness, "a build as hard and dependable as a good rifle" (she, in fact, had pilfered one of Clive's contraband American novels just to see what they were about), not to mention something in his brooding attitude, spoke of a possibly harsh, very physical existence.

Her imagination put him in a big, tooled-leather saddle on a horse caparisoned in silver stars down its breast. To his black hat with silver beads she added silver guns in holsters at his hips and American spurs that jingled as he walked. She remembered what such spurs looked like and, more memorable, what they sounded like: a lot of metal to them, a silver band low on each heel, silver chains underneath, with jagged, spinning wheels at the back. Nothing like an English riding spur with its single, neat point affixed to an English gentleman's boot.

Something about his posture, his attentiveness, made her call over the road noise, "Are you awake?"

After a second, he pushed his hat brim up enough with a finger so that his eyes were visible, if shadowed. "Yes, ma'am."

He had a nice voice when polite, like a bow being pulled slowly over the lowest groaning strings of a bass. He took his time saying things, slow-talking his way over sliding consonants and drawn-out vowels. His diction was full of *ma'am*s, *thanks-you*s, and *you're-welcome*s. A politeness that turned itself inside out when he used it to say surly things.

"Who's Gwyn?" she asked.

Sam sat there slouched, watching a lady he'd been sure wouldn't utter another word to him, while he chewed the inside of his cheek.

Why not tell her? he thought. "The woman I was supposed to marry this morning." He sighed, feeling blue again for simply saying it. Hell, what sort of fellow left the woman he'd courted for almost two years at the altar in front of all their friends and family? He expected a huffy admonishment from Miss Prissy Brit now—

"I'm so sorry," she said.

The coach turned sharply, and they both leaned to counter
the force of the motion, him stretching his leg out to brace himself with the toe of his boot, her swinging from the handgrip.

Over the noise of their travel, she asked, "What happened?"

Sam frowned. Now where had this little lady been five
hours ago? Because that was the one question he had been
dying for someone to ask all day, though not a soul till now
had thought to. Her concern and his needy longing for it
from someone, anyone, shot a sense of gratitude through
him so strong he could have reached out and kissed her.

He said, "I was on the way to the church, when out the
window of my hackney, I saw the robbery I told you about.
The fellow stopped the woman on a Plymouth street and
grabbed at her purse. She fought him. He was puny but wiry
and willing to wrestle her for it. It made me crazy when he
dumped her over. I figured, with me being a foot taller and
sixty or so pounds heavier, I could hop out, pin the punk to
the ground, then be on my way with very little trouble. I
wasn't prepared for his four friends." Sam sighed. "I spent
the morning at the doctor's when I was supposed to be
standing at the altar."

"But your bride—"

"My bride won't talk to me long enough to hear my explanation."

Their eyes met and held. Hers were sympathetic. And
light brown. A kind of gold. Pretty. Warm. He watched her
shoulders jostle to and fro as she said, "Well, when she saw
you like this, she must have—"

"She didn't see me. She only called me names through
her front door. No one would let me in."

"How unreasonable."

"Exactly." What a relief to hear the word.

"You could send her a note to explain—"

"She returned it unopened."

"You could talk to someone, get a friend to tell her—"

"No one will speak to me. I had to bribe the stableboy to get me to the coach station."

Her pretty eyes widened. "But people have to understand—"

Exactly what he wanted to hear, the very words he'd been telling himself all day. And now that he heard them, he realized how stupid they were. "Apparently not. 'Cause not a person I know does."

Bless her, her mouth tightened into a sweet, put-out line. "Well, how unreasonable," she said again. Oh, God bless her.

"Yes." But no. He looked down. "It is unreasonable. Until you realize that I left Gwyn at the altar once before, eight months ago."

She straightened herself slightly in her seat, readjusting her wrist in the leather strap. Aha! her look said. Maybe it just wasn't the right woman.

There's something about a man who works with his hands . . . his self-reliance and ruggedness—along with his lean, muscled body—make him oh, so appealing.

So if you're seeking a strong, silent type—a man of the land—you might want to check out Wyoming. Yes, this is someone who seems like he's only willing to speak when he's asking you out to a Saturday night dance—but once he takes you in his arms, you'll know he'll never let you down . . . and he'll probably keep you up all night long. Because this is the place you'll find . . .

The Last Good Man

COMING MAY 2001

by Kathleen Eagle

She heard the scratch of gravel, turned, and caught the shift of shadow, a moving shape separating itself from a stationary one. It was a horse.

"Where did you come from?" Savannah asked, approaching quietly, assuming it had wandered up there on its own, and she was all set to welcome the company. Then she got close enough to make out the saddle.

"The Lazy K."

The deep, dearly familiar voice seemed to issue from the mouth of the cave.

"Clay?" She jerked the hem of her skirt free from its mooring in her waistband and let it drop. Another shadow emerged, bootheels scraping with each step as though they were taken reluctantly. He looked bigger than she remembered. "Clay, is that you?"

"The real me." He touched the brim of the cowboy hat that was pulled low over his face. "Are you the real Savannah Stephens?"

She laughed a little. "I was hoping it wouldn't matter up here."

"It matters to me." He reached for her hand. "Welcome home."

He seemed to surround her entirely with a simple squeeze of the hand. She stepped into the shelter of him, her nose a scant inch below his square chin. She had yet to see his face clearly, to assess his life by counting lines, but it didn't matter. She knew Clay Keogh. Reflexively she lifted her free hand, her fingertips seeking something of him, finding a belt loop, a bit of smooth leather. All she wanted was a proper greeting, a quick embrace, but she heard the sharp intake of his breath, and she knew she had the upper hand. She'd turned the surprise on him. He was big-man sure of himself one minute, shaky inside the next, simply because she'd stepped a little closer than he'd expected.

A power surge shot through her.

She lifted her chin, remembering times gone by and aiming for a little humor with her old dare. "You can do better than that, Clay," she purred. Her own throaty tone surprised her. Having no humor in her, she couldn't help but miss the mark.

He touched his lips to hers, tentative only for an instant. His hunger was as unmistakable as hers. His arms closed around her slight shoulders, hers around his lean waist. He smelled of horsehide and leather, tasted of whiskey, felt as solid as the Rockies, and kissed like no man she'd ever known, including a younger Clay Keogh. She stood on tip-toe to kiss him back, trade him her breath for his, her tongue for his.

"Savannah . . ."

She couldn't understand why he was trying to pull away. There'd been a catch in his breath—she'd heard it distinctly—and it was that small sound that had set her inside aflutter. The surprise, the innocence, the wonder of it all. Good Lord in heaven, how long had it been since she'd been kissed?

"Shhh, Clay," she whispered against the corner of his mouth. "It's so good, finding you here."

"Glad to see—"

"But don't talk yet. Just hold me. It feels so good. You're not married or anything, are you?"

"I'm something." His deep chuckle sounded a little uneasy, which wasn't what she wanted. She wanted him easy. "But not married."

"Let me see you," she said, reaching for his hat. He started to duck away, but she flashed him a smile, and he stopped, looked at her for a moment, then bowed his head within her reach. "Girlfriend?" she asked as she claimed his hat and slid her fingers into the hair that tumbled over his forehead.

"No."

"Me neither."

"How about boyfriends?"

She laughed. "Completely unattached," she assured him, learning the new contours of his cheek with her hand.

"Well, I've never been to New York, but I hear there's a lot of variety there."

"There's variety everywhere, Clay. Don't tell me you've turned redneck on me. I won't have that."

"You won't, huh?" His smile glistened with moonlight. "Not much has changed here."

"That's what I was counting on."

It's one thing to get away from it all . . . and it might be an-other to visit the town of Gospel, Idaho. Still, even though it's not near very much, you can always have some eggs at the Cozy Corner Café and get your hair done at the Curl Up and Dye Hair Studio.

And there's the added attraction of Gospel's sheriff. He's easy on the eyes and not above breaking the laws of love to get what he wants. Before you know it, you'll have plenty to talk about in the way of . . .

True Confessions

COMING AUGUST 2001

by Rachel Gibson

"Can you direct me to Number Two Timberlane?" she asked. "I just picked up the key from the realtor and that's the address he gave me."

"You sure you want Number *Two* Timberlane? That's the old Donnelly place," Lewis Plummer said. Lewis was a true gentleman and one of the few people in town who didn't outright lie to flatlanders.

"That's right. I leased it for the next six months."

Sheriff Dylan pulled his hat back down on his forehead. "No one's lived there for a while."

"Really? No one told me that. How long has it been empty?"

"A year or two." Lewis had also been born and raised in Gospel, Idaho, where prevarication was considered an art form.

"Oh, a year isn't too bad if the property's been maintained."

Maintained, hell. The last time Dylan had been in the Donnelly house, thick dust covered everything. Even the bloodstain on the living room floor.

"So, do I just follow this road?" She turned and pointed down Main Street.

"That's right," he answered. From, behind his mirrored glasses, Dylan slid his gaze to the natural curve of her slim hips and thighs, down her long legs to her feet.

"Well, thanks for your help." She turned to leave, but Dylan's next question stopped her.

"You're welcome, Ms.—?"

"Spencer."

"Well now, Ms. Spencer, what are you planning out there on Timberland Road?" Dylan figured everyone had a right to privacy, but he also figured he had a right to ask.

"Nothing."

"You lease a house for six months and you plan to do nothing?"

"That's right. Gospel seemed like a nice place to vacation."

Dylan had doubts about that statement. Women who drove fancy sports cars and wore designer jeans vacationed in nice places with room service and pool boys, not in the wilderness of Idaho. Hell, the closest thing Gospel had to a spa was the Peterman's hot tub.

Her brows scrunched together and she tapped an impatient hand three times on her thigh before she said, "Well, thank you gentlemen for your help." Then she turned on her fancy boots and marched back to her sports car.

"Do you believe her?" Lewis wanted to know.

"That she's here on vacation?" Dylan shrugged. He didn't care what she did as long as she stayed out of trouble.

"She doesn't look like a backpacker."

Dylan thought back to the vision of her backside in those tight jeans. "Nope."

"Makes you wonder why a woman like that leased that old house. I haven't seen anything like her in a long time. Maybe never."

Dylan slid behind the wheel of his Blazer. "Well, Lewis, you sure don't get out of Pearl County enough."

Coming Soon from
HarperTorch

CIRCLE OF THREE

By the *New York Times* bestselling author of
THE SAVING GRACES

Patricia Gaffney

Through the interconnected lives of three generations of
women in a small town in rural Virginia, this poignant,
memorable novel reveals the layers of tradition and responsibility, commitment and passion, these women share. Wise,
moving, and heartbreakingly real, *Circle of Three* offers
women of all ages a deeper understanding of one another, of
themselves and of the perplexing and invigorating magic
that is life itself.

"Filled with insight and humor and heart,
Circle of Three reminds us what it's like
to be a woman."
Nora Roberts

"Powerful . . . Family drama that is impossible
to put down until the final page is read."
Midwest Book Review

"Through the eyes of these strong, complex women
come three uniquely insightful, emotional perspectives."
New York Daily News

0-06-109836-1/$7.50 US/$9.99 Can

COT 0401